MEMPHIS
7.9 (REVISED)

What Reviewers Say:

"Kind of like the movie *Twister*, but for earthquakes, Penny's novel imagines the highly possible scenario of a nervous New Madrid Fault finally breaking down ... Penny weaves a readable tale in this first book of a three-part series." John Lovett, Hot Springs Sentinel-Record.

"Excellent. The plot is compelling; the characters are fleshed out and believable. The technical parts are interesting and simplified enough for lay people. The implications are horrific." Bev K, California.

"Penny takes a different approach to spreading the word about the New Madrid Seismic Zone and its associated risk. He approaches the issue as a fictional account based on information from the Federal Emergency Management Agency and the U.S. Geological Survey. *Memphis 7.9* pulls the reader in and captures the imagination while adding an element of "what if" that raises awareness to the hazard facing the central United States." Jim W, CUSEC, Memphis, Tennessee.

"*Memphis 7.9* is a gripping novel I couldn't put down. The characters, who seem real, are fiction, but the account, which may seem like fiction, is all too real." Dr. David Stewart, Marble Hill, Missouri.

"A book that I could not put down until I finished it, a graphic picture of what could possibly happen ... along the New Madrid fault." Roundtable Reviews.

"*Memphis 7.9* should be a wake up call for middle America, cities like Memphis, Little Rock, and St. Louis. Concerned citizens, civic leaders, and emergency preparedness workers will find this book to be of value in understanding the risk and educating the population." Trent F, Florida.

"Wow, what a wonderful book, a great job! I had almost finished the book when I realized that the research for this book is true and this earthquake could really happen, even though the story is presented as fiction." Stephanie B, author, Tuscon.

MEMPHIS 7.9 (REVISED)

A Novel
Book 1 of The 7.9 Scenario

SAM PENNY

TwoPenny Publications

First TwoPenny Edition

1 2 3 4 5 6 7 8 9 10

ISBN 978-0-9755671-2-8 - 0-9755671-2-8

Published by TwoPenny Publications

205 Rainbow Drive #10503
Livingston, Texas, 77399-2005

www.the79scenario.com

TwoPennyPubs@the79scenario.com

Library Of Congress Number: 2005903471
Printed in the United States of America

Back cover photograph courtesy of USGS

An earlier version of this book was published in 2003
by Booksurge, LLC, ISBN 1-58898-920-8

Dedicated to

Alice Mae Voris Penny

My wife and companion, who always believes in me.

TABLE OF CONTENTS

APPENDICES

FIGURES

PREFACE

I began this book over seven years ago to satisfy my need for an avocation in retirement, to continue my interest and studies in geology and seismology, and to publicize the seismic dangers along the Mississippi River.

Having lived in California for 35 years, I had become an experienced temblor-jock, well versed in the need for earthquake preparedness. After reading about the New Madrid Fault Zone and its potential for disaster, what I saw of the condition of highway and building construction from St. Louis to Memphis on a vacation to the area shocked me. I found the complacent attitude of many residents regarding seismic dangers to be appalling.

When I used FEMA (Federal Emergency Management Agency) numbers to estimate the total impact of a magnitude 7.9 seismic event—the size of the 1811 event—I found it could injure over a quarter million people and kill tens of thousands. The impact on the United States economy would be disastrous. The estimated probability of one in ten in the next 50 years should be a level most rational people would not ignore. And yet, it seemed most of the country had put its head in the sand with respect to a giant earthquake in the central United States.

I began writing a piece of fiction to illustrate the mechanics of fracturing in the earth's crust and how the energy released by those fractures would impact structures along the Mississippi. The story grew into several tales told in what I now call *The 7.9 Scenario* series. This first book, *Memphis 7.9*, is the story of the earthquake and the city. My second book, *Broken River*, tells the story of what the earthquake does to the Mississippi River in an earthquake. *Phoenix of Memphis*, to be published in 2006, chronicles the successes and failures of attempts in Memphis and around the country to recover from the worst catastrophe to ever strike the United States.

This is a work of fiction. I am not a seismologist; I do not predict a specific earthquake. My background and experience are in physics and geology, and I have read what is available in the literature and on the Internet. I have translated that information into a scenario of what might happen, making several simple assumptions about the structure of the New Madrid Seismic Zone and how it could fracture.

Memphis 7.9 is the story of a fictional earthquake that strikes a real place. Where necessary I have used specific architectural structures to describe the events; in other cases I have invented fictional places as I saw fit.

The truck stop at New Simon does not exist, nor does the I-55 exit at Stateline Road. Interstate-255 is fictional because I needed a different structure for the Boothspoint Bridge to cover a plot element. The Memphis Department of Seismic Safety is fictional, but its basement office in the Memphis City Building was at one time the home of the Memphis Emergency Management Agency.

All characters in this book are fictional, though I have liberally used observations of those around me and in Memphis to create persona to act out the story.

Some things have changed since the publication of my original book. FEMA has been moved into Homeland Security, and some notable progress has been made in the central United States with regard to planning and preparing for a repeat of 1811 and 1812.

I have been both gratified and dismayed to learn than my estimates for damage and casualties are in line with estimates made by others in the field. I also found people who are very concerned about the danger in the local, state, and Federal Emergency Management Agencies, and in the seismological and earthquake centers in the Universities and U. S. Geological Survey.

What I did not find was a general willingness in the government agencies to share with the public the full extent of the **earthquake**danger to our country. There seems to be an over-riding concern with "don't scare the public" and keeping control, and locally with concerns about inhibiting development.

I have revised and updated *Memphis 7.9* to reflect these changes and am republishing the book with the imprint and ISBN of TwoPenny Publications. The story is substantially the same but incorporates changes that reflect what I have learned in the past two years. I have also added several maps, a glossary, and some of the results from the analysis forming the basis for *The 7.9 Scenario*.

A giant earthquake will happen on the New Madrid, probably within the lifetime of my grandchildren. My greatest concern is the need to plan and prepare for recovery. We must make our structures, lifelines, and economy more resistant to a disaster such as this. We must build for a future that includes a catastrophic earthquake in the center of the USA. It is inevitable.

Sam Penny
May 2005

and now

MEMPHIS 7.9 (REVISED)

A novel that tells
what happens WHEN,
not IF, a giant earthquake strikes
on the New Madrid Fault, just 45 miles
from Memphis, Tennessee.

Book 1 of The 7.9 Scenario

Prologue

Chris Nelson snored in harmony with the humming fans that cooled the electronics at the University of Memphis Seismic Center. He lay sprawled across the old canvas cot, asleep after a nightlong session of fine-tuning his earthquake prediction model, the graduate thesis project that he expected to bring him imminent fame.

The unruly blond mop of hair on his large head coordinated with his wrinkled khaki shirt and shorts. One errant sandal hung on his big toe; the other had already fallen to the concrete floor. His left hand twitched in response to some unknown stimulus, and he dreamt of the praise he would receive as the true prophet, as the discoverer of the Holy Grail of Seismology: a method for predicting earthquakes.

In the early dawn 28-year-old ex-marine and *fem fatale* Pamela Weekes, dressed in sweatshirt and shorts, jogged up to Center Lab door and knocked.

"Hey, Chris, are you in there?" Hearing nothing, she opened the screen door and tried the door handle. Finding the door unlocked, she pushed it open and entered the darkened lab to turn on the lights.

Chris sat up on cot and blinked in the bright light. "Oh, hi, Pamela. What are you doing here?"

"I was jogging by and saw your car. I just wondered about you." She pulled up a lab stool and sat. "What did you do, work all night again?"

"Yeah, I made some improvements on my prediction model." He rubbed his face then looked up and smiled. "And I did some more work on my scenario video of what it would be like if the 1811 earthquake struck again today."

"When are you going to let me tell my boss at Seismic Safety about your work?"

Chris sat upright with a worried look on his face. "Come on, Pam. You know what the University will do to me if I publicize I'm trying to predict earthquakes. I would be out of the graduate program faster than you could shake a stick. You promised me you wouldn't say anything."

Pamela smiled apologetically. "I know, but I'd like to at least tell everyone about your scenario. They need to know what it will be like when another magnitude 7.9 earthquake hits this part of the country. And it would really help our department get the attention it needs."

"Well, maybe I can share that, but it needs a little more fine-tuning." He picked up his lab book from the side table and tapped it. "But more important, I have a prediction for today: a moderate 4.4 magnitude earthquake later this morning up near Dell in Arkansas. If that one happens, I'm one step closer. When I can prove I can predict an earthquake, I'll let you be one of the first to tell the world."

Pamela stood. "I'll take that as a promise, and I will keep totally mum in the meantime. Hey, I better get on with my jog. Gotta stay in shape. You look like you could use more sleep." She smiled as she started out the door, then stopped to turn out the lights.

Chris lay back on the cot and placed his forearm over his eyes. She was right, he could use more snooze time.

Three hours later, at 9:11:51 A.M. Central Daylight Time, the sun reflected off the window of the admin building across the parking lot into the lab, lighting the computer console.

In seconds a moderate earthquake on the New Madrid Fault would shake the small town of Dell in the northeast corner of Arkansas. The prediction that Chris Nelson had made would become fact and raise his record to two in a row, one step closer to his dream.

But earthquakes happen all the time, all across the nation.

Twenty-two seconds later, an unexpected temblor would occur 45 miles east of San Francisco, California, at the north end of the Calaveras Fault, and relieve some of the strain accumulating from the half-centimeter per month of inescapable creep of the Pacific Plate along the San Andreas Fault.

CHAPTER 1: PRECURSORS

Three miles north of the impending epicenter in California, Judy Fox watched the effortless way her husband Tom picked up five plastic bags of clothes and a sack of groceries to carry from their Danville townhouse to the camper downstairs. She took pride that her insistence of his twice a week walks around the golf course kept his 52-year-old body in such fine shape.

Tom turned and said, "Hurry with that last sack, then start locking up."

Judy glanced at the mirror and swiveled her hips. She thought her petite figure looked exceptional for a woman in her 40s. She admired how well Tom's good looks matched her own, considering the seven year difference in their ages. She spoke as an afterthought, "I need to phone Jenny and tell her we're leaving. I have to remind her we'll reach Memphis next Saturday."

Her mind focused on her daughter. The time had come to speak with her face to face. Email and telephone calls handle some issues, but Jenny sounded like she was serious about that graduate student, Chris Nelson. Judy mused, I know what it's like to marry a genius, and an engineer besides. Jenny simply cannot comprehend the suffering that's ahead for her.

Tom stopped at the door. "Dammit, I wish you'd told me earlier that you planned to call. You know I wanted to hit the road by 7:15, and that's only five minutes away." He scowled.

Judy looked toward her husband. "What's so special about 7:15? Why put us in the middle of the commute? Besides, I didn't think you were serious."

"No commute—it's Saturday." He shifted the bag to his other hip and turned to leave. "Oh well, keep Jenny on the line so I can talk to her, too."

Judy's left eyebrow arched up beneath wisps of her short blond hair, flinging virtual daggers at Tom's departing back. That's just like him, find something to bitch about. She snatched the telephone from its cradle, punched the speed-dial for her daughter, and tucked the headset onto her shoulder as she returned to her packing.

That exchange between the two in California took 49 seconds. At that instant, beneath the small farm community of Dell, Arkansas, 1750 miles to the east, the New Madrid Fault fractured.

Torsional forces in the earth's crust ripped the opposing surfaces of the fault apart. An oval-shaped crack, over half a square mile in size, sliced through the basement rock at a depth of 11.3 kilometers. At the oval's center, opposing sides of the crack slid almost four inches past each other, 9.5 centimeters to be exact, generating a blast of seismic waves from the magnitude 4.4 temblor. The primary *P-waves* from the seismic rupture would reach Memphis, 47 miles to the south, in 13 seconds; the secondary *S-waves* would take 26 seconds.

On the Calaveras Fault in California, 22 seconds of tranquility remained.

Chris jerked taut on the cot when the alarm bell startled him awake seconds before others in Memphis would feel the earth shake. He bolted upright and gaped at the blinking yellow light representing the remote sensing station at Dell on the wall-sized map.

"Yellow, that's moderate." Lights glowed green for the more frequent small temblors, red for the rare large events.

He stumbled as he stood and stepped on the fallen sandal. A light representing a second station glowed yellow to report the seismic activity, then another and another. He sat to arrange his footwear and watched as the seismic wave spread outward from Dell in a circle on the map depicting the seismic sensor network that monitored the New Madrid Fault.

Chris estimated the time sequence. "Dell means it'll take less than 13 seconds before the seismometers record the *P-waves* here at the University."

The remote sensing stations transmitted information by radiotelephone back to the University at the speed of light, 300,000 kilometers per second. The seismic *P-wave* produced by the fracture moved through the underlying rock and sediments at only six kilometers per second. Chris sprang from the cot to his computer workstation to prepare.

Judy took the headset in hand as her daughter's voice announced the connection. "Hi, Jenny here."

"This is your mother, Jenny. Are you well? How's school going? Do you still like your apartment?" Jenny Fox, a junior majoring in seismology at the University of Memphis, lived just off campus.

"Oh, hi, Mom. I'm doing just fine. My finals have gone okay and everything's fine. I'm finishing breakfast and was about to sit down to do some more cramming. How's Dad? What's up?" Sounds of kitchen clatter filled the background.

"I called to let you know we're heading out. We'll be in Memphis next Saturday. Your father's antsy about getting on the road, like always. He'll be up in a minute to talk with you."

"Okay." Jenny mumbled as she took another bite of her breakfast.

"When do you expect to meet us? We'll stay at the Sundowner RV Park just east of the University. Do you know where it is? I found it in the camping guide. How's the weather been? They say it has full hookups. Have you talked with your friend Chris recently? You're not sleeping with him, are you?"

Jenny's response blurted over the phone. "No. Mother. Besides, I wouldn't tell you if I did." Her voice calmed. "I've heard of the Sundowner. It'll be okay for you and Dad. I'll probably be busy if you get in early, but I'll see you by noon. Just sit tight. I'll show up. And Chris is doing fine, though he's awfully busy with his research and hardly makes time for me."

The north end of the Calaveras Fault had collected stress from the San Andreas Fault for years without relief. Molecule slid past molecule, granule past granule, vein past vein in the black basement rock, moving the strain from one point to the next along the fault's trace—but not enough.

Seven kilometers beneath San Ramon the microscopic molecular flow of solid rock reached its limit. All nearby points along the Calaveras structure reached their yield point, the state where the rock could deform no more. With no stretch left to give, catastrophic failure remained the only option.

In one-sixth of a second, the blink of an eyelid, opposite sides of the fault moved three centimeters past each other. The movement tore a fracture in the rock a half-kilometer long and a quarter-kilometer high, converting the potential energy stored in the ruptured structure into heat and seismic waves characteristic of a magnitude 3.5 event.

The *P-wave* traveled 12.1 kilometers from the fracture to the surface in Danville in two seconds, its low frequency sound just perceptible to active people. The *S-wave* arrived in four seconds, snapping the hill under the townhouse from side to side in the physical motion that people most often associate with an earthquake.

"Jenny, you know you'd be much better off not getting involved with that boy. I've always told you that you should wait…" Judy stumbled sideways from the jerk. "What?" Judy's voice rose an octave, "Oh my God, Jenny, we're… we're having an earthquake."

Jenny's yell came from the handset. "Mom, do you feel that shaking? We're having an earthquake, too. Wow, it's jerking around. Oh boy, this is something. It keeps going. Mom, are you okay? Is your's still going on?" Jenny paused. "Mom, are you there?" She screamed. "What's happening?"

For a rare instant Judy could say nothing. Instinctive fright response controlled her body. Blood drained from her skin. Hair at the back of her neck stood straight out.

Tom sprinted through the door. "Honey, are you okay? Did anything fall? I just felt one hell of a jolt coming up the stairs."

Judy sank back into the couch, astonishment contorting her face.

"Mom. Dad. Is anyone there?" A tinny voice called from the handset.

Tom grabbed the telephone, "Jenny, is that you?"

Judy stared about the condominium. Everything appeared stable, but the room kept spinning.

"Yes, I'm okay, but your mother must have swallowed an ice cube. She's pale and speechless." He massaged his wife's arm as she looked up in relief. "We just had a really sharp earthquake. We must've been right on top of the fracture." Tom listened, and then exclaimed, "What? You felt an earthquake at the same time?"

Judy looked up in surprise. Her daughter had felt the earthquake.

Tom continued, "Yes, but … The shaking here was strong and quick, a couple of really hard snaps, but it stopped. What about yours? … Good, your shaking's stopped., but if the shaking in Memphis lasted nearly ten seconds, it must have been a pretty big one. Hey, young lady, don't you remember what I told you about the New Madrid Seismic Zone when you talked about going to school in Memphis? I …"

Judy recalled how Tom's avocation of earthquake watching began six years ago when the family moved to California. It had been pivotal in Jenny's selection of seismology as a major.

"That's right," Tom said. "You're sitting 45 miles from the most dangerous fault in the country. In the early 1800's three major earthquakes rocked that area in less than two months, each of them bigger than the 1906 San Francisco earthquake … I know that's why you wanted to go there for school."

Judy swallowed. She imagined her daughter covered by falling buildings, the ground opening around her and pulling her down. Judy's eyes stung.

Tom continued, "Just remember I was the one who first told you someday the New Madrid Fault will shake the hell out of Memphis. Pray you're not there when it does." He glanced down at Judy. "Hey ladies, we can talk more about this later. Your mother and I have to hit the road."

Judy appreciated the pat on the shoulder and the fact that Tom was ending the conversation.

"Jenny, say good-bye to your mother and calm her down so we can travel. And get ready for the Big One like I told you. It's inevitable."

A subdued Judy accepted the telephone as Tom grabbed her half-packed bag of clothes to carry to the camper. Her stomach cramped from worry. Her daughter would hardly be married to that weird genius before she died in an earthquake.

For years the University of Memphis and other Universities surrounding the New Madrid Seismic Zone, in cooperation with the U.S. Geological Survey—usually just called the USGS—had placed instruments throughout the region, gathering information about the geological structures each time any small fracture occurred.

A few seismologists like Chris hoped they would be able to predict when and where the next great New Madrid earthquake would occur. In the meantime, the USGS and the Universities shared the information they collected, and everyone in the program agreed on one thing: another great earthquake was inevitable, and soon.

For three years 24-year-old Chris had labored on his seismic prediction theory with an intensity noted by his peers as remarkable. Larry Snow, one of his fellow-graduate students, declared at a departmental beer-klatch, "Chris, you not only act like a mad scientist, you look and smell like one. We professional seismologists know that it'll never be possible to accurately predict earthquakes. Why can't you understand that?" Larry's opinion carried weight in the department, and Chris felt the growing alienation.

Chris shared his thoughts and progress less and less as others scoffed at his ideas. Then, the fine-tuning paid off. Three weeks ago he had noted in his journal, "*Using Nelson Model version 3.04.422 I predict a magnitude 2.7 event at 35.82N, 90.11W around 3 A.M., April 30.*" Jenny Fox had witnessed and initialed the entry.

On April 30 he wrote, "*Success. I met the criteria. Little River experienced a 2.6 at 6:15 A.M.: within 5% on magnitude, 3 hours on timing, 2 kilometers on location.*"

A few days later he asked Robbie Browne, one of the undergraduates in the weekly Geology Lab that was Chris's responsibility as a Teaching Assistant, to witness and initial a new entry: "*Using Nelson version 3.05.033 I predict a magnitude 4.3 event at 35.85N, 90.04W at 7 A.M., next Saturday.*"

He continued in his journal. *"With the latest adjustments, I now expect over 90% of the temblors will occur within the zones I predict. Although the magnitude estimate usually comes within 10% of the actual value, the estimates for the timing of the temblors have not been good. The model still needs improvement. I still need more computing power."*

In the middle of Chris's second year, Dr. Paul Kenton, his graduate thesis advisor in the Seismology Department, had given him permission to use the Laboratory's newest Quad 3.8 Gigahertz workstation computer to develop and test his seismic model, the computer program he called Nelson. Chris now spent most nights and weekends working on his pride and joy, adding to his image as a mad scientist.

"Come on, baby, give me the data. What do you look like? Are you that 4.3 shake I predicted? It's past due." He watched as the computer compiled the initial summary of readings downloaded over the telephone lines from the remote seismic stations. The automated monitoring system did not require that anyone be on duty, but Chris's sleeping habits gave him a unique opportunity to watch the new data arrive and be analyzed.

He bounced on the stool in front of the computer console snapping his fingers in time with the tune running through his head. He made unintelligible sounds to accompany the music, "Da, da, da-da-da," and tapped a drum roll on the desktop, his hyperactivity masking the shake of the *S-waves*.

The screen filled with more and more detail as other stations reported. When data from the large monitoring station at Little Rock was triangulated with that from Memphis, they pinpointed the exact location of the moderate earthquake. "Hot dog, I scored again." His gloating face reflected on the computer screen as he moved the mouse and entered commands on the keyboard. He had enough information to run a detailed analysis with his model.

Even with all four processors working full-bore, the workstation took three minutes to complete its computations. Chris beat time on the desktop and bounced on the stool. "Dum-ditty, dum-ditty, da-da-da."

He shouted when the results flashed on the screen. "That's it. Magnitude 4.4. Over a square kilometer of the fault broke loose, just like I said it would." He pumped his fist into the air in triumph. "And its focus is right on that little asperity south of Dell. I knew it'd be there. Nelson, you're on target again. That's twice in a row.

"Wait until they hear about this one." Chris bounced on the stool as he celebrated victory with his computer and scratched his itchy scalp. "Nelson, you're getting better, lots better. One more event like this, and I can prove to everybody that I'm the primo earthquake prophet of the world."

CHAPTER 2: NEW SIMON

Four hours earlier, the alarm clock had awakened Tina Washington in her apartment in the soon-to-be-shaken town of Dell. The display glared 5:15. She moaned and rolled out of bed, muttering. "Fudge, why did I take the early shift. With Daylight Savings Time, the sun's not even up."

Tina hurried to shower, dress, and drive 16 miles to the café on Stateline Road off I-55 at the Missouri and Arkansas border. As the sun rose at 6:01, she arrived for her job as Saturday's day-shift waitress.

"Morning, Cookie," she said. The day cook was a 73-year-old length of skin and bones who some claimed to be the best short-order cook in the Missouri Bootheel country.

"Hi, Miss Tina." He smiled, showing the gaps in his teeth. "You ready for today?"

Tina smiled back. "Guess so. It's Saturday, so things should be quiet here at NASTY'S." She used the nickname for the New Simon Truck Stop.

When Tina began working at the cafe, Cookie had related the history of the place. "Originally," he told her, "Simon Kenton and his son built a settlement on the banks of the Mississippi River after he purchased land below New Madrid in 1809. Then during the 1812 earthquake, most of his land slipped into the river and all that remained became a swampy tangle of fallen trees and sand boils. A couple of the settlers moved back to the old Indian mound behind us. They called the place New Simon.

"My grandpa told me that 42 souls lived here once. He said that before things dried up, the truck stop got a reputation as a place to get a good deal on fuel, get work done on your truck, and do shady business at the state line."

He grinned and wiped his hands on the dirty towel. "You see, Stateline Road belongs to the state of Missouri, but the truck stop sits on the Arkansas side. Bootleggers used to move from one side of the road to the other depending on which deputy was here."

"Then one night sheriffs from both states showed up at the same time. That gunfight is the real reason this place got its name." He cackled. "That's when things got really NASTY."

Within two weeks Tina realized that in modern times NASTY's still served the same basic functions, but now for different crimes. The action made her uneasy.

At half past eight JQ McCrombie stepped from the small duplex on a back street in Hayti, Missouri. He admired the warm glow of the morning sun on Loretta's dark arm as he handed her three twenty-dollar bills.

"You come back soon," said Loretta, the sultry black prostitute JQ kept in the small town just off the Interstate in the Missouri Bootheel. She reached up with two fingers to capture the money between her long, painted fingernails.

"Sure, Baby. I'll be back as soon as I can."

JQ sped away, raising a cloud of dust behind his two-year-old red Porsche. At 35 years of age, his aggressive ambition and football-hero countenance commanded far more attention than usual for blacks in the Mississippi Delta. He felt utter disdain for anyone who thought it their business where he spent his nights.

He accelerated onto the freeway heading south. With the convertible top down, the wind blew up from the windshield and whipped his short, curly black hair around, streaming it back across his head. At over 95 miles per hour he overtook and screamed past an eighteen-wheeler.

As he sped past the Steele exit, the wail of a siren pierced the roar of motor and wind. JQ glanced into the rearview mirror to see the flashing red lights of one of Missouri's finest.

"Ah shit, him again." JQ grinned and shoved the accelerator to the floor. The speedometer needle moved past 115. He laughed. "If Smokey wants to race the five miles to the Arkansas border, let's do it."

With half a mile to go, Carl, a proud member of the Missouri State Patrol, conceded he could not make an arrest in his home state. JQ streaked across the state line as Carl slacked off to take the freeway exit at the border.

Unwilling to admit defeat, the officer called on the radio to his Arkansas counterpart down the road. "Jerald. That damned son-of-a-bitch in the red sports car I been telling you about is heading your way at over 100 miles per hour. Do me a favor and bust his damned ass. Bust it really good."

The sound of a belly chuckle trumpeted back over the radio from the Arkansas patrol officer. "I'll shore do that, Carl. You flush them out of Missouri like a good bird dog, and I'll bag them on the fly."

Past the border, JQ eased off the accelerator and laughed. Once again he had flipped off the Missouri Patrol. Gearing the sports car down to second, he pulled off at the next exit to return north. Turning left at the top of the ramp, he found his way blocked by a blue and white Arkansas Highway Patrol car parked sideways across the overpass right-of-way. He stopped and waited.

The State Trooper stepped out of his car, his stiff hat perched atop his round face, and with hands on his hips, he swaggered toward the offender. "Dammit, JQ, I wish you'd stop tormenting those Missouri officers. Carl just called me on the radio and told me to, quote, get that damned son-of-a-bitch in the red sports car, end-quote. I suspected it'd turn out to be you."

JQ raised his hand in greeting. "Hi, Jerald. Sorry to interrupt your day, but I'm late for a business meeting back at New Simon." He remembered a rule he had once read that would be helpful in his move ahead: show concern. "How's your wife?"

"Oh, Claretta's okay, but she's dreaming about them earthquakes again. The doctor says if she gets morbid on the subject once more, he's going to put her in an institution." Jerald placed his hand on the Porsche's door. "I don't know, maybe it'd be best if he did. At least I wouldn't have to listen all the time about how the ground's going to break into pieces and swaller everyone up."

JQ laughed as he pushed the invasive hand from his car. "Jerald, tell Claretta that JQ McCrombie knows everything there is to know about earthquakes, and I say there's nothing going to happen. She's going to have to find something else to be morbid about." JQ grew impatient. "Now, hurry up and move your damned car so I can get back to NASTY's for my meeting."

By nine o'clock the Saturday morning crowd had come and gone. Alex Smyth hoped Tina would take more time to chat. As she refilled the coffee cup beside his plate of disappearing biscuits and gravy, she said, "Alex, you can't be serious about this sky-diving thing. You're plumb crazy to be going up in an air-o-plane and jumping out."

Alex's grin dimpled the point of his chin as he looked up. "Tina, I'll only jump when I'm wearing a parachute, I promise. It's perfectly safe. Nothing can go wrong. You can come over and watch if you want. The airfield's only two miles from here down Stateline Road. You'll do that sometime, won't you?"

She looked perplexed, like maybe she wanted to reach out and take hold of him. She seemed so serious trying to find some argument to keep him from going about skydiving.

Alex remembered her from high school, nine years before, in Marked Tree, Arkansas, 45 miles southwest as the crow flies. He was a senior when she was a sophomore. He recalled how everyone said she was the cutest girl in school, and how everyone considered him a nerd. He made good grades and went away to college and heard that she didn't. He was surprised that she turned out a lot more intelligent than he remembered.

They became reacquainted four weeks ago when Alex started coming into the truck stop every Saturday for breakfast. They chatted about old times at school and their lives since leaving Marked Tree. She had been frank with him. "I spent my time in high school as a cheerleader. I dated around and finally became a waitress. I decided to move out of town when all my old boyfriends got married and started raising families. They kept coming around and suggesting quiet get-togethers—like they didn't have any respect for me."

Last Saturday Alex had spent the entire afternoon sipping coffee and occupying Tina's attention during her slack time. She had looked dismayed when he told her, "I'm a student at the new skydiving field two miles east." It never occurred to him that she would think he possessed a streak of madness.

Today he said, "This morning I'm going over to do my first solo jump." Alex sat up straight on the stool and puffed out his chest. "They don't let you do one of these jumps solo without training." He stressed his experience. "I've already been through seven levels of instruction, and I've learned how to fall—I mean, how to land. I've practiced going out of the plane with the instructor holding onto me and everything.

"Tell you what, if this jump turns out to be so dangerous that I'm killed, I'll drop out of the class and come back and admit that you're right. Okay?" He winked and reached out to squeeze her hand.

Alex felt electricity when he touched her. She squeezed back and smiled, though traces of worry still lined her face. "Alex, I'm concerned about you. I like things better when they're peaceful and not dangerous." Plucking the unused setting from next to him, she moved down the counter to check her other customers.

As Tina brought the coffeepot back for another refill, Alex glanced over his shoulder, surprised to see his employer coming through the café door. He leaned over to whisper. "Whoa, looky there. That's JQ McCrombie. I would've thought he'd be over in Memphis at his new office building. I wonder what he's doing here, and with a creep like that." He referred to JQ's companion, a small-boned skinny man with slicked black hair and a cigarette drooping under his short moustache.

Tina glanced at the new patrons and back to Alex. "Hey, Mr. McCrombie owns this place, so be careful what you say around here. He can be touchy. He comes here from time to time for business meetings."

Ignoring her own advice, she grumbled. "He gives me the creeps. Sometimes he hits on me and acts like I should give him extra attention." She asked, "Where do you know him from?"

Alex leaned closer. "Really? He's my boss, too. I'm a network computer programmer at McCrombie Enterprises in West Memphis. I had no idea he had an outside business like this truck stop."

Tina dropped her voice. "I don't trust him one iota. He acts like every woman must think he's a god."

"Yeah? Well I've seen how he ogles the secretaries in the office, and a couple of them have complained about it. Maybe that's his style." Alex scowled as he watched the two men find an empty corner booth and sit down.

"Tell you what, let's get together and compare notes." Checking the time, he said, "Hey, I got to go, or I'll be late. See you after my jump." Hesitating, unable to muster the nerve to ask until he stood to leave, he stuttered. "And … say … would you like to go see a movie tonight?"

Tina laughed with excitement. "Come back and let's talk about it. Sounds like it might be fun." Alex smiled and winked as he strode out the door.

"Hey, can't we get some service over here?" JQ's loud booming voice jarred Tina's reverie. She grabbed two menus and headed to the booth where JQ and his companion waited.

"I'm sorry, Mr. McCrombie. I was just finishing with my last customer." She put the menus in front of the pair and stepped back. "I'll get you some water and then take your order. Would you like some coffee?"

"Finishing with your last customer, my ass. I saw you wiggling your butt at him. You go for pipsqueak guys with no muscles like that, huh?"

She blushed at the crude remark and the sound of his laughter.

His smile appeared taunting. "Sure, bring two coffees, donuts for George and eggs over easy with toast for me."

As she left for the coffee she heard JQ speak to George. "Nice legs, don't you think? Someday I'll take the time to try her out. Figure she'll be a nice piece of ass." Outraged, she blushed even deeper and went into the coffee station, almost picking up a dirty cup for spite.

George Besh stared after the young waitress and tapped the ashes from his cigarette onto the floor. He stretched his pants around his crotch, then his mind returned to the reason for the meeting between him and JQ.

As Tina disappeared behind the plywood partition to hand Cookie the order, George leaned closer to JQ and, in a guarded, raspy voice, asked, "So, are you buying into this next shipment or not? It's costing me $50,000 cash, and I still need twenty thou'. You kin have a fifty-fifty cut if you give me that $20,000."

Tina poured coffee on the other side of the thin curtain as George pushed JQ for a decision. She almost dropped the pot when she heard JQ agree, "Okay, I'll get $20,000 to you this afternoon, but by God, you better return me $125,000 in two weeks or one of my crews will find a hole to bury you in. That's understood, right?"

"Sure, JQ, sure. Just so long as the creeks don't rise, and the Feds keep their booties cool." His voice dropped as he made his last point. "But you remember one thing, if the shipment gets busted, you don't get nothing— except nobody tells them where the money came from." He leaned back, again tapping his cigarette over the floor. "That deal work for you?"

While the two conspirators continued to discuss details, Tina fled to the kitchen, trying to cleanse her mind of what she had just heard. No doubt it involved a dope shipment. She knew it was not healthy for her to know of whatever the two men discussed.

Cookie dinged the bell and pushed the eggs, toast, and donuts from the kitchen to Tina's side of the serving shelf. He tilted his head and lowered his voice. "Don't let JQ get under your skin, girl. Just hold your head up high." She half-smiled at the old man as she picked up the hot plates and walked to JQ's booth.

As she placed the order in front of JQ, the shaking from the Dell earthquake jerked the floor from side to side. The walls creaked. Dust fell from the ceiling. The plate of eggs lifted from the table and crashed upside down into JQ's lap.

"Holy shit." JQ jumped from the booth pushing the hot eggs and toast to the floor. The ceiling fans swung. The toothpick holder fell from the counter. The windows rattled. "What the hell's going on?" He looked at the ceiling, at the windows. George held onto the edge of the table and stared.

Tina backed through the swinging doors into the kitchen and clutched the shelf on the wall, waiting for her dizziness to end.

The shaking slowed, surged again, and then stopped. Cookie asked, "You all right?"

"I guess so, but what happened?" She grasped his arm in fear.

"We just had an earthquake, honey—a pretty strong earthquake, I'd say, like we had all the time when I worked back in San Francisco." A look of nostalgia swept his face. "Yep, it almost felt like home."

Tina stared at Cookie. She could not comprehend why he seemed so pleased.

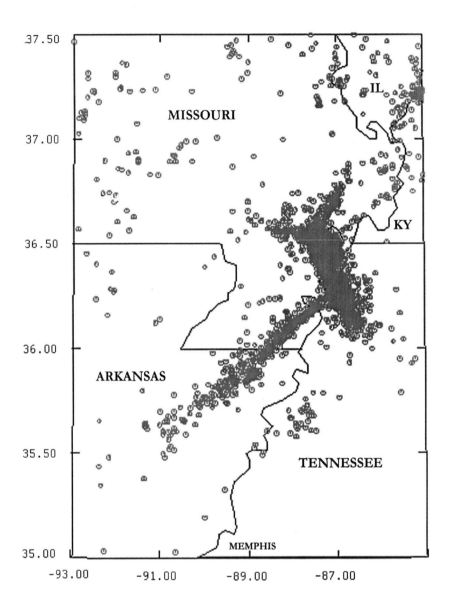

The New Madrid Seismic Zone (NMSZ) is mapped by the many
microearthquakes recorded since 1975. For more information see
www.eas.slu.edu/Earthquake_Center/SEISMICITY/
newmadrid1975-1995.html

CHAPTER 3: PREDICTION

Dr. Paul A. Kenton, PH. D., Associate Professor of Seismic Studies at Memphis University, felt the temblor while eating breakfast, seconds after his beeper alerted him of a seismic alarm at the Seismic Center Laboratory. The duration and strength of the shaking indicated a moderate event, and he jumped onto his bicycle to hurry down the path to the cluster of old frame buildings making up the Seismic Center on the south side of campus.

The presence of one of his graduate students surprised Paul when he walked into the Laboratory. Chris handed him a computer printout with the preliminary analysis of size and location of the morning's event.

"Thanks, Chris." Paul looked over the summary. "Well, it wasn't as large as I guessed after all, so we can put everyone's mind at ease."

Chris explained. "I was here when the alarm sounded, and I've been collecting data from the field stations and compiling it with the reports coming from other major seismic stations."

Paul noticed Chris offering another paper for his attention. "That's fine, Chris. Just let me make this phone call, then we can talk."

Paul dialed the recording system and dictated the generic telephone message, reporting the latest data about the earthquake. "At 9:12 this morning a magnitude 4.4 earthquake occurred at a depth of 11.3 kilometers with an epicenter near Dell, Arkansas. While this temblor is stronger than usual, events like this are a common occurrence on the New Madrid Seismic Zone, and there is nothing to worry about."

Finished, Paul turned back to Chris, steeling himself for the onslaught. As he had explained to the Department Head, "While Nelson is a brilliant student, he's excitable and hyperactive to the point of distraction. When I accepted him, I didn't realize what I was letting myself in for. But I do believe he should be allowed to continue this research, even if some of the other faculty thinks it's bogus." The Head was reluctant but agreed.

"Yes, Chris."

"Dr. Kenton, I did a comparison of the waveforms from the Dell temblor with my database and found a match in the mid-range spectrum, just like I thought I would. Do you see the similarity between this event and the 2.6 event further south 14 days ago?" Chris placed a second summary page from the Little River temblor into Paul's hands and waited, fidgeting.

Paul scanned the two sheets and answered. "No, ... not really." He looked at Chris, his patience wearing thin. "I know you've been checking for trends, but I don't see any relationship. I'm afraid you're letting your desires get in the way of proper scientific methodology."

"But, Dr. Kenton, my computer model shows the relationships between the spectrums. The correlation is good to three-sigma."

"You know your expectations influence how you designed your model." Paul felt it necessary to again expound on the dangers of biased research.

"But the spectral signature two weeks ago showed where ..."

"Chris. I don't have time for this right now. If you think your model is showing something, write a paper and submit it to me for approval. Now, I have to get back home to plant my tomatoes."

Paul picked up his satchel and headed out, closing the door behind him, unable to hear Chris blow out his breath and hiss. "Why do I bother? You won't even listen, asshole. My model predicted this Dell event from that temblor two weeks ago. And from the Dell event it predicts another earthquake at the Missouri border in the next eight days."

Only the walls heard the news. Chris turned and stalked back to the restroom to wash his face. "You want a paper? So, I'll write a paper after this next one. Maybe then you'll listen."

Tom Fox maneuvered the camper through the slower traffic up the grade on I-580 out of California's Livermore Valley. Emerald green hills dotted with white windmills flashed by on each side.

Out of the corner of his eye Tom could see Judy studying some question for a long moment. Then she spoke. "Tom, why are you so sure a big earthquake will happen near Memphis? I thought California was earthquake country, not Tennessee."

Tom leaned back into the seat of the truck. It felt good to be on the road again, and now he had time to explain the temblors they and Jenny had felt.

"Judy, you know I told Jenny about earthquakes around Memphis before she enrolled there. Where there's been one earthquake, expect another.

There are 150 miles of the New Madrid Fault north and northwest of Memphis, and there have been some mighty big earthquakes on it."

"But I haven't heard of any big earthquakes there recently. Maybe the fault quit."

"Have you already forgotten this morning? From what Jenny described, she must have felt a moderate earthquake. It'll make the news. Another shaker like that one hit Marked Tree, Arkansas, a few years ago. In fact, they record about 200 temblors on the New Madrid every year."

Judy sat upright and grabbed the armrest. "Two-hundred," she exclaimed. That's more than we have here in the Bay Area."

Tom shook his head in the negative. "As a matter of fact, the San Francisco Bay Area has more than twice that many each year. Most are very small with magnitudes of one or two. People living on top of a fault don't even feel most of them, but when they happen, seismologists can measure the seismic waves and see where the faults are located and how much they're slipping."

Looking outraged, Judy's cheeks turned rosy. "You didn't bother telling me that more than 400 earthquakes happened each year when we moved here from Colorado."

Tom could see her blood pressure must be rising. He said, "I've read about earthquakes for years and told you lots of things, but you always found something else to think about. You never paid attention."

"Well, you always wanted to lecture and talk over my head." She glared at him. "But now, it's important. I want to know why Jenny's going to have an earthquake."

"Good—then listen—I'll explain again." Tom licked a satisfied grin across his lips. "By measuring small earthquakes, seismologists can estimate the likelihood of different size earthquakes on a fault. Little earthquakes are the most likely, then mid-sized earthquakes, and the least likely earthquake is . . ." Tom's voice dropped as he said, "the Big One." He looked over and winked.

Judy ignored the attempt at humor and focused on her concern. "So what's the likelihood of Jenny having a big earthquake?"

"Though there've been some recent papers that suggest the chances are lower than previously estimated, I've read that some scientists say there's a 30% chance the New Madrid Seismic Zone can expect a magnitude 6.0 to 6.5 earthquake within the next ten years."

"Oh, thank goodness." Judy sighed with relief. "If it's ten years, then she has time to move."

With a patronizing smile, Tom punctured her optimism. "No, that's not the way it works. When scientists say there's a 30% chance that an earthquake will occur within the ten-year period, they mean it could happen anytime in the next ten years, even tomorrow, next week, or next year. You cannot assume it will happen at the end of the ten years."

"Oh." Cut off from relief, Judy chose alternate logic. "But a 6.0 earthquake isn't that big, is it? I don't think an earthquake that size is enough to hurt Jenny. If that's all the earthquake they'll have, I don't need to worry about it."

Tom smiled and escalated the issue. "Agreed, a 6.0 magnitude earthquake probably won't hurt Jenny unless she's very near the epicenter, but that estimate is for earthquakes of that size. Seismologists also say there's a one in ten chance of a major earthquake with magnitude greater than 7.5 somewhere on the fault within the next 50 years."

In a plaintive voice, Judy asked, "What about the next ten?"

"Well, let's see." Tom did a quick calculation in his head as the road leveled out over the pass. "I suppose you could say there's maybe a two percent chance of it happening in the next ten years. That's one in fifty."

Judy manipulated her logic to the conclusion for which she searched. "Good, that's pretty small so I don't have to worry about it." Tom shook his head in amusement, again astounded by Judy's approach to logic.

With the tomato plants all in the ground, Paul Kenton draped his lanky body over the wooden deck chair and doodled on the pad of yellow-stickies as he thought about the latest in a series of minor but disturbing confrontations with Chris.

Chris was an excellent student, brilliant but immature. He wanted to be a star when what the world needed were good, sound team players, serious workers who would collect the data and grind away on the details.

Paul recalled his graduate days—how he had been a lot like Chris—so sure of being right. It took 12 years of fieldwork and some big screw-ups to convince him that he didn't know everything. He lucked out and succeeded in spite of those mistakes, because so few knew about them.

He chewed on the end of his pencil and thought. I don't know. Maybe I shouldn't be so hard on the boy. After all, his enthusiasm keeps him in the Lab around the clock dealing with the monitoring systems. He's exceptional at installing and maintaining the computers, and I'd trust him with any field installation. He just seems more like a computer whiz than a seismologist. Maybe he chose the wrong vocation. Maybe he should be in a line of work more willing to tolerate genius.

In California, Judy remained focused on earthquakes. "Tom, why do they make those probability calculations about the earthquakes? Isn't there some way scientists can just keep them from happening?"

Tom finished his careful scan of the new levees as he crossed the San Joaquin River Bridge on I-205. Then he said, "Nope, afraid not. But the calculations help the government figure out how to plan in their zoning regulations and such. It's like planning for the 100-year flood out here on the river. It helps them figure out how big to build these levees. By knowing the chances of a big earthquake, they can establish building codes that will improve survival rates."

"But you said the other day the floods this last winter were 500-year floods, and that's why so much of this valley flooded."

"That's right. People and government agencies plan for some particular level of disaster, but there's always the danger that something bigger will happen. Society trades off the cost of preparation against the chance of failure."

"So, just because it's going to cost more money, you're saying they plan for smaller floods in the hopes bigger ones won't happen?"

"You've got it. Very often people's perception of how likely it is for something to happen don't jibe with reality. From what I've read that's one of the big problems in the Memphis area—too many people in control just don't believe it could happen on their watch." Tom slapped the steering wheel to emphasize his point. "Lots of people in the central United States just don't want to think a big earthquake will happen anytime soon, so they plan and build as if it never will."

Chris munched on the crumbs of the chocolate-covered donut Pamela Weekes had dropped off when she stopped back by on on the way home from her Saturday morning jog around the campus. "I didn't feel a thing," she had said. "If it was that big, I better get home. Seismic Safety policy is to come into work whenever there's an earthquake anywhere close, even on the weekends."

"You won't tell anyone about my prediction coming true, will you? I'm not ready to let the word get out."

Pamela had smiled as she left. "Don't worry, Chris. Everything you tell me is just between you and me."

An hour later the Laboratory alarm bell rang again. "Yipes, another one." Chris watched as the light on the map for Lepanto, Arkansas, at the southern end of the fault glowed green. "Less than magnitude 3.0, but it moved stress somewhere. Let's find out if it made a difference."

Chris worked at adding data from Lepanto to his database. "Dum-te-dum-dum. Dum-dum." He beat time on the desktop as his Nelson model worked on the new information. "Hot dog. The convergence is more definite. Let's see, now it's good to three-point-two sigma for the temblor north of Dell. And the time's come in to 8.0 days. Magnitude's still about 4.5."

The door to the Laboratory banged open. "Hey, Chris, whatcha doing here on such a fine Saturday morning?" He looked up to admire the lithe, young body in tight jeans and baggy rugby shirt.

Jenny Fox walked up to look over his shoulder. "You should be at the soccer game," she opined.

"Too busy chasing earthquakes—like always." He leaned back in his chair, pushed away from the computer screen, and stretched, pleased to have an opportunity to talk about his recent success to the undergraduate he dated from time to time.

"That Dell event was just what I expected, and I collected a lot of good data this morning. Then a temblor near Lepanto a few minutes ago fit right into the trend that's developing."

"Trend? Does that mean you're tweaking that theory of yours again?" A look of dismay crossed her face. "I heard Larry Snow talking and laughing again over a beer last night about your theories. He wonders when you're going to give up on that dead horse. Jeez, you were almost run out of seminar when you presented your results last quarter."

"I gave that seminar before I made my latest refinements. Now my model fits the data a lot closer," Chris felt defensive, and the joy of seeing Jenny ebbed in reaction to her comments. "And I really don't give a damn what Larry Snow thinks. He'll never do anything to make himself famous."

"Is that what you want, to be famous? Then why'd you go into seismology?"

"Why not? You know, those turkeys at that seminar were all alike." He leaned forward in the chair and stared hard at Jenny. "They've let their collective fear of being wrong convince them that it's impossible for someone to make predictions. They're so afraid they might make a mistake, they've decided it's not professional to even try to predict an earthquake."

Jenny barked back, "Well, sometimes you act so smug about it all, like you know everything, like everyone else is a bunch of idiot teenagers. You're going to fall on your face some day, Chris. Why don't you get a life, anyway?"

"This is my life."

She challenged Chris. "I wouldn't be surprised if you told me that you predicted this last earthquake."

Chris paused, started to say yes, and then hesitated, "Let's just say I'm getting closer and closer to being able to make a valid prediction."

"Do you take into account the position of the sun and moon and the level of the earth-tides?" Jenny taunted.

"No, dammit. Iben Browning made his 1990 New Madrid prediction based on external causes. He was wrong. But just because his prediction received widespread publicity, and some people in the town of New Madrid actually moved away in anticipation of the event, that doesn't mean a legitimate prediction can't be done." Chris pounded the desk for emphasis. "My theory's not based on remote causes. It considers the geological structure and how stresses move along the fault. It's based on science and solid mathematical modeling."

"So what makes you think your ideas are any better than Browning's?"

Chris's anger overcame his better judgment. He blurted the news. "Because my theory works. You bet I predicted that last earthquake and, if you remember, there was the one three weeks ago that you witnessed. I was right on for that one, too. And I know where the next one's going to be—at the Arkansas-Missouri border. He took a deep breath. "I predict a 4.5 in eight days." Chris felt the heat of sudden disclosure color his face.

Jenny looked incredulous, stunned that what Chris told her might be true. For a long moment she let the thought sink in. "Chris, if anything happens that's even close to what you just said, it will make you famous. But everyone knows you can't predict earthquakes."

"There you go again. You don't have any faith in me. Why don't you just get out of here and leave me alone."

Jenny jerked, then turned and walked out the door, hiding the tears streaming down her cheeks.

Chris realized what he had said and done. Jenny and Pamela were the only ones who came close to understanding. Why did he attack her? Why?

Unable to think of a good answer, he turned back to the console and shaking his shoulders, forced his thoughts back to the problems with his computer model, a subject he could understand.

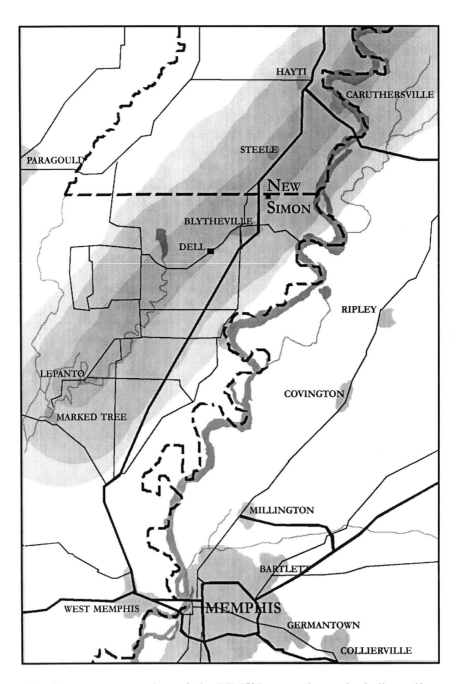

Southwestern extension of the NMSZ, a nearly vertical slip-strike
fault extending from near Marked Tree, AR to near Realfoot Lake
in TN. Dell and New Simon are north of Memphis.

CHAPTER 4: THE SCREW TURNS

JQ sat in his booth at NASTY's, doodling on a napkin with his wet spoon as he made notes on his plans for the day. He sipped his iced tea.

George had said before he left that he'd be by JQ's West Memphis office for the money about six.

JQ had half of the cash at home, but he needed to call Harry the Shark for the rest. He shook his head in disgust. Damn, he hated dealing with the mob, but at least this would give him a big stake to grease the skids on the deals coming up, and nobody would know he had the cash.

In the background Tina and Cookie laughed over some joke, and the sound brought his mind back to the girl. Tina was such a cute piece. He wondered about a different relationship. With things going this well, he would need a wife to move up in Memphis society. People would admire Tina's good looks and body. He and she would look good together, and she definitely was higher class than Loretta.

Tina had stayed in the kitchen with Cookie, avoiding JQ as he sat in his booth. But when the mid-morning lull hit full swing, she had to refresh the tables for lunch. "Pardon me, Mr. McCrombie, may I have the salt and pepper shakers for refill?"

"Sure, Tina, here you go." He handed her the shakers, touching her hand with his fingertips and smiling with half-closed eyes. "Say, why don't you just call me JQ and drop the Mr. McCrombie thing."

Her face showed a mechanical smile. "Yes, sir."

JQ ignored the distant look. "Have you recovered from that jolt this morning? It was a real bumper, wasn't it?"

Tina stared at the man with distrust, then answered. "Yes, it came as quite a surprise. A strong earthquake like that hit Marked Tree when I was a kid, but I was visiting my aunt in Atlanta and didn't feel it. Everyone said it rocked things around pretty well. I didn't know what they felt like."

JQ kept Tina's attention with a new subject, "Say, did you know I'm about to open my new office building down in Memphis? I've renovated the old Walker Hotel on the riverfront."

He beamed with pride and explained. "The city fathers didn't much like my renaming it, but when I bought the place a few years ago, it was an eyesore and naming rights came along with it. It's now the McCrombie Building."

"That sounds nice, Mr. McCrombie. I guess I did hear Cookie talking about your new building."

"Yes, it's quite a beauty. From my penthouse you can look right out across the tip of Mud Island and see the river, and the sunsets are really pretty. And it's JQ, remember?" He winked and holding up his glass, asked, "Could you fetch me some more iced tea? I'd really appreciate it."

Tina took his glass. Their fingers touched again, and she felt a chill run up her spine. "Sure ... , JQ, ... I'll be right back."

When she returned with the refilled glass, JQ persisted. "Look, I'm scheduled to be in Memphis on Tuesday to check how things are going with the renovation. I know it's your day off, so why don't you come down and see my building? I'll buy you lunch."

Tina's stomach tightened when JQ made the invitation.

A smooth smile spread across his face. "There's this really great place on Beale Street to get some gumbo and crawdads if you like Cajun." His tongue slipped across his lips. "I really want to see more of you. It's time we got to know each other better." His reptilian eyes stared at Tina.

Tina's fear that JQ would take a direct interest in her had become reality. She did not want to be alone with the man. She did not trust him, and in an empty building with no one else around, she would have no hope. But JQ was her boss, and her job could be on the line. She lied. "Gee, I don't think so. I already have something planned for Tuesday."

He again licked his smiling lips. "Then you'll just have to change your plans, don't you think?"

"Oh, I'd have to check before I did that." She grasped at the hope that Alex could help her think of a good excuse that wouldn't get her in trouble with JQ. "I take a break in a bit and maybe I could let you know after I get back. Is that okay?"

"That's just fine, Tina. You take some time to get used to the idea, but I'm sure we need to get together and learn more about each other. You know what I mean." The silkiness of his voice did little to hide the implication behind his words.

Dismissing her, JQ turned his attention back to the papers before him. "I have to make some phone calls and take care of some business in Hayti before I head back to Memphis. Check on your plans, and let me know what you've decided when I come back." He picked up his glass of tea and headed for his private office.

Tina stared at his back and shuddered.

"Da, Da, Da. Dum-de-dum." Chris beat the desktop in time with the silent music in his head as the Laboratory's computer workstation pushed the analysis as hard as it could go. He had continued working on the Nelson Model through the noon hour, refining his estimation algorithm, waiting for the workstation to re-compute, plotting the partial results, and checking on convergence.

When not doing music, he talked to the monitor. "Oh, Master Computer, why can't you tell me what's with those two asperities northeast of Dell? Are they bends in the fracture path? Are they cross-faults? Are they a change in material?"

His model kept pointing to one or the other locations as the most probable places for the next earthquake to happen, depending upon his estimate of the stored energy. It would not choose. The most probable choice was beneath the old town of New Simon by a narrow margin over the asperity two and a half kilometers southwest.

"Dum-de-dum. Come on, Nelson, I know there's some fine structure in the fault affecting the results. What is it? Is it their close proximity?" He scratched his head. "Does it really make a difference anyway?"

Alex pushed open the screen door at NASTY'S with a flourish, strode into the cool room, and straddled a stool at the counter. "How about a big, cold root beer for the newest qualified sky-diver in the Missouri Bootheel?"

Reaching over the counter he grabbed Tina's hand and boasted with a wide grin on his face, "I survived the fall to earth without being killed, and I am now a fully qualified parachutist."

The look on Tina's face was not what he expected. She seemed tense and distant. "Do you really want a root beer, or are you just blowing hot air?" she asked.

Dropping her hand he said, "Sure, I'll take a root beer. It's too early for a real beer. And look, I survived. Now what do you think?" He grinned at Tina, putting his thumbs under his armpits to hold out his shirt, trying to flirt and be funny.

After another meager response, he asked as she went to the soft drink dispenser, "So, what's with the long face?"

"Oh, Alex." She sighed. "Things are just getting to me." Tina set the frosty glass of root beer in front of him and leaned on the counter. "First, I got all worried about you jumping out of that silly airplane. Then that earthquake shook us all up. And if that wasn't enough, JQ McCrombie hit on me trying to make a date. I don't know what to do." Teardrops appeared at the corners of her eyes, and she sniffled.

Alex covered her hand. "Well now you see you didn't need to worry about me. And yeah, they told me about an earthquake when I got to the field, but I was driving and didn't even feel it." His squeeze was gentle. "You'll have to tell me about this thing with JQ. But hey, nothing's worth crying about. If you have a break coming up we could go for a ride and talk about it." He smiled and tugged on her wrist.

Tina wrapped her other hand over his and stood erect, grinning with spontaneous optimism in spite of her frustration. Alex had a way of making her feel better. "Sure, I'll get my purse." Pulling off her apron with a flick of her wrist she called. "Cookie, I'm taking my break now. Be back by three."

"Okay, Miss Tina. You just take care of yourself and watch out for that young jasper you're with. He looks a little too fresh to me." Cookie smiled at Tina and winked at Alex.

Alex drove east along Stateline Road between fields of sprouting soybeans towards the Mississippi River levee. After pointing out the small airstrip from which the airplane flew for the parachute jumps, he turned off onto a gravel farm road to find a shady spot at the base of the levee three miles beyond. Stopping his car and shifting sideways in the seat, he asked, "What's really bothering you, Tina? You can tell me." He reached over to massage her shoulder.

"Alex, my biggest problem is JQ. He invited me to lunch on Tuesday and says he'll show me his new building. I don't trust him at all, going into an empty building with him and the like. My feelings are all bad about this."

She leaned her head on Alex's hand. "I know he'll try to take advantage of me. Alex, he could even try to rape me." Tina's voice mirrored the tension in her face. "But he's my boss, and I'm afraid he'll get even if I don't go with him. I really can't afford to lose this job." Again tears filled Tina's eyes.

Alex rubbed her shoulder and neck. "Oh, come on, Tina, he wouldn't try something like that. You're letting your suspicions get the best of you." Alex rationalized to justify JQ to Tina. "I know he has a bad reputation, but he can't be that bad. He's a respected member of the business community in West Memphis." Yet, despite his attempts to reassure Tina, Alex had a niggling suspicion she could be right.

Tina looked up and pleaded. "Alex, can I tell him that you and I are going together, that I have a date with you, so I can't go with him?"

Unprepared for such an emotional request, Alex hesitated. "I don't know, Tina. After all, we haven't even had a date unless you go to the movies with me tonight." Alex felt pressured. "You have to remember, JQ's my boss, too. Don't you think telling him a lie like that could create problems for both of us?"

Tina lost it. "Look, it's just to get me out of this Tuesday date with him. If you let me do that, I'll really be beholden to you." She squeezed his hands in hers and peered into his brown eyes. "Please—for me?"

"Well." Alex hesitated, and then her passionate plea overcame his reluctance and better judgment. "I suppose so, but couldn't you just tell him no?"

Alex felt the tension flow from Tina as a soft smile filled her face. "Thank you, Alex, you're so wonderful." He wondered why he now felt so tense.

Alex and Tina returned from their drive to the river and parked in front of the café just as JQ walked out the front door. He stiffened, and marching to Alex's car, clutched the window-ledge and growled past Alex's face at Tina, "Still flirting with this little butt-head, huh?"

Alex drew back. "Hey, JQ, knock it off."

JQ looked down and sneered. "I'm not talking to you, asshole." Looking back at the girl he asked, "Well, Tina, have you checked your schedule? Are you coming down Tuesday to have a good time with me in Memphis?"

Tina leaned against Alex's shoulder and looked up at JQ. "Mr. McCrombie, Alex and I are going together. We already have something else planned for that day, so I just won't be able to meet you." Tina looked for Alex to give his affirmation.

JQ shifted his gaze back to Alex, directing his wrath at the young man. "I know you, Mr. Smyth. You work in my West Memphis office, don't you?" Alex felt a sudden wave of apprehension. "What do you mean butting in where you're not wanted?

"Now wait a minute, JQ. Tina and I have a date. You're the one who's butting in."

JQ pressed closer to Alex, almost nose to nose, "Tuesday is Tina's day off—not yours. You work for me, but if you take time off for nooners, your ass is fired. Pronto. Do you get the message?"

Alex winced. He wanted to help Tina, but at the expense of his own job? "Yes, sir, Mr. McCrombie, I understand. I won't take any time off."

Tina sucked in her breath and looked with dismay at Alex. Alex realized he had forgotten his promise to help her stand up to JQ. Instead of support he had caved in.

"Just you remember."

"I said I won't take time off. Isn't that enough?"

"Stop it." Tina screeched. "Just stop it." Wrenching the handle, she stumbled from the car and slammed the door behind her.

JQ straightened and glared across the car as Tina rushed toward the restaurant. "Well Tina, your baby-butt boyfriend just dried up. Are you gonna meet me to see my new building, or are you still starry-eyed about this sniveling puppy?" JQ's deep-throated chuckle added insult to injury, and Alex gritted his teeth from the abuse.

"Sure, JQ, I'll meet with you in Memphis," Tina shrieked with anger over her shoulder. "I can't expect anything from Alex, not when he's so spineless." She ran into the restaurant. Alex blushed when he realized what Tina had said, what she must have thought of his behavior.

Alex looked up and gritted his teeth. "JQ, Tina has the right to choose who she wants to spend time with. If she wants to be with you, that's fine. But if you pressure her or try to force her in any way, I'll do more than take next Tuesday off." He could see JQ's eyes narrowing. "I'll shove my job up your ass, and make you pay for it."

JQ squeezed the window-ledge harder and leaned close to Alex, his jaw set. "Mr. Smyth, don't you ever—ever—threaten me again. Now head out of here, and by God, be sure you don't take any time off on Tuesday. I intend to check on it. And I'll give you a prediction: as soon as you get out of line in any way, you're fired on the spot. From now on, that girl's my territory, not yours, do you hear?" JQ stepped back from the car.

Alex started his engine and backed out. He spun the tires heading toward the Interstate. His eyes grew cloudy. He felt like shit.

Chapter 5: The Word Spreads

For a time Judy Fox watched the rich green irrigated fields of crops as the truck cruised through the San Joaquin Valley. She tried another approach. "But that's all about probability. Why don't they just know when the next earthquake will occur?"

Tom chuckled. "They've tried, but so far without success. The U.S. Geological Survey predicted an earthquake in 1988 near Parkfield, California, based upon the 22-year periodic seismic history of the area. They missed by 16 years, and it didn't happen until 2004. And in 1990 a fellow predicted a major earthquake on the New Madrid based upon the positions of the moon and sun."

"Was he right?"

"He was run out of town when no shaking occurred." Tom shook his head. "No, science hasn't progressed to the point where they can say precisely when and where an earthquake will occur."

"Maybe they'll learn how." Judy sighed.

Tom agreed without conviction. "Maybe. But even if someone did figure it out, from what I hear, nobody would listen to them."

Chris sat at the computer console, watching the data accumulate from yet another small earthquake, this one near Blytheville, Arkansas. That made three in one day. Using the new data, his computer model converged to a prediction with an even higher degree of confidence.

When the telephone rang, he reached for it without looking. "Seismo Lab, Chris here."

"Hey, Chris. This is Robbie Browne. Remember me? You asked me to witness something about an earthquake prediction a week or so ago. When I felt the shake this morning, I wondered if that was that one."

Chris smiled and said, "Sure was, Robbie. It happened just like I said it would. It was a moderate temblor near Dell, Arkansas, at a depth of about 11 kilometers with a magnitude of 4.4." Chris continued in his most professional manner, mimicking Paul Kenton's statements on the message phone. "There have been two more small earthquakes since then, a 2.6 and a 2.8, the first near Lepanto, and the second just happened near Blytheville, not far from Dell. Other than that, things are mostly normal."

"Wow, my dad told me I lived near an active fault, but I didn't realize it could be that active. Is the New Madrid as dangerous as they say?"

Pleased that someone wanted his professional opinion, Chris replied, "Well, the New Madrid Seismic Zone released more energy in two months in 1811 and 1812 than the San Andreas has released in California during the past 200 years, and it could do that again. So your dad's right. It can be very dangerous." Chris could not resist the opportunity. "I predict there will be another earthquake on the New Madrid in a week or so, and it'll be even stronger than this last one."

"Really? Any idea where that'll be?" Robbie asked.

"Just north of this last epicenter. I've looked it up on the map, and it should be right under the old town of New Simon on I-55. I figure it'll be a 4.5 and happen Sunday afternoon, but I'm still working out the details." His confidence increased as he shared his information with Robbie.

"Wow, that'll be something. Wait 'til I tell my girl friend. And maybe you'll let me witness this one in your journal, too."

Realizing he had spoken with too much authority, Chris hastened to explain. "Well, that's just my theory. Not everyone agrees with me. Plus, the University's not fond of graduate students making predictions." He emphasized. "Please don't go spreading around anything that I told you. If you tell your girl friend, make sure she keeps it quiet, too. Okay?"

"Sure, Chris, don't worry." Robbie responded with reassurance. "My dad taught me how to keep quiet about things. And thanks for the heads up."

Chris replaced the telephone. That conversation had been fun. It felt good to have people listen about his prediction and success. Maybe he should call his twin sister and tell her.

Jenny popped the last of the sandwich into her mouth as the telephone rang. "Jenny here," she said through the mouthful.

"Hello, Jenny, this is your mother. Are you okay?"

"Sure I'm fine, Mom. What did you expect me to be?"

"Oh, I've just been worried about that earthquake you had, and Tom's been telling me how dangerous it is in Memphis, and I've been thinking that maybe we shouldn't come there after all. Maybe you should come back to California where it's safe."

"Mom, I've already accepted a summer job at the orphanage, and I can't come home. Besides, I'm still trying to get Chris to pay more attention to me, and maybe I can get something going by being around this summer. He's just so focused on his work."

"But they have those big earthquakes where you are."

"Mom, the last earthquake of any size around here happened over 100 years ago near Charleston, Missouri. I admit, that's a little bit closer to me than it is to you. We studied it in class last quarter, and they estimate it measured about the same as the 1995 Northridge temblor down in southern California."

"Yes, your cousin Julia told me about Northridge. She was there, you know. It was pretty bad."

"I admit there was one big difference. The Northridge earthquake damaged an area of about 600 square miles. Of course, that's a lot of prime California real estate. But the Charleston earthquake damaged over 6,000 square miles, ten times more area." Jenny joked. "Only there weren't so many Californians living in Missouri back in 1895, so the damage wasn't considered serious."

Judy sighed. "At least Tom says he's pretty sure the Big One probably won't happen in Memphis while we're there, but I just don't know what to do about it."

"Mom, I wish you'd quit worrying. Chris says the earthquake they're having up north of Memphis this next week is going to be moderate. Just take my word for it."

"What do you mean moderate? Why didn't Chris just say there won't be any more earthquakes?" Jenny had not anticipated Judy's paranoia. "Is there something you're not telling me? Has it been shaking some more?"

Jenny's head spun from her mother's rapid-fire barrage of questions. She wondered if her mother had grown flakier since she left home—maybe she had even developed Alzheimer's.

"Slow down, Mom, slow down. Look, Chris predicts there'll be another earthquake next week up near the one today, but it'll be moderate like this last one, so you and Dad can still come to visit me."

"Is Chris some kind of prophet? How does he know?"

"He has a computer model he runs. He's made a couple of predictions that were on target in the last few weeks. When I saw him this morning, he told me about another temblor he expects to happen up around New

Simon on the weekend. But, Mom, I don't understand him. He got all mad at me when I asked him if he had thought of everything. I really like him, but sometimes he gets so difficult I could ..."

Judy screamed. "There's going to be another earthquake?"

"Well, I'm not sure he's right." Jenny tried to placate her mother. Her voice became plaintive. "You'll still come, won't you?"

Judy said nothing. Jenny waited in vain. Finally her father's voice came on the phone.

"Jenny, this is your father. What did you say to your mother? Are you having another earthquake? She looks like the ground's shaking again."

"Oh. Hi, Dad. I just explained to Mom that Chris predicts there'll be a magnitude 4.5 earthquake up north a week from tomorrow. And then Mom seemed to go berserk."

Tom sounded very interested. "Really. Don't worry about it, Honey. Your mom's had a hard day. But hey, a chance to be around a predicted earthquake, that's what I call a treat."

"Dad, Chris doesn't want me to talk about his prediction, so keep this under your hat, will you? And, Dad, if you can think of how I can get Mom to calm down, let me know."

Tom laughed. "Sure, Jenny, I'll keep quiet on the prediction thing, but you're on your own with your mother."

"I appreciate y'all showing up for this status review." Director Marion Roberts looked over the Seismic Safety Department staff assembled in their basement offices at the Memphis City Building on Main Street. "I know each of you understand the importance of striking while the iron is hot whenever Memphis residents feel a temblor, even on weekends. And as the newest department in the city government, like the new kid on the block, we need to build our reputation in the city. It's good to see that everyone came in like we planned."

He continued, "I was playing golf with the Mayor, and she really paid attention to the shaking. She told me how hard it has been getting things going as a new mayor. And she said how appreciative she was for the new renovation guidelines we issued like she promised in her campaign, but she also told me how much trouble they're having getting businesses and people to respond. It's imperative we use every opportunity to preach the message to the public, especially our local businessmen and city bureaucrats, about the need for earthquake preparedness."

He grinned. "Besides, on Saturdays you get overtime, and I take everyone to lunch."

The small group cheered, looking forward to visiting Marion's favorite deli on the Main Street mall.

"Roger, What do you hear from the University?" he asked his Technical Deputy.

Roger Thomas stood and reported. "I contacted Professor Paul Kenton. He said this is just another in the ongoing series of events on the New Madrid Seismic Zone." Roger reported its attributes. "We got some reports of some books knocked to the floor at *That Bookstore* in Blytheville, but that's all. I called to check, and there're no problems at the power plant outside Dell." He sat down.

"Thanks, Roger. I talked to the Operations Officer at Emergency Management, and they had no reports of any problems in the city. Did anyone else hear anything, talk to a neighbor for reaction, get a phone call, or whatever?"

The group discussed the earthquake and rumors they had heard that morning, comparing the event with past earthquakes. Marion let the conversation continue for ten minutes and then ended the discussion. "Good, let's try to get the news-hounds interested in the books on the floor if we can. George, you do that, please. Any news is good news in this business. Pamela, what can we do for follow-up PR?"

Pamela Weekes, the Department's Public Relations Deputy, stood and pushed the tight red skirt she had changed to from her running shorts back down around her thighs like an exotic dancer. Marion suspected such performances were on purpose.

"Well, I have a great story coming out of the University, but it isn't ready yet. In the meantime we could work on the human-interest angle. I met JQ McCrombie at a mixer last week." She enunciated each word with care. "His company in West Memphis does highway earthquake retrofits, you know, fixing the freeway overpasses."

Her quizzical look told Marion she was testing him to see if she should continue. He nodded.

"I could write a feature article for the next newsletter on ways he is helping prepare for the next Big Earthquake, how his staff is rushing to save us from falling freeways."

Marion smiled and visualized sweet Pamela prying information from JQ McCrombie. He personally didn't trust the man and had heard JQ was quite a womanizer, and he told himself that it might not be fair to turn Pamela loose with JQ. But, he thought, a grown man like JQ should be able to take care of himself. He wasn't worried about Pamela.

Smiling, he gave her the go-ahead. "Sounds like an excellent suggestion, Pamela. Please keep me informed of your progress."

Returning to matters at hand, Marion reminded his staff. "Now y'all know what a struggle it is to get people's attention in the Memphis area regarding the danger of earthquakes. But we're making progress. Let's keep it up. Any questions?"

Glenda Watson, the new clerk, raised her hand and spoke. "Mr. Roberts, the girls in Finance say the earthquake maps show a line goes right through this building. If the building's going to crack in two, are we safe here in this basement?"

Nervously, Marion laughed. She had touched on a most sensitive subject. "Glenda, those lines on the map simply show the border between levels of damage in the event of a major earthquake. That doesn't mean there will be a crack through this building." He looked down to avoid her eyes.

"You asked if we're okay in this basement? Well, it would be better if we had our offices some other place, and the Mayor promised me this morning she's working on that, but she just hasn't found a place where we can go as yet."

"Thank you, Mr. Roberts. I just wondered. I sure hope she hurries."

"I hope so, too." Marion grimaced and looked around to be sure everyone appeared spirited after his pep talk. "Okay. Now let's go have lunch and hit this thing full-bore Monday morning."

Robbie looked over his meager supply of cocaine, knowing his mother would not send his next allowance check until the first of the month. He wondered how he could supplement his stash. "Maybe that earthquake prediction is worth something. George Besh might be interested in knowing." He and George had had a good discussion just a week ago when George shared a small bag. Robbie didn't know what George did for a living, but he seemed to have money and connections for good dope.

He dialed George's number and after a moment heard a muffled, "Yeah?"

"George, this is Robbie Browne. Whatcha doing, old buddy? I want to talk." He heard the sound of someone moving things around, like taking covers off a bed. He heard a small giggle in the background as George spoke to someone away from the telephone.

"What do you want? It's two in the afternoon, but I'm kind of occupied. Robbie, is it?" George sounded sleepy and uninterested. "Oh, now I remember. I was over to your place last week with a sample. You ready to buy?"

Robbie heard George light a cigarette. "Well, another sample would be nice, but you know parents don't give us students much money. I thought maybe we could just hang out together and share." He paused, hoping.

After no response he continued. "But that's not why I called. Remember, I told you about how I know this guy with the earthquake theory? Well, he's getting lots better at it. He predicted the earthquake that happened this morning, and he told me where another one's going to be next week."

"Hey, I felt the shaking this morning. Scared the shit out of me, it did." George's voice sounded more awake now. "What do you mean, he predicted another for next week? There's gonna be another quake?"

"Yeah, that's what he said. He said he can spot trends in the earthquakes and tell when they're leading up to something bigger." Robbie's voice rose in anticipation. "This next one's going to happen up near New Simon, Arkansas."

"Hey, that's where I was when that quake happened this morning, at NASTY's Café." George wanted more information. "Did he say how big the one this morning was?"

"Oh, it was a magnitude 4.4 centered near Dell, fifteen miles southwest of New Simon."

"And what about the next one?"

"He said it'll be closer to 4.5, and right under New Simon. That old town will really jump. Chris is working on the details, and he said he'd let me know more during the week as more small temblors report in." Robbie made his own prediction. "And I expect he'll install one of the University's seismic monitoring stations up near New Simon next week."

Robbie heard George running his stubble of chin whiskers against the telephone, then, "Hey, old buddy, keep collecting that earthquake data. I'll bring over some really good stuff tomorrow for free, and we'll talk more about this." George baited his hook. "And if you get me some really good information on this next earthquake, I'll supply all the happiness you need."

"Hey, that sounds great. See you about four o'clock at my place." Robbie felt rewarded but cautioned. "George, you won't tell anyone else about this prediction, will you? Chris said the University doesn't want anyone publicizing it, so you got to keep this quiet."

George laughed. "Sure thing, old buddy, don't worry. I understand. I won't tell a soul. Talk to you later."

George hung up the telephone and reached over to slap the bare buttocks of the girl on the bed beside him. She yelped and rolled away. "Hey, what's that for? Don't bruise me like that, or I'll leave. I gotta dance tonight, and the boss don't like us girls to be marked up."

George grinned, snubbed his cigarette in the dirty ashtray, and reached for a tuft of the girl's pubic hair. "Oh, I'm not going to hurt you, baby. But, boy, do I have a great one for JQ. He's sure going to be surprised to hear his truck stop's gonna shake again. He'll pay really big for this news."

Chapter 6: More Meetings

Later Saturday afternoon Paul Kenton sorted his papers preparing to go home when he heard a knock on his office door. He looked up. "Yes, Chris, what can I do for you?" He watched Chris swallow.

"Dr. Kenton, I was just getting a soda and saw you here. I believe …" He swallowed again. "I want to install a sensing station in the New Simon area. I've been analyzing the data we received today." He took a deep breath. "I think there'll be another fracture northeast of Dell sometime within the next couple of weeks. I would like to be near the epicenter so I can get a good recording of some of the fine structure and short range vibrations."

Paul stared at the young man in total amazement, the skin crawling up his back. "Chris. You just prance in here and predict an earthquake. Don't you know the University policy concerning predictions? DON'T. You can talk about probabilities, but do not say you predict an earthquake will happen." He pushed his pen aside. "You and I need to have a serious talk about what you just said, and the impact such a statement could have on your career."

Paul looked down at the doodles on his desk pad and blushed as a memory flooded through his mind. My God. That's exactly what my advisor told me. That old man was so pedantic and ossified, so totally judgmental. Have I become that kind of pompous ass?

Paul paused a long moment feeling his face grow red hot, and then looked back at Chris. He must not make the same mistake his advisor had made.

"Chris, I apologize. You might be correct. I had no right to blast you for what you believe. I admire your belief in yourself."

Chris shook and looked ready to run. "Did you say I might be right?"

Paul cocked his head to the side. "Do you truly think you can predict an earthquake?"

Chris raised his shoulders. Paul heard him take a deep breath. "Yes, Dr. Kenton, I do. My seismic model predicted the Little River temblor and the Dell temblor this morning. I have witnesses for those predictions in my lab book to back me up. And with the latest activity, my model indicates there will be a significant earthquake in about a week near New Simon." He blinked, as if waiting for the guillotine to drop.

"You have witnesses?" Paul felt surprise and pride that his student would be so thorough. He shuffled the papers on his desk. "Look, a field station is due back Monday from the repair depot. It hasn't been assigned. Maybe I can arrange for you to use it for a couple of weeks—but you can't tell anyone what you are using it for. Tell them you're just doing a field test for me."

He smiled. "Tell you what, let's talk about this Monday. I'd do it now, but I'm supposed to meet a friend in a quarter of an hour at home."

Chris flushed, flabbergasted by Kenton's response. "Really? You mean it?" He waited, and Paul nodded. "Thank you, Sir. Thank you. Could we meet real early Monday morning so I could get started on it? Would that be okay?"

Paul face broke into a broad grin from the contagious vibes of enthusiasm pouring from the young student. "Sure. I'll see you at 7:45."

Chris danced as he turned to leave. "I'll be right on top of an earthquake I predicted with a full bank of instruments. Now they'll believe me."

"Oh, Chris," Paul called. Chris stopped and turned. "Do you know the history of that area? One of my ancestors, Simon Kenton, was involved with the original town on the river that moved to New Simon after the earthquakes of 1812. And New Simon is near where Otto Nuttli determined the epicenter of the first of that series to be. How's that for coincidence?"

JQ called a special meeting Saturday afternoon in West Memphis for all the foremen of his 17 crews installing earthquake retrofit cabling on highway bridges. Some of the crew chiefs drove as far as 200 miles from jobs in Missouri, Arkansas and Tennessee to be at the meeting; JQ would have fired them had they not appeared.

As the last arrived and sat down on a folding chair in the McCrombie Enterprises garage area, JQ moved to the front of the group and leaned back on the bare table behind him. A slight breeze cooled the large building, but he could see most of the foremen sweating in anticipation.

"Okay, you guys, quiet down and listen up. I didn't call y'all here for a tea party." He waited a couple of moments more until their undivided attention focused on their boss. "I wanted y'all here so we could talk about how things are going, and how some things aren't going so well."

JQ paused to let his words sink in and fear start to build. He did not say what was wrong. Every one of those assembled had been the brunt of at least one of his noted tongue-lashings, and he was sure none wanted to be on the receiving end again. He smiled.

"First, I want to warn you. I suppose y'all know we had a little earthquake this morning." He stared from face to face, moving left to right. "Well, I was up at NASTY'S pretty near where it happened, and it made everybody, including me, sit up and take notice."

He leaned forward. "Earthquakes make people know what we do is important. That's good. But it also makes certain folks up tight so they want to check on how things are going. That's bad." He wagged a finger at one of the men. "Watch out and make sure that anyone who comes around only sees what we want them to see. If you get a snoop, find out who it is and call me. Call me quick. Understand? And hear this, don't roughhouse them unless I tell you to.

"Second, I got some good news, I just got word that McCrombie Enterprises received the next contract for earthquake retrofits on I-55 from Cape Girardeau to the intersection with I-255, and then on I-255 from Caruthersville across the river to Jackson." He smiled with the news. "That means you guys who are making a good profit will be extra busy for the next few months. That's the key, folks: a good profit."

JQ let the thought sink in, then continued. "But there's some of you turkeys who don't understand what that means. There's some who don't seem to understand how to make a profit." He pounded on the table, jutting his jaw forward. "Your goal is to make a big profit, not put some stupid cables on a bunch of dumb bridges. That's just the work you do to make that profit." His voice raised. "Y'all got that? Huh?"

JQ's face clouded, and he paced back and forth. "Now, there's some of you who are falling down on the profit end of things. Some of you aren't keeping your costs in line. Some of you are taking too damned long on piddly jobs."

Stopping with an abrupt slap of his foot on the cement, he turned and picking one of the men at random, glared into his eyes. "If that keeps up, and you don't get the message damned quick, you and a couple of others will be hunting for work in Oklahoma because there sure as hell won't be any work around here for you."

JQ looked over the other crew chiefs, letting each feel the sting of his stare. Adrenaline coursed through his body from the thrill of putting in the screws and twisting.

"Some of you children don't seem to understand how to cut the corner on costs. Che-rist, people, some of your expenses on these jobs are getting way out of line. Where the hell're you buying cable, the jewelers? What's with you guys, can't you get anything right? I want profit, a big profit." JQ shouted and pounded harder on the table.

"This worry about earthquakes is a bunch of bull-shit. Big earthquakes don't happen around here, but they make for good work." He whirled to look at the other side of the group. "All you got to do to keep the golden goose laying golden eggs is get the work done quick and cheap."

JQ stopped, smiled a knowing smile, and winked. "Just be sure you pass inspection, even if you have to pay a little extra for it."

He put on a wondering face for his crew chiefs. "Y'all remember how to put something like that on your expense reports, dontcha?" They all laughed on cue at the in-house joke. "I bet I'm the only boss y'all know who'll cover the cost of a whore provided you write in who, when, and where and get a receipt."

An hour after returning to his apartment in Jericho, just north of West Memphis, Alex remembered his planned date that evening with Tina, neither confirmed nor canceled after the blowup with JQ. Fighting a sense of shame, Alex made a quick decision. What the hell, he'd at least go back and check. Maybe he could explain to Tina his reactions to JQ. Maybe after she calmed down, she'd understand.

Alex drove the 64 miles to New Simon, and then scanned NASTY'S parking lot when he arrived. If he saw JQ's red sportster still there, he'd take a side trip to the river. He'd rather speed away than face JQ again.

Seeing the coast clear, he turned off his car's engine and stepped out. The air hung close and humid, without wind. Sweat ran down his cheeks. He had an hour until Tina ended her shift; he might as well wait inside.

Opening the rusty screen door and pushing aside the squeaky front door, he walked across the worn wooden floor and sat down at the counter. A tall, skinny redhead he didn't remember brought a menu and laid it before him. "What d'ya want?" She synchronized the words with chewing the gum in her mouth.

"Is Tina here?"

"Tina? Sure, she'll be out in a minute. Say, you wouldn't be the reason she's so upset, would ya? She's been crying all afternoon." The redhead pulled back, putting her hands on her bony hips with scorn. She waited for a response.

"I don't know. Maybe."

"So, I guess you're still a customer. Ya already et or d'ya want something?" When she finished speaking, she imitated a wide grin showing off her shiny teeth.

"I'll have an iced tea, sweetened," Alex replied in defense, wanting to send the waitress away. He felt bad enough about letting Tina down and didn't want to hear anyone else's comments.

Tina walked out of the Women's Restroom that also served as the waitress's dressing room. "Bye, Cookie. Bye, Janet. Thanks for letting me take off early. See you guys tomorrow." As she turned to walk out the door her eyes fell upon Alex.

"What're you doing here?" She exploded.

"We had a date, remember? I'm supposed to take you to the movies." Alex's smile was crooked, the best he could do.

Tina looked ready to hit him, and then her face softened. "Alex, how could you leave me out on a limb like that?" Tina wailed and stamped her foot in despair. "Now I've got to go with JQ for lunch, or I'll get fired. Why didn't you do something?"

Alex spread his hands on the counter and took a deep breath. His shoulders slumped as he pleaded. "Tina, I'm sorry. I know how you feel because JQ did the same thing to me. He almost fired me on the spot, and I was so scared I couldn't help myself." His voice cracked. "There wasn't anything that I could do to stop him from walking all over me—and you. Can't you understand?"

She hesitated, then relented, her eyes tearing. "Oh, I know you're right. I guess he really put you on the spot, especially about taking time off for a date with me. But now I have to go to Memphis to meet with him, and I don't know what he'll try. I'm scared, Alex, I'm scared." Drops flowed down her cheeks.

"Tina, let's go to the movie and let this sit a while. Maybe we can think of something. Please?" He reached towards her hand.

Tina wavered, then took his hand. "Oh, I guess so." Shrugging her shoulders as if to throw off the weight, she smiled and said, "But I need to drive my car back home to Dell. Follow me, then we'll go in your car, okay?"

"Sure, I'll follow you, but what's your address and phone number just in case I get lost." Alex smiled, hoping the tension would evaporate as the evening progressed. She wrote down the numbers and handed them to him. At least now, he knew where she lived.

Chris leaned back in his chair in front of the workstation and stretched. The clock read 6:15. "Damn, I've been in front of this console for another nine hours straight." His eyes blurred. He took another sip of stale soda.

His recent results, after adding the latest data, still perplexed him. He asked his computer model, "Nelson, why don't you want to converge like with the Dell event? This next temblor's really giving you fits."

Chris did a drum roll on the desktop and verbalized his situation, trying to find some way to a solution, "I've got a major problem because the calculation keeps jumping between two solutions, but why's that? Okay. The solution 2.5 kilometers south of New Simon's has grown to a magnitude 4.7 event, the one under New Simon's to 5.2." He scratched his mop of hair. Either solution would be significant, but he couldn't make Nelson choose between them. "I don't know. Maybe a smaller shock this week will pinpoint which one's correct. I sure the hell don't want to be wrong on this next one, not after Dr. Kenton's promise."

He played with the mouse and the keyboard, adjusting parameters and rerunning the simulation. "Let's see what happens if I reduce the strength of the southern asperity." He reran the simulation several times to test its sensitivity to asperity strength.

"Okay, let's try zero." This time the computer continued to calculate, longer and longer, not reaching a solution. "Damn, Nelson, you're hung in a loop." He waited a moment to be sure before resetting. Then results began to flash on the screen. Chris sucked in his gut in astonishment. "It's not stopping."

The simulated earthquake grew larger and larger. The depicted rupture in the fault spread further and further beyond the epicenter, northeast and southwest. The magnitude meter kept climbing. When the fracture reached 92 kilometers in length with the estimated magnitude over 7.7 the simulation ended. Chris stared at the screen and exclaimed, "That's one hell of a fracture. It looks like my 7.9 scenario."

Remembering Dr. Kenton's comment about New Simon being the epicenter for the 1811 earthquake, he asked his computer, "Is that what happened 200 years ago? Surely the southern asperity was in place back then."

Setting the second asperity back to its original strength, he reran the computer program and within three minutes his original predictions reappeared. "I'll be damned. Maybe that southern asperity is what keeps the one under New Simon from really going off."

Shaken, he rubbed his eyes. "God, Nelson. I'd better figure out how to make you handle two asperities. Things could be more complicated than I thought."

CHAPTER 7: MAKING DEALS

JQ paced back and forth in his West Memphis office. After collecting cash from the office and more from his home, he had visited Beale Street to get a quick loan—at an astounding daily rate of interest. By mid-afternoon he told George Besh over the telephone, "I've got the $20,000 in twenties and hundred dollar bills like you require. Come by and pick it up."

"Sure thing, JQ. I'll come by your office about seven this evening."

The clock pointed to eight, George had not arrived, JQ was pissed. "Where the hell is that guy? Doesn't he own a frigging watch?"

JQ sat in his office chair and lifted his boots onto the desk, chewing on a pencil eraser. He felt queasy, wondering if the tension from this dope deal had gotten to him. He needed that extra money for the payoffs coming up. There was no other way to get the cash, except to borrow more from that bastard in Memphis. At the interest rate he would have to pay, he'd never get out from under the debt.

JQ had already checked the building to be sure people in on Saturday had left the office. He recalled the morning meeting with his crew chiefs. It had been good. They all took what he said to heart. They knew their business; they'd find better ways to squeeze money out of the contracts. They were people of his own kind.

Afterward Elmer, one of his foremen, said, "Iffen you want, JQ, I'll bring my crew down from New Simon to help move stuff from West Memphis to the new building on Friday. They can make up the missed time on Saturday."

"Sure, do that. I've got a bottle of moonshine you can share with the five of them. I'd invite y'all to stay for the open house, but you're too grungy to be seen in public."

He remembered the caterers and made a note regarding further arrangements for the Friday open house. He hoped the Mayor would visit. He missed dealing with his old cronies she had defeated in the last election. She was an old coot and a bit crafty, but he could work on her. He had a good way with women.

His thoughts drifted back to Tina at NASTY'S. She had agreed to go to lunch on Tuesday, but she didn't seem enthusiastic. He needed to teach her a lesson, soften her up a bit. Once he got her upstairs in the penthouse, he'd bring her down a notch or two.

JQ made another note to talk with the head of his computer department, *"Geoff – is it important to keep Alex?"* JQ had twisted the screws on Alex. He wondered just how the young man would take it. Maybe he'd quit. That way there'd be no problem.

JQ dropped his boots to the floor and again paced about his office. "Where's George?"

Judy brooded and worried more and more about her daughter as her husband drove the truck toward the foothills on US Highway-50. "Tom, are you absolutely sure Jenny's going to be okay with this earthquake danger?"

"Hard to say. The New Madrid Fault places more people at risk than any other fault in the United States. It's the most dangerous fault in the country. The last time it failed in 1811 and 1812, the earth shook so hard that people felt it over 1,000 miles away in places like Boston and Charleston, South Carolina. For the next five months aftershocks were so strong that people over 250 miles away felt them. The fault continued shaking for another five years."

"Five years?"

Tom guided the truck from curve to curve along a winding four-lane road as the grasslands east of the Sacramento merged into the tree-covered foothills. Digger pines and oak gave way to ponderosa pines and fir. In the canyon below ran the American River where pockets of gold had lured thousands of forty-niners to the land over a century and a half before.

"Scientists estimate the largest temblor in 1812 to have been magnitude 8.2 to 8.6. For the United States, only the Alaskan earthquake in 1965 was a larger magnitude, and that one, relatively speaking, consisted of a single event compared to the series of New Madrid earthquakes."

Judy struggled to concentrate on what Tom said, envisioning the destruction from earthquake after earthquake after earthquake, never stopping. The pounding of the tires on the pavement and the swaying of the truck as they went from mountainous turn to turn began to feel more and more like shaking of the earth itself. Judy's back ached and her stomach cramped.

"There have been a few strong earthquakes in the New Madrid region since then. In 1846 an earthquake estimated at magnitude 6.3 hit the region, and in 1895 a magnitude 6.8 temblor struck near Charleston, Missouri.

"Most everyone agrees that another great earthquake will strike along the New Madrid Fault in the not too distant future. There's evidence that a large earthquake occurs as often as every 270 years, though the really big ones may be 400 to 1,000 years apart."

Judy took a deep breath in relief. Tom stated a fact to which she could cling, and she did the arithmetic. "Thank God. That means Jenny doesn't need to worry about a really big earthquake for another 70 years," she declared.

"No, no, Judy. The 270-year estimate is only the average time between major earthquakes. A large earthquake can happen in the region anytime. It might be another 400 years before the next big earthquake happens, or it could happen next year, even next week. You just don't know."

"Then the 70 years isn't right?" Judy asked, her voice cracking a tiny bit.

"No, I'm afraid not. But more importantly, it's been over 100 years since any sizeable, damaging quake has struck along the fault. People who live there are complacent. One thing is clear," Tom preached, "The longer it's been since a great earthquake, the higher the probability it'll happen. So the chances only get worse. Jenny and everyone else near the New Madrid Fault should spend time worrying about the fact that a big earthquake can occur and prepare right now."

Judy sat in silence a moment, then asked in a quiet voice, "Tom, did our earthquake this morning cause the one in Memphis?"

Tom shook his head. "No, the two earthquakes were not related. However, the San Andreas and other faults around the edge of the continent transmit stress throughout the North American continent. The accumulated stress in some places in the interior of the continent, like the New Madrid, is sufficient to cause earthquakes."

"Why on the New Madrid?"

Tom collected his thoughts. "I read where the New Madrid fault became active about 200 million years ago as a rift, a break in the crust of the earth that spread apart. It's still a weak part of the crust."

Judy said, "I remember a special on the Discovery Channel about how the earth condensed from dust around the sun into molten rock with crust on top."

"Right. That crust is composed of minerals that floated up from below, sort of like the scum that collects on top when you make jelly. As the crust cooled, that scum collected into what are called continental plates. These plates move around like parts of a jig-saw puzzle." He looked at Judy and asked, "Do you get the picture?"

Judy asked, "Is any of that scum left?"

Tom smiled. "Sure, look at the road cut we're driving through. Those rocks you see are the scum that make up the continental plates."

He continued. "Our continent is mostly all one piece called the North American Plate, but it also has other plates attached to it, like the Pacific Plate. It averages about 60 kilometers thick—that's 36 miles. Thinner ocean plates cover the bottoms of the oceans. All these plates float on the molten rock called magma. Today about 20 continental plates float around the world."

Judy's patience began to wear. "So what does all this have to do with Memphis?"

Tom pointed ahead to the Sierra Nevada Mountains rising in the distance, their snowy peaks visible in the clear mid-May air. "When continental plates move around on top of the magma, they collide with one another. Those mountains are the result of plates that collided. Earthquakes happen when the crust fractures from the forces of continental plates colliding or rubbing against each other. It's called plate tectonics."

Judy asked, "What does plate tectonics look like?"

Tom frowned but continued, "Well, one prime example of plate tectonics in action is right near our home. Our townhouse rests on the North American plate. On the other side of San Francisco is the San Andreas Fault and west of that is the Pacific Plate. The San Andreas Fault is where the two plates rub past each other. That rubbing is what causes earthquakes along the San Andreas."

Judy thought of their drives along the coast and asked, "I remember one time on a drive south from San Francisco we stopped at the San Juan Bautista mission. Didn't you say that the dirt bank we saw next to the chapel was the San Andreas Fault?"

Tom smiled at Judy's recollection. "Sure thing. That bank marks the actual trace of the fault where the land on one side of the fracture has dropped during past earthquakes, leaving the other side about ten feet higher."

"But the bank is right next to the chapel. Is the fault really that close?"

"Yes, Judy, the fault's trace, as it is called, is within 20 feet of the chapel."

"What about our earthquake this morning? You said it had to be real close to be so strong."

"The earthquake we felt must have occurred on the Calaveras Fault, an offshoot of the San Andreas. Do you remember when we bought our townhouse five years ago we signed a paper acknowledging that we knew our home sat atop the north end of the fault?"

Judy thought. Paper about the Calaveras Fault? She remembered signing papers, but she didn't remember signing anything about a fault.

Shaken, she straightened in her seat and asked, "Tom, just how close is the Calaveras Fault to our townhouse? I haven't seen any bank like at the chapel around our home."

"The fault trace in Danville is not visible like in San Juan Bautista. All the earth-slides from past earthquakes cover it. But it's directly under our home." He smiled, as if taking pride in making the revelation.

Judy realized she had reason to be disturbed. She searched for a comparison, "Tom, what do you mean about the Calaveras being an off-shoot of the San Andreas? Does that make it a big fault?"

"Well, think of the Calaveras Fault as a stretch mark, like on your legs. As the Pacific Plate slides alongside the North American Plate, frictional forces along the San Andreas stretch neighboring rocks and create other faults parallel to the main fault that can be just as bad as the main fault."

Depression and revulsion overtook Judy. Bad luck must run in her family. First Jenny, and now she and Tom, living on a fault line. And Tom compared their fault with her stretch marks. She shifted in the bucket seat. "Tom, I consider your remarks to be utterly gauche."

JQ saw a beat-up Buick sedan pull behind the building and park. "Finally, the bastard's here. Wonder what his excuse is this time." JQ rose from his desk and walked to the back of the offices to let George in.

"Hello, JQ. You having a nice day?" His temporary business associate's slimy smirk as he walked up the steps irritated JQ. He felt uncertain what it was, but George always reminded him of a salamander.

"It's about time you arrived. Where you been? Sleeping?"

"You could call it that. Just catching up on some unfinished business with a girl I know." He smacked his lips. As they walked back toward JQ's office George whispered, "Anyone else here?"

JQ turned back to George and replied in a loud voice, "No. It's late. They left a couple of hours ago, about the time you were supposed to get here, so we don't have to whisper."

They entered the office and JQ closed the door, just in case. Reaching under the desk, he pulled out an old, battered briefcase he had found at the

Thrift Store and placed it on the desk. Opening it, he turned it toward George. "There it is, $20,000 in twenties and C-notes. Count it."

"Oh, that's okay, JQ. I trust you. I know you wouldn't stiff me on anything." George licked his thin lips and added, "Besides, with what I just found out, I think you might want to give me some portion of the profits when you get the one-twenty back."

"One-twenty—god-dammit." JQ yelled. "We agreed I'd get $125,000. You're already trying to stiff me on this deal. I thought you were making your own profit on this deal, and now I know how."

George looked hurt, "You're right, JQ. It's 125, just like you said. Just checking if you remembered." He chuckled.

"Bullshit. And what's this crap about me giving you a rake off the top?" JQ watched George like he would a cottonmouth in the swamp.

George closed the lid to the old briefcase and put it on his lap. "Cause I've got some really important information for you, something nobody else knows anything about."

"What's that? You tell me this information. I'll decide if it's worth anything."

"Well, I got a call from an old buddy of mine at the University, name of Robbie. He knows one of them graduate students on earthquakes, and he told me all about the quake this morning." George lowered his voice. "This graduate student, Chris, says we're going to have another shaker up at New Simon next week. He's got a theory for predicting quakes, and he's getting real good at it. Now if you want to know more, you might shell out some cash to pay for the dope I'm providing to Robbie, say a couple of grand." George rubbed his thumb across his fingertips.

JQ ignored the suggestion. "Going to be another quake, huh. Now that's interesting." He leaned back in his chair and folded his hands under his chin. "What makes you think this Chris guy knows what he's talking about?"

"Well, he predicted the last one, the one we felt, and Robbie says the University's going to send him up there with some instruments to check out this next one, so I guess they must believe there's something about what he's saying."

George put his finger to his lips. "Except, Chris told Robbie to keep his mouth shut about any earthquake predictions. Robbie told me because I'm his special friend."

JQ considered the information for a moment. With earthquake retrofit work as the focus of his company, there must be some good way to use information about earthquakes before they happened, like maybe increase the price for the work about to be done. But he was not about to be taken in on one of George's scams.

"Okay, you keep getting information from this guy, and we'll see if it's worthwhile. I'm not making any promises. If it's good, I'll see that you get what you deserve. Hell, I don't even know if this guy can predict an earthquake or not."

George smiled again like a snake flicking its tongue. "Sure, JQ. I trust you'll give me what I deserve, old buddy. And I remember, it's one-twenty-five, right?" George reached across the desk to shake JQ's hand.

"Right. Now take the money and get the hell out of here."

As George left JQ rubbed his hand on his pants leg, trying to wipe the slimy feeling from his skin.

After a fine dinner in the casino steakhouse, Judy felt happy to follow Tom to his favorite sport, the roulette wheel. She enjoyed following the white ball round and round the wheel and then into one of the numbered slots. At times it proved almost hypnotic. Occasionally she felt that she could guide the ball into whatever slot she wanted.

Tom had his own system, which he again explained to Judy. "Whenever a dealer gets into a groove spinning the ball, I watch for a pattern of successive plays that moves the ball's final resting-place around the wheel in a regular sequence." He turned away from the table to complete his explanation. "Then I place one- or two-number bets on those numbers most likely to be next in that sequence. That's when I win big." He smiled in anticipation.

Though he won a couple of times, Judy watched Tom's stack of chips dwindle to a quarter of its original size in short order. "You keep missing the groove," she commented.

"Yeah, or maybe the dealer's too smart and is avoiding consistency."

Judy leaned over and whispered. "Tom, the number 13 hasn't come up in a long time, ever since we've been here. It's time for it to hit."

Tom leaned back and whispered. "That doesn't make any difference. The probability of hitting 13 is the same as it's always been, one chance in 38. It doesn't get any higher even if 13 doesn't come up all day." He leaned closer and asked, "Why are we whispering?"

"I don't want the dealer to know I've noticed." Then Judy remembered their earlier conversations and questioned, "After all, you said the probability of a big earthquake increases as time goes on. What makes you think the probability for 13 doesn't increase when it hasn't hit in a long time?"

Tom explained. "Well, each roll of the roulette ball is independent from every other roll, that is unless the dealer gets into a groove, which he isn't. So the probability is always one in 38 for each number every time." Tom placed two chips on 29, the next number he expected to come up.

"But earthquakes are produced when the moving plates increase the stress more than the rock can stand, and the plate cracks. Since that stress continues to grow, the probability of an earthquake increases in time. Doesn't that make sense?"

"I suppose, but I still think you should play 13. Being a roulette ball shouldn't be that different."

The ball completed its journey. "Thirteen, Black" the dealer called and placed the marker over the chips of another players.

Judy looked at Tom with disdain. "See, I told you so."

CHAPTER 8: TENSION GROWS

"The place is full." Tom raised two fingers to the hostess as he spoke to Judy. "Looks like seven o'clock Sunday morning is a busy time for casino coffee shops."

The hostess smiled. "It'll be a ten minute wait."

Tom frowned. "Can we sit at the counter? We need to head out of Carson City sooner than later." The hostess indicated two empty counter stools next to a black gentleman in faded jeans and flannel shirt. Tom led the way and sat next to him. The man nodded hello and stirred his coffee, waiting for his breakfast plate.

The buxom waitress deposited two waters and the menus. Judy spoke before she could depart. "Two coffees, and I'll have biscuits and gravy."

The waitress brushed her gray hair away from her eyes and, writing the order on her ticket book, looked at Tom. "Well?"

Tom felt his first irritation of the day. With no chance to study the menu, again he must order his standard fare. "I guess I'll have two eggs poached, sausage, and whole wheat toast, no butter." On impulse he added, "and bring me an orange juice."

Judy smiled at the waitress. "No, change his order to Canadian bacon—it's better for him—and I want orange juice, too, so make that one large orange juice. We'll share."

Tom creased his brow, determined to ignore his wife's micro-management. He stirred sugar into his coffee and leaned his elbows on the counter. "Do you have more questions about Memphis, or did I come too close to putting you asleep yesterday?"

"Tom, I understand most of what you said. And I did stay awake." The tone of her voice told him he had scored. "But I'm still worried about Jenny being in that big Memphis earthquake."

"Excuse me." The low voice came from the crusty fellow next to Tom. "Did you say something about an earthquake in Memphis?" He looked worried. "My daughter lives near there."

Judy leaned forward to look around Tom. "Yes, we're talking about earthquakes. Memphis had an earthquake yesterday while I was talking to our daughter who's going to school there, and we had an earthquake in the Bay Area at the same time." Her eyes widened. "It just seems so strange that they'd occur at the same time, don't you think? There's no damage in Memphis, so you don't need to worry about your daughter." She smiled in comfort. "We're Judy and Tom Fox. What's your name?" Judy's persistence in making instant acquaintances oftentimes embarrassed Tom.

"Oh, hi. I'm Mel Washington. I felt it, too—the one in the Bay Area. I drive an eighteen-wheeler, and I was picking up a load in San Leandro when that shaking hit yesterday. It was the strongest earthquake I've ever felt." He leaned forward to better see Judy. "It made me jumpy, and then I heard you mention earthquakes in Memphis. Well, I'm scared for my little girl, even if she is grown and moved out."

"We understand. We worry about our daughter, too, what with the really big earthquake that's going to hit there real soon." Judy replied in empathy. "What's your daughter's name?"

Mel started at the news, "Her name's Tina Washington. What do you mean a big earthquake's going to happen in Memphis? When?"

Tom intervened. "Whoa there. Mel, don't get all upset. My wife sometimes makes things seem bigger than they really are." He put up his hand to cut the dialogue. "It's just that scientists predict that sometime in the future the New Madrid Fault west of Memphis will let go again like it did 200 years ago, but it's not likely it'll happen anytime soon."

Mel twisted his shoulders. "I'd better check when I get home and talk to Tina about it. Maybe she should move away from there."

Judy said, "Yes, and Jenny's boyfriend, who's a scientist at the University of Memphis, says there's going to be another earthquake next Sunday." She did not want Mel to become complacent.

Tom exploded. "Judy, for Christ's sake. You can't go around making statements like that." Turning back to Mel he once again tried to restore calm to the conversation, "I'm sorry, Mel. Don't let Judy's hysterics infect you. She worries excessively. There are dangers everywhere, and there are always predictions, mostly wrong." He took a deep breath. "If someone moves away from every danger, they'll just trade one danger for a new one. Your daughter will be safe in Memphis."

"Tom, I have reason to worry." Judy turned back to confront her coffee. Her face showed she was pouting.

The waitress delivered the food and tensions eased as the three ate their breakfast and discussed their respective families. Tom explained. "We're driving to Memphis to visit our daughter and see her new place. And the trip's a great chance to try out our new truck-camper with all its gadgets."

Tom saw Judy glance up to raise the proverbial eyebrow. He felt a perverse joy emphasizing his other agenda, knowing her reason for the trip to be a consultation with Jenny.

"What kind of rig and gadgets have you got?"

"Well, my rig's a three-quarter-ton, heavy-duty pickup with four-wheel-drive and a big turbo-charged diesel engine and five-speed trannie plus over-drive." Tom enjoyed talking about his recreational vehicle. "We're carrying an eleven-foot cab-over camper, self-contained, with solar-power and three extra batteries. I installed a 30-gallon fresh-water tank and two 20-gallon waste water tanks."

"Hey man, I'm impressed. Sounds like you got a boss rig there."

"I actually planned it as a survival vehicle for when the next big earthquake hits the Bay Area. I also installed a GPS satellite positioning system with a laptop, a satellite TV system and one of the new Low Satellite telephones."

"You're really set up. What kind of firepower do you carry?"

"Firepower?" Tom had to think a moment to catch the drift of Mel's question. "Oh, I don't believe guns are necessary. We don't plan to be any place where people use guns, and I'm not a hunter."

"Well, there's some pretty scary dudes out on the road, and we haven't even had a disaster. If you're going to survive after a big catastrophe like a giant earthquake, you better carry a gun."

"No. Guns aren't necessary."

"Hey, that's your call." Mel stood and collected his bill. "I'm headed back to Memphis myself. Maybe we'll see each other on the road along the way, though I go south from here, and I'll probably push on ahead of you folks. See you down the road. Take care." Turning he walked away.

Judy leaned closer to Tom. "Tom, could he be right about having a gun? You know, we hear all those reports of car-jackings and everything else on the road."

Tom turned to his wife and glared. "Judy, I wish you'd quit worrying about everything. I don't want a gun. I don't need a gun. I'm not going to have a gun. That's final." His irritation level approached ten.

Tina rescued a newspaper left by one of the truckers and glanced over the Sunday comics. She blushed as her mind wandered back to the evening before. She remembered how she and Alex sat in his car at the drive-in movie and necked, just like back in high school. Only these days, the gearshift between the bucket seats presented a real problem.

They talked of many things, what happened to each other after high school, where they wanted to go in life. Later they got around to talking about JQ.

"JQ just has too much control over our lives," Alex asserted. "That can change if we want it to. It'll just take time."

Tina rationalized her fears of having lunch with JQ. Alex gave her moral support. "I promise I'll help if any problems develop. In the meantime, we can still see each other, but let's keep our relationship secret from JQ." He sounded so sure and pragmatic.

The ringing telephone broke Tina's reverie. Cookie answered, then whispered, "Hey, Tina, it's for you." Putting his hand over the mouthpiece he added, "Sounds like the boss-man."

Tina took the telephone. "Hello, this is Tina," she said, striving to keep her voice steady and calm.

"Hi, Tina, this is JQ. I called to apologize for pushing on you so hard yesterday. I was kind of uptight from some business dealings I was doing, and I imagine I came across a bit heavy."

"Well, you did do that, but thanks for apologizing." Tina marveled at how smooth the man could be when he wanted.

"I just wanted to be sure you'd be going to lunch with me on Tuesday. I'm looking forward to showing off my new building and penthouse office."

Tina, resigned to the fact she had to go, answered, "Yes, I'll have lunch with you, and I'm sure I'll enjoy seeing your new offices."

"Great. Say, I'll be working in the city that morning, so you drive down to Memphis by yourself. Park in the basement of the new building, and I'll meet you there. I'll let the work crew know you're coming. Be there a quarter before noon. Got that? " She felt his firm charm even over the phone.

"Yes, I'll be there at 11:45. Bye, JQ." She placed the handset back on the wall cradle and shuddered. She felt an icy wind blow by, stripping her of emotion except for her underlying fear. She again wondered what the man would do when they were alone.

"You okay?" asked Cookie as he headed out carrying a sack of trash.

"Sure, I'm fine. I'm just cold. It's cold in here." She reset the thermostat and returned to attend to her remaining customers.

"Cold? She thinks it's cold? It's hot as hell today. That girl's got problems." Cookie muttered as he turned the thermostat back down and walked out the back door of the kitchen.

Chris sat in front of the workstation as the Sunday morning sunbeams filled the outer office. He beat a random rhythm on the desktop as he ran another series of tests with Nelson and worked on plans for the monitoring station he would set up near New Simon.

Jenny wrinkled her nose as she walked through the door, "What's that smell? Did someone leave their dirty laundry behind the desk again?"

Chris looked up from his list. "Oh, it's you." He sniffed the air and realized his 32-hour marathon in the Lab had affected the environment. "What're you doing here on a Sunday?" he asked.

"After your comments yesterday about the action at Dell, I thought I'd check to see what's happening on the New Madrid." Jenny sounded flip, but Chris suspected curiosity about his earthquake theory had lured her to the lab.

Chris checked his notes. "Let's see, two more fractures hit yesterday afternoon, then three little ones last night. More and more stress is pouring into that asperity at New Simon." He challenged the young girl. "It's due to break in about a week, and it may be bigger than I thought. At least, that's what Nelson says is going on." He waited for her to challenge him like the day before.

"So what're you doing about it?" she asked.

Though he felt gun-shy, Chris still needed to discuss his work. "Dr. Kenton said I could set up a mobile sensing station in New Simon to get a better handle on that asperity. I'm working on the list of what I need. I'll install it Tuesday and capture details on small temblors in the area."

"Hey, that's great. What do they put in a monitoring station?"

"It's a standard model. It'll have a string of accelerometers to catch all surface vibrations from any nearby earthquake. I'll also use a high-precision GPS and three laser-positioning systems to track slow movement." He checked off items from his list. "Just for good measure, I'm activating the ultra-low frequency radio wave detector as well as the magnetometer to measure changes in the earth's magnetic field around the fault. This station uses a radiophone telemetry link to the lab here. I'm adding solar power so I don't need to depend on the power at the monitoring site. And I'm trying to think if there's anything else." Chris had considered every detail in a thorough and complete manner.

"That sure sounds like a lot to set up. I hope it's worth all that work." Jenny showed a curious glint in her eye. "But what makes you so sure there will be a significant earthquake at New Simon? And why so soon?"

"Come off it—you're just setting up to poke fun again." Chris backed into his defensive shell like a hermit crab.

"No, Chris, I'm sorry about yesterday, I didn't mean to sound bitchy about it all. I really am interested in what you're doing." She put on her best repentant face and fluttered her eyelashes.

Chris ached to tell people about his ideas, and she seemed serious. "Okay, but don't you go repeating this to anyone else. Okay?"

"I promise, cross my heart," Jenny answered like a child, stroking Chris's attention.

"I won't tell you my whole theory, but I'll give you an idea of what's going on." He picked up a rock sample from beside the workstation. "Remember how in geology lab we looked at some of these metamorphic rocks we knew came from extreme depths and hot environments, and how you could see an orientation in the slick crystalline structures of the serpentine?"

Jenny took the green sample and turned it in her hand. "Yeah, that was one of the most interesting labs I attended last year."

"Well, I've worked out how forces are transported over the length of the fault, and that crystalline structure plays a major part in the process." He pointed to the striations along one shiny surface. "Then I found a *P-wave* signature for rock with that crystalline structure. I used that signature to locate asperities where the stress transport is being restricted and determined how much energy flows through them along the fault. Follow?"

"I think so."

"Okay then, by monitoring energy flow along the fault I can locate which asperities don't pass energy so well, and using another correlation I'm not telling anyone about yet, I can determine how much stress it'll take to break each asperity." He took back the sample. "If I do this for all the asperities along a fault line, I can determine which one will be the next to go.

"And by knowing how much energy has collected at the asperity, I know how big the temblor will be. Doesn't that all make sense?" Chris waited for her approval.

"Yes, but how do you know how much energy has collected at an asperity if you haven't been watching it since the last time it broke?" Jenny's quick mind picked out a factor still bothering Chris.

"Oh, I have to estimate how much stress collected in the past. But I've been pretty good at making those estimates on the earthquakes I've studied so far. I think I can tell."

"But if you're off on the energy, does that affect when the earthquake will happen and how big it'll be?"

"Sure, but it shouldn't make that much difference, except for the magnitude. What is this, an inquisition?" Chris again switched to the defensive. "Hey, I've got work to do. If you want to develop your own theory, come back later when I'm not so busy."

Jenny took the hint, "Sorry, I'll head back to the library and do my homework. I didn't mean to bother you. Maybe I'll see you tomorrow." She walked out of the lab.

"Bye," Chris said, sad to see her go. He realized his belligerence had again driven her away. He shook his head to push those thoughts out of his mind and turned back to continue work on his list.

Dialing JQ's number, George waited as the call went through.

"Yeah, what d'ya want?" JQ's gruff voice answered the phone.

"George here, JQ. I just visited my contact with our budding earthquake scientist and gave him a small hit of coke. The latest report is that the next quake'll be at New Simon at 1:00 A.M. next Sunday. He said it'll be magnitude 5.2 plus. This Chris fellow's putting a remote sensing station up near New Simon this week. I told Robbie to keep me up to date, and I'll keep you posted if I hear anything new. That what you want?"

"A 5.2, huh? That's bigger than the one that hit Marked Tree a few years ago. Woke people up but didn't do much damage. That should be about right to get people's attention, especially after the one yesterday. Yeah, that's what I wanted to know. Keep it up, George. You may earn your keep yet."

JQ broke the connection.

CHAPTER 9: MAKING PLANS

Chris paced back and forth like a caged lion in front of Paul Kenton's office. Awakening with the rising sun, he had showered, shaved the soft whiskers from his face, and returned early to the Seismic Lab wearing his cleanest socks and jockey shorts, a slightly rumpled shirt, a wrinkled pair of jeans, and well-worn sandals, ready to face his thesis advisor.

When Paul arrived at the appointed 7:45 A.M. Chris confronted him in the hall. "Dr. Kenton, you said there's a monitoring station I could use at New Simon."

Paul considered the young graduate student whose eagerness bordered on aggression and smiled. "I guess we better check on its status and make sure it's ready to go." He unlocked his office door and they entered. Chris squirmed on the 40-year-old oaken chair reserved for visitors, expectant as Paul placed a telephone call to the repair shop to verify the readiness of the equipment.

"Good, John, I'm glad to hear it's ready for a field test. I'll send Chris Nelson, one of my graduate students to pick it up. He'll be taking it out for a two-week test. His name's spelled N – E – L – S – O – N, … that's right."

He listened a moment then put his hand over the mouthpiece and asked, "Chris, do you have transportation for the equipment?"

Chris had not considered that factor. "Gosh, no, but I'll find whatever I need."

Paul spoke into the telephone. "Chris will provide the transportation. What do you suggest he have?" He paused, and then said, "Okay, a small pickup will do. Great." Again away from the mouthpiece, "Chris, can you bring a pickup to the repair depot by two o'clock this afternoon?"

"I'll find some kind of transportation in a couple of hours, Dr. Kenton." Chris replied, confident that he could find a pickup somewhere.

"He'll be there no later than two, maybe earlier. Why don't you get everything ready to go by ten, just in case, okay? Thanks, John." Paul hung up the telephone.

"You'd better get busy and find a truck." He smiled again, empathizing with Chris's spirit. "Understand the equipment must come back within fourteen days? Think that's long enough?"

"Sure, the earthquake will be over in less than a week." Chris answered, and then realized what he had said.

Paul looked at Chris with a questioning eye. "Still sure it will happen on schedule, huh? Well, be careful about letting word get out."

Chris let out his breath in relief. "Sure, Dr. Kenton. I'll keep it all to myself until I can prove to you that I have something to go on." He paused, then said, "But Sir, there's one thing. Under certain conditions my model predicts this could be a great earthquake with a magnitude over 7.7. Shouldn't we warn someone?"

Paul shook his head. "Chris, people don't like prophets, and they sometimes burn them at the stake, at least figuratively. Please don't embarrass me, or the University, by making public predictions, and for God's sake, don't say anything to anyone about a great earthquake, okay?"

"I understand, and thank you, Sir. You won't be disappointed with the results from this station." He rose and reached over to shake Paul's hand.

Chris mumbled as he hurried back across the parking lot to the lab, "How could I forget transportation? Now I have to borrow a truck."

Alex filled his cup at the community coffee bar of the McCrombie Enterprises offices, added powdered creamer and stirred the mixture. He chatted with Helen Stowes, the programmer in the Information Systems Department, as they loaded up with fresh coffee before meeting with their supervisor regarding the new file server system Alex had installed the previous week.

Alex looked up as JQ walked through the front door. "Oh no. He's coming right at me," he whispered. His stomach clutched. The skin on his arms rose into goose bumps, but he stood his place, unwilling to give way.

JQ stopped three feet away and sneered. "So you came back to work. I figured you'd stick your tail between your legs and call in sick." He snorted and pushed past Alex on the way to his office. Glaring back from the door, JQ said, "And remember what I said about taking time off for nooners. You do that, and I'll fire your ass."

"Wow. What was that about?" asked Helen. She stared at JQ as he closed the door to his office then turned to Alex. "Well?"

Alex blushed. "Oh, I had a run-in with JQ at the truck stop he owns up at New Simon on Saturday, and he's still after me about it."

"What kind of run-in? You must've really gotten under his skin." Alex knew from office gossip that Helen did not shy away from seeking out any news she could find, the juicier the better. He tried to explain without adding anything lurid to the story.

"Oh, there's a waitress up there that I knew in high-school, and she and I were talking. JQ has the idea that she's his own private territory, because he ran me off like a bull protecting one of his herd." Alex could still feel the stings from the tongue-lashing he received two days before. "He threatened to fire me if I didn't leave her alone."

"Alex, you can't let someone push you around like that. Go to Human Resources." Helen always provided instant advice for personal matters.

Alex's scornful laugh prefaced his reply. "Sure, I just tell HR my boss is butting into my love life. Lotta good that'll do. They know who calls the shots around here. No, I'll just stay in the background and keep my eyes open." Shrugging his shoulders, he followed Helen back to the small conference room for their meeting.

Chris hurried into the Seismology Lab, dropped his satchel on a bench and reached for the telephone.

"Hi, Chris," called Jenny from the other side of the room.

"Hi, Jenny," Chris answered and grinned. "Paul, er, Dr. Kenton just located a monitor station for New Simon. Now I've gotta borrow my Dad's pickup." Chris dialed the number for his father's home in south Memphis. "Hi, Dad, this is Chris. How're you doing?"

His father's loud voice filled his ear. "Oh, it's you. I'm doing fine, but Carla told me about you making some stupid earthquake prediction. Are you making a fool out of yourself again, boy?"

Chris pounded his forehead with his fist. When he talked with his twin sister yesterday, she had ridiculed him and laughed at his prediction. Damn, he thought, she's already spilled the beans. He just hoped her bias hadn't infected their father.

"Dad, I did not make a stupid prediction. I have a perfectly good theory to predict when the next earthquake will happen, and it's working." He wanted to yell but refrained. "Carla doesn't happen to believe me, but she's no seismologist. She doesn't know what she's talking about and never has."

"So it's true."

"Dad, the University believes in what I'm doing." He played his ace in the hole. "Dr. Kenton, my graduate advisor, believes enough to give me permission to take one of the department's portable seismic stations out to New Simon so I can monitor the area and test my theory."

"What's New Simon got to do with it?"

Chris took a breath. "That's what I'm calling you about. I need to borrow your pickup to take the equipment up there."

"What's your prediction?"

"I predict that there will be an earthquake underneath New Simon next Sunday morning, and I want to monitor the area in detail in the days before that happens and during the earthquake itself. That'll help refine my theories."

He repeated his request. "But I need to borrow your pickup for a week so I can take the gear up there and bring it back. I can leave my car with you so you won't be on foot." Chris prayed for an affirmative answer.

"I guess that would be okay, but how big's this quake going to be? Will I be able to feel it down here in Memphis?"

"Great, Dad, and thanks. Yes, you'll be able to feel it. It shouldn't be too rough here, a little stronger than last Saturday. But it'll be a good-sized jolt in New Simon. Can I come over and get the pickup now?"

"Suppose so, but what time of day will the quake happen?"

Chris realized much of his persistence came from his father. "I don't know the exact time as yet. I'll call you when I know more, but I need to transport the equipment to the site as soon as possible to get more detailed information to find out when it will be. I'll see you in less than an hour. Does the pickup have gas in it?"

"Has enough gas to get you to a filling station. Pick it up about noon." True to habit, his father hung up the telephone without saying goodbye once he believed the conversation had ended.

Chris pushed the silent handset away from his face and stared at it. "Gee, thanks, Dad. I thought you'd at least keep your truck filled with gas like I told you to." He let the handset fall back into its cradle. "Dammit, now I've got to find money to buy gas."

Jenny's small voice came from behind him. "I can loan you money for gas and food. Sounds like you'll need it if you're going to be up at New Simon very long."

Chris turned to see the girl standing with five twenty-dollar bills in her hand. "Here's a hundred dollars Mom sent me for my birthday. You can repay me after you get back, and then I can take you out to dinner for my birthday." She verified her offer with a big smile.

Chris stuttered from the largesse of the young student. "Thanks, Jenny, thanks a lot. This'll really help." It occurred to him that she could be even more help. "Say, maybe you could work with me from here at the Lab to see that the connections from the monitor station are set up right? Would you mind doing that for me?"

Jenny beamed with excitement. She had finally found a way into Chris's world. "Sure thing. I'd really like that," she said. "What can I do?" clasping her hands together in front of her chest.

JQ sat at his desk as the telephone rang. "Yeah. Who is it?" he demanded.

A sweet, feminine voice answered, "Am I speaking with JQ McCrombie?"

JQ adjusted his manner to the fact that the call must be from outside, not from one of his subordinates, and replied in a silky voice. "Why, yes ma'am, you are. Who is this, and what may I do for you?"

The answer came in a slow melodic drawl. "This is Pamela Weekes. We met three weeks ago at the Mayor's business community mixer, and you told me about the work you're doing on highway overpass retrofits. It was 'soooo' fascinating. You said I could call and talk with you about it anytime I wanted."

JQ squeezed his eyes, trying to recall the face that went with that voice. "Yes, I remember," he said, still searching his memory for the match.

Pamela not only spoke slowly, she spoke with detailed diction, "I work in public relations for the Memphis Department of Seismic Safety, and we are preparing some new collateral material to help people in the community understand what is needed for earthquake safety."

Now he remembered. That tall, slinky redhead who stood next to him at the mixer and kept gyrating her hips one direction while stirring the olive in her drink the opposite way and talking incessantly. He had not bothered to listen to what she said. His mind focused on the rhythmic counterpoint between olive and hips.

"I just thought it would be 'soooo' interesting to tell our public about all that marvelous work that you do, especially after this last little temblor." Emphasizing the personal touch, she asked, "Mr. McCrombie, did you feel the earthquake?"

The question brought his mind back. "Oh yes, as a matter of fact I did feel it. Not much of a jolt for someone like me," he expounded, though the recollection of the hot eggs in his lap still made him wince. "But I didn't realize you were with Seismic Safety. You say you want to write something about my company doing earthquake retrofits, is that right?"

"Why yes, and can I call you JQ?" She paused. "It would be 'soooo' interesting, JQ, to put the story into the City's monthly newsletter that goes to all the citizens of Memphis and surrounding regions. It will assure everyone to know what an important service your company performs for all of us."

He lifted his eyebrows and marveled how she laid it on 'soooo' thick, then responded. "Yes, I suppose it might be good for people to know about the work we do and why it is so necessary. Do you want to interview me over the phone?" The temptation of again seeing those hips grew. "Or maybe we could meet somewhere more comfortable and talk about it face to face?"

"Why, a comfortable face to face meeting, so to speak, would be splendid, JQ. When do you suggest we get together?"

JQ struggled to focus his mind on the reason for their meeting, and with effort he pushed his fantasies aside. "What about today? I'll be in Memphis visiting the new offices we're opening in the renovated McCrombie Building just off Main Street. It used to be the old Walker Hotel. We could meet there and talk over lunch."

"That would be 'soooo' nice, JQ. Maybe you could even show me your new offices. I have wondered what was being done with that old hotel. It needed so much repair and strengthening, and I was 'soooo' pleased when I heard someone was renovating it for office space." Her voice cooed. "It must have a spectacular view."

"As a matter of fact, the view is marvelous. I'll take you up to my penthouse where you can enjoy it to your heart's content. Tell you what. I'll see you in front of the building at half past noon. We can grab a bite to eat up Beale Street at Presley's and then tour the building."

"That will be grand, JQ. I will see you at 12:30. Good-bye, JQ."

"Good-bye, Ms. Weekes."

"Oh please, JQ," she purred. "Just call me Pamela. Until we meet again, goodbye."

After a pause, the line disconnected. JQ held the telephone in his hand, his mouth agape, shaking his head. "My God. What a nooner this is going to be." He licked his lips and grinned.

Chapter 10: Road To Fame

Chris drove to his father's home in south Memphis. Parking on the grass beside the pickup in the driveway, he walked to the house. He rattled the screen door and stepped inside into a cloud of stale smoke. "Dad, it's Chris."

"I'm in the kitchen." The white-haired old man sat at the old kitchen table holding a half-smoked cigarette, using a bent tin can as his ashtray.

Chris hated that his father would not quit his dirty habit, but had stopped trying a year ago to dissuade the confirmed smoker. He just held his breath whenever he visited and minimized his time in the cloud of second-hand smoke.

"Here's the key to my car. Where're the truck keys?" His sinuses ached already, and Chris wanted to leave.

"I'll give them to you when I'm good and ready. Sit down and talk to me for a while." His elbows on the table, the old man squinted at his son through the smoke. "You and Carla don't come by to see me much any more, and I miss the company. Since your mother's gone, it gets too quiet around here." Chris' mother had died two years ago, and over time both he and Carla had drifted away from their father, although they all lived in the same town.

"I'm sorry, Dad. I know I haven't been over to see you very much, but I've been really busy at school." Chris adopted the subservient role to avoid another tirade from his father like the last time he had come around. "So how're you feeling?" he asked in an attempt to put the focus back on his dad.

"I'm the same as I'll always be, and you know it. Now tell me about this earthquake. You're telling people you know when the next earthquake is coming?" His father chuckled and took a drag on his cigarette. "That's pretty good. Finally my son's starting to make a name for himself." Blowing the smoke to the side, he asked, "Well?"

Chris pulled out a chair and sat. "Well, Dad, I've been watching earthquakes along the New Madrid and found a trend that no one else noticed on how the energy seems to flow through the fault zone and collect at asperities." He tried to keep it simple so his father would understand.

"What's an asperity?" His father flicked the cigarette at the can.

"That's a rough spot on the fault, like a bend or a cross fault. Anyway, asperities are where a lot of the energy collects. When an asperity finally gives away, all the energy it's collected gets released into the earthquake. The more energy it collects, the bigger the earthquake."

"That makes sense, but how do you know how much has collected and how much it takes to break it loose?"

"Oh, that's all in the scientific and mathematical theory that I've learned in graduate school. In any case, I've figured out how to answer those questions, and I can watch the energy collect at the major asperities and tell when one of them is supposed to go." He paused.

"So what about New Simon? I used to deliver soda pop there."

"There's an asperity on the fault right under the old town, and that's the place where my model predicts the next significant earthquake will occur. There'll be other temblors, but they won't happen on asperities and will be small."

His dad snuffed his half-smoked cigarette into the can and lit another. Chris moved around to get away from the smoke. Unable to resist, he said, "Dad, I wish you'd give up that ugly habit. Your smoking killed Mom."

"That's poppy-cock." His father sat back with belligerence on his face. "Just because your mother died of lung cancer doesn't prove that my smoking caused it. I've smoked for over 50 years, and it never killed me. I'll die of something else before smoking hurts me any." Having parried Chris' thrust, he returned to his subject. "So what should I do about this quake that's going to happen? You're the expert, so you should be preparing me."

"Dad, you've already tied all your heavy furniture and fixtures down like I told you before. Keep your first aid kit handy, and be sure there's some water and food stored up. Be prepared to turn the gas off at the meter." Chris had trained his family well.

"But I'm a little worried about this next one. The latest run of my computer model says it should be just over magnitude 5.2, and it'll be over 60 miles away, but under some conditions the model indicates it could grow into a monster earthquake. Hopefully, you'll only feel a bump or two."

"Glad to hear that." His father cackled. "How about that. I can tell the gang I got it straight from the horse's mouth."

"Dad, don't go around telling anybody else about my prediction, please. The University gets very upset about people making prophecies. Now, I need to get that equipment out into the field. Can I have the truck keys, or is there something else you want to say?" Chris shifted in the kitchen chair.

"Just one thing, Chris. Take this advice from an old man. You're cock-sure of yourself, which is good. You may be about to make yourself famous, but you should never believe you're always right." He looked Chris straight in the eye. "You need to develop some humility and realize that God sometimes doesn't let people know everything. You may not be right on that earthquake prediction. It may not happen, or it may be even bigger than you thought. Have some humility, and if you're wrong, admit your mistake."

Chris realized his dad was being a father, and though he resented the intrusion, something like this was so rare that Chris felt nonplussed. Returning his father's look he thought a moment then replied, "I hear you, Dad. I'll try to develop humility, but I'm a hard nut to crack."

"That's because you're my son, and you take after me. I'm the hardest nut there ever was in this family." The old man laughed and handed Chris the keys. "I'm proud of you, son. Here you go. Just don't wreck her on your ride to fame."

Pamela arrived at the McCrombie Building in her small blue sports car. She wriggled her legs and hips through several contortions to extricate her tightly clad body from the machine. JQ had trouble keeping his mouth closed and salivated as he admired the voluptuous body.

"Pamela, it is so good to see you again." JQ said as he reached down to take her hand in his and help her stand. In her four-inch high-heeled spikes, she stood as tall as he and looked him straight in the eye.

"JQ, I'm 'soooo' happy to see you. You're stronger than I remembered." She smiled as she gave his hand a slight squeeze and then removed it to reach back into the car for her purse. JQ watched the curve of her thigh stretch her short, blue skirt even tighter.

Turning, Pamela smiled and said, "I'm hungry. Shall we eat first?"

"Sure thing, and it's my treat." JQ counted the ways he would make time with this lady. His fantasies grew more and more interesting.

Over pulled barbecue pork sandwiches, Pamela questioned JQ about the work his company did in the earthquake retrofit for bridges in the area. She soon knew the time it took to complete each overpass and the names of his primary contacts in each of the state capitals. "I had no idea you had 17 crews in the field and you work in three states. That's truly amazing."

JQ basked in the praise.

"Which method are you using for the bridge retrofits? Are you attaching the roadways to the abutments with cables, or are you rebuilding the abutments with deeper overhangs?" Pamela asked in all innocence.

JQ winced as Pamela caught him off guard with the question. "Why, as I remember, all the work is done using cables. That seems to be the fastest and most economical method."

"Yes, it is, but, of course, you know it is intended only to keep the overhead section from falling onto the roadway below, and the cable must have a substantial anchor to support the dynamic weight of the concrete section. It is not intended to keep the overpass from being a total wreck when a major earthquake is finished with it."

"Of course, I am aware of that." JQ recovered and parried. "Oh, but then we don't really know just how strong the next earthquake will be or how much damage will be done, do we?" Changing the subject to get away from more uncomfortable questions, JQ continued, "Say, why don't we go back to my office so I can show you around?"

"Just as you wish, JQ. And lunch was 'soooo' delicious. Thank you." Pamela smiled and pushed the check to his side of the table just in case he had second thoughts and wanted to split the bill.

The signs of construction abounded as they entered the parking basement of the building. "The front lobby isn't finished, but we can catch the elevator here in the basement and go up to my offices in the penthouse." JQ walked over and inserted his key to call his private elevator.

Pamela stopped beside the wall next to the elevator and looked it over with care. "JQ, are you sure there is enough re-bar in those columns to support this structure? The columns look rather puny." She cast a critical eye around the parking basement. "And I don't see the shear walls that I would expect to be running from the elevator column to that opposite wall. Are you sure you used a good architectural firm to plan the renovation of this building?"

JQ stammered. "Why, everything's just fine with the renovation. I mean, I checked it myself, and there's nothing wrong with it. It meets all the codes." Aghast at her direct and specific questioning, he asked, "What do you know about this stuff?"

"Oh, didn't I tell you, JQ? Even though I'm responsible for the Public Relations in the office, I am also one of the licensed structural engineers in the Department of Seismic Safety." She smiled and added, "I earned my Masters from Georgia Tech."

The next hour proved to be one of sheer misery for JQ. His plans for a seduction forgotten, he became the object of an inquisition. He longed to be drawn and quartered if that would get rid of the bitch.

As JQ walked Pamela back to her car, she commented again on the basement walls, "JQ, I really think you should review the plans you used for this renovation. When the next earthquake hits, there could be some problems." She shook her head. "In fact, I wouldn't want to be anywhere near this building if anything larger than a magnitude 6.0 strikes on the New Madrid Fault."

"Thanks for your advice, Pamela. I'll certainly look into it. And you have a good day. I know you must be very busy." JQ stood back, waiting for her to leave the parking lot.

As her car accelerated onto Riverside, he turned and started back towards his building. Damn, he just hoped she didn't talk to anyone else about this. He better get everything buttoned up and hidden before someone else came snooping around. JQ felt depressed.

Crossing the threshold, a sudden wave of fear coursed across his shoulders. He stared at the walls on either side, now wondering about their safety. He questioned if his belief that a large earthquake wouldn't happen was right. After all, his trust in the timing had been a big factor when he cut the corners on design and saved the money in the renovation.

He shook his shoulders like a wet dog and spoke to the empty garage, "I can't let that bitch get me nervous. This building's okay. I know it is." With confidence he strode to the elevator and rode it up to his penthouse. But as he stepped into his office, another attack of anxiety spread through his back.

As Chris stowed the last of the equipment into the back of the pickup with Jenny's help, he asked, "So how are your mom and dad? Have you heard from them recently?"

"Actually, I heard from Mom last night. They were stuck on a mountain somewhere in the middle of Nevada, hoping someone would come along and tow them out. She sounded just a bit ticked when she talked with me and described what she's going to do to Dad when she has the chance." Jenny laughed.

"Really? Stuck on a mountain? Then how did she call you?"

"Dad's got one of the new LowSat phones for emergencies, so they can call from anywhere on the globe."

She continued, "I think they're dropping down to Las Vegas and then coming across Interstate-40 to go through Oklahoma City and see my grandparents. They'll get here Saturday. And I'd really like for them to meet you. I've told them all about you. I hope that's okay."

Chris felt embarrassment. "Sure, I guess so."

Two hours later at the Arkansas-Missouri border, Chris used the master key provided by the power company to let himself into the electrical substation grounds surrounded by the six-foot-high chain link fence. He looked around. "This should be safe and quiet enough." Located in the middle of a cotton field, the substation rested a quarter-mile to the west of I-55, just off Stateline Road.

On the drive north Chris had thought about his father's words. Yeah, they were both hard nuts to crack, but he felt proud being bullheaded like his father.

Chris worked at a steady pace unloading the equipment from the pickup and placing it around the grounds of the substation. He kept away from the transformers, not from fear of their power, but he wanted the equipment as far removed as possible from their electromagnetic interference.

The sky darkened as the sun set, and Chris concluded the best time to bring the equipment up and running would be tomorrow morning. Besides, Jenny would not be available at the Lab to check the installation until then. He drove to the other side of the Interstate to the old truck stop for supper.

Tina had traded for Janet's Monday night shift in exchange for time off on Thursday when she hoped to spend more time with Alex. As she placed the hamburger and fries in front of the rumpled young man, he asked, "Were you here when the earthquake hit Saturday morning?"

Tina exclaimed, "Oh my God, yes. It really scared me. I'd never been in one that big before and it came as a real surprise. Did you feel it?"

"Yes, I was at work in the Seismology Lab at the University of Memphis. I got a complete recording of it on my workstation and laptop. It was a pretty strong temblor you know, right under Dell."

Chris took a bite of his hamburger and chewed on it as Tina started to walk away. "My name's Chris Nelson. Did you know there's going to be another one?"

Tina stopped and turned. "What do you mean, there's going to be another one? You mean another earthquake?"

"Yep. This next one's going to be right here under New Simon, and it'll be even stronger."

"How do you know that? Are you a prophet?" Tina's suspicion that she was the brunt of some kind of joke sounded clear in her voice.

"Seriously, I'm a graduate student in seismology, and I'm working on a theory that predicts earthquakes. That's why I'm up here at New Simon. I just set up a monitoring station across the freeway at the electrical substation." He took another bite from his burger. "Nelson, my computer model, says there'll be an earthquake with its epicenter right here next Sunday morning about one A.M. It'll measure 5.2 on the Richter scale." He paused, then added, "Nelson says it could even be larger, but I don't think that will happen."

Tina stood in place, at a loss for words. She didn't know whether to believe Chris or not. "Well, at least I won't be at work then. I work the early morning shift on weekends."

As she returned to the kitchen Chris heard her comment to the assistant cook. "Boy, you get some weird ones in here at night, don't you?"

His appetite satiated, Chris paid his bill and drove back to the substation to set up his tent. In the middle of May the weather was variable and he expected it would still be a little cool, maybe even damp with dew, but he had camped in the field before and had prepared for the inconvenience.

Chris slid into his sleeping bag, consumed with pleasure. He lay atop his asperity. He could almost feel the tension in the earth's crust. Six more days, and then it would fracture—the crack that would make him famous.

Looking through the open flap of the tent he spoke to the few stars that peeked through the broken clouds. "What the heck. I'm not doing anything special this next weekend. I'll just come up here and wait for my earthquake. I'll be the first to know when the Nelson Earthquake happens. What a gas."

The quietness of the evening brought slumber to Chris. As he slept, another small temblor ten miles northeast passed more stress along the fault. Below him another set of molecules slid past each other, striving to compensate for the additional stress without failing. The rock matrix neared its yield point.

Chapter 11: Preparations

Chris had most of the equipment operational and passing its local test by the time the sun rose in the east. He buried accelerometers at the corner posts of the substation plot to measure movements in the East-West, North-South, and Up-Down directions. A laser beam alongside the fence would measure earth displacement. As he placed the magnetometer in a distant corner, he looked at the transformers. "Sure hope the electromagnetic fields of those transformers don't disrupt the local magnetic field too much. I'll just have to set it up and see."

At last he eased the control panel and un-interruptible power supply off the bed of the pickup. Putting the solar panels to the side, he plugged the UPS into the convenient external 50-amp power outlet provided at the post next to the power station shack. Its batteries would power the seismic station for at least 36 hours in case of a power failure.

By nine o'clock, all the pieces were in place, checked and rechecked. "Ready, set, go. Time to connect everything to the RSCS." He called the Seismology Laboratory number using the University's cell-phone.

"Jenny, here. Is this Chris?" Her bright voice matched the morning.

"Hi, Jenny. The station's all set up, ready to connect to the Remote Station Control System."

"I'm ready at this end."

"As I explained, I initialized an entry for the New Simon station before I left, and all it requires is turning it on. Do that now." Chris moved the phone to his other ear in impatience for her to complete her task.

"Okay, here we go. You told me to enter the STATION ID as *New Simon* on the RSCS, set the station status to ON and press RETURN. Done, and yes, the screen says the RSCS recognizes that the station is there. Now what?"

"That's great. Now enter command SYSTEST, and we'll make sure everything's running okay."

Chris could hear Jenny striking the keys. "Starting SYSTEST on New Simon," she read from the screen. "All tests are passing … Done. Is that all?"

"Yep, that's all. Easy, isn't it?" He blew his breath through his pursed lips to relieve his tension. "Now we just wait for something to happen down below."

As he finished speaking, Jenny yelled, "Hey, what did you do to the station, kick it?"

Her shout surprised Chris. "No, of course not, why?"

"Well, then we just recorded our first event. Yes, it's lighting up the map in Dell and now in Caruthersville. Chris, it's an honest-to-God earthquake."

"You're kidding me. I didn't feel a thing."

"Well, that means a seismic event of intensity I or II happened where you're standing, and you wouldn't notice the slight jerk."

Chris grinned, happy to hear Jenny's enthusiasm in what had happened but disappointed, too. "Well, I'll be damned. I'm standing right on top of an earthquake and didn't even feel it. Now, that's the pits."

"Hey, Chris, I've got to run off to class. The analysis should be complete on your workstation when you get back. See you later."

"Thanks, Jenny. You've been a real help, and we've recorded our first earthquake. Things are really heating up in this part of the country."

Chris laughed as he terminated the call and headed to his dad's truck for the return trip to Memphis.

When Tina drove into the parking lot at the McCrombie Building, she saw JQ talking to one of the building workmen. He motioned for her to drive forward and park next to his red sportster.

After giving final instructions to the workman, he walked over. "Glad you made it. You're right on time. Let's go upstairs so you can see the view." He opened the door to her car and helped her out, his smooth smile and fluid motion indicating he had done this many times before.

Tina did her best to eliminate any sensuous innuendo in the touch of her cool hand. She thought, it looks like he's thinking I'm here and handy.

JQ ushered her up the steps and through the ornate doorway framed with dark green wood and polished brass trim at the top of the entry steps to the old brick structure. Inside the foyer Tina saw a security desk and a hall leading back to two elevators. "That elevator is for the tenants, this one is my private elevator to the penthouse." He inserted a key into the lock with an affected smile and turned it. The polished brass door slid open with a whir.

Tina admired the mirrored interior of the elevator. "This is so elegant." She felt the surge of being rushed to the top of the seven-story building.

When the elevator opened, she saw the expanse of a wide-open room, 30 by 40 feet in size, with floor to ceiling windows on the west and north sides. Solid oak flooring accented the brick walls surrounding the windows. An open door to the right side of the elevator led to a fully furnished bathroom and toilet, the door to the left to a serving area and a service elevator.

A selection of new, elegant furniture already decorated the penthouse office. Several comfortable chairs and a padded leather couch were a fine complement to the large oaken desk and executive chair, placed with its back to the north window.

A well stocked bar covered the east side of the room. "Fix you a drink?" JQ entered the bar and started to work on his own. "I'm having a mint julep. It matches the southern tradition I want to show."

"No thank you, but I'll take a glass of water, please." Tina walked over to the western windows and peered down at the street below. With the window glass installed on the outer edge of the building, she could almost see the building entrance beneath her feet. She backed away towards the center of the room, vertigo tickling her back and neck.

"Isn't this kind of dangerous? I mean, what if you fall against the window, and it breaks."

JQ laughed. "These windows are truly unbreakable, and they won't pop out. The fellow who put them in proved it to me. You maybe heard the story of the guy who thought he had unbreakable windows, and when he showed them off by running and trying to bounce off, the window shattered and he went flying out. He fell 16 stories and didn't live to tell about it.

"Well, I told the dude who installed these windows that he had to guarantee them and prove to me they wouldn't break. He swore everything was just fine. So after he installed the windows, I came up here with him to check the work. I told him to run and bounce off the window to prove it was safe." JQ chuckled. "He wouldn't do it, but I told him I wouldn't pay him if he didn't test the windows. Then I showed him my pistol and told him he didn't really have a choice."

JQ laughed again. "It was the funniest thing you ever saw, but the dude finally did it. He ran up to the windows, and he bounced back real good. Wet his pants. I paid him and gave him a $100 bill as a bonus for good work."

Tina stared at JQ, wondering what kind of man could be so cruel. He walked over and handed her the glass of water. Her hand trembled as she took the offering.

"Cheers." Lifting his glass in salute he strode to the window to look out at the tremendous view of the boat harbor and the tip of Mud Island just down river. A trolley rumbled by below.

"Nobody in Memphis—and I mean nobody; even the Mayor—has a view like this." He stared out the window and drained his drink, then turned.

"Hey, let's walk over to Beale Street and grab a bite to eat." JQ lead the way to the elevator, and they dropped to the ground floor. "They're still putting the finishing touches in the offices on the other floors. It'll be a couple of weeks before the new tenants start moving in. But my offices are ready now. I'm having an open house on Friday afternoon."

The waitress on Beale Street knew JQ by name. The meal tasted great, and the service made everything extra special. Tina said little. She marveled at the elegance of the dining room and the courtesy of the service. The number of people who stopped by to say hello made it obvious that JQ had lots of pull in Memphis.

After lunch they walked back to the McCrombie building. Since moving to Dell, Tina did not often come to Memphis, and she could see how much things had changed. "There sure are a lot of construction projects going on. Do you think the city can maintain its flavor with the new additions?"

JQ looked around. "There's no other way. We have to have progress. Building means taking control. That's the way we businessmen do business."

As they rode the elevator back to the penthouse, JQ stroked her arm. "Nice, isn't it. Doesn't this all just give you a feeling of well-being, seeing everything so nice and comfortable?" His arm encircled her shoulders as they stepped out of the elevator.

Tina tried to move away, but JQ's hand clasped her arm, and he pulled her to him. "Hey, nobody can see us up here, so we can do anything we like. And I've locked the elevators so we can't be bothered." He showed her the elevator key on the end of the watch chain hanging from his belt.

"So now let's just take it easy and get to know each other." He reached up and put his hand behind her head, stroking her neck.

"JQ, this isn't something I want. Please stop." Tina pushed back and moved around the chair to get away from him. "I agreed to come down for lunch, but I wasn't planning anything else."

"Hey lady, I thought you understood. Don't tell me you were just leading me on. Or are you just playing hard to get for the fun of it?" With a lecherous smile he started to follow her around the chair.

"JQ, leave me alone. I never said anything about us doing anything but going to lunch."

"Tina, I'm really being nice with you. Don't run like this. Just calm down and come here." He edged to the other side of the chair, cutting off her escape.

Things could only get worse, she thought—panic welled in Tina's breast. It became clear where this little dance would lead, exactly as she had feared. The advice of her mother sounded in her mind. *Attack. That's the only way to protect yourself, Tina. Attack.*

As JQ stepped around the chair, she grabbed his watch chain and jerked, tearing it from his belt. At the same time she shoved him hard in the chest, pushing him backwards, and he fell over the padded arm. Tina ran to the elevator and unlocked the door. She stepped in and pressed DOWN before JQ could rise. He rushed towards the elevator and tried to open the closing doors with his palms, but not in time.

The elevator jerked and then dropped toward the lobby below. She heard him yelling. "Come back, you bitch. Come back here." The elevator descended as the sound of JQ's cursing faded into the distance.

When the elevator door opened at the bottom, she threw the keys back inside and ran outside to her car. The work crew grinned as she rushed by. She blushed. They must imagine what had happened, and she knew they'd joke to each other about it after she had sped away.

The sound of the diesel motor in the dark purple Peterbilt made music in some trucker's ears. A talented painter had labeled the driver's door with the word *Hulk* in flowing yellow script letters. The driver could be seen in the dim light at the end of the row of big rigs, sitting at the wheel, drinking a cup of coffee, and smoking a cigarette.

Bugs flew in swarms around the parking lot lights in the Tuesday evening blackness, and George looked all around and over his shoulder before he walked towards the *Hulk* and rapped on the driver's door. The driver rolled down the window and stared at George below. "Who're you?" he asked with a scowl, blowing smoke into the wind.

"My name's George. I got a call from Murphy, and he said the *Hulk* had a package for me. I came by to trade for it." George showed the edge of a thick manila envelope inside his sports coat.

"Yeah, Murphy said you'd be here at New Simon. Come on around and get in." The driver rolled the window back up. He reached over to unlock the passenger side door, then pushed it open. George walked around the front of the rig and climbed up into the cab of the big tractor.

"Why'd you guys pick this place for the pickup?" asked the driver. "I thought we only delivered in West Memphis, then I got this call from Murphy to stop here."

"Just didn't want to start a pattern, you know. Besides, I've got friends here. This was an old bootlegger stop, you know. We're just keeping the tradition alive." George pulled the thick envelope from under his jacket and tapped it with his thumb. "So, you got a bundle for me?"

The driver reached back into the bunk space and fetched a cardboard box a foot on each side filled with packages the size and shape of small bricks, each wrapped in brown paper and string. "Here you go. I've got orders to check the money's all here, so let me count what's in the envelope."

"Okay, but I check the kitty at the same time. Okay?" The two traded packages and the driver slit the top of the envelope with his pocketknife.

George counted the packages and picked one at random. "Borrow your knife?" he asked. The driver handed the pocketknife to George and started counting the bills inside the envelope. George made a small slit into the side of one brown parcel and squeezed it a couple of times to force a small dusting of powder out of the hole. He wet his finger, touched the powder to collect a sample, and brought it back to his tongue. Smiling, he looked at the driver and asked. "Tastes good. Is the count okay?"

"Seems to be. You satisfied?" replied the trucker.

"Okay by me." George slipped the box under his arm inside his coat, opened the door, and climbed back down to the pavement. "See you around." He waved as he slammed the door and walked back to the rear of the truck, toward his old Buick.

He heard the Peterbilt rev its engine, and then the driver settled the rig into first gear. Lights from the truck came on, lighting the way for George a little better. He looked across the parking lot at his car. The truck pulled forward as he walked out from behind the rig.

The headlights of a speeding car caroming down the rear of the row of parked trucks blinded George as he stepped forward. He jumped back, and a couple of packages fell from inside his coat to the ground. Some of the powder splashed on the pavement. He could hear music pouring from the open windows of the oncoming car.

The car straightened, pointing at him, gathering speed—at least 40 miles per hour. George saw the end of his days in those blinding, bright lights.

The car came within 20 feet of George before it swerved to its left, missing George by inches. He heard a loud laugh mixed with rap music, and the wind from the passing car flapped his trouser legs as it squealed back to the right and around the departing Peterbilt. George shook as the loud blare of the truck's air horn issued a stern warning to the car cutting across its path. The sound of the car's rushing off into the distance faded into the purr of the diesel as the truck pulled on out of the parking lot to return to the freeway.

"Oh shit." said George as he looked down. In the dim light he could see the darkening stain of urine on his trousers. Then he noticed that the car had run over a package, and though not broken open, the slit he had cut had expanded, and almost a cup of the white powder had spilled onto the asphalt. Looking around to see that no one watched, he picked up the remains of the package with care and tried to scoop some of the powder from the ground onto the brown paper.

Seeing that he would not succeed, George carried the box to his car and laid it on the fender so he could unlock and open the trunk. He stowed the box and found an old bucket inside and placed the broken package in the bucket. Glancing back at the small pile on the asphalt, he climbed into his car and started the engine.

"Are you just going to leave that shit on the pavement back there?" growled a voice from the shadows at the side of the car.

George spasmed and looked up to see JQ standing beside his car in the dim light. He almost backed out to speed away, but JQ admonished him, "You didn't say anything about dealing the dope in my truck stop, you asshole. And now you're about to run away and leave evidence lying out in plain sight. Get out of your stinking car and clean it up."

George almost panicked as he looked around. "What if someone sees me?" he asked in a plaintive voice.

"Then your ass is in a sling. I'm just a stupid passerby wondering what you're doing on your hands and knees in the middle of a parking lot."

George shook with fright, not just from the near miss of the speeding car, but also from the fear that someone would come out and see him with the dope. He resolved that never again would he take a delivery at the New Madrid Truck Stop.

CHAPTER 12: COMPLICATIONS

Chris spoke into the telephone. "When I came in this morning there was nothing. Not one bit of data from New Simon, and all the other stations reported a 2.4 event under Dell this morning."

"Did yesterday's event help?" Jenny still sounded sleepy from the 7 A.M. call.

"Oh yes. It looks like that fracture occurred right at the edge of the southern asperity. Then I used data from surrounding stations to add in this morning's event, and it moved a big pile of energy up from the south. There's some kind of weakness there I haven't seen before."

Chris's voice reflected his tension. "Now the model's predicting a 5.5 three hours sooner. It's absolutely critical I not miss any more data from the area. I've got to fix that station—quick. Please, could you come over to the lab in a bit so we can go through the set-up procedure again once I get it fixed?"

"Well, sure, I guess. How soon do I need to be there? I haven't even showered yet." He could hear Jenny stretching and moving about.

"It's 80 miles from here to the New Simon, and at this time of morning I'm going to fight some commuter traffic, so let's say in two hours. Make it nine o'clock. Will that work for you?"

'Okay, I have a ten o'clock mid-term, so I can fit it in. I'll come by the lab at 8:45. Talk to you then."

"How're things going?" The voice startled Chris. He looked up to see Paul Kenton standing behind him.

"Oh. Hi, Dr. Kenton. Okay, except my station at New Simon went belly-up last night. I'm leaving in a few minutes to get it going again. My assistant's available at nine."

"You have an assistant?" Paul showed surprise and pleasure that Chris had involved someone else in his work.

"Yeah, Jenny Fox is helping me. Hope that's okay."

"She's a good student. So long as she's not shirking her classes, that's fine. This is her third year you know, and she has to pass the coursework to stay in the program. So, tell me, what have you found so far?"

Pleased with Paul's interest, Chris still sensed he should be cautious. "Well, there've only been two events in the general vicinity of New Simon since I installed the station. The first occurred right after it started, and the second this morning after New Simon went down. But both provided some really good input."

"Were they consistent with your theory?"

Reluctant to expose his ideas until he had proof, Chris hedged. "Yes. I'm making good progress in fitting the data to some of the equations, but I need more data to get better convergence. I'm still seeing the trend. My biggest problem now is to account for two asperities that are close together. It's like they mask each other."

"Do you still predict an event around New Simon this weekend?"

"The probability computed by my model is substantially higher than average, and as other activity occurs the chances keep increasing."

Paul smiled as if pleased with the diplomatic way Chris handled the inquisition. As he turned and started back to his office, he said, "Keep up the good work. If you get anything definite, let me know."

An hour and fifteen minutes later, Chris sped along I-55 past Blytheville towards New Simon, still agitated and tense. Pulling off the freeway onto Stateline Road, he drove around yellow construction trucks labeled with the McCrombie Enterprises logo parked at the base of the overpass and men slogging about in their rubber boots, working on what looked like a bridge retrofit.

He continued west a quarter mile to the power substation enclosure holding his monitoring equipment. Unlocking the gate he entered the compound.

Chris stared at the obvious cause for the outage. The charred remains of a raccoon that must have taken great interest in the orange power cable connecting the control unit to the UPS and its batteries reposed next to the power supply. "Ouch," Chris exclaimed in sympathy.

With its front feet planted on the metal sides of both pieces of equipment, the raccoon had taken a great bite out of the cable insulation, right through to the live wire of the 12-volt, 50-amp cable. Its teeth had melted, stuck to the copper wire for several seconds as the stored power of the UPS batteries shorted through the small body. The futile scrapes in the dust and grit told the story well.

Chris turned off all power on his equipment and the UPS, unplugging it from the substation panel. Knowing the batteries might still contain some charge in them, he found two dry sticks and lifted the burnt body off the equipment. "Poor bugger, you must have really been surprised." He pitched the remains over the chain-link fence into the cotton field where the crows could pick it clean. Then he returned to his equipment.

Carefully checking each step along the way, Chris brought the monitoring station back to life. Luckily the breakers and fuses on the system had performed as intended, and all electronics remained functional.

Finally, Chris leaned against a warm tire and sat in the dirt beside his dad's truck. The sun felt good, and he dozed, making up for some of the long hours he had spent in the lab.

His wristwatch finally read 8:45. Standing back at the control panel, he hit the reset button one more time as he called the Seismic Laboratory.

"Hi, this is Jenny." He welcomed the sound of her voice over the telephone.

"Hi, Jenny, Chris, here. A stupid raccoon got too curious and took a big bite out of the power cable, but now the station's back up. Please give it a check from your end."

Jenny entered the command sequence on the RSCS to recheck operation of the unit, and within 45 seconds she reported. "Got a full green panel. Your fixings worked. What happened to the raccoon?"

As Chris walked back to the pickup he told her in gory detail the effects of the power surge on the raccoon. "So, I moved the cables around so it'll be hard for his cousin to get to them." He closed and locked the gate behind him and headed back along Stateline Road.

Chris slowed as he approached the freeway overpass. "Hey, Jenny, looks like they're doing some earthquake retrofit work up here." He watched the construction crew working on the understructure, installing cables from the crossbeams to the concrete abutments on either side. "I want to take a look, so I better go. I'll talk to you when I get back."

"Okay, see you later." Chris heard the telephone go to dial tone as Jenny terminated the call.

Chris stopped the truck and got out. He walked over to where the men worked and looked at their installation. Puzzled, he watched the crew drill holes for the cable anchors into the concrete abutments. He expected them to drill at least 18 inches to reach through the concrete facing, but they appeared to drill only a few inches deep into the concrete.

Even as he watched, one of the crew inserted a three-inch long bolt into one of the holes and filled the space around with quick-setting epoxy-concrete. When installed, Chris realized he couldn't tell whether they had drilled three inches or a full 18 inches all the way through the facing.

Elmer Jones, the foreman of the crew, noticed Chris standing to the side watching the work. He walked over. "Hey, bud, this is a construction site. You can't stand around here. Get in your pickup and head out."

"Are you putting earthquake retrofits on that overpass?"

"Yeah, now move along." The burly foreman walked up close to Chris, trying to block his view.

"Well, you're using short bolts for the cable anchors. That's not much help. Those cables are supposed to keep the overpass roadway from moving away from the abutment, and with any sizeable temblor, those anchors will rip right out."

"What do you know about this, and who are you?" Elmer frowned, unaccustomed to dealing with someone who understood the work being done.

"My name's Chris Nelson. I'm a graduate student in Seismology at the University of Memphis. My seismic sensing station's over at the power substation. One of the things we study is earthquake resistant construction, and I can see you're not doing the proper job here."

The foreman now became belligerent. "Like I said, Mr. Nelson, this is a construction site, and you're not welcome. You're not one of the state inspectors, so you ain't got no rights to judge the work we're doing. Just get the hell out of here while you still can."

Chris could see the rest of the crew lay down their tools and start towards him. Realizing the jeopardy of his criticizing the work, he jumped back into the pickup and hurried on down the road to NASTY'S. As he drove away, he again saw the McCrombie logo on the trucks. "I'll damn sure check that out when I get back to Memphis."

"No, Priscilla, you're just going to have to call your mother and have her go over to the school and pick up your kid. We've got too much to do today for you to take the time off. So you better get back to work, now."

The young mother looked at JQ in misery. "But Mr. McCrombie, the nurse said that Tommy was pretty scared from the fall, and they needed me to come by."

"Priscilla, you'll just have to call them and explain you can't get off right now. And you better get busy calling your mother to go in your place."

"But Mr. McCrombie. I ..."

JQ glowered at the girl and raised his voice. "Priscilla. I'm telling you one last time, go call your mother. If you insist, we can send your last paycheck to your home and you can go get your kid right now. Which way do you want it?"

The girl bowed her head and choked back a sob. "Yes, sir. I'll go call Mom." She headed back to her desk while the others in the office looked down at their work, afraid to be seen with their heads up watching the proceedings.

The white phone rang, JQ's direct link to his crew foremen in the field. Only they knew the number of that line. It required an emergency for them to call. He called, "Priscilla, please come back and close my door." The girl returned and closed the door before continuing on to her desk.

When the door shut he picked up the handset. "JQ here. Who's this?"

"Elmer, boss. We're working the Stateline Road overpass on I-55 at New Simon."

"What's the problem?"

"Well, sir, you said to call if anyone comes nosing around the job, and this kid showed up a little while ago. Thought you should know about it. Said his name's Chris Nelson and that he's a seismologist. He's got a monitoring station up here and knows about earthquake construction. He saw we was using three inch anchor bolts and said that wasn't enough."

"Now why the hell did you let him see you using those bolts? What did he do, stand around all morning. You know you're supposed to be extra careful when you put those babies in. Elmer, get on your crew and tell them to be more careful."

"Yeah, boss, but what about this kid?"

"I know about him. An acquaintance of mine is keeping me informed about an earthquake prediction he's doing. The kid says there's going to be an earthquake under New Simon this weekend. I guess I better do some more looking into things down here."

"Do you want me to get rough next time?"

"No, not yet. Check with me before you do anything physical, but keep him the hell away from the construction site, and that goes for anyone else who wants to stand around and lollygag at the crew installing the anchors or cables."

"And, Elmer, glad you called me about this. You did the right thing. I'll handle Mr. Nelson from this end. I've got some muscle I can use on him. I'll just have to let him know where things stand."

JQ hung up the telephone and considered how he might get at Chris through the folks at the University. He'd arrange things through George.

"So, Billy, like I told you, for a hunnerd bucks you can try some really good stuff before you buy in for a bundle." George led the potential purchaser of a block of the dope into his room.

"George, get serious. Sure I'll have a hit, but I ain't paying you no money for it. I'll pay for the bundle once I know it's worth the price, but if you want to make the sale, I get a free sample. Now do you understand that simple and clear, or do I just walk out of here?"

George shrugged his shoulders and put his palms out. "Okay, okay. I'm just kidding you anyway. Sure, you can have a sample. I'll be right back with it." He went into the kitchen to prepare a cutting board with the dope and required paraphernalia.

"Crummy place you got here, George. Why don't you move?" Billy could see George spent too much time high on dope and not enough on taking care of his surroundings.

"Aw, you get used to it." George returned with the board and set it on the old coffee table beside the couch. "There you go."

Billy tasted the cocaine to be sure it had not been laced with something else. Some dope heads tried to run stuff through with strychnine to give it a kick. Others tried reducing the concentration with aspirin or sugar. Billy always relied on his taste buds to determine the purity of the goods. The sample seemed fine. Leaning forward with his favorite C-note rolled for pleasure, he took the whole snort and rocked back into the couch to let it take effect.

George eagerly bent forward and partook of his share. He too leaned back to enjoy.

Earlier in the day George had lost track of the lines he snorted, and the levels in his body climbed even further as his blood stream absorbed the narcotic. Suddenly, he grabbed his pounding chest as he gasped for breath. "Holy shit. That stuff really kicks." He tried to stand but fell backward.

Billy had seen the same reaction a few times before. Without question George had overdosed. He stood and hurried for the door. "Hey man, I'm leaving. I'll call tomorrow, and if you're still around I'll buy a block.

But right now you might want to call 911. You don't look so good." Billy locked the door behind him wondering if George would survive. Someday he wouldn't, not hitting the dope that way.

Tina listened as Chris explained, understanding only a portion of what he said. "So what I think's happening is that the second asperity is like blocking the primary one that's directly under us. If the second one weakens, then there's a chance that when the first one gives way, they'll both break."

He drew a line of coffee on the counter, then cut it with the spoon. "Once you have the stored energy from both moving down the fault, that wave will clear out everything else holding the fault in place until it gets near the end of the old fracture. At least, that's the worst-case scenario."

Tina stared at Chris sitting at the counter. "Then you're saying we're going to have a really big earthquake."

Chris picked up his hamburger and took a large bite. "No." He chewed a couple of times before he answered. "I don't really believe that's what's going to happen, but the earthquake might be a little bigger than I first thought. What I've got to do is change my computer model around to consider two interconnected asperities. Then I can tell you what's really going to happen."

George still freaked from time to time. He mumbled to himself, "This dope's some powerful shit, stronger than anything they've delivered before." His calves twitched from time to time. His whole body felt like one big raw nerve.

When the telephone rang he almost popped out of his skin. Shaking, he reached over to pick up the receiver. "Yeah?"

"George, this is JQ. Anybody with you?"

George looked around. "Naw, I don't see nobody. I'm just sitting here being mellow." His voice slurred.

"You dumb freak. You're snorting away your profits. You better get busy peddling that stuff before someone finds you with it. If you don't bring me my money, I'm sending down one of my crews to cut it out of your butt."

George felt alarm. JQ pushed on him hard, and how did JQ know he took a hit anyway. George looked for a hidden TV camera in his room. "Now, JQ, don't you worry. Everything'll be okay, and you'll get your money. Don't you worry about it any. Everything'll be just fine."

In a smoother voice JQ said, "George, do something for me." He waited for a response. "George. Are you listening?"

"Oh, yes, sure am, JQ. What d'ya need?"

"I want you to call that kid friend of yours, Robbie, and have him invite Chris Nelson to my open house Friday afternoon. Have Robbie tell him I've heard about his earthquake station up at New Simon and want to talk with him. Tell him I heard he's upset with the retrofit crew, and I'd like to talk with him direct about that, too, you know, give him a chance to take the problem right to the top. Can you remember all that?"

George thought a moment. "Sure, I can do that, JQ. I'll give Robbie a call right after I finish with you. Is that okay?"

"That's okay, and George, leave the dope alone. It's for sale, not for consumption. You screw this up and you won't have nothing left to screw with." George heard JQ bang down the telephone.

"Oh shit, I better get busy." He sat back in the chair and closed his eyes, letting the buzz creep over his head once more.

CHAPTER 13: DISCOVERY

Alex sat at his computer monitor playing a game of solitaire, taking advantage of a slow Wednesday. The trouble queue listed nothing to fix, all the servers reported normal, nobody complained of a hang-up on their personal computer, the Internet connection to the outside world had recovered from yesterday's outage, and Alex didn't feel like working on the next set of system modifications. Besides, only five minutes remained to closing time and the rest of the computing staff had left for the day.

Alex closed the solitaire window, logged off, and reached to power down his computer when Harry Perkins, the head of the Accounting Department, came to his cubical. "Alex, we've got some kind of problem with the network. Alice's PC won't shut down properly. Could you take a look?"

"Bummer. Sure, Harry. Be right there." Alex liked working out networking problems, but he hadn't planned on staying late.

An hour later, he turned to Harry. "I don't know how she did it, but Alice kicked the hell out of the file server. I'm going to have to do a complete reboot to clear this up. You might as well go home. It'll be another three hours before you can get back on-line."

"Okay, see you tomorrow. It's vital that everything be back up and ready by 7 A.M.. Think you can do that?"

"Sure. If I run into serious problems, I'll call you at home." Alex walked back into the server room and sat down at the master console to start on the file cleanup and reboot.

It took two hours to complete most of the work. All that remained consisted of cleaning up the file garbage left from the system crash. Fragments of files had been cloned or orphaned in the crash, and he hoped to find a disposition for all of them before he did the final reboot.

The air conditioners sounded loud in the quiet building. Everyone, including JQ, had left for the evening an hour ago. The janitorial service would be in after one in the morning. Alex took his time, investigating each fragment of data with care.

He opened a new fragment and looked it over. It appeared to be rich text, so he pressed the control sequence for the rich text display. Part of an email appeared on the screen. Alex glanced over the fragment and moved his finger to the DELETE key to discard it. Then he became aware of what he had read and he scanned it again.

The fragment appeared to be part of an email message from JQ to someone in Nashville, someone at the state government. Alex read in part

"...just so we both understand, so long as you keep the other inspectors on projects other than the retrofits, I will put $5K per week into your Bahaman account. The three I mentioned all know the ropes and can be trusted. Now we do not want anything to go wrong with this project, so do your part and I'll do mine."

Alex shuddered, staring at direct evidence that JQ had bribed state officials for the retrofit work. Even though his screen showed only a fragment, he knew the secret way to locate the complete message in the email backup transaction file. Alex mused. How ironic—JQ didn't realize that whatever he sent across the Internet became accessible to anyone who knew where to find it.

Looking over his shoulder just in case, he copied the original email to a floppy disk and stowed it in his shirt pocket. Someday it might come in handy.

Alex searched further, finding more fragments of other emails involving JQ. Most were innocuous, but one mentioned some of the construction in the restoration of the McCrombie Building. Alex laughed to himself when he realized that JQ not only cheated on the overpasses, he cheated himself in the rehabilitation of his own building. He saved that email to the floppy disk as well.

Once he had processed all fragments and determined that they were not vital, he deleted the orphan files and restarted the system. It would be back up and functional in 30 minutes.

Alex patted the floppy disk in his shirt pocket. "I guess there's always a silver lining in every emergency. Now, what do I do with this?" He considered a couple of alternatives as he turned off the lights, locked the door, and headed home.

When Chris began work early Thursday morning, he included data from a couple of small events from the vicinity of Dell into his database and reran the model with his newest approach for handling two asperities.

"Tum-ditty-tum-ditty-tum." He did a drum roll on the edge of the keyboard, and then stopped as the results appeared and talked to the monitor. "Tension on the fault sure has increased, but Nelson's gone crazy. I put in the new feature and what does it do? Gives me two solutions: a 4.9 magnitude event to the south and a 5.8 magnitude event to the north. Like it's saying both will happen. And the time's moved forward again. Now it says 3 p.m. Saturday afternoon, plus or minus two hours."

Chris scanned over the latest results and conclusions he had written in his lab journal. He added the note, *"This is really looking good. It'll form the basis for a great paper. And if I add a personal note about my own experiences, it'll be even better. I sure want to be in New Simon for the big event. After all, it's my earthquake that's about to happen. They'll just have to call it the Nelson Earthquake."*

The more he thought about calling it the Nelson Earthquake, the more excited he became. He picked up the telephone and dialed. It rang four times, and then Chris heard the answering machine recording. "Hello, this is Jenny Fox. I'm unavailable right now. Leave a message at the tweedle and I'll call you back when I get a chance. … Remember, tweedle."

Chris started to talk and then the machine tweedled. He began again. "Hi Jenny, this is Chris. Thought I'd give you an update on my prediction. It now looks like Saturday afternoon, same place around New Simon, but now it says there'll be two earthquakes, a 4.9 and a 5.8. That'll shake a few cans off the shelf. Maybe they'll call it the Nelson Earthquake. What do you think of that? Give me a call when you have a chance."

Chris replaced the telephone on the cradle and returned his attention to the screen of his workstation. His plans to go for a cup of coffee faded, and he focused his attentions on how to handle two asperities without giving two solutions.

JQ and Herb Wright walked towards the front of the parking basement of the McCrombie Building. "What do you mean my crew's going to have to tear out that wall so you can see how the shear supports were installed? I'm in the earthquake retrofit business myself, and I know how to do it right. I inspected it myself." JQ stopped and stood in the face of the city inspector performing the final inspection of the building before allowing it to be opened to the public.

Herb stepped back and lectured JQ. "Mr. McCrombie, the rules are that city inspectors are to visually check the construction of all renovation of these older Memphis buildings. That means we have to see it, and there is no record that I can find in any of the files that any city inspector has seen how your crew installed the cross-stress relief in these walls."

He stopped and swallowed, trying to organize his thoughts. "You know that in the event of an earthquake, old brick walls need even more shear strength than anything else. That's what this renovation is all about, making it so these buildings don't fall in the event of an earthquake. You say the shear supports are installed, but I can't see them because you put up a drywall and plaster in front of them before I had a chance to inspect them."

JQ next tried logic instead of an aggressive voice. "Herb, I know you have a job to do, but it's Thursday, and I have already scheduled an open house here tomorrow afternoon. The Mayor is going to be the guest of honor." He paused to let that fact settle in. "You know, it'll take probably 12 hours to get a crew in here to tear out the wall, have you come back to inspect it, and then put the wall back up. I don't think we have a chance in hell of getting all that done before 2:00 tomorrow afternoon—unless everyone works around the clock."

JQ put his hands on his hips and looked Herb in the eye. "But, if you really want to force the issue, then I'll get the crew in here immediately. Let's see, that means you need to be back here about 1:30 tomorrow morning. Okay?"

Herb balked and put his foot down. "Mr. McCrombie, I'm sorry, I cannot be here until 10:00 tomorrow morning at the earliest."

"Well then, Herb, I'll just call the Mayor right now and tell her that the opening of one of the jewels of her renovation project for the Memphis waterfront has been delayed and the open-house has been cancelled— all because one of her numb-skulled city inspectors wouldn't come early in the morning to finish an unnecessary inspection that he ordered in the first place."

Pleased to see the way Herb blanched, JQ remembered hearing the previous Mayor had given the inspector hell the last time he pushed one of his friends the wrong way. "Now Mr. McCrombie. It's not necessary to bother the Mayor about this. I'm sure we can work something out. It's just that there is the city requirement that all construction be inspected. There are the forms that must be signed."

"Tell you what. I personally inspected the work. I can personally verify that it's fine. I could sign the forms." JQ tilted his head and looked into the eyes of the inspector.

Herb blinked and thought a moment. Caught between two hard rocks he needed a way out. Shrugging he said, "Well, I suppose that would meet the requirement. Okay, let's do that." He pulled out the forms and offered them to JQ, pointing to the spot where the building inspector should sign.

JQ marked an illegible, scrawling signature on the form and dated it one week earlier.

"Okay, now you just sign the official release so we can open this building tomorrow." Herb pulled the paper from his briefcase and signed the two copies, giving one to JQ. "Thanks, Herb. We'll both just keep this conversation between us. And please let my secretary know what your home address is so I can be sure you're on my Christmas list."

Herb Wright walked back out to his car parked next to the old building. He looked up the side of the old brick structure. "Hope they did it right," he said to himself as he got into his car to drive away.

"Hey boss, what was that all about?" Charlie Simmons, one of JQ's bridge retrofit crew chiefs putting 20% of his chargeable time into the building renovation, asked as he walked over to JQ. "We never put any shear walls into that area of the basement."

JQ turned to his crewman. "Charlie, you didn't hear or see that conversation, and so help me God, if you say anything about those shear walls, I'll personally see that your ass winds up on the bottom of the river. Now get back to work and finish up the rest of the building for the opening tomorrow." He turned and walked over to the elevator and inserted his control key to call the elevator to take him to his penthouse office. He needed a drink to celebrate having passed inspection of his new building.

Judy asked Tom, "Jenny said her apartment's in a two story brick building. Will a building like that be safe in an earthquake?"

"Probably not in a big earthquake. I understand the building codes have not been strict until recently back in that part of the country, so even low buildings can be a problem. A bigger problem will be the taller brick buildings, especially those that have not been properly reinforced. As the ground oscillates beneath them, they get to pitching back and forth and crumble very easily. You can see examples of that in the old pictures from the San Francisco earthquake."

Judy peered down the pavement of I-40 where it disappeared into the distant countryside of the Texas panhandle. "What's that?" she asked. A strange looking water tower could be seen in the distance.

"That's one of the Groom, Texas, landmarks I've heard of. It's a regular water tower, but it tilted over almost 15 degrees to the side after they got it built."

Judy said, "I bet that's something that's sure to fall in an earthquake, but a regular water tower would be pretty safe, wouldn't it, Tom? After all, it's up off the ground."

"Not really. Water weighs just over eight pounds per gallon, and a typical small town water tank holds 50 to 60,000 gallons or more. That's approaching half a million pounds. In the vicinity of a magnitude 6.0 quake, the sideways acceleration can peak at 15% of gravity."

Tom did the calculations in his head. "Let's see, that means the water at the top of the tower can push on the sides of the tank with a force of 75,000 pounds, double that if the water gets to sloshing back and forth. With that much force it'll effectively move the center of gravity outside the legs, and the tower can simply pull its back legs out of the ground. The front legs will start to buckle and tower will just fall over."

Judy pointed to a nearby farm. "What about those tall grain elevators we've been seeing?"

"When grain starts shaking, it flows like a liquid, so you can have the same problem. But Todd Crowe at UC Berkeley told me that an even bigger problem in some of the grain elevators could be the generation of static electricity by the shaking. Sparks could ignite the grain dust and cause some horrendous explosions."

After her one o'clock class Jenny strolled through the campus of the University by the Seismic Lab to check for Chris. To her satisfaction, she found him staring at his console.

"Hi there." Jenny pulled up a stool and sat just to the back and side of Chris so she could see the screen. She rubbed his back and shoulders. "I got your message about the magnitude increasing. How's it going now?"

Chris concentrated on the screen, and it took a full minute before he typed in a final phrase into the formula being composed on the screen. He pressed RETURN. "Huh. Where'd you come from?"

"Oh, I just happened to be walking around and saw you, so I thought I'd check it out. Are you gonna work all night again on your model?" She leaned on his back.

"Yeah, I'm still trying to figure out how to properly handle two asperities. That's my problem with the Nelson Earthquake. Every time I take out the second asperity the model goes berserk. But when I leave it in, the model keeps giving me two solutions. The solutions are becoming more and more bizarre as more stress is added. I'm not sure just what's going to happen when it finally lets loose." He typed the command to run the model and turned to face Jenny.

"Guess what. I've been invited to an open house at the McCrombie Building tomorrow afternoon. McCrombie is that guy I told you about whose crews are doing the retrofits on the freeway overpasses up around New Simon. It should be fun. Want to go with me?"

Jenny felt disconsolate. "No, I'm entertaining some kids at the orphanage tomorrow afternoon, but what're you doing afterwards? Maybe we could take in a movie or something."

"Afraid not, I'm heading back up to New Simon after the party to be there when the earthquake hits. It'll really be some experience to feel the earth shake, almost like I told it to." He grinned in anticipation.

The computer beeped, indicating another completed run through the model. Chris looked at the screen and scowled. "Oh shit. It still doesn't work, but I'm close to knowing how to make it work. Hey, I've got to get back on this problem, so I can't talk any more." He turned his back on Jenny.

"That's okay, I need to get some studying done sometime anyway. Sorry you can't go to the movie." Jenny looked like she felt, unhappy, and Chris turned back, his face showing a tinge of regret.

He tilted his head and smiled. "Tell you what, I'll give you a call back here at the lab Saturday morning from New Simon. We can talk and recheck that everything's running okay. Can you do that for me, say about 9:30? I'll leave the latest model ready to run for you to look at when you get here."

"Sure, why not. I don't have much of anything else to do until my folks get here." Jenny stepped down off the stool and headed for the door. "Talk to you Saturday morning." She felt strange as she walked out the door, sad and just a little jealous. Somehow, she had lost to the earthquake.

CHAPTER 14: RETRIBUTION

Stunned by Alex's declaration that he had solid evidence of JQ's bribing state officials, Tina hung the telephone back on the wall and picked up her next order from the heating shelf.

Alex seemed so sure that the two of them now had a way to keep JQ off their backs. Tina had asked, "What if JQ decides to get rough? How do you know he won't get even?" She had pushed Alex with her concerns, consumed by her doubts.

"Honey, I didn't order eggs and bacon. Mine was a hamburger." Tina looked down at the lady before whom she placed the order she had picked up from the service counter.

"Oh, I'm sorry. You're right. These go to that other table." Tina felt embarrassed as she retrieved the plate and took it to its rightful owner. She always took pride that she never forgot what each customer had ordered. Alex's talk had just thrown her mind out of kilter.

In a quandary Tina asked herself, "Oh, what do we do, what do we do?" She wanted to strike back at JQ for his attack yesterday, yet she feared the kind of violence he might create in retribution. Alex's evidence might be the weapon to get to JQ, but it could also blow up in their faces. She just didn't know.

The telephone rang again. Cookie answered and called out, interrupting her thoughts, "Hey, Tina, it's for you again." Cookie put his hand over the mouthpiece. "It's the boss-man this time."

Tina took the phone. "Hello, this is Tina." Her voice cracked, and she almost stuttered.

"Tina, this is JQ. I'm just calling to apologize about yesterday when you were down. I figure I might have given you the wrong impression. I'm really sorry if I upset you in any way."

Tina exploded with anger. After that episode in the penthouse, JQ had the gall to call and try to apologize. "A wrong impression, Mr. McCrombie?

I'm absolutely and totally upset about what happened. I really am. Where did you ever get the idea that I'm that kind of woman?"

"Look, I understand, I really do. I don't know what I was thinking, and I'd really like to make it up to you. Really, I would." She could feel him turn up the charm. Her ire rose in reaction, and her thoughts turned vile. That asshole, who does he think he is kidding.

She stuttered, and then responded. "Well, you just try to think of some way to make it up if you can, but after your actions on Tuesday I'm sure you don't know how." She felt emboldened by her conversation with Alex, and as she stood up to JQ, she felt better and better.

"Look, I'm sorry. Tell you what. Why don't you come by my open house tomorrow afternoon? There'll be people around if you don't feel safe. We can find some time to talk about it a little, and maybe I can make amends."

Tina realized this could be the opportunity to set things straight with JQ regarding her relationship with Alex. Why not?

"What time is the open-house?"

"The party starts at four o'clock, but you could come by a little earlier if you wanted, and we could talk about how to work …"

"No, I'll come after four. And I'll bring a friend."

"Whatever you say. I'll just be glad to see you again. And I mean it, I'm really sorry for giving you the wrong impression."

"I will see you tomorrow afternoon, Mr. McCrombie."

"It's JQ, remember."

Tina slammed the handset into its cradle on the wall, cutting JQ off from any further conversation. Fuming, she reached a resolution. Now she and Alex needed to plan what to tell JQ tomorrow. Whatever they decided, she wanted it to hurt.

"Helen, I'm taking off. Something's come up with a friend of mine that requires my immediate attention. Cover for me, will you?"

"Sure, Alex. But you'll owe me one. I know our boss is out, but what if JQ comes back and finds you gone. What do I tell him?"

"Tell him to stick it up his ass." Alex seemed most foolhardy.

"I'll tell him you told me to say that. It's been nice knowing you." Helen sat back in her chair and shook her head.

"I don't think he has a hot date this time of day, but then you never know about these young kids," she said to Priscilla.

Alex drove the 66 miles from the McCrombie Enterprises offices in West Memphis to NASTY'S in less than 50 minutes. Tina's call indicated a dramatic urgency to speak with him in private and as soon as possible. He was lucky no Arkansas State Troopers patrolled I-55 that afternoon.

In the dim lighting of NASTY'S, Alex and Tina sat in the back booth in quiet conversation. The clock showed 3:10, and no trucker had come in for coffee for ten minutes. Cookie even took a break to go out back to smoke a cigarette.

Alex said, "Let me explain how this works. When someone sends an email, the server saves a copy in case there's a transmission problem while the message is transmitted over the Internet. As with most email servers, ours doesn't bother deleting its copy until there is a general cleanup of the system." He spoke softly, as one conspirator to another.

"After the system crash last night I happened to find a fragment of an email that started me looking, and now I've got copies of five emails that JQ sent to Harley in Nashville where he makes reference to the arrangements for the bribes. There are other emails as well about the shoddy work he's been doing, including work on his own building."

Tina thought a moment then asked, "How will someone know your email copies are not fake? That's what JQ will say, for sure. Or he might just destroy all the files."

"Well, the beauty of email is that there's a server at each end. The one at the state capital keeps a copy of all emails received. Both JQ and this fellow Harley don't realize there's a copy of every email there, too, and they don't have any way of getting rid of those copies. All the authorities need to know is the email date and time, and with some searching they can find everything, even if JQ somehow does destroy the copies at the McCrombie Enterprises office." He chuckled. "I called a friend of mine who works for the state Information Systems group and he confirmed they never throw anything away."

Tina sipped her iced tea. "So you're sure there's no way JQ can get out of this, just like you said over the phone at noon."

"Absolutely not. No way."

"How do you know JQ won't get rough? How do you know he won't just rub us out? And what do you want to get out of this?"

"I don't think we're dealing with a murderer. And we can tell him if he gets rough that we'll notify the authorities and blow everything wide open." Alex recounted the various ways he had considered to put the screws to JQ. "I guess the main thing I want to do is get him to leave us alone. And I'd like to force him to do good work on the retrofits. I don't really want to put him out of business or anything, just make him do it right."

"Alex, you're being naïve. JQ's a criminal, and the best thing for a criminal is to put him in jail."

"Tina, maybe you're right, but right now I don't think we have to go that far. The first thing is to get his claws off of you." Tina had sobbed in agony when she called Alex the previous evening and told him of the incident in the penthouse. He had almost been angry enough to go hunting for JQ to extract retribution himself.

He asked, "By the way, what was the important thing you wanted to talk about? I assume it's to do with JQ and the way he attacked you on Tuesday."

"Well it does. I've decided it's time to get even with Mr. JQ McCrombie. I'm not going to let some low-life like him do what he did to me yesterday and get away with it. Then after you told me you had evidence that he bribed state officials, I decided it's time."

"So, what's the rush?"

"JQ called this afternoon and tried to apologize. He made me so mad. Then he invited me to his Memphis open house tomorrow afternoon, and I said I'd be there and bring a friend. That'll be you. That's the best time to throw this bombshell of yours in his face and tell him." Tina's resolve had grown hard as nails, and now with Alex's ammunition, she seemed ready to extract her pound of flesh and more from JQ.

Alex realized Tina was out for blood and the sooner the better. He knew he better calm her down before she found some gun-shop and bought the tools to do mayhem.

"Hey, let's keep cool on this. We want to get JQ, but we don't want to get ourselves in trouble." Alex now pressed for caution and reason.

"Tell you what," Tina replied. "It's close enough to quitting time for me to leave. Come over to my apartment, and we'll talk more about this." She stood and whipped off her apron.

When the alarm clock buzzed, Alex bolted upright. Accustomed to keeping computer programmer hours when he seldom arose before nine, waking at five in the morning came as a big surprise.

A slender arm reached across the bed and silenced the alarm clock. Alex looked around in the half-lit, unfamiliar room, and then he remembered the night before.

"Well, are you going to keep sitting up in bed, or are you going to snuggle back down here next to me?"

Alex looked at the female form under the sheet next to him. "Tina?"

"Who'd you expect? Yogi Bear?"

Dropping back onto his elbow, he ran his hand under the covers to touch her bare skin, stroking it from her thigh to the back of her arm and around to her breast.

"I forgot where I was. I thought I was dreaming."

"Silly boy, it is a dream. Come here and let's dream again."

Alex leaned over and kissed her waiting lips, first lightly and then more firmly as his hand searched more and more of the warm body next to his.

Half an hour later, the buzzer sounded again, waking Alex from the doze he drifted into after their passionate early-morning lovemaking. Tina had finished showering. He could see her putting on makeup in the bathroom.

"Second call. Time to rise and shine." Tina looked out the door and smiled. "I suppose you're not used to waking up so early, but we grunts get a move on and go to work. Do you want to come over to NASTY'S for some breakfast before you start back to Memphis?"

"Sure, I guess so. I've got to get up sometime." He rolled out of bed and pulled on his clothes from the previous day. He sat on the side of the bed and scratched his chin, wishing he could shave.

Tina walked from the bathroom over to the bed next to Alex and reached down. "You know, you're a really great guy, especially good in bed. I enjoyed last night and want us to spend more time together if it's okay with you." She rubbed his shoulders with her hands and brushed her bikini-panty-clad thigh by his face.

Alex reached around her body and drew it to him, rubbing his chin into her abdomen above the panties.

"Ouch, be careful with that sandpaper face of yours. It might leave scars." She bent over to kiss him on his upturned lips as his hands cupped her dangling breasts. He squeezed, and she stood up. "Hey, we better stop this, or I won't get to work until noon."

Later at the cafe with a coffee in front of him on the counter, Alex considered their situation and asked as Tina walked by to serve the three truckers in the back booth. "Do you really believe JQ will back off the way we want him to?"

Tina returned and poured warm coffee into Alex's cold cup. She spoke quietly but firmly. "I'm sure. Look, Alex, I made a big commitment to you last night. I want you to be with me and back me up on this. Promise me you won't cave in again. I couldn't take it if you did."

Alex thought of the evening before, how Tina kept saying they could get even with JQ and asking if Alex could think of any way JQ could get out of the trap when they sprang it on him, when they showed him the information Alex found in the emails. Alex came to realize her absolute intention to build a perfect case against JQ. She wanted revenge in the worst way.

Alex tried to preach reason and caution. Tina began a campaign of seduction, using every way she could think of to get Alex on her side, to convince him that their goal must be to punish JQ, to make the man suffer for what he had tried to do. She didn't care that much about the poor construction and the bribes. She wanted a woman's revenge.

When Alex agreed, she sealed the agreement with the wild trip to bed. The passion of the lovemaking surprised Alex, but it ensured his complete cooperation. And yet, underneath, he still wondered if her strategy was best.

Alex looked at Tina, concerned by his lingering doubt of her plan to use the email evidence to exact some kind of physical retribution from JQ. Alex just wanted JQ to leave them alone and let them keep their jobs as if nothing ever happened. He wondered if his sexual desire for Tina clouded his better judgment. He just didn't know.

"Okay," he agreed with reluctance. He stirred his coffee again and lifted the cup to drain most of its contents and glanced at his wristwatch. "Hey, I better get going. Come by the West Memphis office about 3:30 and leave your car. You can ride with me over to the city." He stood up from the stool, leaning over the counter to give her a quick kiss.

"Will you come back home and stay with me tonight after the party? I'd like that." Tina smiled with half-closed eyes at Alex, stirring the coals of his ill-damped passions.

"Sure, and this time I'll bring some clean clothes and a razor," he answered, then continued, "but I just remembered. Tomorrow morning I'm signed up to go over to the airfield to make a parachute jump. Of course, I won't have to get up quite so early if I'm staying at your place." He quipped as he winked at her.

"Oh, Alex, I wish you'd stop doing that sky-diving thing. It's so dangerous. It worries me." Tina frowned at him with her head cocked.

"Yeah? Well I don't make a life out of wrestling alligators named JQ, like some folks I know." He grinned the dimple back onto his chin as he tossed her another kiss. As he turned and left the café, he saw Cookie watching from inside the kitchen, smiling at the terms of endearment exchanged between the two lovers.

CHAPTER 15: BLOWOUT

After checking that the cleaning service had finished the floors in the McCrombie Building, JQ watched his crews take the furniture up to the penthouse office. "Be careful," he yelled.

The caterers arrived at 10:00 A.M. to do the initial setup and would return at 3:00 to set out the food.

"Finally, it's ready." He sat down and looked at his watch. "Damn, it's only 10:45. What am I going to do for the next five hours?" His drummed his fingers on his clean desk.

The buzzer for elevator access to the penthouse rang from the lobby below. "Those dumb caterers must have forgotten something." JQ punched the intercom. "Come on up." He hit the button to open the elevator doors downstairs.

He sauntered back to the center of the room and took in the view. "JQ, you've really done it big this time. You're definitely top dog." He walked over to mix a drink at the open bar and turned as George Besh stepped off the elevator.

"What the hell are you doing here? The party doesn't start until four. You know I don't want you to stand out around this place."

George strolled into the room. "Now, JQ, calm down. I think you'll appreciate me being here. I brought you your profits from our little venture."

JQ had given no thought to the dope deal for several days, and George's bringing the money so soon surprised him.

"Is it in that briefcase?" JQ asked as he looked at the hand luggage George carried. His face glowed with greed.

"Shore enough, all 125 big ones." George placed the briefcase on the desk, and taking a key from his pocket, opened it. He handed the key to JQ. "You also get one fine briefcase."

"Thanks," JQ said. Inside he could see bundles of $100 bills, 1,250 of them if George had not stiffed him.

"How come you're so quick with the money? I thought you said it'd take a couple of weeks."

"Let's just say that some eager buyers showed up and were willing to take the whole load off my hands. Besides that, you don't want to know anything. So, are you going to count it?"

New to banking drug deals, JQ had not handled so much loose cash before. "Yeah, guess I better." He looked at the clock. "I'll count it, and then we can take it by the bank and get some lunch."

"Take it by the bank? Are you crazy?" George sounded aghast. "You can't just walk into some bank and lay down 125 Gs without them calling the Feds and every cop in the city. It just ain't done that way." George paced back and forth. "JQ, you gotta find someone to launder this money for you so you can bring it back in slow, like it was normal. Boy, are you ever dumb."

"I know that, ass-hole. I was jerking you around." JQ laughed, but inside he felt chagrin. He had not thought far enough ahead to plan for this, and now he faced a new problem: what to do with the money in the meantime.

"Okay, let me count it, and then I'll stash it." He sat down at the desk and started. It took over 30 minutes before he looked up at George and said, "Seems to all be here."

JQ put ten $100 bills into his billfold, and then pulled off 20 more and handed them to George. "This is for the earthquake info, just like you asked. You launder that part yourself. Now, George, go take a leak or something in the bathroom, and close the door I don't want you around when I put this money away."

"I can understand that. Sure, back in five." George ambled off.

JQ looked around. "Why the hell didn't I put in that safe? The only secure place I've got is the locked file under the table by the sofa." Dropping the briefcase into the wide file, he grinned. "Nobody will ever suspect there's a $125,000 hidden under their drinks during the party this afternoon. What a kick." He laughed at the irony as George returned from the toilet.

After showering and finding his least rumpled shirt, Chris dressed and drove his father's pickup over to park near Robbie Browne's apartment. He honked and waited only five minutes before Robbie came out the door. "Howdy, Chris. Sounds like it should be a fun party, doesn't it?"

"It should be, but, Robbie, I'm worried. I found what's wrong with my earthquake model." Chris's voice echoed his distraction.

"You mean it doesn't work?"

"Oh, it works alright. It's just on this latest round it's been giving me two solutions for the earthquake at New Simon. Now I see it's trying to tell me that both could happen—at the same time. That would be a disaster."

"What you need is a rest. We'll get that at this party. Take your mind off it." Robbie continued, "Say, I'm going to need my car to pick up my date later tonight, so how about me following you over to where the party is, okay?"

"Sure, I'm driving back to New Simon tonight anyway. That'll give me time to check on the instruments before it gets too late."

JQ's Rolex read 4:00, time for his open house. The caterers had finished with the setup and deposited the extra food outside the stairwell door of the penthouse suite, the servers stood ready at the food tables, the bartender shined glasses behind the bar. Suzie, his new secretary, bustled about the room moving the different knick-knacks from one place to another and then back. JQ felt very satisfied with the ambiance of his new showcase office.

Snatching an olive from the bar, he walked to the floor-to-ceiling window on the west side and looked down upon Riverside Street and then out to the Mississippi River. "What a view. What a view," he mused to himself, sucking on the olive. "JQ, you've finally done it. You've really come a long way." A smug feeling enveloped him.

Hearing the elevator bell, he walked to the double doors of the lobby and opened them. "Suzie, we're on. Are you ready?" The first guests stepped from the elevator.

"Welcome, Madam Mayor." On Friday afternoon everyone came ready for a blowout, even the city officials. The head of the city government had arrived with the first contingent. JQ shook hands with the Mayor and members of her party, including the Director of Seismic Safety, Marion Roberts, followed by Pamela. Avoiding eye contact with his lady nemesis, he showed them the way to the *hors d'oeuvres* and bar.

As he started to turn away, JQ felt a light touch on his arm and a voice behind him said, "Mr. McCrombie, I just wondered if you're applying the same effort on earthquake mitigation in your overpass retrofit business as you applied in the renovation of this building."

Caught by surprise, JQ turned and scowled at the smiling black gentleman for a brief moment before his face returned to its normal beguiling countenance. "Mr. Roberts, isn't it? Well, sir, like most of Memphis's businessmen, I am very concerned about earthquake safety. As you obviously know, one of my primary enterprises is to retrofit all the bridges and overpasses around Memphis so they can withstand earthquakes."

He raised his voice a notch so others would hear. "And I am most concerned that this building meets all the earthquake standards you and your staff have been putting into effect here in Memphis, even though it has added substantially to the cost of renovation." Underneath, JQ felt a strong surge of irritation for the interference this man's staff put on the crew renovating this building. Had he not been able to find ways to get around some of the standards, it would have been even worse.

"I'm so glad to hear that. You know, we must all worry about what will happen with the next big earthquake in this area. Most people just don't seem to be taking it to heart that a major earthquake will occur on the New Madrid." He smiled. "And I'm sure your crews must be doing a fine job on those bridge retrofits. The government is paying enough for us to rest assured that we won't have some bridges fall down like that overpass did down in Los Angeles a few years ago."

JQ saw others arriving and excused himself to greet his new guests, weaving among the gathering throng, putting as much distance as he could between him and Marion Roberts. This talk about earthquakes got on his nerves.

By the time Chris and Robbie arrived, the crowd filled the room. Chris looked around and spotted the bar. "I'll get you a beer if you'll get me some food." Robbie nodded his agreement, and Chris joined the line at the bar.

A scrawny man in a rumpled gray suit walked up and slapped him on the shoulder. "Hi there, old buddy. You must be Chris Nelson. I'm George Besh. Glad you could make it down." Leaning closer, he said in a low voice, "Whatcha' doing tonight. I've got some good dope that just came in."

Chris stepped away from the little man invading his space. "I'm not into that kind of thing, and I'm going to New Simon tonight. I'll pass."

"Sure, kid. Anyway, good to see you. And I know JQ wants to see you."

"JQ? You mean Mr. McCrombie?" Chris felt ready to refocus his frustrations and put McCrombie in his place.

"And hey, Robbie told me about you predicting earthquakes, and I mentioned your ideas to JQ, you know, and he's interested in how it's going." George patted him on the back. "I'll let him know you're here." George walked away.

"I see you met George," said Robbie as he brought two plates loaded with goodies.

"Robbie, I told you not to say anything about my predictions. Now I find out you told George, and he's told JQ McCrombie. If Dr. Kenton hears about this, my name is really mud."

Beneath the surface JQ fumed from the conversation with Marion, worried that the Seismic Safety Department might get involved with some of the inspections. As he walked by the open door to the lobby, he heard Tina's laughter. He turned and moved toward her voice but slowed upon seeing Alex.

"Hello, Tina. Hello, Alex. Welcome to my open house." He held out his hand and shook the hands of both of his employees. "Glad you could make it, but I'm surprised you would come together." Already up tight, he took the upper hand. "Alex, why don't you go get Tina and me a drink?"

"Sorry, Mr. McCrombie, I'll just take Tina over and get her a drink. I don't know which kind of snake poison you like." Alex turned away and taking Tina's arm moved towards the bar.

JQ stood very still, considering the rejection. He clenched his fists as his blood pressure rose.

"Hi, you must be Chris Nelson." Chris looked at the well-dressed gentleman who stuck out his hand. "I'm JQ McCrombie. Welcome to my open house." His booming voice jarred Chris' ears, and he drew back. "So you're the kid with those crazy notions about earthquakes."

Chris looked at JQ for a moment and then answered in a matching loud voice. "I don't think my ideas are crazy. I think we're going to have a big earthquake, and if you're the guy who has those crews out working on the bridge retrofits, you better tell them to do the job right, not the shifty way they're doing it now."

Chris's belligerence surprised JQ, and he did not like what he heard. "Now look here, kid. I'm sorry if I suggested your ideas were crazy, but don't go putting down my work crews. They're good people, and they're doing a fine job." He paused and took a different tack. "So just where do you get the idea we're going to have a big quake real soon? You some kind of genius?"

"I may be. My mother thought so," Chris answered. "I'm a seismology graduate student at the University, and over the past three years I've developed a theory about how earthquakes happen and how to tell when one's developing." Chris warmed to his lecture. "My theory has been pretty successful over the past year, especially this past month. I was right on for the last sizable temblor in Dell."

JQ grunted. "That doesn't prove anything."

"I've been monitoring the small event activity since that time, and my calculations show there will be a significant temblor near New Simon, probably tomorrow."

He turned square to JQ, jutting his chin out at the taller man. "I've installed a seismic station at New Simon, and I saw your crews doing the work on the overpass there. I'm thoroughly appalled at the work they're doing."

JQ glanced around as he listened to the exposition. He saw Marion Roberts and Pamela standing to one side looking his way, possibly listening in on the conversation as it became ever more heated and loud.

"Whoa there. Come on, let's talk about this in a more reasonable way." JQ took Chris by the arm and guided him to one of the private corners of the large room. "Okay, so you're a seismic genius, but don't go spouting off about some earthquake about to happen. You just make people nervous."

Chris continued his crusade, "They should be nervous. Earthquakes destroy and kill. If an earthquake the size of the ones that hit 200 years ago struck the New Madrid now, it would totally destroy this city and severely damage all the other major cities within 600 miles." He pushed his finger into JQ's chest. "You're the one who should be nervous."

"Look, kid, just quiet down," JQ said, dropping his voice. "I hear what you're saying, but you can't prove anything, so don't go around stirring things up and scaring people, especially at my open house. There are people here I don't want to get upset about this earthquake stuff and the retrofit business."

Reaching the limit of his patience, JQ decided the time had come to use a strong arm to keep Chris quiet. "Besides, you wouldn't want me to drop by my old friend, the Chancellor, and tell him you are making earthquake predictions, now would you? A 5.8, huh? This weekend at New Simon, huh?"

It dawned on Chris why he had been invited to this particular party, and his stomach churned at the direct threat. Dr. Kenton would be livid if the Chancellor asked about a graduate student making public earthquake predictions. Any hope of support would be lost. Chris almost panicked, and his face showed it.

"So, keep your trap shut about quakes and have yourself a nice time at this party. I'll take care of the bridges." JQ stared at Chris while he adjusted his tie and shirt collar. "You understand?" He turned and stalked away. Chris stood rooted to the carpet.

Robbie walked up with an empty bottle in his hand. "What's the matter, old buddy? You swallow a pickle?"

Chris said, "I guess I shot my mouth off one too many times. Now, I can't even talk about it. All I can do is prove I'm right."

George stepped close to JQ and, pointing towards Tina and Alex, said in the knowing tone of a co-conspirator, "Look's like you're losing out on that piece of ass, don't it?" Having stomped on one of JQ's hot buttons, George shifted to another sore point. "Did you get what you wanted from Chris? Or is he still doing his thing on the earthquakes. And say, do you want to come through with some cash for the next shipment?"

JQ's emotions poured over their limit. He directed his pent-up fury onto George. Reaching out, he took the small man by the neck of his shirt and walked him backwards towards the elevator. "You prick, you son-of-a-bitch, you stinking asshole—you're leaving. I'm sick and tired of people pissing me off. So get out." Ignoring his gaping guests, JQ shoved George into the just vacated elevator, reached in and pressed the DOWN button. "Don't call me, I'll call you."

JQ was on a roll, and he headed towards Alex and Tina. Stepping between them, he looked Alex in the eye and said, "I just decided you insulted me a few minutes ago, and I don't like it. Get out."

Looking his boss straight back, Alex laid it on the line. "Mr. McCrombie, Tina's my girl, so keep your hands off her and shut your damned mouth. Tina's had enough of it, and so have I. If you bother either of us again, I'll tell a few people what I know about your emails to Harley in Nashville and just how you run your company. And the proof of that is safe where you can't get it."

The statement stunned JQ as he realized that Alex knew something more than he should about his business dealings in the capital. Truly amazed that Alex would dare threaten him, JQ responded, "Buster, you're fired as of this instant, and your little whore is fired as well. Get the hell out of here, and take your slut with you." He stared after them as they headed for the elevators.

Tina squeezed Alex's arm as they stepped on board the elevator. She turned, smiled at JQ, and said, "You lost." He stared at her triumphant look of defiance as the elevator doors closed.

Chris heard Marion Roberts talking about earthquake safety and joined the conversation. He nodded to Pamela and told Marion of Dr. Kenton's research and described some of his own work in developing a scenario model. He felt comfortable having found someone at the party with similar interests.

JQ talked for a moment with the Mayor, but when he noticed Chris in deep conversation with Marion, he assumed Chris must be spreading bad words to one of JQ's enemies after being told to keep his mouth shut. JQ walked over and grabbed Chris by the shoulder. "Okay, that's it. I told you to keep your mouth shut. Now you're out of here." He shoved Chris towards the elevator.

More people stared at JQ, wondering at his bizarre behavior in this series of confrontations and speaking amongst themselves. "Come on … Let's go … It's time to leave." Several picked up their wraps and purses and headed for the elevator. Although scheduled to last two hours, a mass exodus soon stood waiting for the elevator as everyone left the open house with excuses about dinner plans and the need to beat the commute. Within ten minutes, only JQ, Suzie, and the caterers remained.

"Damn." JQ picked up a cocktail glass and hurled it at the large plate glass window. The cocktail glass shattered, leaving a wet track running down the unbreakable windowpane. "Damn."

Suzie picked up her jacket, entered the elevator, and pressed the DOWN button. "I quit," she told her reflections. "No job is worth being with that kind of boss. If I have my way, that's the last time I'll ever see you, Mister JQ McCrombie."

Chapter 16: Calm Before The Storm

The alarm clock announced Saturday morning. Judy lifted an eyelid and peeked out the crack under the window blind next to the camper bed. The rising sun caught the edges of the clouds, and the orange glow of the eastern sky became lost in the bright yellow that followed.

She whispered, "Hey, sleepy head. Time to wake up. We've got miles to go and places to see." Pushing the sheet back, she rubbed Tom's bare back, feeling the ripple of muscles under the smooth skin. Tom moaned with pleasure. Judy's fingers tingled and she turned her hand over to run the backs of her fingernails down his back. As she reached the skin below his beltline, his body gave a mild involuntary jerk, much like a cat that raises its tail when its back is rubbed.

He rolled to his side and reached for her. "I'll do the places to see first," he said with a grin. "Come here." He pulled her to him. It took 35 minutes for them to get out of bed, and by Judy's reckoning. that seemed pretty fast.

After six days of practice in the camper, they dressed like two sardines sliding around a can, very adept at the dressing dance. Downing a quick bowl of cereal and a banana, they packed for travel. The air felt cool and humid, foretelling a pleasant run for the final leg of their trip to Memphis.

Tom winked at Judy as they turned onto the freeway, "We did pretty well this morning, getting out at 7:10. I must say you're becoming a good traveler."

"I hope Jenny doesn't have to study Sunday." Judy found her worry for the day, and she could be expected to cover it from many different angles before discarding it. "You know, she sounds like she's really taken with Chris. Do you think she's ready for someone, or is she just looking around?"

"I can't read her mind, Judy, but when I listened to her, she sounded pretty definite this time. We'll just see how it is. You can't live her life for her, you know."

"Well, just so we have a chance to talk with her. I'll worry about it until I can really know, I know I will." Judy dabbed at her eyes and turned her head to look out the window at the trees. They would reach Memphis by 9:30 A.M.

It seemed like he had slept only minutes when the sound of keys in the door, the door's opening, and a bucket being pushed into the room awakened JQ. He sat up to look out at a rapidly expanding dawn. Almost eight hours had passed since he fell asleep on the couch. Sunlight touched the trees across the river, lighting them like beacons in the west. He saw that the shadows of the Memphis skyline would soon be off the water.

"Oh, I'm sorry, Mr. McCrombie. I didn't know you was here." The janitor stopped when he spied JQ. Joe had come up in the service elevator, not expecting anyone else to be present in the building.

"That's okay, Joe. You got to clean this place sometime, and after the party yesterday, it really needs it. I'll use the bathroom and shave, and you go ahead in here." Joe had worked with JQ from the beginning and had cleaned at the West Memphis offices for years. When JQ rewarded him with the responsibility of the new building, Joe seemed pleased.

JQ washed his face and hands at the new gold inlay faucets. He found the emergency living supplies his secretary had stored and did a good job scraping the whiskers from his chin. He looked at his watch, 8:35 in the morning.

While Joe cleaned the restrooms, JQ unlocked the cabinet beside the couch and pulled out the briefcase. Opening it, he sorted through and counted out $13,500, the payoff with interest for Harry. He put the money into an envelope and placed the two-inch thick package inside his coat pocket. Closing the briefcase, he returned it to its hiding place and relocked the cabinet.

"Hey, Joe. I'm going down to Wheeler's for breakfast, and then I'll be back. See you in a bit." JQ turned his key in the elevator lock and waited for the lift to reach the penthouse floor.

JQ entered the cafe and waved at the hostess. "Pour me some coffee, I'll be back in a minute." He walked to the rear of Wheeler's and called to the cook. "Harv, I've got a package for Harry. He said you'd take it. Okay?"

"Sure, JQ, jest leave it on the counter." JQ placed the envelope next to the cutting board, amazed at the nonchalance of the loan sharks in this town.

JQ returned to the front and enjoyed a hearty breakfast, a quick scan of the paper, and four cups of coffee, He began to feel much better.

Jenny sat in front of Chris' workstation screen. She had come to the Seismology Lab after her early morning walk and now waited for Chris to call. It seemed so still and empty without him around.

Chris's strangeness worried Jenny. At times, she wanted to mother him, and at other times she wanted to fight tooth and toenail with him, shake him until he paid attention. She wondered if what she felt might be love. But then she couldn't be sure Chris would ever look at her as a woman long enough to get interested. He didn't seem gay, but she didn't know.

As promised, Chris had not logged off his workstation when he left Friday night, so Jenny could run the latest model. She reviewed the command log.

"Looks like the program automatically updated its database with a magnitude 2.8 event under Cooter this morning. That's pretty close to New Simon."

She redisplayed the command sequences Chris had run last night. She could see where he had changed some parameters around and then run the model, producing a prediction for a magnitude 6.1 event for that afternoon.

She picked the latest set of parameters and re-executed the program. The workstation spent three minutes processing, then displayed the results.

Jenny stared in amazement. The display showed a map of the southern extension of the New Madrid Fault, from Reelfoot Lake through the Missouri Bootheel down to Marked Tree, Arkansas. A bright red gash cut through the map, running from south of Tiptonville to just north of Marked Tree. The caption at the bottom read:

```
"Nelson Connected-Asperity Model, Case 141.
Prognosis based upon latest activity at 08:32.
Epicenter on asperity #1 at 89.85W, 36.05N, secondary
on asperity #2 at 89.97W, 35.89N; initiate 09:33
CDT Saturday; magnitude 7.9"
```

Jenny looked at the big clock on the wall. It read five minutes after nine. She reran the model and got the same result. She rechecked her watch and mumbled to herself, "Now Chris wouldn't construct some practical joke, would he?" She decided to wait in the lab to find out. After all, if the display meant what it said, she need only wait another half-hour to find out.

Besides, Chris had said he would call by 9:30.

"Ladies and Gentlemen, most of you have finished breakfast so I would like to introduce our speaker for this morning, Dr. Todd Crow from the UC Berkeley National Lab." The program chair for the East Bay Breakfast Club meeting in Danville waited for the group to pay attention.

"Dr. Crow will speak this morning about earthquake phenomena, providing us with a step by step summary of how an earthquake happens. He has done detailed analysis with the USGS of the 7.9 magnitude earthquake in India a few years ago and has developed some new insights into the mechanics of such an event. This should be a very interesting subject for us residents of the East Bay." He helped Todd arrange the writing pad.

As Tom approached Memphis he glanced at his watch. "9:30, it's 7:30 back home. The Breakfast Club is probably getting ready to listen to Dr. Crow speak about now. I was lucky to get him to come out. Just wish I was there to hear what he has to say."

"Tom, you know these were the only three weeks you could get off from work." Judy sounded pleased as they sped onto the I-40 Bridge into Memphis.

"I know, but ..." His voice echoed a small disappointment. Changing the subject he commented, "The Memphis skyline's really pretty, isn't it?" Tom had developed an admiration for the fine old city during previous business visits.

"Yes, it's gorgeous. But, oh my, Tom, the Mississippi River is huge. I didn't know it was so wide." As often happens in the spring, the mighty river flowed above flood stage from the spring melt to the north and covered the low-lying flats between the channel and the levees protecting West Memphis.

Tom pointed out the landmarks, "See those bridges to the south? That's where I-55 crosses the river along with a railroad bridge. Those bridges are much older than this one." Tom stayed in the right lane so he could travel slower than the Saturday morning traffic and allow Judy to have a good view of the city. "And on the north side of this bridge you can see the Pyramid."

"Where're we going first?"

"We'll go to the Visitor Center to pick up the latest event schedules. It's at the first exit off the bridge. By the way, as you look towards the city, the shore you see next to the water is Mud Island. The channel of the Wolf River is on the other side and separates Mud Island from the real riverfront."

Judy continued to admire the skyline as they approached the center of the bridge.

Joe had finished vacuuming the carpet in the penthouse when JQ returned. The old man stowed his tools back on the cleaning cart and prepared to leave.

"You have a good day, Mr. McCrombie, you hear," Joe said as he pushed his cart to the service elevator and inserted his key to call it. JQ looked at his Rolex. "9:31, that's pretty good, Joe, to clean up all that party stuff that quick. I guess that means you're going fishing today?" The jibes about Joe's not working hard unless he wanted to go fishing had been a standing joke between them for a number of years, from the time Joe had watched over JQ as a child.

"Well now, that sounds like a good idea, JQ. Maybe I'll do just that." Joe smiled at the younger man. The elevator door opened, and Joe pushed his cart into the elevator, pressing PARKING to return to the garage and the utility rooms where he was stationed. "I suppose I'll see you next week, Mr. McCrombie," he said as the doors closed in front of him.

JQ stared at the shiny brass elevator portal. He felt detached, like at the end of a play when the curtain draws closed, and the world played out on the stage ceases to exist. But he couldn't think of what had ended, and the importance Joe had in it. JQ wondered if his mind had gone wrong.

Jenny again ran the simulation on the workstation. Again the map of the southern extension of the fault showed with the bright red gash down the middle. Only the case number had changed in caption at the bottom.

"Nelson Connected-Asperity Model, Case 142. Prognosis based upon latest activity at 08:32. Epicenter on asperity #1 at 89.85W, 36.05N, secondary on asperity #2 at 89.97W, 35.89N; initiate 09:33 CDT Saturday; magnitude 7.9"

Jenny looked at the master display clock on the wall. It read 9:31, two minutes to go. Panic clutched at her throat. Chris still had not called.

In desperation Jenny pulled out her electronic assistant and searched for Dr. Kenton's phone number. " ... 5412." She dialed the number and waited as it rang several times.

About ready to give up, she heard an answer, "Paul Kenton here."

"Dr. Kenton, this is Jenny Fox. I'm at the Seismology Lab, and I'm worried. Chris's computer says a big earthquake is about to happen. He hasn't called yet, and I don't know what to do. I'm just worried ..."

"Whoa there. Where's Chris? What do you mean his computer says there'll be a big earthquake?"

"I told Chris I'd come into the Lab this morning to help him calibrate some of the equipment at New Simon. He went up there last night, but he hasn't called like he said he would. But he left his computer logged in so I could rerun his model. Another small temblor up near New Simon early this morning seems to have changed the results. Anyway, the model now says there will be a magnitude 7.9 earthquake at 9:33 this morning at New Simon. That's less than a minute from now."

Paul voice reflected disbelief. "Jenny, I know Chris has been working on that model of his for months, but he doesn't have one chance in a million to actually make a good prediction. Don't get all worked up about it. I'll talk to Chris when he gets back next week, and we'll put an end to this foolishness."

"But, Dr. Kenton, maybe he's right."

"If he's right, then we'll have an earthquake, but don't plan on it. I suggest you just calm down and wait and see. If nothing happens, then you'll know Chris was wrong. Don't let some wild dream like this suck you into panic."

"But, Dr. Kenton …"

"Jenny, I have to take care of some other business right now. Please log off Chris's computer before you leave the Lab and make sure everything is in proper working order. I appreciate your calling me, but believe me, there's nothing to worry about. Okay?"

Jenny could think of nothing to counter the arguments. "Okay, I guess. I'll see you next week. Bye"

She hung up the telephone and turned back to the screen. Just in case she clicked on the PRINT icon and took the single page of the screen image from the printer.

Looking at the master clock on the wall she saw it turn over to 9:34. With a sense of relief but some regret, she realized the prediction had been wrong—the earthquake had not happened at 9:33 like the model said it would.

It was all a joke. She felt embarrassment after her panic episode and began to plan what she would say to give Chris a piece of her mind, if he ever called.

Alex had already eaten his breakfast and headed for the airstrip down the road when Chris walked through the door of the cafe and waved at Tina.

"What happened to you?" Tina asked as Chris sat down on a stool near the kitchen. His rumpled clothes and uncombed hair accented the two-day growth of fuzz beginning to show on his face. "I thought you were going to stay for the whole party."

"I got kicked out shortly after you did. What are you doing here? I thought you were fired, along with Alex."

"Well, maybe I am, but I knew Cookie couldn't handle things this morning if I didn't come in. Besides, Alex wanted to get up early for his parachute jump, so here I am. But what happened to you?"

"I'm not sure, JQ went ballistic and sent me packing. I went back the the Lab and worked on my computer model some more, so it was late when I got to my camp. I just sacked out in my sleeping bag." He yawned and scrubbed his face. "Can I have a cup of coffee and the breakfast special? I need to get some food in me so I can call the Seismo Lab and see how things are going."

"Sure, just be a minute." Tina wrote the order on her pad.

"The last run I made on my model last night said that about three this afternoon we should have a pretty strong temblor up here, probably a magnitude 6.1."

"Really? My shift's over at two, then I'm out of here for sure." She didn't know whether to believe Chris or not. He seemed such a strange person, with all his predictions and everything. She handed the order for the biscuits and gravy special to Cookie and grabbed the coffee pot to take back to Chris.

Once served Chris wolfed the food down and drained his coffee cup. As Tina refilled his cup, he asked, "What are you and Alex going to do?"

Tina poured herself a cup of fresh coffee and glanced at the clock on the wall—the second hand raced past 9:33. "Alex will be back in an hour. Then we're going to start planning the rest of our life together."

CHAPTER 17: T+0

"How many of you have felt a strong earthquake?" Todd Crow addressed the May assemblage of the East Bay Breakfast Club in the restaurant banquet room. Several raised their hands. "Did it shake moderately, or was the shaking strong enough to scare you? How long did it last? Do you remember?"

Todd looked over the 22 Saturday morning attendees, ranging in age from 20 to 70. "You all know earthquakes are caused by fractures in the rocks beneath us, but have you ever wondered exactly how that fracture happens? That's what I'm here to tell you." He took the black marker in his hand. "I hope to give you a clear sense of how an earthquake happens over time, sometimes lots of time.

"First I want you to visualize the spread of a fracture causing an earthquake." Todd drew a jagged line from the bottom left of the page towards the top. "It's like a crack across the windshield of your car. It starts in one place and moves outward from there. The longer the fracture goes, the longer it takes to spread." The line reached the top left as he finished his sentence.

"Take a little magnitude 3.0 earthquake. The fracture will be a quarter mile long and a hundred yards high. It happens in about one-tenth of a second." Todd turned, flipped the page, and drew a tiny dot on the paper.

"On the other hand, the fracture that causes a magnitude 8.0 earthquake in this part of the country tears up 90 miles of fault line and takes from 25 to 50 seconds to complete." Marching in place, one step a second, he drew a jagged line across the bottom of the pad and counted, "1,001, 1,002, it goes on and on, 1,005, 1,006. To some it seems to go on forever. 1,010, 1,011."

One of those eating breakfast raised his hand and asked, "Why such a large range in time?"

"The area fractured determines the magnitude. On a vertical slip-strike fault like the San Andreas, if the fault fractures in both directions from its focus, it takes about 25 seconds for each side to extend 45 miles. If the fracture is mostly unidirectional, like the event in Northridge a few years ago, it starts at one end and travels to the other, taking twice as much time." The questioner nodded.

"But even if you're at the epicenter of a temblor, you don't feel an earthquake the instant the fracture starts." Todd drew a horizontal line near the top of the paper. "That represents the earth's surface, and here is a stick-man standing there. Shock waves take time to rise from start of the fracture to the surface." He traced a series of arcs rising from the fracture line to the surface. "People a long distance from the fault may not feel the earthquake until long after the fracture causing the earthquake has ended."

Todd looked over his audience and paused to let the information take root in their minds

Alex nodded as the pilot boasted over the roar of the engine, "It's a perfect day for skydiving. There're only a few puffy clouds above the Mississippi River this morning. It's 74 degrees on the ground, winds four knots from the southwest, normal for a Saturday morning in May. It's perfect, just like I told you it would be."

Alex crouched just out of the whistling wind next to the open door of the single-engine airplane, strapped to his parachute, standing with one foot on the step outside above the strut, waiting for the call to jump. He swallowed and thought of his folly. Come on, it's the same as last time. Don't sweat it. His heart pounded and burning acid rose in his throat as he looked down at the ground, 10,600 feet below. Okay, it's only the second time he'd gone solo, and it's not that much of a thing. Stay calm.

"Remember," the pilot yelled, "When you step out of the airplane, you'll reach your terminal velocity of 180 feet per second in about ten seconds, that's over 120 miles per hour." He tapped the altimeter. "From our current elevation, if you pull the ripcord in 50 seconds, your elevation should be 1,800 feet above the surface, and your vertical velocity will drop to 12 feet per second. That'll give you two and a half minutes to sail around the field and finally walk to a soft landing in the grass beside the jump school."

"Sure." Alex chided back. "That's if this piece of cloth in the bag strapped to my butt works and stops me from making a messy stain in the grass." He told himself everything would work.

The pilot smiled. "Trust me, there's nothing to go wrong." He circled back for the jump run and called, "Five seconds." Alex clasped the side of the fuselage with his hands. "Three, Two, One, GO." Alex sprang through the open door of the airplane, diving headfirst into a pool of air.

Todd flipped to another blank sheet. "Here in California, we all have a lot of preconceived ideas about our local faults, so to keep away from our biases, let's consider the New Madrid Seismic Zone as an example of how an earthquake happens."

He pointed to the map of the Mississippi River valley he had pinned to the sidewall. "You can see the red smear showing where microquakes have occurred in the past 20 years. They mark the primary fault area. It runs southwest to northeast from the eastern middle of Arkansas, through the Bootheel of Missouri then beneath the Mississippi River past Cairo, Illinois, touching Kentucky and Tennessee along the way.

"The earth's crust in the central United States is being shoved and twisted by forces deep within the planet. West of the fault, these forces push the basement rock northeast. To the east, opposing forces push the rock formations to the southwest.

"For eons the torsional stress from these forces has accumulated along the fault, straining the rock closer and closer to its limits until it breaks. The earthquakes in 1811 provided major relief along the entire fault, but stress immediately started to re-accumulate and the strain began to rebuild.

"Somewhere along the fault is a place where the fault will soon fail catastrophically once again. The place it starts will be deep, between 15 and 20 kilometers." Todd put a black dot at the middle of the page and a horizontal line across the top.

"In West Texas gas wells, exploration crews drill their deepest holes to depths of over 12 kilometers, little more than half way to the depth where the greatest strain accumulates in the basement rock of the New Madrid." He drew a small tower on the top line and a black line half way down towards the dot. Tapping the black dot, he said, "We have no direct way to observe actual events that deep in the earth's crust. We can only imagine the earthquake as it happens.

"Imagine how hot it is. The temperature 17.5 kilometers down is about 380 degrees Celsius, that's 720 degrees Fahrenheit. Overburden pressure, the weight of the rock and fluids above that point, measures 52 tons per square inch, so great that fluids in the rock cannot boil. Under these conditions the rock becomes somewhat plastic and is able to deform to some extent to accommodate the increasing stress."

He placed one palm atop the other and pushed them in opposite directions, showing how his hands moved without slipping. "However, the rock is still not hot enough to flow, though strain within the rock becomes enough for rock faces to develop micro-fractures and slowly slide past each other, moving one molecule at a time.

"The rock matrix accommodates the stress with deformation and micro-fractures along the fault. But the adjustment is miniscule compared to the movement necessary to fully relieve the growing stress. Seismologists watch for spots where the stress accumulates without much deformation. Those points are candidates for major fractures of the fault." Todd took a drink of water and looked at his watch.

"Let's label the instant when the fracture begins T+0."

As Alex leapt into the thin air, his digital wristwatch read 9:34:09. At that instant, the rock far beneath the surface at New Simon fractured.

Like a knick in a pane of glass, a microscopic crack materialized between the two sides of the fault at the point of maximum stress. Friction holding the two sides in place could no longer overcome the shear stress, and the two sides broke apart, moving past each other, right and left, along the direction of the fault.

T+0 had arrived on the New Madrid.

"Fractures start at one single point called the focus or hypocenter." Todd pointed to the black dot on the paper. "As the rock fractures, it releases some of the stored energy as pressure waves, compressions and dilations of the molecules in the rock. In air we call those waves sound. In rock we call them Primary or *P-waves*, seismic waves that move outward in all directions from the focus at a speed just under six kilometers per second.

The rest of the released energy goes into Secondary or *S-waves* that physically move the rock. These waves travel more slowly, at about three kilometers per second.

"It will take three seconds for the *P-waves* to reach the surface from a focus 17.5 kilometers below." He drew concentric waves rising toward the top of the page.

"The southern segment of the New Madrid Fault is a vertical slip-strike fault. When a fracture happens there, the shear forces align the physical crack in the rock to expand upward, downward, and to the sides along the direction of the fault. It forms a rough circle in the vertical plane of the fault."

Changing to the red marker, Todd drew a three-inch diameter circle around the dot.

"In ten microseconds the fracture grows to a circle six centimeters in diameter, half the size of my palm. Edges of the tear propagate outward at three kilometers per second as the *S-wave* initiated by the first fracture and amplified by the subsequent rock-breaking action physically transfers the strain that is released by the failure as added stress to the unfractured rock matrix."

Todd drew an expanding series of concentric circles, each an inch outside the last. "20 microseconds, 30 microseconds, 40, 50. As you can see, it expands rapidly, the radius growing linearly with time as the fractured area grows as the square of the radius."

"In one millisecond, the edge of the circular-shaped crack following the front of the *S-wave* moves outward to three meters on either side and up and down from this dot. The ruptured area is about the size of a large trampoline, 28 square meters."

"The edge of the fracture becomes ragged. Rock matrix strength varies across the area and some places rupture more quickly than others. It may take several microseconds for the transfer of stress to collect sufficiently to break the stronger points in the rock matrix."

Another young man asked, "So you're saying it's the *S-wave* that propagates the fracture?"

"That's right."

"Is it always a circular area?"

"No, it does not remain circular. As the broken area continues to grow, the greatest transfer of stress in this case is horizontal along the fault, and the fracture assumes an oval shape, spreading faster horizontally than vertically. Got the picture?" Todd waited for the questioner to nod.

"Now the surfaces of the rock fracture at the focus begin to slide horizontally in opposite directions, by now with a physical displacement approaching half a millimeter, the thickness of the toenail on your little toe. With a pressure of 52 tons per square inch, the frictional heat generated is awesome."

Todd raised and waved his index finger. "These dimensions may seem small, but remember: this has all occurred in only one millisecond."

"At T+3 milliseconds, the front edge of the *P-wave* is 18 meters from the focus, the *S-wave* is 9 meters. The fracture covers 260 square meters, the size of a midsize suburban home. Over 1,700 tons of rock are in motion."

Todd took another sip of water. "Once moving, the rock does not stop. The sides of the fracture continue to slip past each other in jerky starts and stops, searching for equilibrium with the rest of the formation until the total displacement of the rupture is reached.

"The fracture grows. After seven milliseconds the fractured area measures 30 meters high and 42 meters long, involving 1,000 square meters with a maximum displacement of two millimeters. By this time the energy released is sufficient for the event to register on a seismograph as an earthquake of magnitude 1.0.

"The tear grows and grows. The earthquake reaches a magnitude of 3.0 at T+65 milliseconds when the fractured oval has grown to 400 meters in length by 130 meters in height. Its surface area is 50,000 square meters, room enough for six full-sized baseball fields. At that time the *P-wave* is still 17.4 kilometers from the surface."

Todd's audience sat silent, spellbound.

"At T plus half a second the *S-wave* has moved 1,500 meters from the focus and the *P-wave* almost three kilometers. Horizontally, the edge of the fracture continues to closely follow the *S-wave* front but begins to encounter strong points in the rock matrix that resist the tearing force of the *S-wave*. The crack covers over 2.5 square kilometers of fault surface, nearly a square mile, with a maximum displacement near the center of the oval of almost half a foot. The temblor is approaching the magnitude of the event that struck near Marked Tree, Arkansas, in 1976."

Todd put his glass down on the table. "Gentlemen, half a second of fracturing—that is all it takes to generate a magnitude 4.7 earthquake—half a second."

On the New Madrid, the propagation of the fracture ran into more and more resistance. It required more and more accumulated stress to extend the crack. The rock matrix resisted. The chances were high that the earthquake would end within the next one-tenth of a second and be limited to a magnitude of 5.0.

But when the leading edge of the *S-wave* passed through the second asperity 2.55 kilometers southwest of the focus, sympathetic fracturing began.

The second small kink in the fault could not contain the impulse of the added stress, and it, too, failed. The second fracture propagated backward towards the malingering points that resisted the first passage of the wave front. The second lurch was too much and those points resisting the growth of the fracture plane gave way, adding their stored energy to the ever-expanding seismic event.

No strong points along the fault remained in the vicinity. No place along the fault closer than 44 kilometers to the northeast or 64 kilometers to the southwest had the strength to stop the spread of the fracture. By T+0.85 seconds the die had been cast. It had become inevitable that the 5.1 magnitude temblor would grow into a giant earthquake.

Todd continued, "If the fracture keeps growing, by one second the maximum displacement between the opposing surfaces of the fault at the focus will exceed ten inches. The earthquake has reached a magnitude of 5.3."

In one second Alex had fallen 16 feet below the airplane's altitude, though wind resistance had already pushed him 30 feet behind. The *P-wave* had climbed to within 12.8 kilometers of New Simon, streaking upwards at eight times the speed of a rifle bullet from a 30-06 hunting rifle.

An exponential growth in power resulted as the fracture involved more and more of the fault. More of the rock matrix along the fault began to move. The energy released increased 30-fold in the next second, and the earthquake reached a magnitude of 5.9 at T+2.0 seconds, sufficient to wreak significant damage to man-made structures near the epicenter. Within seconds, what seemed vital and important to those at the surface would become of little consequence.

Chapter 18: Six Seconds To Hell

When the initial fracture launched the earthquake, most people in the five states surrounding the New Madrid Fault—unmindful that such an event could even happen—continued with their normal lives. From ignorance sprang their sense of well being, or at least normal.

George Besh drove north on Memphis's Riverside Drive toward the I-40 Bridge, his heart pounding like an overblown balloon. His mouth felt dry, his stomach nauseous, but most of all, his head felt high. A mixture of euphoria and panic coursed through his shoulders, and he tried to remain calm, but the strong narcotic coursing through his bloodstream warped his mind.

His eyes crossed, then drifted apart, and he shook his head to keep them pointed ahead. He saw the traffic light turning red, and after some heavy, slow motion thinking, he muttered, "Stop. I got to stop the car." He reached out with his foot and slammed the brake pedal. His car pitched forward then rocked backward as it screeched to a sudden stop, well short of the intersection.

George looked out his car window and blinked. "What're they staring at? What do they care about me?" He wondered if some carried guns, searching for him. A chill of fear and paranoia found its way into his body. Spasms rose in his gut and another taste of acid burned the back of his throat. He could find no way to control it. "Shit, man." He blinked again, trying to clear his eyes.

Steve Pauli drove his old pickup truck north on Tennessee Highway 22 from Tiptonville toward the old landing town of Bessie at the base of the New Madrid loop on the Mississippi River, his daughter Juliana sitting on the bouncing, slick truck seat beside him.

"There, isn't that a pretty honeysuckle vine?" Steve pointed out the scattering of delicate white flowers.

Too late, Juliana turned her head to look in the direction her dad pointed. Steve could tell she obviously wanted him to understand this was not her idea of a fun trip. "Oh, guess I missed it."

Steve felt the alienation. He wondered if he would ever convince his daughter to enjoy his company with their visits limited to two weekends a month. He still had to earn a living, and his vocation of photography took him into strange places. This time he traveled along the old road to the half-mile wide isthmus that separated the two bends of the Mississippi River: Winchester Towhead to the east from Point Pleasant Chute to the west. Some called the isthmus Bessie's Neck.

"Hey, see that squirrel scooting across the road up there?"

"What squirrel?" Juliana turned her hand to inspect the purple nails she had painted that morning.

The paved road turned left, away from the levee, but Steve bore right "We'll pop up this dirt road. It goes over to the other side of the levee to a turnaround beside the river. I've done some great photo shoots along here."

As the road dropped into the trees and rounded the turn, he came to an abrupt stop. "Holy cow. The turnaround's covered with water. No one told me the river would be running this high."

The river east of Bessie's Neck flowed northward at an elevation of 298 feet above sea level. The river level dropped a full ten feet while making the 19 miles around the long bend past New Madrid and then south to Compromise Landing, only three quarters of a mile west. Behind Steve the top of the levee separating the two bends stood at an elevation of 305 feet. Seven feet of levee was all that kept the river from cutting through Bessie's Neck to take a much shorter path.

"Guess I'll have to back out this time, but we can still get some good pictures." Steve set the brake. "Come on, let's get out and walk around."

"Do I have to?" Juliana looked her pouting best and slumped her shoulders to show how weak she felt.

"Yes, you have to. Come on. I only get to visit with you two weekend days every month, and I'm not going to waste any of my time with you sitting in this truck while I take pictures. Move your little butt out of the truck. Now." He grinned to show the big bluff behind his gruff voice.

Juliana could not help but grin back. "Okay, Daddy, but really, this trip is just 'soooo' boring."

JQ leaned back on the couch in his new office atop the bluff overlooking Mud Island. He rubbed his eyes and squeezed his temples. The digital clock read 9:31, and his head still pulsed. He had to stay away from those Wallbangers.

He rose and walked to the west window, looking across the Mississippi River toward the Arkansas shore. He could see tourists below parking on the thin strip of cobblestones beside the river, thronging to the excursion boats. The Jazz Festival was heating up in Lee Park. A few clouds hung in the west, indicating the possibility of another rainy afternoon. At least the bright sun shown from the other side of the building. He stretched the skin of his scalp back from his eyes to help relieve the pain.

Squinting to the north past the Pyramid, he thought of his fracas with Tina and Alex, He didn't know about Tina, but it felt good to fire that smart-ass. It would probably require something more with Alex. The information he had could really hurt. Maybe he ought to call one of the crew chiefs to put Alex in line.

Shaking his head, he remembered the scene with Chris. He wondered what he should do about Chris's prediction of an earthquake. Chris kept talking like it would happen sometime today. JQ laughed. It'd be funny as hell if it turned out the little prick knew what he was talking about.

Marion Roberts pulled the driver from his golf bag and walked over to tee his ball on the par four 13th hole at the MidTown Municipal Golf Course. This morning he played with three old friends, all good players and moving along well.

Marion had finished with par on the 12th by avoiding the mid-fairway sand trap, unlike two of his golfing buddies. "I guess that's the advantage of not hitting so well," he joked. "It keeps me out of the sand on my first shot." He took several practice swings, and then stood back to study his tee shot.

"Hey, Marion, hurry it up. We don't have all day," called Henry Spocket, his partner in the foursome. At that instant the basement rock cracked 47 miles away beneath New Simon.

Marion put his club head down on the ground, turned around and smiled. "Henry, I thought we were partners. You shouldn't rush me, else I won't be able to win the hole for us like I did last time."

"Okay, you're right, but don't take all day."

Marion took the club in hand and again settled in his grip. He approached the ball on the tee, looked down the fairway, and declared, "I'll take all the time I need."

Todd asked the audience, "So what do you think it will be like when the *P-wave* reaches the surface after three seconds?"

One intrepid member of the audience held up his hand and spoke. "I remember a moderate quake I felt, and there was a growl coming from the ground. It took a couple of seconds before the real shaking started."

"Growl is a good way to describe it. And you did hear it. Not many people do. *P-waves* are like sound, and when they pass from the earth into the air, they become sound. It sounds like a growl because by the time it reaches the surface, it is mostly the low frequencies that remain. Higher frequencies are absorbed into the rock matrix.

"Now if it is a really big earthquake, the growl will grow and grow into a roar because there is more and more fracture sending *P-wave* energy to the surface. Strong *P-waves* can raise dust particles and make dishes clack together. If they are strong enough, you can feel them in your feet."

By T+3.0 seconds, a chronological time of 9:34:12 Central Daylight time, Alex had fallen 130 feet below the elevation of the departing airplane.

The fracture along the fault covered 102 square kilometers in an oval 17 kilometers long and 5 kilometers high. The top edge of the fractured zone had climbed to within 15 kilometers of the surface. No life form on the earth's surface yet knew of its existence.

In Arkansas the fracture tore unabated to the southwest under the runways of the Gosnell Airplex toward Marked Tree, while in Missouri it sped northeast under Cooter toward Tiptonville at almost 3,000 meters per second. The maximum displacement at the focus had grown to three feet, and the magnitude of the temblor had climbed to 6.3.

Alex began to organize his trip to the earth's surface, face down with his arms and legs spread wide. He checked the second counter on his wristwatch and calculated that he should pull the ripcord at 9:35:00. That would give him another three minutes to reach the ground.

Alex turned the palm of his hand in the wind and spun around for a better view of the Mississippi River, just three miles east. With the goggles protecting his eyes, the rush of the wind in his face excited and exhilarated him.

Chris sat on the stool at the shiny counter of NASTY's Café stirring the remains in his half-filled coffee cup. He worried over the confrontation with JQ McCrombie. He hoped JQ would not expose his predictions, at least before he had his proof in order. He knew the University wouldn't be happy with any premature news.

Chris felt sure that with this earthquake he could show that his theory worked and he could pinpoint earthquake location, time, and strength, and that would get the doubters off his back. He daydreamed of the accolades and recognition he would receive.

Tina stopped with the coffeepot. "Warm-up?"

"Sure, why not?" Chris continued to stare into his cup, watching the cream and coffee mix in a swirl. Tina moved down the counter to serve a couple of truckers talking baseball. Cookie placed an order on the serving shelf under the red lights.

A rumbling growl filled the room from the floor.

The sound grew as the leading edge of the *P-wave* spread across the earth's surface. The residents of New Simon felt the vibrations and heard the wakeup call before all other creatures on the surface of the earth.

Chris noticed his coffee dance and felt the floor beneath his feet vibrate. Deep sounds like an underground train filled the room. The stool shook his buttocks. Glasses and silverware danced and clacked together.

Already sensors at Chris's remote monitoring station west of I-55 had flashed the news to the Seismic Laboratory in Memphis.

Chris looked up and around in wonder, realizing the earthquake had begun. "Earthquake," he yelled, coming off the stool and running headlong for the door. "My earthquake's here. It's early, but I've got an earthquake. I've got to check my instruments. I've got an earthquake."

His voice rang with joy as he dashed out the door of the café to jump into his pickup and speed to his instrument station on the other side of the freeway.

The rumbling increased. *P-waves* lifted dust from the floor. The whole world vibrated up and down as if it were the leather head of a large kettledrum on which King Kong pounded with ten-ton pompoms. It became hard to keep firm footing. Cookie dropped his plates onto the serving shelf and grabbed for the wall. Tina slopped coffee from the pot onto the cups of the truckers as they lifted themselves by their hands away from the counter.

Outside, truckers and attendants stared around and yelled to each other. Some thought a train had derailed on the tracks west of town. Others knew a squadron of Air Force jet bombers must have passed overhead at supersonic speeds, shedding shock waves with abandon. Some felt the sound in their feet; a few thought it came from the ground below. Dust danced in the sandy paths along side the road.

Mixed with the continuing blast of the temblor was a cacophony of howls and barks as the 12 dogs around the truck stop were jolted awake from their sleepy dreams or were caught scrounging in the garbage can next to the kitchen door. All ran. Some swerved and leapt into the air while racing across the grass.

Birds burst from the trees, darting in random flight to escape the unseen monster.

People driving on the freeway a quarter mile west noticed little except a cloud of dust rising in the cotton fields around them. A few felt their steering wheels vibrate and started to slow. Some wondered if a tire had blown or the lug nuts had fallen from one of their wheels and their car had lost the whole tire.

The portion of the earth experiencing the rumblings grew outward in a circle from New Simon. Within a second the circle of vibration had grown to a diameter of 10 kilometers. Within two seconds *P-waves* struck at the I-255 Bridge over the Mississippi River.

Vibrations began the process of liquefying soils in the surrounding fields. Pressures began to build to force the fluids in those soils to the surface. Residents would soon relearn why the Indians had named the surrounding county Pemiscot, the old native word for "liquid mud."

When the *P-waves* had shaken New Simon for two seconds, the fracture centered beneath the old town had grown to 28 kilometers in length and 9 kilometers in height, involving a ruptured area of 240 square kilometers, with a maximum displacement of four feet. The earthquake's magnitude had climbed to more than 6.6. The fracture expanded relentlessly; the magnitude of the resulting earthquake growing as the fault released more and more of its strain into the seismic event.

Todd continued his lecture, "Finally, at T+6.0 seconds in our hypothetical earthquake, the *S-waves* will reach the surface and begin the serious destruction.

"If the fracturing has continued to this time, the energy release after six seconds is that of an earthquake of magnitude 6.8, the same as the 1996 earthquake in Northridge, California.

"By this time the fracture on the New Madrid will have grown to an oval over 33 kilometers in length and 11 kilometers in height. But the top of the oval fracture is still 12 kilometers beneath the surface."

The fury of Hell found its way to the surface of the earth at 9:34:15.0 Central Daylight Time.

The sediments underneath New Simon gave a chaotic twist. Lands to the west jerked northeast and fields to the east whipped southwest. In the fraction of a second, the waves reversed direction to twist the other way—back and forth—back and forth—then up and down and around as well.

A monster stirred the surface of the earth. An earthen tornado exploded outward from the epicenter, snapping trees, buildings, telephone poles at their base, tearing asunder everything that tried to resist, consuming more and more of the peaceful fields and groves of trees that surrounded the small Arkansas town. It reached out, further and further from New Simon.

It had taken six full seconds from the tiny beginnings of the earthquake before the seismic energy of the *S-waves* could begin its serious destruction of all structures built by man in and around New Simon.

The shaking and destruction in New Simon would continue for over a minute. In the minds of those who survived at the epicenter, it would seem that Hell would last an eternity.

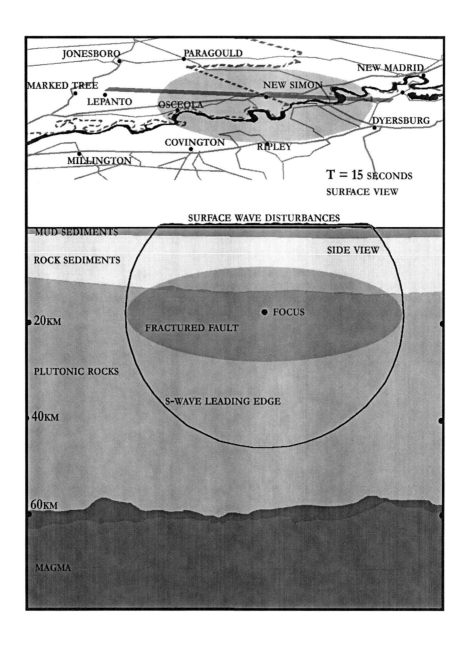

At T=15 seconds the fracture is 60 km long and 20 km long. The surface being shaken is 45 km in diameter and growing. The fracturing will continue until T=23.4 seconds.

CHAPTER 19: THE SHAKING BEGINS

Nervous and sweating from her apprehension, Jenny Fox sat at Chris's workstation in the Seismic Laboratory waiting for 9:33, the time predicted by his Nelson model.

The time came. It passed. No earthquake happened. Filled with mixed feelings of relief and disappointment, and incensed at Chris's lack of response, Jenny gathered her books to leave.

The sound of an alarm resonated through the lab. A temblor had been detected.

Jenny turned and saw the map showed shaking at Chris's station near New Simon, then at Steel, Missouri and Dell, Arkansas. The lights glowed yellow then turned red. In the thrill of empathetic pride, Jenny jammed her fist into the air and screamed, "Right On. Chris's earthquake is really happening. His prediction's right. His model worked."

Chris slammed the screen door open just as a violent jerk pulled the world to the side. Tina, Cookie and the two truckers drinking coffee remained in the café. Two more truckers talked checkpoints next to one of the fueling rigs while the truck mechanic read a magazine and smoked in the garage. Just down the road at the small airfield offering parachute jumping, the mechanic dozed in the tool shed while the pilot started his circle to lose altitude for a landing. Alex fell towards the ground, counting the seconds to open his parachute.

The initial motion of the *S-waves* moved the earth forward and backward in the direction of the slip of the fault. The two sides of the fault fracture moved in opposite directions making the jerking at New Simon torsional in nature, twisting clockwise then counter-clockwise.

The foundations of the café lurched from side to side. As Chris started his pickup, Tina stumbled and fell beneath a booth table. "Umph." She expelled her breath just as a ceiling beam ripped lose from the roof and crashed across the counter, splintering tables and chairs from its force.

Every square meter of the fracture generated *S-wave* energy as it ruptured, contributing to the lateral vibration of the rock matrix. The waves came from many different sources along the fracture. Incoherent, they did not beat together like a rhythmic chorus of drums. Wave packets interfered, sometimes adding, sometimes canceling each other out. The earth did not sway back and forth, but lurched and spasmed like an epileptic giant in seizure.

The *S-waves* themselves produced little sound, but their effects created the sounds of crashing windows, cracking trees, falling buildings, and screaming people.

As Chris's pickup accelerated to the west, coffee slopped from the coffeepots and burned Cookie, "God-damn, that's hot. Oh it's hot." He fell, dropping his hand onto the burning stove in an automatic reflex to brace his fall. "Ahhhh. Oh no. Oh no." He clutched his blistered hand and screamed from the searing pain, writhing on the floor in agony.

Gas lines to the stove ripped from the wall and propane gas whistled into the disintegrating café.

When the *P-* and *S-waves* reached the surface, a portion of their energy vibrated and tore at surface features where they emerged. But since the energy from neither wave could be transmitted into the air, some of their energy reflected back into the earth to reappear at some other point.

Like a stone skipping across the water, wave packets glanced against the surface and reflected down. And then the curvature of the earth and the varying density of rock with depth warped the path of the packet back up until they returned to the surface at some other place to do further damage and be reflected again.

Under the truck fueling station canopy a trucker grabbed the windshield washing station and warned, "Get away from that truck. It'll bounce on top of you." Both drivers scrambled away as the truck did the herky-jerky, twisting back and forth on its springs until they broke.

The act of reflection oftentimes doubled the amplitude of the seismic waves at the surface, especially near the trace of the fault where the waves aligned with the fracture. At these points the wave coming to the surface and the wave being reflected interfered to produce enhanced amplitudes, an effect strong enough in some places to throw objects into the air.

Chris swerved his pickup around the mechanic who ran from the barn under the oldest oak with its base trunk 18 feet around. A trucker shouted, "Watch it, the tree's falling." The tree literally disintegrated. Long branches spread out over the parking lot twisted out of their sockets and one dropped to the ground, pinning the trucker beneath. Another crushed Cookie's old car into the asphalt. A longer branch out over the road ripped down the power lines strung between the utility poles, breaking lines that snapped back and forth, shorting them, one to another then to metal structures on the ground. "Get away. Get away." screamed the mechanic as he cowered amongst the fallen wires.

Some *P*- and *S-wave* energy converted into surface waves, waves that followed the lay of the land out from the epicenter, the most destructive kinds of waves.

One surface wave, called the *Love-wave*, tossed the surface back and forth, perpendicular to its direction of travel, like a snake slithering across the land. The wave front tracked along the surface, amplifying in alluvial sand, soft dirt, and mud.

Chris guided his heaving truck pell-mell down the road towards his instrument site, ecstatic to be at the epicenter of an earthquake. The acceleration of the *Love-waves* threw his pickup and everything else about and back and forth, like a carnival ride. "Wow. There's a car being shook off the freeway." He stepped hard on the accelerator and swerved to miss the Lincoln rolling down the embankment.

Chris ignored the flash of an explosion in his rearview mirror. "I've got to check my instruments. I've got to make sure they get all the data."

Some energy converted into *Rayleigh-waves*, surface waves that rolled the soil up, around and down like an ocean swell coming onto a beach, about to become a breaker. When people spoke of seeing the earth moving like waves of the ocean, they described the *Rayleigh-waves*.

Chris's hurtling pickup reached the Interstate just as the road rolled up in a swell and the southbound lanes of the freeway overpass lifted. The land jerked eight inches north, yanking the short cable anchors from the southern abutment. The huge block of concrete fell, missing its south support, hurtling towards the pavement below.

Chris stared ahead at the substation where he had placed his instruments. "Oh God, the transformers are sparking all over the place. Come on, truck. Go. Go. Go." Chris sensed a shadow as he sped beneath the Interstate, quick but not quick enough. The collapsing concrete overpass crushed the pickup into the asphalt of Stateline Road.

At 9:34:35.8 Central Daylight Time, Chris Nelson became one of the first victims of the New Simon Earthquake.

For 12 seconds NASTY'S café withstood the wrenching vibrations, and then it began its total collapse to the ground. Tina scrambled from under the booth, looking for an escape route.

The old wooden structure rested on a concrete slab, its walls unbolted to the slab. The foundation bounced them up and moved out from under them, ripping apart all the piping for water and gas.

Unsecured objects like the water heaters, coffee pots, stoves, and ovens slid over the concrete floor ripping their power cords and pipe connections from the wall, tumbling over when their base hit something that got in the way.

Several large beams constructed from discarded telephone poles supported the roof of the café. The poles balanced on unsecured pillars. As the pillars moved to the side, the roof caved into the center of the building. Tina ducked into the coffee station, crouching under the workbench.

Plates, glasses, utensils, and menus flew into the air then to the floor. The garlic odor of escaping gas filled the room. Tina scrambled from her temporary shelter and raced for the side door.

The base of tall objects such as trees, power poles, and supports for the fueling shed whipped back and forth at speeds exceeding 80 centimeters per second—two miles per hour, less than a moderate walking speed—but the earth moved in a different direction every quarter second. Just as the top of an object caught up with its meandering base, the base turned and went some other way.

Trees standing close together became tangled in their tops, adding to their distress. The brutalizing actions bent then snapped all the larger trees and power poles in the area within a few oscillations. Overhead power lines whipped back and forth, yanking insulators from the supports and crossing wires with great displays of sparks and broken lines. Telephone and electric power lines, some still sizzling, flew about until most lay about the ground.

One of the power lines flying through the air landed across the roof of the café and shorted to the metal base of the sign at the front door, igniting the escaping gas.

The café blew apart in a huge ball of flame.

Tina stumbled through the screen door just as the explosion blew the entire wall into the parking lot. Pieces of the exploding building crashed down around her. The screen doorframe fell across her legs.

The blast torched the cook, two dogs, and a trucker. Tina could hear their screams competing with the sounds of breaking trees and roaring earth.

She sobbed, unable to move as those inside cried of their horrible death in the flames. The fire in the café grew from the supply of broken kindling scattered throughout the area. Flame and black smoke boiled into the air from the shaking coals.

North in Missouri at T+6.5 seconds, the same destructive scene as in New Simon played out in the small farm communities of Holland, Cooter, and Steele as the shaking swept through those towns half a second after it began in New Simon.

Gary Lincoln walked along the railroad track on the south side of town, next to Polk Street, wishing. "Sure wish I had an old railroad spike. Sure wish a train would come. Sure wish they had an arcade here in Steele."

He looked for any piece of old treasure that might interest a ten-year-old. The sun shined warm on his shirt. His dog, Rusty, beat through the weeds, hoping to scare up a cat or cottontail or any life form to chase. Gary's folks had begun fixing the old house they would move into, and Gary had been left to fend for himself, just so long as he did it somewhere else.

Looking down the tracks, "I wish a train would come this way. I wonder if Daddy's right. But he said if the tracks were slick, and that means there's a train." Gary hoped it would happen soon. He'd never lived close to a railroad track before, and it would be exciting to see a train go by.

He turned over an old can. "Now I hear it. It's roaring down the track. The railroad ties are vibrating, too." He looked to the south, but saw nothing. He whirled around. "Where's the train? I hear it, but I don't see it."

Rusty barked, bounding onto the railroad right-of-way. Gary turned to the dog, "What, Rusty? Do you see the train?"

The railroad ties beneath his feet jerked northward, tripping him. Gary grabbed his dog's neck and dropped to his knees. The gravel of the roadbed dug into his kneecaps as the ground accelerated and then snapped back.

"Ouch. That hurts." Pained from the gravel gouging his knees, Gary sat down, still hanging onto his dog. He sat between the two rails. "No, no, train. Don't come now. You'll run over me."

Rusty kept barking, trying to break free, but Gary hung onto his collar and neck for dear life. The old house across Polk Street vibrated from side to side, skipping across its yard, crushing the roses planted next to it.

Gary hung onto one of the steel rails until he looked south back along the track and saw the rails bending from one side to the other, coming like a snake in his direction. They started lifting like someone cracking a whip.

As soon as he realized how they were moving, the rails and ground upon which he sat began the same motions, throwing him from side to side and up and down, then out from between the rails. He wrapped both arms around his dog and buried his eyes into the canine's fur.

When he peeked out he saw where the two rails had spread apart and had torn the ties from the ground, throwing railroad spikes into the air. "Now I'll find some spikes." The rails next to him again vibrated and jumped, almost with a life of their own.

To Gary it seemed like forever, though the shaking diminished over the next 28 seconds. Then it accelerated as waves reflected from the mantle coursed through the town. Though not so strong as the initial blast, they continued for twice as long.

At last the shaking stopped, though Gary's body still twitched. He lay on his side in the ditch beside the rails, sobbing from the adrenaline coursing through his body, still clutching the dog in his arms, covered with dirt and grit. Where his skin had touched the ground, it felt like fire and looked scratched raw, as if he had been drug across a field on the end of a rope.

Gary sat up and looked around, sobbing, "What happened, Rusty? Everything's different." He sat beside the rails, but they had been torn from the ground and bent all around. Pieces of railroad ties propped up part of the track or just lay askew. No train would ever travel these tracks again. The right-of-way by which he sat showed large cracks and in places it had sunk into the ditch alongside. "The train track's all broke."

He stared across the road at the house he had seen walking across its lawn, now a pile of broken lumber. An old woman struggled to pull up one side of a wall calling for her cat.

Gary remembered his parents at work on their new house. "Does our house look like that now?" Gary scrambled to his feet and pulling Rusty along, ran crying back alongside the tracks toward his parents and their new home. "Mommy. Daddy. Mommy."

At T+6.7 seconds, to the south in Blytheville, the train that Gary expected, the next train up the line, transitioned through the switch from the east-west sidings in the industrial section of Blytheville onto the main line.

The train had begun with 17 cars from the Osceola Landing destined for several cities to the west. Following them was the standard collection of 30 tanker cars and nondescript boxcars retrieved from the Gosnell Aeroplex staging dock, all labeled with various defunct rail companies and tagged by graffiti hounds.

In their midst were three hazardous materials candy-striped tankers carrying toxic chemicals to Hannibal from a plant in southern Louisiana, so dangerous that the state of Louisiana refused permission for them to be hauled overland. They were shipped up the Mississippi by barge to Osceola for transfer to rail in Arkansas.

Two Burlington Northern diesel engines towed the collection of 47 cars.

The voice on the radiophone told Ben Smothers, the engineer, "You've got the all clear through to Hayti." He pushed the throttle forward to hurry the line of cars out onto the main line. Half of the train pointed east and west and half north when the *S-wave* began rocking the train north to south. At first Ben thought an engine had blown. Then he saw the drive wheels slipping on the steel rails.

He looked back at the rear of the train coming onto the main line. To his horror he saw several cars tilt, then fall to their side, including the three haz-mat cars with their red flags.

"Jerry, the train's derailing. Emergency stop, NOW." He pulled the throttle back as his assistant pushed all brake controls full on, locking the airbrakes of every car on the train.

The train tore apart. Cars moving east rocked off the tracks, uncoupling from the rest of the train. As the *Love-waves* jerked the northbound section of the train east and west, cars remaining with the engine left the rails. The warping and tearing of the rails from the right-of-way added to the chaos, leaving the engines standing upright but without a path for locomotion.

The train reached a complete stop in 15 seconds. The engines dropped their high-pitched exhaust and then Ben could sense the sounds, shaking and rocking of the earthquake.

"Call Central Switching and tell them we're having an earthquake and the train's derailed. I'm going back to check the hazmat cars." Ben clambered down from the rocking engine and ran towards the rear of the train, his 285-pound frame stumbling over the heaving ground. His concerns grew when he saw clouds of gas spew from the red-flagged cars. The shaking hobbled him and slowed his speed.

In the distance he saw workers streaming from a factory next to the tracks. They stood around in the parking lot and held onto whatever they could find that might be stable. Their factory building rocked back and forth, losing portions of its exterior every time the earth moved in a different direction.

Some workers pointed towards the gas coming from the cars, and a few wandered towards the cloud. "No, No. Get Back." Ben yelled at the top of his lungs, trudging along at his best speed. The cloud spread, and it blew towards the crowd in the parking lot. "Watch out for the gas," he called, hoping someone would hear his warning.

As the cloud drifted across the fence, the workers nearest the broken cars threw up their arms and fell to the pavement. Other evacuees from the factory called to their fellows, pointing out the approaching danger. The crowd turned as a group, and seeing the cloud bearing down on them, turned again and ran up the road towards the center of town. The gas cloud followed them, sweeping along like the grim reaper.

Ben stopped, his head sagging, "Oh, my chest. It's hurting too much. I can't move. Oh, shit." He brought his right hand over his heart and leaned his left hand on the wheel of one of the cars.

Looking up he watched the cloud move over the factory building to the other side as the pain swelled in his chest. His breath became shallow and a cold sweat broke across his face. Clutching his left arm he collapsed onto the gravel beside his train.

CHAPTER 20: FRACTURING ENDS

Early Saturday morning Spencer Travis drove his jeep onto the levee road north of Barfield, Arkansas, for his first day of levee patrol. The river ran eight feet over flood stage, within nine feet of cresting the levees, seven feet higher than the elevation of the farmlands just to the west.

Spencer's trainer on Thursday had emphasized, "Just watch for water boils along the landward base of the levee. Their presence indicates when seepage is working its way through the dikes, a sure sign of a weak spot that needs attention."

Spencer whistled an old Disney tune in competition with the sputtering sound of the engine as he guided the jeep along the dirt ruts atop the levee. Happy to be at work, he bounced on the cracked vinyl seat, held in place by the new seat belt and shoulder harness. He looked over the Johnson grass growing on the sides of the levee at the waters of the river to his right and the cotton fields to his left.

Near Ditch 14A the high level of the river pushed against the levee for the fifth week in a row, saturating its foundations with water. Spencer stopped next to the ditch. He could see water in the bottom. It seemed to be flowing—flowing away from the river.

With his binoculars he scanned the area around the base of the levee and spoke in amazement to the old jeep, "Well, I'll be darned. There's one of them boils. It looks just like a little water spring on the side of the dike. First day out and I've already paid for my keep."

Spencer picked up the microphone for the two-way radio and called the Osceola Dispatcher. "Hello there, this is Spencer Travis, and I'm patrolling the Barfield levee. I'm at Ditch 14A and a real live boil's coming out the side below me." He continued with a more detailed description of what he saw.

The radio emitted static until the voice of the dispatcher answered, "I copy that. Y've got an active boil at Ditch 14A above Barfield. I'll dispatch an evaluation crew within the hour to take a look."

"Great. Now what do I do? Keep going north on the levee or wait here?"

"Move on up north, and keep a real close lookout. Where you find one of those water boils, you most often find another."

Even as the dispatcher answered, thunder rumbled through the ground surrounding Spencer. The surface of the river to his right turned frothy, no longer reflecting the sky and trees from the banks across the waters. The levee began to sway.

Spencer asked, "Osceola Dispatch, this is Spencer again. The levee's shaking real hard. Does a boil make it do that?" Static obscured any answer.

The fracture passed nine miles west of Barfield. At T+7.7 seconds the leading edge of the *S-wave* reached the levee under Spencer. For the next 48 seconds direct *S-wave* energy pounded the area from the entire length of the fracture. Reflected *S-waves* from the mantle added their energy 27 seconds after the start of the direct waves. A total of 73 seconds passed before the severe shaking subsided.

"Osceola. Can you hear me?" Spencer's voice quavered as he yelled into the microphone.

Typical of levees along the banks of the Mississippi River from Cairo, Illinois, to New Orleans, the Barfield levees just happened to be the closest to the epicenter of the earthquake, the first to be stricken. Composed of the same Mississippi sand and mud that make up the farmlands of the former flood plain of the river, the levee loosened and crumbled from the shaking, sagging towards its lowest possible level.

"Osceola. The levee's starting to sink. Osceola." Spencer let out the clutch of the jeep and accelerated along the levee road, bouncing in and out of the ruts.

Where water saturated the soils of the levee, as evidenced by water boils that search out such weaknesses, the loosening and crumbling spread even faster. The levee became the consistency of quicksand. It did not sag— it flowed. Within 13 seconds the water pressure of the river punched through the earthen dam and poured onto the land to the west.

Spencer drove like he had never driven before, screaming into the microphone. A crevasse opened behind him, then 100 feet in front of him, as the levee melted. His jeep dropped into the quagmire to be swept along with the eight-foot deep wall of water from the river. The jeep tilted, then rolled. Water poured through the passenger compartment. Too late, Spencer grappled against the rushing waters to remove the seat belt that trapped him inside the tumbling vehicle.

Bud Stevens had just completed his Saturday morning inspection of the grounds of the CG granary at the foot of the I-255 Bridge on the Tennessee shore of the Mississippi River. No scheduled barges would arrive until next Tuesday, so his job today concerned only the security of the premises. "That means there'll be time to do some fishing this morning," he had told his wife Martha. "I keep seeing that old black man fishing from the bridge pier, and he must be catching something. I'm taking along my rod and reel just in case. I'll be back by noon so we can go into town for groceries."

He heard an ominous growl, and he looked back at the 50-foot diameter grain storage tower in apprehension. He had heard of elevators that burst for some unknown reason, and he first associated the sound with the elevator. Soybeans from last year's crop still filled it half full, so pressure pushed on the sides for sure.

The growl grew in volume. It did not seem to be the elevator. It seemed to be the ground or maybe the bridge. Looking back at the river, he saw what appeared to be a hard wind hit the surface, for it sprayed up in small wavelets. Yet he felt no wind. Fear gathered in his gut, but of what he had no idea.

At T+10.7 seconds the *S-wave* slashed in from the southwest. The ground beneath his feet jerked back and forth, vibrating at a pace faster than he could handle, and he fell onto the gravel. He heard the granary behind him strumming with the vibrations, but his eyes became focused on the bridge.

From his position 200 yards downstream Bud could readily see what the growing seismic waves did to the bridge. Portions of the pavement between the support columns began to flap about, up and down, side to side. Then, as the shaking of the earthquake grew, over on the Missouri side he saw the entire southbound causeway leading to the central structure collapse like a deck of cards, pulling away from the far embankment and falling into the flood plain with a huge splash.

"Oh my God. The whole bridge is going to fall," he gasped as he lay on his side in the parking lot. He had not yet noticed the contusions that the skidding pavement had torn into his arms and legs.

Loretta stood in the little park on the levee just outside the Ward Street floodwall in Caruthersville, Missouri, watching the Bella Queen excursion boat depart the casino dock to head downriver. She could see a towboat and barges a mile up the river coming along the main channel.

She had driven from her bungalow in Hayti to the larger of the nearby towns for groceries. As she told her sister, Fran, "I always get better prices in the larger stores. Besides, it gives me an opportunity to prospect for other business. I wish JQ'd give me more money so I didn't have to go free-lancing."

In May the river ran high. The water pushed against the banks at 279 feet above sea level, eight feet above flood stage and seven feet higher than some streets behind the wall. But seven feet of levee plus the floodwall protected the town.

Loretta's instinct was to reach out to a post set in the levee in response to vibrations from the *P-waves*. She heard a growling sound like a roaring truck. Her feet tingled from the asphalt pavement.

At T+10.9 seconds the earth moved. The levee jerked toward the river, then back. The pace quickened and the motion became more and more chaotic. Buildings along Third Street made clanking and breaking sounds as they fell apart from the shaking. The grain elevators upriver rocked back and forth and one burst, showering the ground with the ochre green of stored soybeans.

As the leading edge of the oval-shaped fracture passed beneath the river two miles southeast of Caruthersville, the rupture in the earth's crust measured 57 kilometers long and 19 kilometers high. The earthquake's magnitude had grown to 7.3.

Loretta watched as the water became more and more choppy from the shaking of the riverbanks and bottom. Large waves washed up on shore. Cracks developed in the levee revetment downstream and the concrete coverings dropped into the water. Looking around, she saw other levee surfaces begin a lemming-like march into the river. The very ground on which she stood sank as the water climbed towards her.

The water table in Caruthersville stood two feet beneath the surface. After a brief period of shaking, granules of sand and silt became suspended in the water, a process called liquefaction. To a depth of several hundred feet the whole area under the town turned into ooze that could flow and into which heavier objects would sink.

The center of town sat at an elevation of 279 feet before the earthquake began. During the shaking its elevation dropped six feet. Some building foundations sank as much as 12 feet into the mud.

Trickles of muddy water flowed over the levee tops, cutting channels into the dirt. Down river, where the riverside lands were lower, the trickles became torrents.

Loretta watched in fascination for a few seconds then, realizing the awful truth, turned and ran back into town without considering where she might go. A blinding flash and explosion behind her gave proof to the fear that the grain dust in three grain elevators would ignite from electrostatic sparks generated by the shaking.

Dodging falling bricks and light poles, she screamed to everyone she saw, "The river's coming. The river's coming. It's coming over the levee." She prayed she could outrun the advancing waters and falling debris.

The strong vibrations continued in the town of 7,400 for 72 seconds while its protecting levees and the soil beneath shuffled into the river channel. During that time another two grain elevators exploded upriver.

In the Seismic Lab Jenny watched the circle of lights spread wider and wider: Little River, Caruthersville, Senath, Ashport, Osceola.

New Simon's light changed to ominous blinking, then Steele's light began to blink. Two seconds later, the Dell station blinked. "Oh no, what's happening? Chris said the lights only blink when the communications link is lost. Could the *S-waves* have hit that hard?" Jenny whispered under her breath.

One by one other stations along the trace and to the sides of the fault reported seismic activity. The big map on the wall lit with an ever-expanding circle centered on New Simon, just as the growing inner circle of stations registered blinking silence.

"Chris's model was right," she cried in amazement. "It's a major earthquake right where the computer predicted it would be, and it must be strong, just like the model said."

Sixteen seconds after the first alarm, the light on the map for Memphis glowed a bright red, like those disappearing. The tiles beneath Jenny's feet vibrated. She heard the terrible rumbling growl of the *P-wave*, signaling the approach of the violent shocks to follow. Jenny ran for the door of the Laboratory.

Pastor William Prather stepped out of his little church at the corner of Poplar and Church Street in Ridgely, Tennessee. He had already planned that tomorrow's sermon would address how to prepare for meeting St. Peter at the gates of Heaven.

After speeding past Caruthersville and plowing under the river, the fracture tracked directly beneath the town of Ridgely, stopping its northeastward advance two miles past the town at T+16.9 seconds. Much of the *S-wave* energy from the northern half of the fracture hit the town of 1,775 inhabitants in the first nine seconds. It had the effect of exploding a huge bomb beneath the street corner.

The ground lifted and rolled like waves on the oceans. Every building in town shattered, every tree and power pole broke. Every car flew into the air with bursting pieces of pavement. People were thrown about as if thrashed like stuffed toys in the mouth of some gigantic mongrel.

It took 66 seconds more for the remainder of the energy from the southern part of the fracture and from reflections off the mantle to course through the town and stir the remains that lay scattered about. Little remained to stir. Pastor Prather would not give his sermon on Sunday. He had already completed his interview with St. Peter.

At T+23.4 seconds the accumulated *S-waves* rushed into the grounds of the Lepanto elementary school where children played on the swings and jungle gyms of the school. At the same time the increasing strength in the rock 18 kilometers beneath the Donnick Siphons on the St. Francis River seven miles west of town challenged the growth of the fracture, bringing its southern advance to a halt.

Julie pushed the old swing so high the chains almost went limp each time she reached the top of her arc. She closed her eyes and kept pumping and pumping to go even higher and higher. If she went high enough, maybe she could just take off and fly. Maybe she could forget what she saw at home, her mother and that man again in bed.

The intensity built as the accumulated *S-waves* from the rupture from New Simon south hit the town with their full fury, the ground moved north and south, coming into the side of the swing platform. Though the earth shook beneath Julie, its frequency did not affect the path of her swing as she pumped harder and harder with her eyes squeezed shut.

When the *Love-waves* pulsed into the schoolyard, they boosted the swing, and the force of her pumping became more effective. She swung higher, and she pumped harder. The brick siding of the old school crumbled, but she did not see that.

As the *Rayleigh-waves* started rolling the land up in knots, they lifted the swing just as she reached the bottom, and she felt like she was shooting into the sky. She dreamed of shooting above the trees, up into the clouds, maybe even to the moon. The front wall of the school fell forward onto the cars.

Children on the playground screamed and ran, but they always screamed when they played hard. Julie felt from the swing her pumping grow stronger and stronger.

The roof of the school collapsed, blowing out the remaining windows and creating a huge cloud of dust.

Julie pumped real hard the next time the swing started down, and she felt a strong push on her buttocks as she reached the bottom of the arc. She just knew this time she would take off and fly. As she rose, the ground rose as well, and the chains went slack. For a moment, Julie flew out of the reach of gravity. "I'm free," she screamed.

The swing fell back, hitting the end of slack in the chains. It bounced hard and hurt. Julie felt cheated; she did not fly after all. As the swing came down it bucked about and tried to swing to the side. Julie opened her eyes to regain her orientation and saw the remains of the school building crumble into a heap. Other children ran as best they could across the road towards their homes, all having a hard time staying on their feet. Some fell on the school grounds or in the road in front of the school.

Julie could not imagine what had happened, but with force of habit she began to pump the swing again. It became a cantankerous swing, not wanting to go as she wished. She pumped harder still to gain control and swung up into the air where she could see across the town. The church had fallen as well as the school, and most of the houses seemed to be jerking about and falling down. The town's water tower near her home twisted and fell into the creek beside it. It all looked so strange.

She kicked her feet back under the swing and pumped hard again to go high so she could again see what was happening. As she rose into the air, she noticed the trees tossing about. Some broke their branches and fell, but she could feel no wind except from her swinging through the air. She saw cats and dogs streaking across the lawns and cars pull over to the side of the road and people stumble out of them.

Julie decided she did not like what she saw. She closed her eyes again and pumped harder and harder on the old swing. The strong shaking continued its destruction of the town of Lepanto for almost a minute, but Julie did not stop pumping the swing until noon.

The fracturing had taken 23.4 seconds. In that time the trace had grown to a length of 113.3 kilometers, 70.8 miles. The rupture along the underground fault surface totaled over 4,000 square kilometers, 1,594 square miles. The maximum displacement far beneath the surface measured 19 feet.

The seismic energy released by the fracture correlated to a moment magnitude of 7.9, roughly the same as the event of December 16, 1811.

It would take another ten minutes and more to spread that energy across the eastern half of the nation.

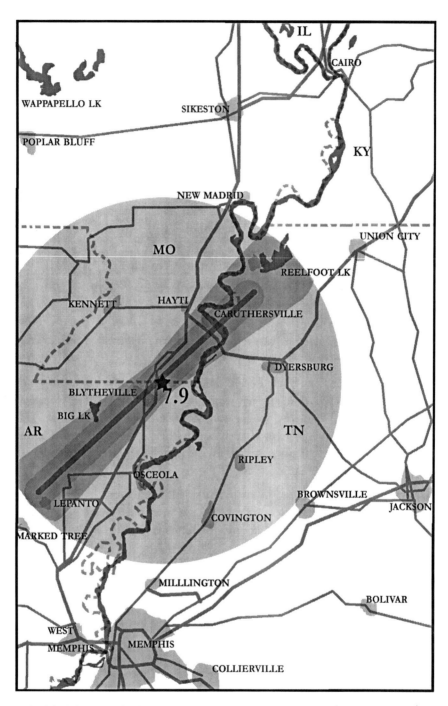

At T=24 seconds fracturing has ended but the circle of shaking continues to expand. The most destructive shaking is along the fracture trace as the "bow" wave moves outward.

Chapter 21: The Shaking Spreads

Todd Crow explained to his audience in San Ramon, "Many people think an earthquake is over when the fracturing stops. Not true. Seismic waves travel outward from the fracture, and it can take minutes more for them to expend their energy. Damage will vary greatly over time and distance."

An elderly gentleman in the back asked, "How much damage would a magnitude 7.9 earthquake do, say in central Missouri?"

"To estimate damage at a particular place, you need to know the shaking intensity, not the earthquake magnitude. Damage depends upon how hard the land shakes and also on the local geology and structures involved.

"Scientists express shaking intensity at various places by a comparison scale of typical damage to structures and land features. Readings can range from Roman Numeral I, which can hardly be felt, to Roman Numeral XII, which is totally destructive. They call this the Modified Mercalli Scale. [editor: see Appendix B for details]

"It's when the high intensity shaking intersects with man-made structures that you have significant damage. For example, in January 1994, the magnitude 6.8 earthquake beneath Northridge, California killed 57 people and caused over $20-billion in damage. In October 1999, a magnitude 7.1 earthquake in the California Mojave Desert—ten times more powerful and less than 100 miles away—killed no one, and the only significant damage was a derailed Amtrak train."

Another member of the audience asked, "Since intensity depends upon observed damage, doesn't that make it subjective?"

Todd nodded. "Yes and no. We have no instrument that gives a direct measure of intensity, but we use a rigid set of definitions for the various levels.

"Reports of the New Madrid Earthquakes of 1811 suggest maximum intensities around the fault were mostly level X. In today's world, areas subjected to an intensity of X are characterized by the total destruction of most masonry and frame structures along with their foundations.

"Most well built wooden structures are destroyed, though some may survive. The ground is badly cracked, and landslides are prevalent along riverbanks and steep slopes. Sand and mud shift, and water in lakes and rivers splash about and slop over the banks.

"Some reports from 1812 have been interpreted as level XI and possibly even XII. When the intensity reaches XI, very few structures are left standing. Bridges are destroyed; railroad tracks are bent greatly. Trees are snapped and broken. Ponds and pools are emptied. The earth slumps, and the land slips about in soft ground, producing broad fissures. Underground pipelines and utilities are totally destroyed.

"At intensity XII objects are thrown into the air, and witnesses's lines of sight and level are distorted. Survivors see waves as if the ground were the surface of the ocean in a bad storm. The damage is total."

Todd took another sip of water. "Remember, in 1811 and 1812 this all happened in mostly forested lands with very few residents, all of whom lived in tents, lean-tos or log cabins alongside the untamed river. If something like that happened now, it would …"

The crashing sound of a stack of plates falling in the kitchen reverberated through the walls of the banquet room, interrupting Todd's lecture.

Steve Pauli squatted next to the dead tree stretching into the waters of the river and pointed to the new strand of grapevines unfurling to its side. "Now what do you think? Will that make a great photo or not?"

Juliana stepped back for a critical look. "Well, if you get the dark bark as a background, it might be nice."

"Say, maybe you take after me after all. You have a good eye for arranging a picture."

As Steve positioned the camera for the first of his five shots, the grape cluster moved, then the camera started vibrating, and Steve could not get it to focus. "Dammit, hold still." He tried to talk the plant into posing.

"Daddy, what's happening? The ground's vibrating, and I feel thunder." Juliana stepped back, tension enveloping her body.

Steve looked up and around. He too felt the trembling in his knees and heard the low-pitched rumble. A wave of fear ran up his spine. Something was wrong in the woods around them, but he could not see what—something terribly wrong.

He stood. "Come on, Juliana. Let's get back to the truck." He reached out and took her hand. They hurried back up the dirt road away from the water.

At T+21.8 seconds a violent jerk of the river bank beneath their feet to the north and then south flung them to the ground. The trees around them snapped and pounded each other. The shaking grew, and Steve and Juliana crawled up the dirt side of the levee on their hands and knees.

A slithering east-west motion accentuated the north-south jerks. The land heaved upward, throwing them into the air. The pair could not even stay on their hands and knees. For eleven seconds the land shook harder than any roller-coaster ride Juliana could ever remember. Then it eased.

"Daddy," Juliana screamed. "The river's coming at us. We'll drown."

Steve turned to see the surface of the river swirling with a chaotic chop and waves over four feet in height. The level of the river climbed through the trees and up the side of the levee. The shoreline that had been 50 feet away now came within ten. Even as Steve watched, water crept six feet closer, and waves washed his shoes.

"We have to run for it." He pulled on Juliana's arm and crawling, drug her up the dirt road away from the advancing waters. The low slope of the road required that they scramble many feet to gain a foot in elevation. The shaking built again, not so violent but the ground kept churning faster and faster. They scuttled like crabs as fast as they could on a surface that did its best to thwart their efforts. A tree fell beside the road, but its branches missed them and did not block their path.

Several times they felt water splash on their feet, urging them to climb faster. As they neared the pickup, Steve watched it buck and dance around. It had slid to the side of the dirt road and turned 45 degrees, but its brakes held. It did not roll down the slope.

"Come on. Watch out for the pickup," Steve yelled to Juliana. "I don't want to get near it right now." They scrabbled past the lurching truck 40 feet farther to the top of the levee. Once there, it became a battle to even stay atop the highest land around.

Their frantic contest lasted 75 seconds before the quaking eased. The waters of the river still tossed and churned, but the river had ended its advance. The front wheels of the truck sat a foot and a half deep in the water as the jolting died down, then stopped.

Steve's entire body shook from fear. He pondered what would happen next. Standing, he drew his daughter next to him, pulled her shoulders tight into his chest, and gasped, hoping to slow the pace of the adrenaline coursing through his body. Juliana sobbed into his dirty shirt.

Steve released Juliana and said, "Honey, I think it's stopped, but I have to save the pickup. Stay here while I back it up here to the top of the levee." He ran down the slope toward the truck.

Wading into the water, Steve opened the door and stepped in. He turned the ignition and cried in joy when he heard the engine turn over and fire. Shifting the gearbox into reverse, he backed the pickup with care back up the rutted path.

Juliana climbed into the cab. Steve killed the engine and wrapped her in his arms. They stared out the window in wonder. River water now lapped to within four feet of the top of the levee. When they had arrived minutes before, they had been unable to see the water through the trees.

"Daddy. The river can't rise that much that fast, can it? It just doesn't happen."

Steve realized the awful truth. "No, the river hasn't changed, it's the land. The levee must have sunk; it must have sagged into the river. And if it drops any more, the water will cut right through the dike. It'll make a huge rapids and waterfall. It'll be catastrophic."

Alex had dropped from 10,200 feet to 6,700 feet in 25 seconds of free-fall, guiding his flight with his hands and feet, sailing back and forth, executing loops and swoops, unaware of the awesome destruction and vibrations taking place a mile and a quarter below.

Out of the corner of his eye he sensed an explosion. "What's that?" Jerking his head around and staring downward in disbelief and dismay, he saw smoke and debris billow from the flames. "NASTY'S Café just blew up. Oh my God, what happened?" Six seconds later he heard the dull thunder of the explosion.

"Oh, no—Tina." In desperation he jerked the ripcord to open his parachute. At 6,300 feet his velocity dropped to 13 feet per second.

He looked at another fire over at Steele, his mind racing to understand. He thought the trees looked like they were breaking. Dust and fog were covering the fields. Flashes. Power lines shorting. Chris's earthquake, that's what it was, all over the place. Chris must've been right.

To the west, he could see cars and trucks stopped on the road at a fallen freeway overpass. In the distance he watched the water tower at Cooter fall to one side. Then, realizing his mistake, he looked up and yelled into his parachute. "That was dumb. Totally stupid. Why did I pull the ripcord? I'd fall ten times faster in free fall."

The small town of Marked Tree, Arkansas lay in the direct path of the shockwave of accumulating *S-waves* that swept southward from the epicenter.

On the west side of town, across the St. Francis River from the main street of Frisco, Jerry Fairchild tapped the pencil on his thumbnail in the showroom floor amidst the newest models from Detroit. He told Henry, "All I need is three sales this weekend. If the credit cards don't foreclose and Millie quits buying dresses, I've got a chance. I guess the good news is that at least things can't get much worse."

A loud roar captured his attention. "Wow, now that's a big engine tune-up." He started toward the garage to check the rumbling, stopping when he noticed the windowpanes vibrating and realized the noise did not come from out back. It came from beneath his feet.

The cement floor became slippery, vibrating like a foot-massage machine. Fear swept through his chest and face as he remembered how it felt when he was a kid, and that 5.0 temblor struck near town. People warned a big quake might happen some day.

The *P-wave* growled louder and louder for 12 seconds, then the *S-wave*'s shock front struck the town.

The first pulse of energy blew apart the windowpanes of every building in town, so violent came its slap. Within two seconds, acceleration back and forth in the north-northeast direction grew to twice that of gravity, peaking in four seconds.

All the utility poles in the town snapped off near the ground, flinging sparking wires to the ground. Trees broke. Chimneys leapt from the tops of the houses, their bricks hurtling through the air and bouncing off whatever or whoever stood below.

Motion from the earthquake slammed broadside into the 34-car Burlington Northern freight train rolling northwest through town at 40 miles per hour on the raised railroad right-of-way. The engines had just cleared the Highway 140 overpass as the right-of-way and track accelerated to the south. The two engines and every railroad car fell as a group to the north and slid on their side for another 500 yards, crushing 14 automobiles and pickups parked or driving near the right-of-way, destroying 22 houses and small businesses.

The concrete bridge over the St. Francis River lifted from its supports and catapulted into the river. Concrete grain elevators sheared off at their base as they exploded or tilted to the side in an ochre and yellow splash of soybeans and corn. The broader, squatter metal grain elevators split around the bottom and burst open.

Brick and concrete-block business buildings lining Frisco Street came apart, their roofs falling down on top of the mixtures of furniture, merchandise, and people inside. Those buildings with walls built of solid concrete lasted a few seconds longer as the walls fell to the side rather than dropping straight to the ground.

Wooden buildings fared no better. The earth tore their foundations from under them. Within all structures the motions of a cement mixer turning at a hundred times normal speed threw their contents about. Gas and water lines ruptured, and a series of explosions and fires erupted all over town.

Jerry's feet flew from beneath him, dropping him to the floor. He saw the new convertible in the middle of the showroom floor skid toward him. Then the floor jerked back to the north, stopping the convertible, but throwing Jerry toward the car as he lay on his side.

The desk in the office next to the walkway bumped into the north wall and then flew back to the south. Henry Withers, Jerry's boss, sitting in the chair behind the desk, screamed as the momentum of the desk crushed his hips through the interior wall.

The concrete block walls of the automobile showroom fell in and out of the building. The false ceiling tumbled to the floor followed by the steel girders holding up the roof, pinning Jerry next to the convertible. The convertible danced up and down, limited in how far it could go by the steel girder holding it down.

The nature of the shaking changed as *Love-* and *Rayleigh-waves* arrived, their intensity spread in time, not coming as one gigantic shock, but rocking back and forth. The mix of waves continued for 70 seconds, fading then growing again as reflected *S-waves* swept through the town. Damaged structures that somehow survived the initial burst again shook, this time to destruction.

By the time the shaking ended, every man-made structure in the town lay in total waste.

Jerry pulled his way through the small cave made by the crushed convertible and the girders. He crawled through the torn ceiling tiles and found a hole in the roof four feet above his head. Clambering onto the fallen rooftop he surveyed the scene around him. "Oh my, God. Everything's gone." He probed his body, looking for damage, amazed to find himself unhurt except for bruised elbows.

He stumbled to the edge of the fallen roof and looked three feet down to the ground below. "Man, was I wrong. Things just got a whole lot worse."

Eighteen cemeteries dotted the immediate vicinity of New Madrid, Missouri, attesting to its age. Settled in 1789 under the rule of the Spanish, the earthquakes in 1811 and 1812 had dropped the old town into the river. Its inhabitants moved to its present location. In the twenty-first century many in the town showed great pride in their seismic legacy and several did a thriving tourist business based upon that reputation.

Madge and Homer Baldwin stood atop the observation platform jutting out from the levee looking to the south across the Mississippi River. Homer expounded on his knowledge of the area. "The old town was halfway across the river, Madge. You can't see it now, but they lost half a mile of riverbank when the big quake hit. Took the old town right with it."

Madge panned the camcorder across the river and zoomed in for a picture of the spot in the river where Homer pointed. Homer would enjoy showing it to the neighbors in their trailer park back home.

"What was it really like back then, Homer? Was it the same as the earthquakes we have in California?" Homer had assured Madge that their hometown of Hollister set the standard for earthquakes along the San Andreas Fault. She knew little about the New Madrid Fault.

"Well, the shaking started at two o'clock in the morning, so they were probably all asleep." A low rumbling sound came from nowhere, and water danced up in a spray on the river.

"The first quake happened south of here. The last one in 1812 took out the whole town." Homer chewed on a grass stem he had pulled a few minutes before and stared out across the waters. Flocks of birds burst from the trees across the river and from the island they called Madrid Bar to the southwest. "Yup, I'd say it must've been a lot like the quakes we have—but milder."

At T+24.4 seconds the *S-wave* swept beneath the platform. Homer looked around, startled by the jerk at his feet. "Why, Madge, I think we're feeling an earthquake right now. It's sure like one of the bigger ones from back home." He and his wife put their hands on the railing and stared across the river. "Can't see much happening out there, but this one's a humdinger." The wooden platform on which they stood rocked back and forth, and its base splintered. It dropped and almost tore away from the levee.

Homer turned and looked back toward the town. "Hey, looky back there, Madge. Everyone's running out. Get a picture of that."

Madge obeyed and pointed the camcorder at the crowds scurrying from the museum with all its earthquake paraphernalia as bricks fell from its cornices. She held the device to her eye and said, "Homer, look at that car bouncing all over the place, and that flag pole. It just bent in half."

The shaking became more intense on the platform and Homer scanned the levee. "Madge, looky at those cracks in the dike. Quick, get that. And over there, the smokestack of that power plant west of here is falling. Hey, this is getting serious; let's get back to the levee."

"I will if I can, but it sure is bouncing around." She filmed the falling stack in the distance as the rock covering of the levee lifted at one end and started sliding into the river. The stairs down the concrete facing to the water pulled apart and areas of mud appeared in the cracks. The two leapt off the platform and onto the cracked asphalt road atop the levee as the wooden structure dropped another two feet.

Even with precarious footing, Homer continued to spot scenes for Madge, pointing out a three-story brick building down the street having trouble. "Catch that building. I think it's going to fall." And fall it did, crumbling onto the cars parked next to it.

"Marge, feel that surging in the ground. That must be one of those surface waves they told us about down in the museum. I'll have to buy that earthquake book now so I can figure out what's happening." Homer grinned and searched for more action.

"Hey, see that dog running. Get a picture of that." They watched a dog tear through town as if followed by a pack of demons, so scared it did not look where it is going. It ran pell-mell into a hog-wire fence, trapping its head in the lattice.

"Homer, do you think this might get us on America's Greatest Video? Maybe we could win first prize." Madge kept the camcorder going, pointing from spot to spot as other acts of destruction tore through the city. The levee offered the best vantage place from which to view the calamity as it happened.

After 59 seconds of violent convulsions the convulsions subsided to mild undulations that lasted for another 11 seconds. Madge dropped the camcorder to her side. "My arm's getting tired, and it feels like the quake is over, so I'm gonna quit for now. Do you want to take some pictures?"

"Sure, let's walk around town and see what all has happened." Homer led the way down the broken roadway to the street below. Their video recorded damage from an earthquake the likes of which had once made the town of New Madrid famous.

CHAPTER 22: MEMPHIS

Earthquakes begrudge large cities and hold a special vengeance for those built near an active fault. The bluffs of Memphis stand too close to the New Madrid.

The leading edge of the *P-wave* touched the banks of the Loosahatchie River on the north edge of Memphis at 9:34:23.5 Central Daylight Time. It reached the riverfront heart of the city in another second and a half. Three seconds later people on President's Island south of Memphis heard the roar of the *P-wave*.

S-waves tore into Mud Island and the Memphis Visitor Center on Riverside Drive at T+32.2, a full 16 seconds behind the *P-wave*. Fracturing along the fault had stopped 8.8 seconds earlier.

Two-thirds of the *S-wave* energy and the resultant *Love-* and *Rayleigh-waves* ripped through the city in the first 23 seconds, with an eight second peak of doubled energy from both direct and reflected waves at the end of the sequence. Reflected waves pummeled the city at a lesser intensity for another 22 seconds, followed by a mild roll for 10 seconds more.

Nearly 1,000,000 souls lived in or visited the Memphis and Shelby County area this Saturday morning in May, each with his or her own story of the earthquake. The experiences of a few tell of what happened to many.

The piers of the I-40 Bridge buried in the riverbed conducted some of the *P-wave* energy up to the surface of the roadbed. Tom said, "Judy, I'm feeling a shimmy in the front tires. I just hope it's not a lost lug nut."

Tom slowed the camper truck as he approached the exit off the bridge. He circled down the ramp onto Riverside Drive, still feeling even stronger vibrations in the truck's steering column.

"Hope we make it to the Visitor Center. Something's wrong." Tom rolled his truck window down for the warm weather. He drove under the Mud Island monorail, stopped at the red light a block past the exit ramp and waited for the green. "Strange, I still feel that shimmy, even though we've stopped." Tom tensed, not yet understanding the incongruity of his senses.

The traffic light turned green. Tom pressed his foot to the accelerator as the sound of an explosion filled the air, coming from the northwest like a sonic boom, but stronger and longer. Tom glanced into the rear-view mirror. "What is that, a wreck?"

The camper truck jumped as if rear-ended by an army tank. Tom jammed down on the brake pedal and fought for control as the truck slithered into the intersection. He could see other cars doing their own erratic dance alongside.

Tom pressed harder and harder on the brakes, smashing the pedal to the floor, but the truck kept moving ahead, backward, from side to side, bouncing. Judy's voice quivered from the vibration. "Tom, what's the matter? What's going on?" She bounced on the seat of the truck, riding a bucking bronco with doors.

Tom beheld the trees ahead of them, the traffic lights, the buildings, everything doing the crazy dance. Windowpanes exploded from business storefronts up on the bluffs; furniture rolled from upper floor windows and fell to the sidewalks below. People staggered out of the buildings, grabbed light poles and parking meters for support, or raced into the street like drunks.

"Judy, it's an earthquake, and it must be a big one." Tom's white knuckles clamped harder and harder around the steering wheel.

On the bridge behind them, cars and trucks reeled from the jerking motion of the pavement, and most drivers slowed. Vibrations of the soil around the foundations of columns supporting the bridge converted the river bottom into mush. The south end of Mud Island settled and shifted its roots further into the Mississippi River, the beginnings of a huge earth slide that reached inland past the edge of Memphis's historic bluffs.

Tom noticed the suspended monorail car from Mud Island rocking above them on its track where it crossed over Riverside Drive toward its landing up the hill on Front Street. The car stopped 100 feet short of home and 70 feet above the street. Faces of people inside the car mirrored the looks of Tom and Judy: the contorted facial cast of people screaming as loudly as they could.

Marion Roberts addressed his golf ball on the 13th tee as the *P-wave* rolled through the MidTown Municipal Course. He stopped in the midst of his back swing and put his driver back on the ground.

His ball rolled off the tee. "No. No," he said to the trembling ground around his feet. The trembling did not stop.

After five seconds of increased rumbling, he turned to his playing partners and said, "Gentlemen, we're having a major earthquake. I suggest you immediately head for your homes. You'll be needed there." Marion picked up his ball and tee and walked over to his golf bag sitting on the golf caddy. With deliberation he placed the driver back into the bag and the ball into his pocket. Then he hurried toward the clubhouse parking lot at a brisk trot, pulling his golf caddy cart behind. The earth trembled beneath his feet; the rumbling thunder rose then subsided.

"Hey, what're you talking about?" called Henry Spocket. "Marion, where're you going? We have a match to play. Marion," he yelled at the back of his retreating partner. Then he, too, noticed the vibration beneath his feet. "What the hell is this?"

The time reached T+32.4 seconds. Seventeen seconds after the first rumblings, the direct and reflected *S-waves* combined to knock the golfers to their hands and knees onto the grass. They clung to the ground as they watched trees sway about them.

Marion staggered and dragged his cart along the path toward his car. The lurching ground tripped him and he fell, skinning his knees on the gravel path, but he got back up and continued. He knew he must reach his offices downtown. The time had come when he would be needed the most.

JQ stood lost in thought before the floor to ceiling window of his penthouse office and stared into the west. He attention returned to the present as the *P-wave* buzzed his feet. He tensed.

The seismic waves hammered on the pilings and supports under the building, starting small fractures and cracks in the concrete, in particular in those areas with insufficient reinforcement. Old mortar between some bricks began to crumble into smaller pieces of mortar. Then, after 14 seconds of hammering came a brief pause. "Thank God, whatever it was has quit." JQ expelled a deep breath.

His relief lasted but for a short time. As the first of the *S-waves* hit the riverfront, the McCrombie Building began to sway back and forth. JQ watched reflections in the windows of buildings to the north. "Oh, God, those windows just shattered, like an explosion." Seven stories below, the hammered supports of the McCrombie Building that had been jarred with the *P-waves* ground into dust as the *S-wave* rubbed them back and forth against their stubs. The building shifted, and then came to rest as the *S-waves* canceled each other out.

"What the hell. This floor's sloping toward the river. I gotta get out of here." He turned toward the elevators.

Another burst of shaking, stronger and more chaotic than anything before, hit the building. JQ tripped and flew across the room, sliding into the plate glass windows of his office. The high strength safety glass did not break.

"Ugh. Get out. Get out." He pushed himself back into the interior of his office as the crazy dance continued. "What's wrong with my eyes? Mud Island's moving. It's coming closer. What's wrong?"

JQ stared in horror, not understanding that what he saw could be true. His window had moved closer to the island and the streets below.

Glenda Watson had arrived at the Seismic Safety Office in the City Office Building at eight o'clock that morning, hoping to catch up on the filing from the previous week. Still learning the ropes, she worried that she did not yet grasp her assigned tasks.

When the first *P-waves* passed through the building, Glenda felt very little, though she heard a dull roar coming from somewhere, maybe the walls. She worked two floors below ground level.

When severe shaking began, she both heard and felt the seismic waves as they threw furniture, filing cabinets, and computers about the office.

Glenda backed against the east wall of the room, fending off panels dropping from the ceiling. The lights flickered, and she stood in darkness. She heard more and more cracking and groaning as the room tossed around. Within two seconds the emergency lights clicked on behind her, and she looked around in their eerie yellow glow.

She grabbed the telephone, dialed 911, and screamed, "There's a crack in the floor near the hall. It's growing wider and wider. We're having an earthquake." In the yellow light the crack looked jet black. The concrete wall to her left cracked. A scar ran up its side as the wall beyond the crack moved downward.

"The crack's growing," she yelled to her telephonic savior. "The other side of the room has dropped. It's cutting the room in half. The ceiling has slid down to the floor." Glenda braced herself against the east wall and stared in shock as the floor from the level above came even with her floor and then slipped further down into the abyss.

"Mr. Roberts said the map the girls were talking about didn't mean there would be an earthquake crack through the building. He must've been wrong." She listened for a response. "Hello? Hello?" Not even a dial tone came from the telephone.

Judy heard Tom screaming, "Judy, it's getting worse. I can't hold the truck at all. It may roll over."

Furious writing of the ground beneath the nearby Memphis Visitor Center tore the building apart. The heroic fifteen-foot statues of Elvis and Handy again danced across the stage in the Visitor Center, then fell from their pedestals upon the tourists cowering below.

"Tom, I love you." Judy said her goodbyes, knowing the fury of the catastrophe around them would sweep them away.

The doubled energy lasted eight seconds, though it seemed eternal. Tom pressed ever harder on the brake pedal as the truck again bucked up and down and from side to side. Both he and Judy watched the landscape change around them.

A building on Front Street fell toward the pavement and exploded in a shower of dust and flying bricks. Two skyscrapers on the bluffs to the east scraped their top towers together, and a shower of glass and flotsam exploded from both buildings and fell toward the streets below. "Oh my, God, Tom. Those are people falling out of that building."

Then the direct waves arriving from the northern extension of the fracture stopped. The fault fractured no more in that direction. *S-waves* arrived from the southern end of the fault and reflected waves continued to shake the ground, but the violence weakened.

Tom stared out of the truck cab at the devastation surrounding his camper in the middle of the intersection. "Wow, what a big wallop. I've never felt anything like that before. The truck's still rocking so it's not over." He looked at his wife. "Did you say something?"

Mel had arrived at President's Island from his trip to the west coast minutes before. He sensed the first grinding sound of the *P-wave* as he climbed out of his eighteen-wheeled tractor-trailer rig and started toward the rear of the trailer to watch over the unloading process. He stopped to check if the sound and shaking indeed came from the pavement beneath him.

"Hey, Jack," he yelled at the teamster on the loading dock. "You're having an earthquake like I felt back in California. It's just starting."

The heaving pavement threw the truck and trailer into the air, and boxed goods tumble out the back door of the trailer onto the dock. Mel did a jig in the middle of the parking area, trying to keep his balance on the concrete. With nothing to hang onto, he dropped to his hands and knees.

Individual sections of the pavement around him came alive. "Oh shit, get away from me," he yelled as he tried to avoid the cracks where paving sections touched. They opened and closed like the jaws of a piranha fish searching for fresh meat.

Down the dock, a portion of the warehouse wall crumbled, and he heard men yelling inside. He could not tell if they were trapped or not. More and more people ran out of the building, jumping to the parking lot from the heaving dock alongside the warehouse.

For a short period the shaking doubled then eased, then it rose again as reflected waves coursed through the waterfront warehouses scattered across President's Island. Much of what started failing in the first period of shaking finished that process in the second period.

More and more of the buildings around him collapsed. Tilt-up concrete walls fell as whole units. Some of the men standing on the dock were crushed as the walls fell outward and over them, pulling parts of the roof with them. Dust poured from the crumbling structures.

Mel flattened his body onto the concrete paving, sobbing in fear.

Panic gripped George Besh's drugged body. He did not realize that what he felt were *P-waves* filling both him and his car with low frequency sound. He only felt panic from somewhere, and it grew and grew.

The fear enveloping George surged as the *S-wave* shook his car like a dog trying to rid his fur of water from a bath, and he shoved the accelerator to the floor, crashing through the intersection in front of Tom and Judy. His clouded mind told him that he must outrun the terror that chased him. He turned his car hard right onto Adams Street.

Judy looked past Tom at the car careening into the intersection at high speed toward them. "What's that man doing?" She screamed in horror then watched George's car turn east and rush up the hill.

As George's car skidded around the corner, a sudden lift in the pavement threw the missile against parked cars lining the street. Sideswiping three of them, George continued to accelerate, smoking his wheels, racing up the incline.

Half a block ahead a four-story office building tilted. Bricks and stone porticos crumbled into the street in his path. The buckling street lifted his car, almost as if to help it jump over the growing pile of brick and stone. But the push was not great enough, and the car fell into the growing pile, its fuel tanks rupturing and bursting into flames. The growing remains of the building pelted the flaming car. The ground heaved again.

George leaned out the broken window of the car screaming. Flames rose behind and under him. With his feet pinned beneath the dashboard, he struggled with no success to climb out the window. His panic grew, like he had again over-dosed on the drugs. Soon, his shrieks disappeared into the sounds of those wailing around him.

CHAPTER 23: THE WORLD HEARS THE NEWS

Frank Howard watched the TV feed from downtown Memphis on the director's newsroom monitor at **NEWS WORLD SATELLITE** broadcast studios in Atlanta. "Okay, Allen, I would like you to do the next shot from the Peabody Hotel. Can you get across the street?"

He watched the Memphis video as Allen Shenks, the reporter from the **NWS** affiliate in Memphis for local events, jaywalked across the busy thoroughfare. With the Memphis Jazz Festival in full swing, the **NWS** ten o'clock evening show needed a 40-second clip of the action.

The digital clock on the screen read 9:34:25. Allen held the headset to his ear as he stepped onto the curb. He looked startled. "Frank, something strange is happening. I swear—it feels like an earthquake."

Frank reacted from habit, hitting the record button and dropping into reporter mode. "Allen Shenks, I heard you say you feel an earthquake. What is it like? What do you see?" Both reporters had years of common experience around the world, sometimes under small arms fire, but never together in an earthquake.

"Right now the pavement's just vibrating a little, and I hear an increasing roar of some kind." Allen looked around. "It's hard to tell with this crowd. I can't see much happening, though people are running for some reason over near the trolley tracks." The *S-wave* cleaved through the city. Allen looked up. The camera view froze then went to the test pattern as the satellite video connection lost synch.

Allen's telephone feed continued. "Oh. Now the ground is starting to lurch. It's getting heavy. Street signs and cars are bouncing. I see buildings along the street swinging back and forth. No, they're jerking back and forth."

Frank could hear vibrations in Allen's voice. "I hear things breaking and people screaming. The windows in the store across the street just cracked and burst out. It's getting harder and harder to stand. I see glass popping out the side of the Cartwright Towers."

Frank listened as Allen's rich tenor rose toward soprano. Frank empathized with the emotion Allen must feel, the sudden fear that strikes every reporter who finds himself in a fire-zone.

"Allen, keep talking." Frank put his hand over the microphone and shouted out the door, "Jack. Get in here. On the double."

Allen spoke faster and faster. "The building above me is swaying farther and farther. That time it almost touched the Peabody across the street. I can see older buildings out toward the riverfront crumbling right before my eyes. The whole side of Kresses just sloughed off and fell to the ground. The noise between the buildings is deafening. Like the world is breaking apart."

His voice quivered then cracked. "I see flashes down the street. Must be trolley lines shorting. I'm holding onto this parking meter to keep from being thrown onto the sidewalk. Now the shaking's getting even stronger and there's noth…"

Dead sound. "Allen. Allen. Can you hear me?" Frank waited, hoping for a response. Nothing. Then a dial tone. The connection had been lost.

Frank scribbled on a piece of paper. "Jack, take this to the news desk as fast as you can and give it to Carolyn. Immediately. Don't let anyone stop you, even if they're On Air."

The newsroom aide ran out of the office clutching the paper, intent on delivering the breaking news to the news broadcast anchor.

Frank sank to his chair trying to re-establish the lost connection to Memphis. "Damn. Come back, Allen. Come back."

Sixteen seconds of tossing seemed like forever to Tom and Judy as the city died around them.

By T+48 seconds liquefaction of the riverfront soils coupled with the huge earth slide into Wolf River began the serious displacement of Mud Island, dislodging supports for the I-40 Bridge and its entrance and exit ramps over the riverfront. More and more of the bridge structure fell to the water or land below.

Drivers of cars traveling eastward at 70 and 80 miles an hour on the Interstate began to slow. When they recognized that parts of the bridge were falling and disappearing before their eyes, they locked their brakes, trying ever so hard to stop. Many did, but several skidded too far, slipping into the opening before them. Some hit those who had stopped and pushed them into the abyss left by the falling roadway.

Below the interchange a trucker with a load of prime beef destined for the Livestock Show in the Pyramid geared down coming through the south gate of the parking lot. He almost lost control of his rig from the shaking. Glancing up, he screamed in horror, "The bridge is falling. It'll hit the truck."

The long piece of concrete and steel checked its 50-foot fall as the shaking shoved it back into the support column, giving the tractor cab time to clear the gap. The trailer did not. The falling bridge section sheared the trailer from the cab and crushed 46 head of prime steers. Four cars and a bus followed the bridge section to the parking lot below.

Judy pointed to a fissure in the road surface to the south. "Tom, the road down there. It's cracking in two," she screamed.

"My God, this whole area is sliding into the river." Tom shoved the accelerator to the floorboard even though the pavement still pitched the truck about. By the time he reached the Union Street intersection three blocks away, the roadbed had moved six feet west and dropped 18 inches.

Tom slowed, shifted into four-wheel drive, and dropped into low gear to climb the growing ridge that separated the sliding ground he was on from the more solid ground beyond the fissure. "Come on, baby, come on," he yelled at his truck, like it driving a team of mules.

The truck smoked its four wheels a moment and then found traction and climbed the two foot slope as the slide sagged farther, weaving a jagged tear across the road and down through the cobblestone slope to the water below.

Glancing in his rearview mirrors, Tom saw the entire monorail system riding the sliding earth to the west. As the slide moved, the track nearest the bluffs dropped lower and carried the station down, creating enough slope that the gondola moved of its own accord to its home nest in the building. The great slide had wrecked the city but saved the passengers in the gondola.

In Atlanta, Carolyn Phelps, the **NWS** anchor for the **NEWS NOW SEGMENT**, let her surprise show on camera as Jack, the newsroom aide, barged to her podium and, in full view of the worldwide audience, handed her Frank's hand-written note.

Like a true professional, she looked down, read the note in her hand, and looked up at the camera to broadcast the news around the world, "We interrupt this broadcast with breaking news. We have just received a report that a severe earthquake has struck Memphis, Tennessee. We are attempting to contact our bureau in Memphis for confirmation and more detailed information. At T+58 seconds Carolyn searched the studio for help, but the staff, busy with their own problems, had not heard the words she broadcast.

Todd again looked over the assemblage in San Ramon. "As I explained at the beginning, I want you to appreciate how long an earthquake takes to happen.

"If our example earthquake on the New Madrid had occurred one minute ago, over 45,000 square miles of land—a circle 106 miles in diameter centered about the epicenter—would now be shaking. That area would increase at a rate of 1,400 square miles per second, and the strength of the spreading waves would be strong enough to inflict damage to almost any man-made structure.

"The epicenter would continue to shake from *S-waves* reflected off the mantle from the opposite ends of the fracture for another five to ten seconds."

Todd walked over and tapped on the New Madrid Fault map on the wall. He looked at his audience. "The central United States has a big, big problem. Apart from the New Madrid Seismic Zone and a few smaller faults, the North American continent is very stable and solid." He moved his hand in a big circle around the fault. "Thick beds of limestone, sand, and shale were laid down for thousands of feet over the past 200 million years. There are very few loose cracks in those thick beds of stone, and the rock is cold.

"On the other hand, here on the West Coast, the land is rife with faults. It's been broken apart and thrust over itself so many times that much of its geological history is still uncertain. The rocks are hotter which makes them more pliable.

"These differences in geology make for a major difference in the energy loss as a seismic wave propagates through the basement rock. In the west, the wave goes a short distance and runs into a fault. The broken rock absorbs some of the energy, reflects some, and lets some go through. After the wave has exhausted itself going through six or seven fractures, there's little energy left to tear at the structures on the surface.

"But in the middle of the country, a seismic wave travels great distances with nothing to interrupt or attenuate it. It goes on and on and on without losing much energy.

"Another factor is that seismic waves in the center of the country are prone to a pancake effect where the consistent layers of sediments collect and channel the energy between the mantle and surface like a wave guide.

"Put these two factors together and the energy of the shaking does not drop off as one over the distance squared like you might expect, it drops off more like one over the distance to the first power. Seismic energy carries about three times farther in the central United States as here in California.

"Let me put this into perspective. The 1895 earthquake in Charleston, Missouri, affected an area ten times larger than that affected by the Northridge earthquake of 1994 in California, even though the two events were comparable in size.

"That is one of the reasons I say an earthquake in the central United States is ten times more dangerous than one on the west coast. It has to do with the pancake effect and the number of faults surrounding the event.

Todd pointed to the center of the central United States map. "Add to that the lack of preparedness in the center of our country, and you have the ingredients for a gigantic disaster."

The *S-waves* tore through Paducah, Kentucky, on the banks of the Ohio River at T+55 seconds. Five seconds later shaking began at the giant dams on the Tennessee and Cumberland Rivers that formed the largest lakes of the Tennessee Valley Authority and created the Land Between the Lakes.

At the northeast end of the mile and a half long Kentucky Dam across the Tennessee River, the 110-foot wide barge lock penetrated 120 feet deep into the dam's structure. Two gigantic metal doors prevented the rush of water out of the reservoir into the Tennessee River below. Lake waters stood 90 feet above the river surface below the dam.

The position and alignment of the Kentucky Dam across the Tennessee River made results of the shaking even worse. Eighty-three miles from the north end of the fracture, the dam's position came within one degree of being in direct alignment with the fracture's trace. In addition, the orientation of the dam paralleled the direction of the fault, the preferred direction of shaking for the *S-waves*.

Dispersion, the differing velocities of different wavelengths, spread the *S-wave* energy from the northern leg of the fracture over 18 seconds, clumping the faster, longer wavelengths together first, then sweeping up through the spectrum to the higher frequencies. Eight seconds later, the pancake effect added reflected *S-waves* to the energy level over the next 21 seconds. When that burst ended, seismic energy from the southern leg of the fracture continued to pour in for another full minute.

The mile-long earth-filled portion at the southwest end of Kentucky Dam resonated at a frequency near one cycle per second. Like a battering ram, it slammed against the third-mile long concrete core of the dam holding the floodgates and electric-generation turbines. The core collected the energy, and with its one-third second resonant period, it thrashed its internal floodgates, aqueducts, and turbines to destruction while hammering into the side of the canyon containing the locks.

The underlying earth, shaking with velocities up to 30 centimeters per second and accelerations more than 35% of gravity, pounded the dam for 83 seconds.

Structural failure of the dam began in the first three seconds. Concrete pillars holding the floodgates along the top of the core cracked and tore lose, unhinging floodgates that fell to the river below.

The shaking dam pummeled the two lock gates, crushing them against the north side of the lock with the lateral wrenching of the dam, bending the four-foot thick metal assemblies in a manner that left no hope for retaining the waters of the lake. Water forced its way through the bent locks until the metal tore away completely, opening a gigantic channel through which the flood could flow.

Within two minutes, the fluid stream through the broken floodgates and locks exceeded 50 million cubic feet per minute, sufficient to raise the level of the Ohio River at Paducah by 15 feet and top the crumbling flood wall that had protected its old downtown. When the flood surge reached the Mississippi River, water levels would increase by 6 to 12 feet, depending upon the location. With the Mississippi already above flood stage, this surge would only add to the waters already flowing over its earthquake-ravaged levees.

S-waves reached downtown Nashville on the banks of the Cumberland River, 149 miles from the fracture, 92 seconds after the fracture began. They shook the city for the next 87 seconds at an intensity level of VII. The city's newer buildings built on the firm hills with rock foundations fared well, but many older structures and buildings along the river suffered severe damage from the shaking.

Violet Washington lifted her hands, wagged her finger up and down to set the time. "Now from measure six, let's try it one more time, and this time put some gusto into your voices." She counted, "One and two and three and four," and swung her hands down and out to restart the *a cappella* choir. As they launched into the chorus, the old Ryman Auditorium again resounded with song.

A deep base rose from the floor, adding flavor to the song, and the group sang stronger and stronger. The whole building joined in the sound of music.

When the strong shaking began, some in the choir did not sense it at first and continued singing, but even they dropped out and looked around when they felt the old flooring move under their feet.

Violet held her hands up to stop the choir. "Ladies and Gentlemen, I think we must leave this building. Let's all please pick up our music and file out the rear doors. Quickly now."

There was a scramble but no panic as the choir moved out through the stage exit door. Within 20 seconds they had assembled in the parking lot. The sounds of clatter and shaking increased, and they heard heavy falling and breaking inside the building. Dust billowed out their exit.

After a moment Violet stepped back and looked inside. "My goodness, the roof just fell onto the stage. It crushed all the chairs and the organ. The Lord be praised. That roof would have crushed us if we had stayed in there a minute longer."

A chorus of "Amen" and "Praise the Lord" filled the parking lot, even as the asphalt pitched beneath their feet. The scheduled performance of the Marabelle Choir for that evening had been cancelled.

At **NWS** Carolyn leaned her head to one side listening to the voice of the producer from her small earphone. Looking into the camera she relayed the information. "We have an unconfirmed report that Nashville is experiencing an earthquake. We are contacting our other bureaus throughout the Central United States asking for their observations about an earthquake somewhere around Memphis, Tennessee. We are checking St. Louis, Kansas City, Little Rock, Indianapolis, and Cincinnati. As yet we have no confirmation of any earthquake.

"We are also contacting government authorities for any information they may provide." Her hand holding the paper shook. "To repeat, we received a report from Memphis just a minute ago that they have been struck with a severe earthquake. That is all we know. Please stay tuned."

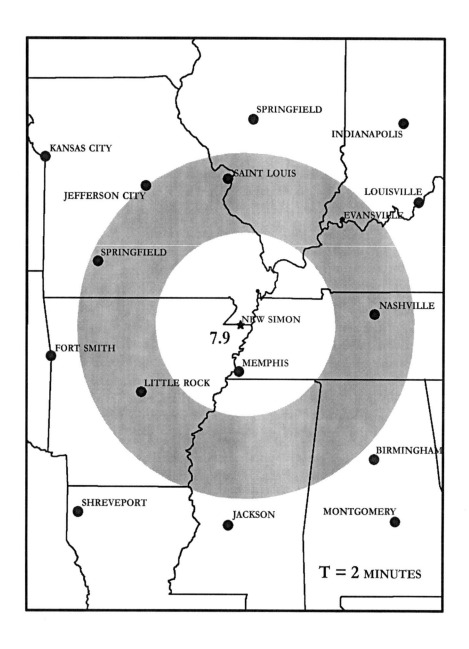

By T=2 minutes, the shaking has stopped around the epicenter but is spreading into the neighboring regions. This donut-shaped zone will spread across the eastern United States and Canada.

Chapter 24: Beyond Memphis

"Judy, I think the earthquake's over, but I'm shaking so much I can't tell for sure." Tom held his wife in his arms as they sat in their truck beside the curb of Riverside Drive, overlooking the excursion boats tied to the cobblestone shore in the Wolf River harbor. To their left the crumbled buildings of Memphis lined the bluffs.

Memphis had shaken for 63 seconds, reaching a shaking intensity level of IX along the riverfront. Even now glass, bricks and cornices from the broken buildings fell from time to time with each small aftershock. People screamed and called for help from the streets and from within the shattered structures, but the relative quiet grew awesome in comparison to the noise that had been moments ago.

A dust cloud hung in the air, created by the falling buildings along the streets intersecting with Main Street. Bricks and concrete blocks lay about, on the street, on the sidewalk, and on the open areas around the riverfront.

"Judy, we're just lucky that nothing hit us hard enough to break anything, but this dust is a problem. Roll up your window before we choke." Judy sat subdued, and after a moment did as Tom instructed. She coughed and wiped at her tear-streaked face with the back of her hand, unmindful of the smears it left on her cheeks.

Even as the shaking ended in Memphis, *S-waves* began tearing into St. Louis, shaking that city for 82 seconds, inflicting major damage throughout the area with an intensity level between VIII and IX.

The most prominent feature of St. Louis, the Arch, stood 702 feet tall on the west bank of the mighty Mississippi. Though the designers had over-engineered the structure to withstand this kind of punishment, people in the top observation platform and riding in the elevators had not been designed to survive the punishment they experienced.

Tossed about with abandon and frightened beyond words, two immediate fatalities occurred from apparent heart attacks. Several more suffered chest pains, many suffered broken bones, and all suffered contusions and bruises.

Seven hours of terror would pass before everyone could be evacuated from the towering structure.

Beneath the Arch, in the museum and shops, falling walls and ceiling panels panicked the Saturday morning throngs. Screaming, the mob rushed up the long, narrow exit halls, crushing each other into the floor, against the walls, and through the glass doors. Eighty-eight bodies, most of them children, were later recovered from the halls.

Four floors of the parking garage near the Eads Bridge pancaked to the height of one, crushing cars, trucks and people with indiscriminate abandon. Witnesses compared its failure to that of the Cypress Structure in California's 1989 Loma Prieta earthquake.

At the old Union Railroad Station, built on lake fill and turned into a quaint shopping mall with a glass roof and ornate stairs, the old lakebed proved most unstable. Much of the structure fell on the Saturday morning tourists that lined the walks through and around the shops. The hotel convention and banquet rooms hosting a Science Fiction Convention collapsed onto the gathered trekkies.

Most older buildings throughout the city sustained severe damage. Gargoyles, cornices and glass rained from on high. Several buildings suffered total collapse. Newer ones fared better.

Ten freeway overpasses around the city collapsed from the shaking. Most of the earthquake retrofits on the other bridges worked to hold the concrete slabs on their supports, though replacement would be required for at least 20% of those left standing.

The MetroLink rail line across the Eads Bridge was demolished as the old structure crumbled onto the tracks and then into the river, taking one train with it.

Other bridges spanning the Mississippi and Missouri Rivers still stood, though damaged. Had the shaking been stronger or lasted longer, at least one of the newer bridges would have collapsed in catastrophic failure.

The suburbs of St. Louis shook with the same intensity. Collapsed malls, damaged shops, and mangled homes lined their streets. Most of the numerous fires that started during and after the shaking burned to completion, unattended by the overextended local fire departments that could extract no water from the broken mains.

Power failed throughout southern and eastern Missouri, and telephone communication was spotty. The cell-phone system continued to work, though sometimes with long delays for no apparent reason.

Though wounded, St. Louis had survived.

At **NWS** Television Carolyn searched the studio for direction, but everyone seemed concerned about their own issues. Turmoil increased as people in the studio fretted about the impending earthquake. She ad-libbed, "We are attempting to locate reporters in other cities around Memphis and will pass word on to you as soon as we hear anything."

Jack hurried to her desk and handed Carolyn another paper which she scanned and then read into the camera, "Now this just in. A severe earthquake has struck St. Louis in the last minute. And Nashville and Little Rock are reporting severe damage from the trembling."

She laughed under her breath, her back stiff with tension. "Meanwhile, here in Atlanta, the mild shaking has stopped, but some people are saying that the more severe shaking—they're calling it *S-waves*—is yet to arrive. Not being a native of earthquake country, I don't know what to expect."

At T+1 minute 44 seconds no one could yet comprehend the extent of the damage. The *S-waves* had reached 185 miles in all directions from the epicenter at New Simon.

Branson, Missouri, and Evansville, Indiana, began shaking at the same moment. Branson clung to the sides of limestone hills and plateaus. It shook for 70 seconds, but its solid rock understructure held in place, and the damage showed characteristics of an intensity level of VII.

Evansville was not so lucky. Sitting on the ancient flood plains of the Ohio River, it was destroyed by the shaking that lasted for 92 seconds. Upstream at Owensboro, Kentucky, the *S-waves* tore at the city for 94 seconds. Liquefaction occurred throughout the Ohio River valley. Damage in both cities was consistent with a shaking intensity level of VIII.

At 9:36:07 CDT, two minutes after the start of the earthquake, the land under Jefferson City, Missouri, began to shake at a distance of 218 miles from the fracture; it was also built on limestone hills. Pounded for 75 seconds, its geography limited the damage to an intensity level of VII.

Birmingham, Alabama, 240 miles south of the fracture, shook for 79 seconds, creating damage at level VI. Everyone considered the shaking to be strong, and many ran out of doors to get away from the noise and falling objects in the buildings. Several people died and many were injured as brick walls, old chimneys, cornices and windowpanes, shaken from their supports in the upper stories by the motion, plummeted to the ground.

Greater distance from the epicenter proved to be a blessing. The ground shook longer but most often with less intensity.

In New Simon, the violent shaking died off to occasional trembles. The café burned, spilling plumes of black smoke into the air and making crackling sounds as the flames consumed the wooden frame and asphalt siding. Screams for help no longer came from inside the burning building.

A trucker with singed eyebrows wandered about in a daze, clutching in his left hand the coffee cup Tina had filled just before the earthquake began. He looked down as a low moan sounded from beneath the wreckage in the middle of the road and saw a leg protruding from under the doorframe.

"Oh, someone's hurt. Let me help." Placing his cup on the ground with care, he lifted the frame along with the door to reveal Tina, her face scraped and scratched, staring into the sky. He threw the door to the side and reached under her to pick her up. "You're going to be okay, little lady. Everything's going to be just fine." He carried her to the side of the road and gently placed her on some grass. He found a tablecloth that had been blown out from the café and covered her.

The trucker returned to pick up his cup. "Wonder where a body can get a cup of coffee around here?" he asked, addressing no one in particular. He wandered back toward his truck, one of two trapped under the fallen fuel shed.

JQ watched in horror during the height of the shaking as the building to the north moved toward his window. It held in place for a moment, and then dropped into a billowing cloud of dust. His own building shifted and settled, then stopped. The shaking lessened, and his building remained in place.

The jarring vibrations ended. "Oh God. Just stay in place. Don't fall any farther. I'm getting out of here." His office floor now sloped toward the west window, but the McCrombie Building had remained erect. Quiet prevailed, except for creaking in the walls and occasional trembling of the floor.

Careful to disturb nothing, JQ stood up from the floor, holding onto the furniture scattered around him. "Step carefully," he told himself. "Don't make sudden motions. Keep calm. Hold onto something the whole way." He worked his way to the elevators and punched at the button several times, but with no response, no light. "Dammit, what's wrong? The elevator must be stuck somewhere below."

"God dammit." he swore at the quiet room. He pulled a handkerchief from his pocket and wiped his brow. "The stairs. I'll go down the stairs." He moved toward the janitorial services door down the hall to his right. When he felt the building lurch left, he reached out to the wall and waited, hoping, praying. Feeling no further motion, he continued down the hall.

He reached the door and turned the knob. "Dammit, the blasted door's locked. Where's my master key?" He searched his pockets for his key chain then remembered the keys were in his coat back in his office.

JQ turned and ran up the incline toward his office. The building lurched again as he turned the corner. "Oh shit." He grabbed the coat hanging over the chair next to his desk and located his keys. Turning he ran back toward the utility door, pulling the keys from the coat pocket. The key slipped into the keyhole, and he turned it to release the lock.

He pulled on the door. "No. No. The door's jammed." Harder and harder he pulled. Nothing budged. "What do I do now? How do I get out?" Searching his mind, he could think of no other way out of his penthouse. He was locked in—trapped.

JQ kicked the door, and the floor shifted again. He reached out to pat the door, apologizing for his rudeness.

He looked at his watch. "Not even two minutes," but it felt like it had been forever. JQ leaned back and breathed a deep breath. He had to think, find a way out of this mess.

Walking gingerly back up the incline into his office, he looked out his picture window toward the river and then north along the bluffs. Across the street and in the distance, through the dust, he could see other buildings that had fallen. Many were burning. "Damn. Part of the bridge is missing and the Pyramid's gone. That was some God-awful earthquake. That kid was right in his prediction."

He thought of his crews working on the earthquake retrofits on the overpasses, and a tinge of guilt shivered his gut. He recalled the shortcuts he had made in the renovation of this building. He felt fear, knowing that his cutbacks had been too much and that the building must be in trouble because of them. A sudden lurch redoubled his fear.

JQ dropped to the couch, his head in his hands trying to think of a way out of his trap, of something he could do. "Damn. There must be a way. How? Damn." His mind drew a blank—he could think of nothing.

In California Todd flipped to a new page and drew three concentric circles. "In one minute the *S-waves* will travel 106 miles outwards from the epicenter. After two minutes they will be at 212 miles and at three minutes 318 miles. By that time the damage will cover 160,000 square miles and the ground will begin to shake in the outskirts of Indianapolis, Peoria, Kansas City, Tulsa, Natchez, Knoxville, and Atlanta.

"The pancake effect I mentioned means that the energy of the waves reaching Indianapolis up here," he said drawing an X on the top right of the outside circle, "will still be half of what hit St. Louis." He tapped a point above the epicenter between first and second circle. "These cities can expect damage consistent with an intensity of VII. That means …"

The door to the banquet room burst open with a loud bang. "Hey. There's an earthquake going on TV. It's happening right now," yelled the busboy. "They say it's tearing up Memphis."

Carolyn looked into the TV camera with a stoic but worried face. Her eyes moved back and forth, glancing around. She listened to her headphone and then said, "Vicksburg has now reported the earthquake. And we have reports that Chattanooga and Birmingham are shaking intensely. The waves certainly seem to be coming toward Atlanta. We can only assume that they are spreading in all directions." Her face turned more ashen in expectation.

Vicksburg experienced a short period of very sharp shocks as all of the direct energy arrived within a period of 50 seconds. The brick antebellum homes along the riverbank crumbled, and those old homes built on brick supports fell to the ground within seconds. The city experienced damage in the VII intensity range while Chattanooga experienced shaking in the VI range.

At **NWS** the reporters began to anticipate where the seismic waves would strike next and called to establish live connections to reporters in those cities. This time there had been only a three-second delay. The news approached real-time, giving new meaning to live-on-camera.

Carolyn Phelps sat chained to her chair at the TV anchor desk continuing her broken report on the progress of the earthquake. "… another report says the shaking may be stopping in St. Louis."

As neighbor yelled to neighbor, wife called husband at work, and people stopped in the stores to stare at the rows of TVs for sale, more and more people across the country and around the world tuned in to her broadcast, wondering what would happen next.

Suspense built in Carolyn's mind and on her face. "Many of the staff here at **NWS** are heading for the exits, looking for safety from the …" At T+3 minutes 4 seconds, her sharp intake of breath told the entire world that the violent shaking had reached Atlanta.

Carolyn struggled for control and held onto the desk with both hands. Her voice quivered as she continued to report live the news as it happened.

"The earthquake is now in Atlanta, and the shaking has become quite severe. Most people in the studio ... Oh, that was a big lurch ... are leaving. The building seems to be rocking back and forth, and some of the cameras are rolling around and falling. I can't hear any noise other than people yelling. There's no noise from the outside ..."

The On-Air view showed equipment and fixtures around the studio moving from side to side and up and down. Lights fell from their supports. Equipment teetered on edge. The image itself vibrated as the floor of the studio bounced and shook, more than the anti-shake circuits could handle.

"Whoa, watch that console, it wants to roll on its own. Joe, can you stop it before it hits someone?"

The studio lights blinked, dimmed, and then returned to bright. "Are we still on the air? ... We are? Okay ... Now I can feel the building bucking up and down, and it's swaying in different directions ... There, a ceiling panel is falling. Hey, watch out." Carolyn pointed out past the cameras. "Someone go help Sherry. I think that cabinet fell on her ..." Viewers around the world watched in fascination as the news staff scrambled for cover amidst studio equipment that shook, churned, and pitched about.

The studio swayed without pause for 68 seconds, then the jolts began to subside, ending after a total of 100 seconds. Damage throughout Atlanta matched with intensity in the VI range, considered strong. Those people in larger high-rise buildings felt it the most. When added to the anticipation of those in the studio this day, it seemed far worse.

Carolyn's knuckles could be seen wrapped around the edge of the desk, white from clenching with all her might. Her face glowed under the perspiration. "Now, the shaking seems to be easing off some. Yes, it's not so severe as it was. I still feel some swaying around, but the hard jerks have stopped. We don't know if more will follow. Here in the studio the scene is pandemonium, but several of the crew stayed with their equipment to broadcast this experience to you."

She stopped a moment and swallowed. "Pardon me, I need to stop and catch my breath. I'm a little dizzy." Carolyn's face grew even whiter as she leaned over to the side and retched onto the floor in full view of her worldwide audience.

CHAPTER 25: ACROSS THE UNITED STATES

President Francois LaPorte pounded on his desk. "What do you mean, you heard it on TV?" His Chief of Staff had rushed into the room with the news a full minute after the President watched in wonder as Carolyn Phelps began to tell the world of the earthquake in Memphis. "Doesn't FEMA or somebody around here know what's going on in this country before **NWS** knows?"

"It was FEMA that called us, Sir. They told us to tune into **NWS**."

"Well in case you're interested, I've already heard everything you just told me."

The President refused to leave his desk in the Oval Office as his staff gathered. "I want an emergency meeting of the cabinet. Convene within ten minutes. And Jerry." He spoke to his personal secretary. "Get the Homeland Security Secretary on the phone."

"Yes, sir, right away."

"And does anybody know what's happening in St. Louis? Sheila's there attending a science fiction conference."

Jerry Worthall slowed his rush to action when the President asked the last question. "We'll find out about your daughter as soon as we can, Mr. President."

When Homeland Security came on the line he asked, "Are there any reports yet on just how bad this earthquake is?"

"Yes, Mr. President, an initial estimate from the University of Arkansas says magnitude 7.6. Memphis appears to be severely damaged, and that's our biggest concern right now. They've lost all power and communications. We assume they're switching to emergency systems as soon as they can."

After a short pause, the report continued. "And we just got word there's been major damage at the Kentucky Dam on the Tennessee River, and it's flooding the Ohio. The flood is moving down to the Mississippi. We're gathering data on that situation."

"How big is this?"

"St. Louis, Nashville, Little Rock, and Birmingham have all experienced major damage, Sir, but it's too early to get a good assessment. The seismic wavefront is still moving outward, so the damage zone is still growing."

"Well, you're paid for this. Get busy and keep me informed. I want a bulletin sent to my office every two minutes, sooner if something important comes up." The President hung up the telephone and turned back to the TV consoles lining the wall across from his desk.

"Thank God for **NWS** news," he exclaimed over his shoulder to his assembled aides.

The Girl Scout troop walked on the sidewalk alongside the Grayson Towers in Chicago. The girls ran over and around the patio fountains between the skyscrapers with their troop leader, Angela Thomas, leading the way toward Lakeside Park where they would have their picnic. Angela had noticed a growling boom a couple of minutes before the earth started shaking, but dismissed it as truck noise from nearby Lakeshore Drive.

The shaking began in Chicago and New Orleans at the same time, and in both cities it lasted for almost two minutes, rocking the downtowns at a shaking intensity above VI, enough for damage.

Many people in Chicago just felt a jarring experience, but in an unprepared metropolitan area with a population of 5,000,000 and its many high rises and older brick structures, the casualty toll climbed.

Angela reached for a tree to catch her balance. She saw light poles swaying, but the wind did not blow. "Girls, girls. Get over here." She called to the scampering troop. "We're having an earthquake. We've got to take cover." Only half of them looked up and started toward her. "Girls," she shouted. Though reluctant, the rest turned toward their leader.

As they gathered, she explained to them, "The ground is shaking. Do you remember what we're supposed to do if there is an earthquake?"

"Go stand in a door," said Maria, one of her brightest.

"That's right, so let's go stand in the doorway of that building over there." She led the troop toward the portico of the nearest of the larger buildings.

She heard a crash, like someone dropping plates and looked around but saw nothing amiss except Lia stopping to pick a flower, "Lia, hurry, come here."

As Lia looked up, Angela sensed, rather than saw, a flash of reflected light and heard the crash of shattering glass as a golden pane from a window high in the skyscraper reached the ground. The sheet of glass had sailed from many stories up, twisting from side to side like a loose kite as the air caught it from different directions on its spiraling path to the ground. Angela never saw the sliver of broken glass that sliced through Lia's arm holding the flower— just the sudden red spurt of arterial blood from the child's arm.

"Run, run. Get into the doorway. Now." She screamed to the troop as she raced back to the bleeding girl. Snatching her up, Angela turned and followed the group rushing for the doorway. Another pane hit to her left, and then another in front. She slipped on the slithering glass, but somehow kept her balance and reached the portico of the building.

Her hands and blouse dripped red with blood. Spurts came from the small arm she squeezed. Hearing the screaming girls, the security guard rushed out the door. He saw the injury and shouted, "I'll call 911. Hang on." He rushed back inside to call for help.

"Girls. Quiet." Angela instructed. "We have to give Lia first aid. Maria, give me your belt, quickly." Taking the small belt, she used it to make a tourniquet around the limp arm and tightened it until the blood stopped spurting. Lia screamed and cried, and then Angela and the whole troop cried with her as they waited for help to arrive.

Houston, Texas, looked northeast toward the New Madrid Fault, like a deer staring into the barrel of a hunter's rifle.

Ed Baker leaned back in his chair, gazing out the large window of his new office on the 43rd floor of the Zapata Building. Named by the Board only yesterday as the new President of Laramie Oil, Incorporated, he had at last moved to the center of power. Now he planned to enjoy it. He had come in this Saturday morning to move some of his personal things from his old VP office into his new digs. He smiled and lit a large, green cigar.

The telephone rang. He punched the voice button on the speakerphone. "Yes, who is it?"

"Ed, this is Lynn. Have you heard about the earthquake coming this way?" Ed's first thought registered surprise that his wife would call. He had told her strictly not to bother him at work. It took several seconds of silence before the message she delivered settled in.

"What are you talking about? What earthquake?" he demanded.

"I'm watching TV, and they just interrupted the morning show to say there's been an earthquake in Memphis. They said that Houston is going to be hit by the shaking. I know you told me not to call you at your office, but I thought maybe you might want to know." Her voice pleaded for approval.

Ed considered what to say to his wife. He knew he should immediately lecture her about calling him, but this did not seem to be the right moment to do that. It would break his feeling of success. He replied, "Thank you for calling. I'll watch out for it. Goodbye," and pressed the button to disconnect the telephone.

Ed again leaned back in his chair and looked out the large floor to ceiling window of his office. From the high-rise, he could see much of Houston laid out at his feet to the southeast. He felt a great surge of personal power. He did not consider an earthquake worthy of his attention.

At T+4 minutes 45 seconds the building's base accelerated southwest. The acceleration measured one twentieth of the force of gravity, but after three seconds the acceleration reversed direction and the base jerked back to the northeast. Then the direction reversed again, and then again, and again. The frequency of the oscillation increased as shorter wavelengths arrived, whipping the base of the building back and forth at a faster and faster pace, increasing to one oscillation every two and a half seconds, the resonant frequency for the building.

Much of the energy from the fracture focused at the city arrived in the first 15 seconds, though shaking continued for a total of 128 seconds. Only the distance traveled, 460 miles, offered protection. Even so, damage in some parts of Houston reached the intensity VI level.

The security officer in the lobby noticed the shaking, but it did not seem strong enough to interrupt his reading of the sports page.

On the 43rd floor Ed Baker suffered pure hell. Within ten seconds his office was swinging back and forth over a distance of 15 feet, and the furniture caromed about the room. Ed fell to the floor, and his new desk fell over him, striking the windowpane and crashing with the shattered glass out the opening.

The desk disappeared from view. Staring at the monstrous opening to the sky, Ed dragged himself with his hands flat on the floor toward the door of the inner office. He trembled with stark fear as a mild wind blew into the office from the south.

The shaking quickened. "No, no, keep away from me," he screamed at the opening as he slid back and forth over the polished walnut flooring then headfirst toward the missing window.

The TV scene from **NWS** held steady, showing pandemonium. No one sat at the broadcast anchor desk, but beyond it people could be seen in the dark background moving equipment around.

After several seconds the TV screen flashed then switched to a feed coming over satellite from elsewhere. A young man holding onto a streetlight pole stood on an asphalt walk atop an embankment. A large body of water could be seen behind him.

"… and as the ground continues to rock back and forth, I can see the river washing further and further up the side of the levee, almost as if the Mississippi River is rising. This shaking has been going on for almost a minute now according to my watch. So far, the water has risen at least four feet up the side of the levee."

The camera panned along the earthen dike to show the choppy brown water starting to wash over the asphalt sidewalk 100 feet away. The scene shifted further along the levee to a dip in the walkway several inches deep, now filled with running water.

"I'm here with Jack Swift, my cameraman. The city of New Orleans is facing disaster. This levee must have sunk from the shaking of the earthquake, and that shaking must have affected all the other levees protecting the city from the mighty Mississippi in the same way. As you can see, the levee has now sunk to the point where the floods are flowing over it to the streets below. I see several places where water is washing over the levee. God help us. The city is lost."

The voice stopped. The camera continued to pan back and forth showing scenes near and far of water spilling into the streets below. It showed a few scenes of fallen chimneys and people standing around in the streets below staring up the embankment at the growing flow of water. Some turned and ran.

The voice came again. "Jack, watch out, under you. The levee's giving away. There's a crevasse forming where you're standing." The camera jerked around, pointed down at an out-of-focus brown stain, and then swooped up to the blue sky above. After a flash of static, a test pattern replaced the video signal.

President LaPorte looked around at his assembled staff. "Is that all there is?" They had just experienced the shaking from New Simon as it coursed through the Oval Office. "Doesn't it do more than that?" He looked at the chandelier still swinging overhead from the level IV intensity shaking.

The swaying motion that started at T+6 minutes 29 seconds had lasted over two and a half minutes, but never became violent. During the entire time, the staff sat in silent prayer that the shaking of the earth beneath their assemblage would either stop or at least not become stronger.

"Mr. President, the motion you felt came from a seismic event that happened over nine minutes ago, 700 miles away."

The Secretary of HomeLand Security had assumed the role of *de facto* expert on earthquakes for the gathering. "It may not feel like much, but it was enough to break some dishes around this city and to do horrendous damage in cities closer than we are."

The President picked up his pen. "Okay, so let's get back to planning. Everything I hear says we have catastrophic damage near the New Madrid fault zone, so we better get the troops moving into that area as soon as possible. Those people need help, and need it fast."

HomeLand Security flinched and said, "But, Sir, that's what we have FEMA for. We can take care of it. There's no need . . ."

"Mr. President." The Chairman of the Joint Chiefs of Staff shifted in his chair for a better angle and chimed in. "I don't think we should be too precipitous on this. After all, we don't want to pull our boys and girls off their assigned duties to take care of some internal matter. Surely there's some better way . . ."

"Harry," the President said. "Your folks at FEMA have the smarts, but you don't have enough manpower to handle this. You need help. The Armed Forces are the only resource big enough to handle this matter. General, I'm declaring a National Emergency and Martial Law. The two of you have got the ball—now get with it and work together. This country needs help." President LaPorte made clear who was the Supreme Commander.

Marilyn sat on the couch in her high-rise apartment in Duluth, Minnesota, clutching her cat close to her breasts, her eyes fixed on the TV. Marianna Rosti, the morning anchor on local cable news arranged the papers and looked back at the camera. "We just received word from Washington, DC, that the earthquake has been felt there. The intensity seems to be diminishing, and there are no reports of damage from the nation's capital. Meanwhile, we have this feed from *NWS*."

At **NWS** Harold Owens turned to his right and received a fist full of papers. "Here are the latest updates from other areas of the country hit by this earthquake, surely one of the strongest any of us have ever felt.

"We have reports that Tulsa, Shreveport, Indianapolis, Cincinnati, Kansas City, and Dallas have all felt the shaking from this earthquake, and the list keeps growing." He shuffled through the notes. "Here is a report from Chicago of shaking. Levees in New Orleans have failed. Omaha, Houston, and

Charleston, South Carolina all report the earth temblor. At this very moment Cleveland and Detroit are coming under attack.

"The shaking is expected any moment now in Washington, DC." Owens looked up past the camera. "Oh, my producer says the shaking started a minute and a half ago in our nation's capital. Reports of damage are as yet sparse. We can only conjecture that the damage near the epicenter must be extreme."

Owens shuffled through more arriving papers and continued, "Here are some additional reports of more shaking. Let's see, these are from Rochester, Minnesota, San Antonio, Minneapolis, Philadelphia, Denver and ..."

Marianna reappeared on the screen in Duluth. "Thanks to **NWS** for that feed. We interrupt this story because we are told the shaking is about to reach Duluth. We will ... Oh—now I feel it. It seems pretty strong. It just keeps going back and forth. But it's not as strong as I thought it would be."

The time was T+6 minutes 40 seconds. Marilyn felt the seismic waves lift her building, and the room oscillated from side to side. Her dishes rattled on the counter and in the shelves from the intensity IV shaking. She hugged her cat closer, pulled the comforter over her head, and curled into a fetal position on the couch to pray. The tension had been worse than the shaking.

At T+9 minutes 45 seconds the seismic waves had traveled 1,075 miles around the curvature of the earth's surface, far enough to reach Boston.

In a northern borough of the city, an Irish priest knelt at the altar in the chapel of the abbey. He had prayed for half an hour, concentrating on his thoughts of reverence for Mary, Mother of Jesus.

The priest felt a wave of light-headedness, almost as if something or someone had touched the top of his bowed head. He looked up at the figure of Christ on the cross in awe, and the bells in the steeple of the chapel began to ring.

"Bong ... Bong ... Bong ..." The priest crossed himself, knowing that the touch he felt and the sound he heard must be a sign from God, Almighty.

"Bong ... Bong ..." On and on, the bells rang out for three minutes and forty-five seconds on the clear spring day. People who had gathered in the plaza in front of the chapel when they heard the news of the earthquake stared in wonder as the seismic waves rocked the foundations of Boston, just as they had nearly 200 years before.

"Bong." People standing in the plaza waited for the next chime, but the ringing had ended. A terrible silence settled upon the land. Thirteen and a half minutes after the earthquake began, God paused.

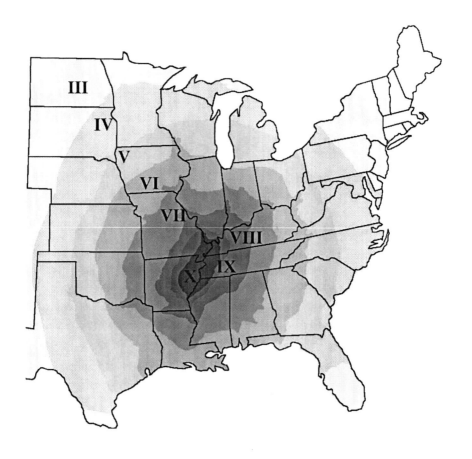

Intensities across the USA from a 7.9 magnitude earthquake:

XI possible over 2,000 square miles,
X possible over another 20,000 square miles,
IX possible over another 23,000 square miles,
VIII possible over another 90,000 square miles,
VII possible over another 185,000 square miles,
VI possible over another 355,000 square miles.

Total damage zone: 675,000 square miles.

Chapter 26: Reality Sets In

Even as the shaking reached Boston, the first major aftershock struck on the New Madrid at a depth of 14.3 kilometers beneath Lepanto, Arkansas. Too much strain still deformed the freshly broken fault. Displacement along the fracture had relieved some tension, but not enough. Huge pockets of stored energy remained.

The 6.8 magnitude temblor ripped another fracture within the seismic zone stretching 20 miles along a northeast bearing from Marked Tree to Athelstan. Another 126 square miles of fault surface slipped 5.5 feet at the focus, sufficient to inflict intensity level IX shaking along the fracture's trace. Little remained that could be destroyed in the small towns along the southern end of the fault.

At nearby points along the river, like Osceola and Fort Pillow, the shaking intensity from the aftershock reached a level of VIII. Accelerations of one-third of gravity stirred the already shattered levees and bluffs with forces that hurried along their destruction. Liquefied mud that had started to settle once again erupted from sand boils on land not yet covered by the flood.

In Memphis, the *S-wave* shook the city at a strong VII intensity for 15 seconds, dislodging many of the already broken walls left standing after the primary temblor. Bricks and cornices again rained to the ground. Little glass fell, for there was little left to fall. The shaking eased for the next four seconds, then the reflected waves swept up from the mantle for another 22 seconds of twisting contortions.

The ten minutes of relative quiet had been enough for many volunteer rescuers to enter broken buildings to search for victims. They had not heard the USGS warnings about the notorious earthquake sequences of the New Madrid Seismic Zone: Big Aftershocks Will Occur.

Most of those buildings that had been left standing lacked the strength to withstand the added assault, and they crumbled in upon themselves, killing half of the rescuers inside and snuffing out the lives of many trapped by the first round of shaking. Those who survived the aftershock had passed the exam on their first lesson: never again trust the earth to remain stable.

Glenda screamed and screamed and screamed. She dragged a huge gulp of air into her lungs and screamed again. She pressed against the back wall of her tiny cave in the second level basement, a cave created by the row of filing cabinets on one side and the broken wall on the other.

Through the dust she could see the ground floor lobby of the Memphis City Office Building, now level with the top of the filing cabinets. The western three-quarters of the building had dropped 20 feet as the bluff supporting the structure had slid into the Wolf River harbor.

Fred, the Saturday morning guard, still sat in his chair at the front desk. His head and chest lay sprawled across the solid oak desk, and his bright eyes stared out from his broken face toward Glenda. After a long moment she realized one of the pillars from the front portico rested across his skull, crushing it to half its original width.

She fought her panic, knowing she had to find the courage to crawl past Fred and escape from the shattered building.

It was a miracle that Glenda remained uninjured other than bruises. "Daddy, Daddy, where are you? Why can't you help me?" She cried and rubbed her eyes, fighting for control. The yellow glow from the emergency light on the wall above Glenda added to the macabre scene, and when aftershocks rocked the building, she could see dust settling through the light while the sounds of further shifting and breaking echoed through the remains.

Taking several deep breathes, almost to the point of feeling faint, she crawled toward the opening of her cave to Fred's floor. She reached up and pulled herself erect with one of the bars of torn metal reinforcing rod that protruded from the concrete remains of the lobby floor. Looking up, she could see the reflection of outside light on the walls and ceiling above Fred.

Glenda searched for a way to climb the five feet to Fred's floor. She pulled over a rolling stool that helped, and she reached for the leg of the desk on the ground floor. Next to it she could see Fred's radio, a tinny voice screaming from it in a language that sounded like Spanish, saying things she did not understand. She pulled with her hands and stepped up on the stool. She was still too low to finish the climb.

She stepped down from the stool and pulled out the second of the drawers of the filing cabinet next to her. Again holding onto the rebar and desk leg, she climbed onto the stool and placed her foot on the open drawer.

As the Lepanto aftershock rolled through Memphis, the earth-slide once again loosened and sank further toward the river. The west side of the City Office Building dropped another six feet, and the front of the building facing east gave way and caved into the entry area, crushing Fred and his desk into the floor. Glenda scrambled to the back of her cave, saving herself from being carried further down the slope with the rest of the building. Dust billowed into the small space, so thick Glenda could not see beyond the second filing cabinet.

When the shaking stopped, the emergency light seemed brighter. It seemed even quieter than before. Fred and the ground floor had disappeared. In its place she saw a flat, unbroken slab of concrete covering the opening to her cave. Now she could see no way out. She was trapped.

Glenda brought her hands to her face to wipe the tears from her eyes, surprised when the thick object she held in her hand hit her forehead. Bringing it close to her face, she realized she held Fred's radio. She must have grabbed it when the shaking started.

The radio came to life. "Help me, Mother of God, help me, please. Can anyone hear me? I'm trapped and hurt. Please, someone help me." The male voice with a Latino accent sounded hysterical.

Fred had shown Glenda the radio the week before. He had been so proud of it. She pressed the button on the side. "Hello, do you hear me?"

When she thought to release the button a stream of yelling came from the radio. "Mother of God. You're there. You can hear me. Please save me, I'm trapped."

Glenda waited until the person who was talking stopped and seemed to be waiting. Pressing the button again she answered, "I'm trapped, too. I'm Glenda, and I'm in the basement of the City Offices. Where are you?"

The radio answered, "My name's Juan Cortez. I'm in the parking garage of the Federal Building. I was making my rounds when the shaking started. A beam fell on my legs and I'm pinned against the wall. Please get someone in here to help me. This building sounds like it is crumbling more and more."

Another small shake ran through the buildings, and Glenda felt the ground settle around her. Over the radio she heard a scream and then silence. "Hello, Juan. Hello, are you there? Hello?" She waited for Juan's answer, but heard nothing, not a sound. Even the building stopped creaking.

"I'm going to move further down the street. I don't like being so close to that slide." Tom restarted the engine of the truck. A few people now drove along Riverside, their distress obvious. He watched with care for those who sped, sometimes knocking the bricks and stones across the pavement.

Hugging the right-hand curb, he slowed then drove past the leaning building labeled Walker Hotel. As they came abreast of the old building the *S-waves* arrived from the Lepanto aftershock. The truck rocked and resumed its cantankerous ways.

"Hang on, Judy. I was afraid of this. We're getting a major aftershock. It could even be bigger than the first." He kept the truck moving on down the street, searching for a safer place to stop.

Judy bent forward. "Oh my God, Tom, that old hotel. It's starting to fall." Tom looked wide-eyed out his left window to see the building rock back and forth and settle even further in front. Bricks shot out of the walls from the pressure in the base. He pressed the fuel pedal, hoping to escape the flying fragments from the falling building. The truck accelerated down the street.

As the facade of the McCrombie Building dropped to the parking lot, the bulk behind it leaned further and further over the trolley tracks, falling in a heap. The shiny unbroken glass windows of the penthouse disappeared into the billowing cloud of dust that rose to hide everything from view.

Jenny sat on the grass watching the smoke and flames pour from the doors and windows of the Seismic Lab. Minutes before she had been inside the building. She had made it out just before the intense shaking started.

During the earthquake she recorded in her mind each of the motions she experienced and tried to estimate the immense energy she felt. She held onto the grass as the ground wanted to throw her into the air. The buildings of the University shook and crumbled. Broken glass poured from the windows. Above her the huge trees cracked, and broken limbs covered the grounds.

Then the shaking stopped. Thinking the earthquake had ended, she started to rise, and another wave coursed through the grounds. Sparks flashed inside the old structure, followed by a growing plume of smoke blowing from the windows of the lab. Something had caught fire, and she dared not go back inside, knowing yet another aftershock could happen at any time.

"What's happened to the Lab?" yelled Paul Kenton as he raced up on his bicycle. He sounded hysterical. "We've got to save the equipment." He ran toward the door, and Jenny ran after him, grabbing at his old sweater to hold him back from the inferno.

"No, no, Dr. Kenton. Don't go in there. It's burning too much."

Paul stopped and turned around, looking with a dazed expression at the young girl holding onto the arm of his sweater. "Why didn't you save the equipment? Where were you?" he demanded.

"I was in the Lab when the first waves hit, and I barely got out in time. All the racks of equipment were being thrown around. The bricks from the old chimney almost hit me. Then I had to hold onto the grass to keep from being thrown into the air. I was about to go back when the fire started. Honest, Dr. Kenton, there was no way to save any equipment."

Jenny's mind suddenly focused on the personal danger she had just experienced, and she reacted to the unleashed anxiety, sobbing as she held onto the professor's arm. "Really, I couldn't do anything. I couldn't." Jenny broke down and cried, sucking in deep gasping breaths in reaction.

The distraught girl leaning on his chest brought Paul back to his senses, and he put his arm around her. He turned and watched the Lab burn. Grabbing his bicycle he pulled it and the girl back from the growing heat. "You're right, we can always get new equipment."

Jenny brought herself back to order, then looked up at Paul. "Dr. Kenton, Chris was right. He predicted an earthquake at New Simon, and that's where it happened. I saw the sensor alarms go off. They were all centered around New Simon."

Paul looked at the girl with disbelief on his face.

"And like I said when I called you, I ran Chris's model on his workstation, and the screen said there was going to be a 7.9 magnitude earthquake at New Simon. It was only a minute wrong on when it started. Honest— it was on the screen. Chris was right." Jenny became more and more excited as she remembered the success of her friend.

"You must have imagined it," said Paul. "There's no way Chris could have predicted this earthquake."

Jenny pushed the page she had printed in the lab at Paul. "Look. That's his prediction. See, the location is New Simon, and this shaking could have been as strong as his model said."

Paul took the printout. "Oh, God. Oh, God. He couldn't be right, could he?" He shook his head in amazement. "Oh, God. We have to talk with Chris. We have to check his results and compare them with what really happened. God knows, maybe he really was onto something."

Jenny looked back at the burning Lab in horror. "But his workstation and all the computer records are in the Lab. They're lost."

"I know, but Chris can explain to us what he did when he gets back from New Simon, and he must have a copy of his earthquake model on his laptop." He looked again at the printout, and his face beamed with joy. He folded the paper and tucked it inside his sweater. "We've found the Holy Grail."

With effort Judy detached her mind from the Memphis around her and remembered the outside world. "Tom, do you think our phone still works?"

Tom had stopped the truck two blocks beyond the fallen McCrombie Building and turned off the diesel engine. The truck again became quiet. He shook but the truck no longer rocked.

To their right the tents and stages for three of the Jazz Festival venues lay strewn across the wide grassy area that reached 200 feet from Riverside Drive to the banks of the Mississippi River, jumbled in a tumultuous mess.

Those who had fled the falling buildings on the bluffs intermingled with those who had paid to hear the performances. They all gathered in the open where there seemed to be some relative safety. Those who could still stand stared back at the city.

The long row of green and blue outhouses lay on their sides, spilling their stinking contents onto the grass and mud.

Pillars of smoke rose from the ruins atop the bluffs, blowing to the northeast away from the river and back across the wreckage. Some buildings on the bluff still had two or three walls standing, waiting for the next aftershock to complete their fall. Most lay in heaps around their foundations. The skyline had disappeared. No one would recognize what remained as Memphis.

Tom looked at Judy for a moment and then nodded his head. "It should. I'll call Jenny." He took the low-sat phone from its charging cradle and searched for his daughter's phone number. Pressing TALK he waited for the call to go to the satellite, back to the ground station in California, and then back to Memphis. Instead came the "buzz, buzz, buzz, …" of the busy signal.

"I should of thought of that. All the phone lines into this area must be down. There's no way to phone in or out of Memphis."

"Do you think Jenny's okay?" Judy looked as if she would break down again.

"We can only hope so." He rubbed her arm and returned the phone to its cradle.

Alex became very adept at controlling the horizontal direction of the parachute. He just could not make it fall any faster.

He drifted over and around the remains of New Simon. A canopy of dark gray smoke hid the cafe. From time to time flames leaped up the side of the column of soot. The tire barn and fueling shed had fallen but escaped the fire so far.

Many of the older trees in the grove behind the truck stop appeared to be broken and down. The electric power poles had fallen. He stared into the distance at the little town of Cooter. It looked strange, and he realized after a minute that the water tower marking the town's location was gone.

Gliding over the Interstate, he looked down on the fallen overpass at the New Simon exit. The hood of some vehicle protruded from under the fallen slab and two more cars lay at the bottom of the embankment. The north and south overpasses were down with trucks and cars stopped at each and people milling around.

The fields of young cotton and soybeans presented the strangest sights. They glistened like lakes, and as he neared the ground he began to see that water covered much of the land. Drifting lower he could discern places where there had been waterspouts, often building mounds of sand and dirt.

At 300 feet, he still had 25 seconds to go before he touched down. Over eight minutes had passed gliding under his canopy from when it opened 6,300 feet higher. A lot had changed in that time, and as he looked for a place to land, he saw several places where he did not want to touch down.

Power lines lay on the road and across the fences next to the snapped electrical power poles along the road. Some wires looked alive. Some of the geysers in the fields still spewed water and steam into the air. He could now sense the putrid smell from those openings into the bowels of the earth.

He gritted his teeth and made a decision. "Oh, crap. Looks like I'd better land in the lake behind the truck stop and swim to shore. What a mess this is going to be."

Alex felt a growing nausea as the surface approached, for he could now see a black scum covering the muddy waters. For all he knew, it might even cover quicksand. He worried he would drown, for he could not swim that well.

Bracing his feet and pushing them forward, he hit the surface, holding his breath for immersion in the water. Three inches beneath the water's surface his heels drove into solid ground, and his forward momentum flopped him over onto his face and chest. He spread his arms to catch his fall.

The six-inch deep muck smelled like pumpings from a septic tank. Alex pushed his hands down into the firm mud below and rose to his knees, his face and chest covered with the sticky goo. Spitting to clear his mouth, he stripped off the parachute harness, and then turned to run through the slop toward the road and the still-burning cafe.

Alex yelled, "Tina, Tina, where are you?" Reaching the road 200 feet east of the remains of the café, he trotted down the middle of the pavement, staring at the scene, his hands dangling out at his sides.

People around the truck stop ceased their aimless wandering and moaning. "Oh my God," one of them yelled. They all stared down the road in horror.

"The earthquake has freed some kind of monster. That looks like the creature from the Black Lagoon." They turned and ran like a mob to the west.

CHAPTER 27: THE NELSON REQUIEM

All the buildings of the old truck stop at New Simon lay in ruins. The smell of burned flesh and smoke from the smoldering remains of the cafe mixed with the sulfurous stench from the sand boils in the surrounding fields, adding to Alex's nausea.

The drying mud on his face, hands and chest started to crumble and fall off onto the quivering asphalt at his feet. Alex walked back and forth around the cinders of NASTY'S café, more and more certain that Tina had perished in the fire.

Oblivious to the image Alex presented, the dazed trucker walked up and asked, "Do you know where I can get a cup of coffee? Nobody seems to have coffee around here anymore."

"Have you seen a girl? She was in the cafe." Alex shook the trucker's arm.

"A girl? I remember. She gave me coffee this morning, but now she's sleeping. She's over there." He pointed to the other side of the road, and then turned and walked back toward his trapped big rig. "But I can't find anybody with coffee."

Alex looked again at the small bundle on the grass he had thought to be a pile of rags. He ran and knelt, turning Tina's face up to the light. He stroked her cheek, "Tina, Tina, are you all right? Honey, wake up."

The stroking of his hand roused her, and Tina opened her eyes a crack. "Alex, is that you? What happened?" She pushed herself up on an elbow to look around, and then fell back as another small aftershock rocked the ground beneath her. "I remember things started shaking, and I fell under a table. I ran for the door. There was a big explosion." She shuddered as memory flooded back.

Looking up, she returned to the present. "Alex. Are you okay?" She reached up and pulled some of the caked crud from his face. "You've been swimming in mud. You're a mess." She smiled. Alex smiled back in relief, tears streaming from his eyes.

"I'm okay, but let's check you out." He felt her arms and legs, and she yelped once when he moved her right knee. He could see a large abrasion on the side of the knee, but nothing seemed to be broken. He helped her sit upright, and though woozy, she had come away without major injury.

As Tina picked the clods of clay from Alex, and Alex massaged Tina's back and shoulders, they surveyed the devastation surrounding them. The fire in the café had exhausted most of its fuel, though smoke still rose from the ruins. Another small rattle shook the coals down a bit further.

They saw a few people pulling timbers and siding from the demolished garage, searching for two thought to be missing. A dog came to them, wagging his tail and shoving his head under Tina's arm, hoping for human kinship amidst all of its terror.

Alex put his arm around Tina. "Guess we're lucky to be alive. There must be a lot of people in more trouble than we are." He helped her to her feet, and after a few staggering steps, she walked forward with a slight limp. Seeing a larger crowd of people around the fallen overpass a quarter mile west at the freeway, Alex led Tina down the road to join them, looking for companionship, wondering what they would find.

Nodding to his director, Owens continued, "Next we have a recorded report from Howard Temple, one of our **NWS** reporters in St. Louis. He phoned this in over his cell-phone."

The tinny voice from a cell-phone began to speak. "I was watching the Carolyn Phelps broadcast on **NWS** at the ninth floor offices of the attorney I planned to interview this morning, so I was warned the earthquake was on its way. I first noticed some vibration in the building, like the feel of a bass guitar when a string is plucked real hard. Then the back and forth shaking started.

"The severest shaking began at 9:35:50 according to my wristwatch and lasted for approximately a minute and a half. During that entire time, the shaking was intense. The initial shaking seemed to move north and south, then it went in all directions, including up and down."

After some static and a pause the voice continued, "I am now on the top floor of this 12-story building. I didn't have a chance to get out of the building when the earthquake hit. I'm trapped on the roof along with 15 other people, with the elevators non-functional and the stairs blocked by falling debris. I must say it has been quite a ride.

"I'm able to look out over the city from here on the roof, near the center of town. It appears most of the higher buildings are missing windows. Some are missing parapets, and at least three to the north and west have crumbled to the ground. Several seem to be tilted over to one side or the other."

"Busch Stadium seems okay, but I can see that Union Station in the distance has crumbled. Smoke and flames are billowing out the backside of the ruins."

"I can see one leg of the Arch. The Arch itself is hidden behind another building, but it must still be standing. However, smoke coming from that direction seems to be growing in intensity. The sounds of sirens from police, fire, and ambulances fill the air around the city, and people are running around in the streets below me. Cars are mostly stopped, and some seem to have crashed into each other or other structures. And now another aftershock is happening. Oh, it's lurching this building around. And again … I'm scared as hell. This building seems to …"

Static came on the line and the recording stopped.

Owens commented live. "We hope to receive further reports from Howard, but for now we have lost all contact with his cell-phone."

Owens turned to look at the new anchor sitting down next to him. "Sherry Kent has joined me at the news desk. Welcome, Sherry, I hope you're okay after that bout with the filing cabinet."

Sherry smiled at Owens and then into the camera. "Harold, I'm fine. The cabinet missed me by inches, and apart from too much adrenaline, I survived. You look like you could use a breather."

The camera focused on her face as she took over the reporting. "Let me continue describing the toll of the largest earthquakes to strike the contiguous United States in modern times. Up to this time we have reports of seismic shaking being felt as far away as Toronto, Canada, in Cheyenne, Wyoming, New York City, Fargo, North Dakota, Orlando, Florida, and Boston.

"All indications are that the further a city is from the epicenter of the quake on the New Madrid fault, the less shaking it receives, though we will have to wait for the actual measurements to be sure.

"We have direct confirmation of damage from Memphis, St. Louis, Nashville, Birmingham, Paducah, Evansville, Little Rock, and Chattanooga. There is an unconfirmed report that there has been a massive levee failure in New Orleans.

All communication with Memphis have apparently been lost, but we are still in contact by telephone with our reporters in the other cities.

"We are trying to contact the authorities in all these cities, but I am sure you can imagine that they are preoccupied at this time. We will report any item as soon as it is received. Please stay tuned."

President LaPorte held his hand up to stop the chatter and pressed the button to increase the volume of the TV as Owens gave his introduction, "… of our **NWS** reporters in St. Louis, phoned in over his cell-phone."

The President listened as Howard Temple reported, "… a number of the higher buildings are missing windows. Some are missing parapets and at least three to the north and west have crumbled to the ground … Union Station in the distance has crumbled. Smoke and flames are billowing out … another aftershock is happening … I'm scared as hell … "

Static came on the line and the recording ended.

The President muted the TV and turned to an aide. "My daughter's attending a Sci-Fi conference at the Union Station in St. Louis. Jerry's already checking on her, but have the Head of Secret Service get through to one of his people there and find out what's happening. I want a report back within five minutes. Move it. Now."

He turned back to the four people seated around the Oval Office and mopped his brow. The earthquake had become a much more personal issue. He shuddered when he thought of Sheila and what trouble she could be in. He felt chilled and started sweating.

Another aide burst through the door. "Mr. President. We just received this analysis from the Army Corps of Engineers concerning damage at the Kentucky Dam and the expected flooding downstream." He paused.

"Well, what are you waiting for? Read me the highlights."

"Sir, the Engineers have calculated that the Ohio River will rise at Paducah by 15 feet within the hour. It will take four hours for the flood to reach Cairo about 40 miles downstream. They expect within one hour it to add 12 feet to the already flooded Mississippi. The river at New Madrid, 70 river miles downstream from Cairo, will start rising within ten hours and will add nine feet to their level in two hour's time.

"About midnight the crest should reach Caruthersville, another 40 miles below New Madrid, and take another three hours to raise the level to its maximum there, adding six feet. The flood should reach Memphis in 30 hours and take four hours to reach its maximum of five more feet. It will take five days for the flood to impact New Orleans, adding probably two feet to the river level."

The President asked, "As I remember, the Mississippi is already above flood stage along most of the river. Is that correct?"

"Yes, Sir, it is six to eight feet above flood stage from St. Louis to Vicksburg. That surge will be reaching New Orleans about the same time as this flood crest does. However, we also have a preliminary report we lost the Old River Control Structure and the Mississippi River is diverting into the Atchafalaya River Basin. That may save New Orleans."

"When will the water from Kentucky Lake stop?"

"Sir, the flow is expected to be cut to half by the falling level of the lakes within three days, but it will be four weeks before the level of the lake drops to the point where water no longer runs through the broken locks."

Taking a deep breath to steady himself, the President said to the others, "Okay, this problem keeps getting bigger. Let's get to the business of saving whatever we can of the heart of this country of ours. May God have mercy on the U.S.A."

JQ coughed from the dust, and then coughed again. The back of his head hurt. He realized he must still be alive, else he would not feel the hurt. When he opened his eyes, it was pitch black, so maybe he was blind. He could hear sounds like creaking timbers and hissing steam or gas.

He lay on his left side on a flat surface that he realized must be tilted. It felt like his head must be pointed downhill. Maybe he lay on his office floor. His right hand could move, and he found obstructions above and in front of his face. Reaching above his head he felt a padded leather surface like the front of his couch.

JQ twisted to his right, and felt opposition. His backside touched something. He pulled on his right foot, but it would not move. At least it did not hurt. His left leg was pinned beneath the right.

JQ's pulse doubled in reaction to another small shake. He started to struggle, but the space where he fit had no extra room for movement. His breaths became shallower and quicker from the laborious panting. As he pushed and shoved, he felt the sides around him come closer, tightening in on him and restricting his movements. He realized that if he pushed too hard, his cave might collapse on him. He became far more frightened than he had ever been before. The wreckage was about to smother him, and he could do nothing about it.

JQ brought his left hand up and saw the luminescent dial of his watch. It read 9:57. He seemed to remember it had been just about 9:35 when the earthquake hit. Over 20 minutes had passed. If he had lived that long, maybe he still had a chance.

At 9:57:06 another strong aftershock ripped along the seismic zone, starting beneath East View, Arkansas, 39 miles to the north. It tore apart another

50 square miles of the fault along a 12.5-mile fracture. The 6.4 magnitude event shook downtown Memphis with intensity VI shaking, enough to shuffle the unstable piles of rubbish that littered the city into denser piles.

JQ felt the trembling increase and the sides of his cave shifted. Something broke and hit the backside of his head. A brilliant streak of light flashed across his eyes. He no longer felt the shaking.

The trucker pointed and commented, "We don't have time to worry about the guy in that pickup under the overpass. He never knew what hit him and never will."

Alex looked at the remains of the black pickup sticking out from beneath the fallen concrete beam of the bridge. Its driver could be seen leaning forward across the dashboard. The crushed roof had shoved his body around the steering wheel, and his bloody skull pushed part way through the shattered windshield.

Another shudder swept the surrounding fields and piles of fallen concrete. The trucker climbed over the broken pavement, avoiding cracks that might open or close, to the late model Lincoln that had crashed head-on into the abutment on the other side of the road passing beneath the Interstate.

"Hey, we've got a woman here who seems to be breathing." He started pulling on the bent door of the automobile, trying to wrench it open. Alex scrambled over beside the trucker. "Let's get this glass out of the way." He picked up a broken piece of concrete and smashed out the window of the car, giving them access to the inside handles and some leverage to pry on the door. With a mighty squeal, the door pulled away from the car. The trucker moved forward to attend to the woman inside.

Walking back to the west side of the fallen overpass, Alex again looked over the edge and noticed a piece of cable with a short bolt at one end laying on the hood of the pickup below. He said to the man standing beside him, "I have a friend who is all upset about how they were doing those earthquake retrofits. That cable and bolt must be part of the retrofit stuff that Chris was talking about. It sure doesn't look like it held much of anything in place."

The earth jerked with violent shaking for a couple of seconds. Everyone stood like grotesque statues with their arms spread to catch themselves if they fell. Then it stopped, and one by one they started to move again.

Looking again at the truck jutting from beneath the 120-ton piece of concrete, Alex yelled, "Hey, I know the guy in that pickup. That's Chris Nelson."

Tina had scurried over the broken bridge to join the pair, and when Alex yelled, she leaned over to look.

"No, Tina, don't look down there. He's dead." Alex grabbed for her arm as she gasped and began to sway.

Tina turned toward the other side of the road and clung to Alex, her face ash white. "Oh, no. Chris was in the cafe this morning after checking on his seismic instruments. I had just served him a cup of coffee when the earthquake started. I remember him yelling that his earthquake was here. He wanted them to call it the Nelson Quake." She sobbed. "He was yelling with joy as he ran out the door—he was so happy. That was the last time I saw him."

She stared back at the smoldering ruins of the truck stop and again cried into Alex's mud-stained shirt. Her eyes were running out of tears.

Chapter 28: Taking Stock

A woman standing on the south side of the chasm left by the overpass pointed to Chris's black pickup sticking out from under the fallen block of concrete. "Hey, the boy in the pickup down there. He moved."

Alex looked back to the road below. Chris's hand beat on the broken windshield. "Tina, Chris is moving. Wait here while I check." He slid down the embankment through the weeds to the asphalt roadbed and ran to the pickup. From that vantage point he could see the cab of the pickup had not been crushed like it appeared from above. He pulled the passenger-side door open with a loud squeal.

Chris's head lay on its side on the dashboard pushing partway through the shattered windshield, blood trickling across his face. His dull eyes stared ahead, looking toward Alex. His right hand rested on the dashboard pushing on the glass. "Chris, you're bleeding. Dead people don't bleed."

Alex reached inside and shoved the windshield glass up and away from Chris's scalp. He could see Chris making gasping motions with his mouth. Throwing the jacket and backpack on the seat beside Chris out the door behind him, he reached in and pulled the limp body toward the passenger side, bringing Chris out of the cab and laying him on the pavement. Feeling Chris's chest, he detected a steady heartbeat.

"Tina," he yelled. "Find some bandages or something and bring them down here. Quick."

Chris twitched from time to time and writhed on the pavement. Alex grabbed the jacket and placed it under Chris's head then used a corner of it to wipe his battered face. "Hold still, Chris. Just lay quiet. We're watching after you." He felt Chris's shoulders, arms, and legs, searching for any obvious breaks.

Chris moaned and rocked his head. "I gotta save my station. I ..." His eyes rolled upward, giving no sign he heard or recognized his surroundings.

Tina knelt at Alex's side with a small towel. "This is all there is. A woman had it in her car. How is he?"

Alex looked up from his ministrations. "He's breathing but he's only semi-conscious. It looks like he may have a concussion, but there're no bad cuts, and I can't find any broken bones. There's no arterial blood flow, but we need to get him to a doctor as soon as we can."

"Alex, my car's back at the parking lot. I don't think it was damaged. Should I get it?"

Alex looked around. "Yes. I'll get help to carry Chris to the other side of the freeway. Here, take his backpack and bring your car up on the other side. The Interstate looks pretty broken here, but we can take the back roads to get him to Caruthersville."

Tina scrambled back up the embankment on her mission of mercy as Alex called one of the truckers to come and help.

Once shaking from the latest aftershock ended, Tom maneuvered the camper truck over the curb and around bricks and fallen light poles to a spot on the grass in Lee Park. The disheveled tents and stages of the Jazz Festival covered most of the park, leaving one small grassy area clear beside the road.

"This place looks safe. There're no big trees, buildings or power lines that can fall on the camper. And I think we're far enough from the river so the bank won't slide out from under us."

People milled across the street and about the park. Judy watched the crowd of refugees streaming down from the city above. Many were black, most were bloody. "Do you think one of those people might steal our truck?"

Tom could see Judy approaching one of her hysterical states. "Judy, cool it." She looked startled at Tom's harsh tone. "Snap out of it. Everyone here is distraught, probably even worse than we are, so just calm down. We're not going any further right now. This place looks safer to me than driving through that mess on the road or around any of those buildings up on the bluffs." Tom stared again at the piles of collapsed buildings lining the crest of the bluff to the north and south.

He opened the door to the truck and started to step out. "Maybe the TV's reporting on the earthquake. I'll set up the satellite dish and see if I can get anything."

Tom touched the pavement just as the P-wave from another aftershock arrived. "Oh shit." he exclaimed as he scrambled back into the truck. "Hang on. Here comes another one." Tom locked the doors to the truck and grabbed Judy to hold her next to him. The truck bounced and jerked to the right. It shook for a few seconds, and then relative quiet returned.

"I'm getting pretty good at detecting incoming quakes, don't you think?" He smiled, trying to make a small joke to relieve the tension. Judy just sobbed into his chest.

Tom looked out the window. People still ran about, and he could see more dust hanging over parts of the old downtown area. "More buildings must've finished falling from that last aftershock."

After a time comforting his wife, Tom opened the door and again stepped toward the back of the truck. Opening the rear door to the camper, he rummaged inside for the satellite antenna and tripod and quickly aimed it to point at the TV satellite. Reaching back inside, he moved the portable TV to the floor pointing out the door, turned it on, and located a signal. From habit he selected the **NWS** channel.

"Damn. Damn. Damn." The President of the United States pounded his fist on his desk. "Why did it have to happen this weekend? Why?" Tears clouded his eyes, and he pulled his bifocals from his head.

Jerry Worthall stood mute to one side, waiting for the anger and sorrow to pass, as he knew it would. Under the worst of tensions and calamities, President LaPorte always found a way to come back. "I'm sorry I can't tell you any more, Sir."

The President's secretary had provided sparse information about the President's daughter and her entourage, missing somewhere in the wreckage of Union Station in St. Louis. The Head of the Secret Service would provide more information as soon as possible.

"I know, Jerry. It's just something I didn't expect, that's all." He wiped his eyes with his fist. Taking a deep breath, he replaced his glasses over his eyes and looked up. "Thanks for bringing me the news. Please find some way to tell Mary our daughter may be one of the casualties of the earthquake. God knows, we're not alone in that kind of grief."

"Yes, Sir, I think she's already heard, but I'll be sure."

The President took a deep breath and turned to the solitary aide standing on the other side of the desk. "Well, back to the problem at hand. Why the hell aren't there any lines of communication into Memphis?" Ten people had responded to the President's order to immediately get in touch with authorities in the Tennessee city, but after 30 minutes of searching for a way, one aide had returned to report their lack of success.

"No, Sir, all telephone land lines, cell-phones, microwave connections, and satellite uplinks anywhere near the fault zone are nonfunctional. There is some spotty communications through the Memphis Emergency Operations

Center, but they apparently are having some major problems and are still trying to get up and running and focusing only on local emergency matters.

"We've gotten radio relays through the river network, but no direct contact has been made with the City or Shelby County mayor's offices in Memphis. All the Military, National Guard and Federal offices in and around the city are also out of touch."

"What about the satellite phones? Surely someone there has a low-sat phone we can call."

"Memphis EMA has four, but they are not answering at this point. We asked the phone company for the phone number of anyone else who lives in that area with such a phone, but they haven't started distributing them in Memphis as yet. It's not hilly enough for satellite to compete with cellular."

"What about a visitor? Can't they find someone with a satellite phone visiting the area?" The President kept searching for a way to talk to Memphis.

"We didn't think of that. We'll ask." The aide hurried off to work on the problem.

"Damn, why don't the local governments get onto these things faster. They need this new technology for times like this."

Jerry looked up and answered, "Sir, they can't afford it. Remember, we told FEMA to cut off funding for such discretionary items two years ago when it was decided that the newer estimates of earthquake risk for the New Madrid did not warrant the mitigation expense."

President LaPorte looked at his companion of many years and frowned. "You're right, of course. We've been cutting back and cutting back. Guess frugality comes home to roost at times like this."

JQ's head hurt. His legs hurt. His chest hurt, and every breath he took seemed to be half dust. It grew hotter and hotter as time passed. He awoke into semi-consciousness and once again realized that he hurt too much to have died. "Oh shit, my leg's bent too far. God, that hurts."

Using his upper shoulder he struggled to push aside the walls of the cave in which he lay. "Hey, something moved." Overjoyed, he wriggled forward on his side under the layer of debris that rested on top of him. He felt the edge of what might be his desk and found a large space under the object. He squirmed and pushed his head into the void.

Another aftershock rolled through Memphis. "Oh, shit. Stop that shaking. Please stop." He screamed. Ominous wrenching sounds of the shifting debris pummeled his ears. With his head shielded in part by the desk, he was protected from some of the heavier bricks and pieces of roofing that found room to fall in the shaking as everything shuffled and resettled.

His coffin grew even tighter, but room remained to breathe, though horrendous dust again filled the space. He gasped. He pushed his nose into his shirt trying to filter clean air from the grime.

When JQ opened his eyes as the dust subsided, he realized a faint glow came from somewhere. "Hey, there's light." It outlined nearby broken edges. Blinking his eyes, he saw bits of debris around him. He moved his hand up his chest and groped in the semi-darkness.

With his right hand he felt the parts of his body he could reach, rubbing arms and neck and torso. He found bruises, but there did not appear to be any major injuries. He felt nothing cut or wet with blood. But when he started to pull his leg under him, he realized a fallen object still trapped his foot.

Searching in the gloom, he discovered he lay in a small cavity lined with bits of ceiling and flooring. His hopes soared. "Maybe there's a way out back there." Struggling harder and harder, he hyperventilated from anticipation as more adrenaline coursed through his body, finally lapsing once again into semi-consciousness.

It took several minutes before JQ calmed enough to again think rational thoughts. Then he listened. He heard what sounded like a person's voice, very faint. In time he became sure he heard the sound of another human being.

His loud yells filled the small space. "Here I am. I'm trapped in here. Look in this pile. Help me. Help."

Outside, the sun lit the three story high pile of bricks and timbers. Thirty-five minutes after the shaking had ended, people climbed over and around the bricks, looking and listening, lifting broken timbers and then dropping them.

"This here's what's left of the old Walker Hotel. They was doing renovation, and there ain't nobody in it," commented one of the searchers. "Nobody lived or worked here yet. It was empty, thank God. Come on, there used to be some apartments up top of this next building."

With scarcely a backward glance the searchers moved on to the next pile of rubble, hurried along by yet another shrug of the earth.

Listening again, JQ heard nothing more. He yelled and listened and yelled again and again until his throat hurt. When he listened, he heard nothing but the continued hissing of gas escaping from a broken pipe somewhere in the building.

His mood plunged. Hope became despair. Trapped. No one knew where he was. Now he realized he could die in this place, and no one would know about it. He started to pull on things around him, trying to find a way out from under the pile of rubble.

Another aftershock pinned him down again and shifted the pile of debris around some more. He waited a few moments to quiet his pounding heart, and then started digging again. There must be some way out of the wreckage, if he could but find it before the continuing shock waves sealed the mound of bricks and wood into a coffin around him.

Marion Roberts had made his way through the littered streets to near Winchester Park, where he parked his car, still half a mile from the downtown City Offices. He wanted to see his offices at the City Building before heading for the Emergency Operations Center out on Flicker. He realized there would be no way for him to reach downtown by auto. He could see an elevated portion of I-40 askew on the ground two blocks south.

He walked alone amongst the wreckage. He saw people pulling victims from the ruins. Many injured lay on the sidewalks. Already the rescuers separated the dead from the living, laying them side-by-side on the street, awaiting the arrival of some kind of funeral hearse.

Throngs gathered outside St. Johns Baptist Hospital, hoping to find help, but the building lay broken in half and smoke poured from the two upper floors. A triage area had been set up in the parking lot.

A block over on Poplar he could see the crumbled ruins of the city jail. "Oh God, any inmates that could must have just walked away." He shuddered and looked around to see if anyone dressed in orange or drab was near.

Marion continued past the crumbled stands of the baseball park, coming to the grass lawn in front of the Memphis City Building, the building that housed his offices. He stopped and stared in consternation.

All the columns supporting the ornate overhangs of both the City Building and the Federal Building had failed. The outer 20 feet around the perimeter of the City Building supported by the sparse columns must have dropped first, stripping the building of its outer garments, leaving it standing like a naked woman.

He turned and stared down the Mid-America Mall, Memphis's beautiful job of urban renewal that had turned downtown Main Street into a promenade of fine new and old structures, flanking a tree-lined brick walkway. Down the middle of old Main Street ran the steel tracks used by the city's early twentieth-century trolleys.

Anchored to the north by the new Convention Center built on the side of the bluffs alongside the six-story City Building and the eleven-story Federal Building with their common Plaza of Flags, the Mall swept south to where it opened onto historic Beale Street. Fourteen side streets offered shopping opportunities in a variety of boutiques and cafes for the tourists who strolled from one end to the other.

"Main Street looks like a ghost town in a Texas gully," he mumbled in astonishment. Marion could see buildings on the west side of the street that had been cleaved in half by an earth slide toward the river. Most structures on the east side had simply crumbled to the ground. The bricks and trolley rails of the promenade had been ripped from the ground.

Screams and cries howled from the canyon between the two rows of broken buildings. Smoke streamed from some piles of rubble down the street of ruins, and flames burst from several. Marion could see people wandering in the valley of bricks, not knowing what to do. Others dug into the piles of debris that had fallen into the street or ventured into the remains of those buildings with parts still standing.

A steady stream of people stumbled toward the open plaza before the City Building, out of the rubble of the Main Street Promenade. Most showed signs of injury. A few policemen tried to direct them to open areas.

Marion walked toward the wreckage of the City Building, evaluating the damage. "The bluff must have carved off along a line running north and south, right through the City Building." He could see a portion of the building resting on top of the bluff at the edge of the break. The landslide had left the front one-quarter of the City structure level with the plaza and dropped the back three-quarters downward at least three stories.

"My God, the Seismic offices two floors down must be under another 40 feet of rubble. I told the Mayor we should have moved."

Marion could see where the earth slide cut south through the heart of the downtown district, tearing the buildings just west of Main Street in half. He could not see how far the slide extended south, but it must go for several blocks. Buildings no longer obscured the view of the Mississippi River from the plaza. The scene reminded him of pictures in his office from the earth slide in Anchorage in 1964, but today the scale looked so much larger.

Shaking his head and squeezing his eyes to clear them of tears, Marion turned his back to the west and looked for help. He pulled his identification badge from his pocket and approached one of the policemen helping people as they came up Main Street.

"Officer, I'm Marion Roberts of the Department of Seismic Safety. Are there any other city officials around?"

"No, sir. You're the first city-man I've seen or even talked to. We're not even getting an answer from Headquarters on Poplar. One of the mounted figured he could get through with his motorcycle and headed down that way to see what was the matter, but he said he was going by his home to check his family first."

"Do you know if anyone made it out of the City Building? Is anyone trapped inside?"

The officer stared blankly at Marion through red, tear-stained eyes. "Me and three other officers were coming up from the Convention Center to start patrol. We drug a couple of people out near the front of the building, then the big aftershock hit and the back of the building dropped another ten feet. That's when the top just fell in. It sounded like there was a bunch of people trapped inside, but I don't know how many. We don't have any idea how to get them out. A lot of them have gone quiet, so I'm not sure what their status is."

"If I'm the first city officer to arrive, I guess we need to start getting some semblance of order together. Would you help me, please?" The officer looked at the badge and nodded his head.

"I'm Sergeant Phil Rowdy, Mounted Patrol. Looks like you're the man in charge until I get orders from higher up."

"Where are you sending the wounded? It looks like half of those coming up Main Street have some kind of injury."

" I've just been directing them toward St. John's."

"I'm afraid they're not going to find much in the way of service there, but it's better than here."

"I didn't know what else to do, sir. We never had a training exercise for something as bad as this."

Chapter 29: Searching For Help

Alex stopped Tina's car to talk with the truckers gathered around the fueling station looking for ways they could extricate their rigs from the fallen canopy of the fueling shed.

"I've got a schedule to keep. I've got to get this thing out of here," said one of the drivers to the mechanic who walked around picking up the new tires that had bounced out of the tire barn.

"Well, there ain't nothing I kin do about it. Until we get someone in here with a welding torch, you're stuck under that shed." He continued his search for more tires.

George, the old man who washed the dishes, still wore his greasy apron and walked around the burned out shell of the café wringing his hands. "Tina, the phones don't work. How can I call the sheriff and tell him about the fire and Cookie being dead?"

"Don't worry about it, George. The sheriff knows we've had a problem, just like everyone else in the county. He'll get here as soon as he can. Alex and I have to take Chris to the hospital in Caruthersville, and if we see some law officer we'll tell him he needs to call Arkansas and ask someone to come up here."

"Well, if you say so, but I sure hope he don't take too long. In this weather, I don't know how long it'll be before Cookie starts smelling." George walked off to sit in his car and smoke a cigarette and wait.

As Alex drove east on Stateline Road beside the open farmland, they saw more signs of the destructive power of the earthquake, but nothing as awful as what they had witnessed at New Simon. Trees lay twisted on the ground, and utility poles tilted to one side or the other. The open fields were wet with piles of sand and debris covering much of their surface. In the patchy forested groves alongside the road they could not tell, but they supposed it would be the same but hidden by the greenery of the brush that covered the land.

Driving the car, Alex could feel how the earth had been heaved about. Though still passable, the road surface pitched back and forth, and cracks had broken the asphalt in many places. Sand blows had covered portions of the road and filled the surrounding fields. Everything smelled of decay.

They passed an old barn that lay in a heap on the ground. "Alex, it looks like a tornado hit it, but all the boards are laying there together. It seems strange how it tore everything up."

She turned and checked when Chris moaned from where he lay on the back seat. "I think he's resting easier, but he doesn't look good."

From time to time the earth rocked again as more aftershocks pounded the land. Some temblors rocked the car enough that Alex came to a stop.

He looked at his watch as they turned onto the road to the jump school. "It's 10:20. Would you believe it's only been three-quarters of an hour since the quake hit."

Tina said, "I know, but it seems like it happened ages ago."

Alex did not see the airplane anywhere about. The hanger lay on the ground beside the tilted tool shed. Pulling Tina's car in beside his SUV, he got out and walked up to the shed. Inside, he saw Harry, the mechanic, playing solitaire on the workbench with an old dirty deck of cards.

"Harry. You okay?"

"Hey, Alex. Good to see you. I didn't hear you drive up. You must've made your jump okay, but I don't see your parachute. You know if you don't bring it back, you have to pay for it."

"Yeah, well at this point it's buried in a pile of mud in the middle of a field up by the truck stop. We'll work it out. Where's Michael and the plane?"

"I don't know. You guys left and then the quake hit, I hung on for dear life. When it was over, Michael radioed he was heading somewhere else to land. I haven't heard from him since. The phones are dead, so I don't know how he'll call."

Alex shook his head. "Well, I don't think he found anything any better than here for a long ways. We just had a really big earthquake, and it tore hell out of everything. NASTY'S Cafe burned down, and there's some freeway overpasses that fell." Turning to introduce Tina, he explained her presence. "She used to work at NASTY'S, but she doesn't have a job anymore."

"So whatcha going to do now?"

"We're taking a friend to the hospital in Caruthersville. I'm going to switch him over to my SUV since it has four-wheel drive. Figured we'd stop at Cooter along the way and check out what's happened to everyone else. You want to come along with us?"

"Michael gave me a ride this morning, and he has the keys to his car. I better wait here for him to come back. That way I can watch the place."

"You're welcome to come, but that's up to you. We'll leave the keys in Tina's car just in case. You can borrow it if you want."

Alex and Tina moved Chris to the back of the SUV on Alex's old sleeping bag. Chris remained semi-conscious and moaned on occasion, but no more blood flowed from his head wound.

Alex pulled out of the parking lot and headed toward the town of Cooter, three miles north. Tina tried the car radio but found only static on both the AM and FM bands. "Even WSM is off the air. That's awful."

Driving up to the small bridge over Ditch Number 5, Alex slowed to a crawl, unsure whether or not the temblor had damaged the bridge over the ditch like it had the overpass on the Interstate. The bridge seemed to be okay, and he eased across it.

"Alex, look at the water in the ditch. It's a lot higher than usual and flowing really strong, away from the river."

Alex glanced down at the rapid current. "These sand boils could've put a lot of water into the ditch, but it might also mean the river levee has busted somewhere." He hurried on up the road.

As they entered the tiny town of Cooter, they saw a frame house to the right of the road sitting askew, and the old lady who lived there walking around it, shaking her head. "I want to talk to her," said Tina. Alex stopped the SUV.

Tina leaned out the open window and asked, "Hi, are you okay?"

"Oh, I'm mostly fine, but my house fell off its bricks. See there." The woman pointed a scrawny finger at the corner of the house that had moved a foot away from its brick foundation. The house tilted to the north, off its foundation in back as well. "Do you know if houses can be put back on their bricks?" she asked in a plaintive voice.

"I don't know, Ma'am, but I suppose so—if someone has the right tools. I don't know how to do that though. But is everything else okay?"

"Oh yes, I'll be okay. Can't say that about some of the others in town. Three houses burned down, and the water tower fell over onto the hardware store. Killed Jerry Peterson right on the spot. Don't know what the town will do about the water tower. I have some water in my hot water tank, but there ain't no water pressure anymore, and I don't know when we'll have any."

Tina remembered what she had seen at the small bridge. "I should warn you, we saw the water running really fast in Ditch 5, so there may be a break in the levees. You might want to watch out for a flood."

"Land sakes. We don't need no flood." The woman shook her head. "This earthquake is enough trouble."

Tina gave the woman her condolences and turned back with a look of dismay for Alex. "She doesn't understand, does she?"

Driving on Main Street into town, Alex said, "Gee, every one of these business buildings suffered terrible damage. Anything built of brick or just old is down." Only a few frame structures remained upright with any semblance of order.

As the woman had described, the water tower had collapsed to its side, and its legs lay through the remains of a two-story store. An old blanket covered what appeared to be a body beside the fallen wall.

"Hey, there's a mini-mart. Let's see if we can get some first aid supplies for Chris." Tina pointed to the remains of the town's fuel stop.

Alex drove around the concrete blocks and lumber in the road into the parking lot. As they stepped out of the SUV, they could see someone moving about inside the darkened building through the broken front windows.

"Hi, there," called Tina. "Are you open for business?"

The girl inside looked up from her job of picking up the bottles and cans strewn about the floor. "Sure, but this place is a mess. Watch out for the broken glass."

"Can we get some first aid supplies and maybe something to eat and drink? We have an injured friend we're taking into Caruthersville."

"You'll just have to pick it up yourself from the floor. And you gotta pay cash. We don't have no way to take credit cards with the phones and power out. And I can't give you any fuel. The pumps won't run with no electricity. I already tried that."

The travelers searched through the unlit store and picked out a selection of food packages they could take with them. Alex found some bottled water and picked up three six packs. They checked their resources and found a total of $35 between them. "Here you go. How much?"

The girl laughed. "You know, I never did learn how to add in my head, and the cash register don't work. You just add it up and tell me how much it comes to."

Alex looked over their purchases and counted. "Looks like about eight dollars and change." He handed her a ten-dollar bill.

The girl stripped two dollars off a roll of bills she pulled from her jeans, added the ten, and stuffed it back into her pocket. "Cain't get the cash register open neither. Call it eight even. You know, the world is just falling apart."

As they returned to the SUV, Tina looked around and then at Alex. "I think anytime we get near where there are a lot of people , we're going to find things a real mess." She shook her head. "So, are we heading over to the river?"

"I'd like to, just to see how the levees are doing, but we'd have to cross Ditch 5 again, and I'd rather not do that." Alex turned west toward the Interstate. Chris moaned again as another aftershock rocked the SUV from side to side.

"I'm getting some chatter on simplex at 146.652 megahertz, but nothing from any of the radio repeater stations. Guess the earthquake wiped out every two-meter repeater in the area. When I tried the CB radio in the truck, it was so full of garbage with people screaming at each other, I couldn't get through at all." Tom clipped the two-meter handheld radio back onto his belt and turned to the policeman standing beside him. "What do you want me to do?"

"You can set up an information center here for the people in this neighborhood. You have a usable radio, so you can get information back and forth to us if it's important. The police are monitoring that frequency for emergency messages. You also have that satellite TV, so you can keep people around here informed about what's going on in the outside world. Just call us if something vital to us comes out.

"And screen the refugees coming down from the bluffs. If it looks like someone is healthy, then send them back up the bluffs into the city to volunteer. If they appear to be hurt or in shock, just have them sit down and take it easy in the park. Treat what injuries you can and call to report the serious ones. We'll send a doctor down here, if we ever find one available."

"I'll do the best I can," Tom assured the officer. The policeman threw his leg over his motorcycle and headed south on Riverside, weaving around the debris littering the pavement.

Judy stuck her head out the camper door, raised her left eyebrow, and looked at her husband with mock admiration. "So now, you're the big man on the block."

"Judy, we've got to do what we can to help. We're in this mess just like all the people who live here." Tom turned to clear some debris from around the truck. Just then came the sound of ringing from the low-sat telephone inside the truck cab.

"I'd forgotten about the phone. Maybe someone in California is wondering how we are." Tom reached in and took the phone. Pressing the TALK button he answered, "This is Tom Fox. Who's calling?"

A strange voice asked, "Mr. Fox, are you currently near Memphis?"

"Why yes, we just arrived and found ourselves in the middle of a big earthquake. Who's this?"

"My name is Jerry Worthall. I'm the personal secretary to President LaPorte. Please hold just a moment, sir. The President of the United States wants to speak with you." The line went silent, and Tom pulled the phone away from his ear and looked at it as if it were crazy.

Judy asked, "Who's calling? Someone I know?"

Tom shook his head. "No, some kook says the President wants to talk to me."

A new voice came over the phone, "Mr. Fox, this is President Frank LaPorte. We've been searching for some means of communication with Memphis, and your low-sat phone is the only personal link we've found so far. Are you in Memphis right now?"

Still incredulous, Tom asked, "Come on, is this really the President of the United States?"

"Yes, it is. Now please, there's a lot to do. Are you in Memphis?"

Recognizing the serious voice of the caller, he said, "Yes, Sir, my wife and I are parked just below downtown next to the river in Lee Park. We came here in our camper to visit our daughter."

"Good, I remember that area. Now I want to talk to a city or county official in Memphis. Would you please contact them for me and have them come to call me from your phone?"

"Sure, I can do that. I have two-meter radio as well, and the police are monitoring a simplex channel we agreed on."

"Great. Here is the number they are to call." Tom pulled his ballpoint pen from his pocket and wrote the number on the palm of his hand as the President dictated it. "Now, may I speak with your wife while you contact the Memphis authorities?" The President's voice had a calming and strengthening effect on Tom.

"Sure you can, here she is." He turned to his wife. "Judy, the President wants to talk to you."

Judy stood with her hands on her hips. "Tom, this joke has gone far enough. Who are you really talking to?"

"Judy, take the phone. I have work to do." He placed the telephone in her hand and moved away to use his two-meter handheld radio.

"This is Judy Fox. Now, who is this?" As she listened her expression changed from skepticism to awe, and then she started to describe to the President and his staff all she could see of the damage in Memphis.

A few minutes later Tom tapped her on the shoulder and said, "Tell him the Mayor is on the way in from the suburbs and should be down within the hour to call him."

Judy nodded, passed the message along, and continued her litany. For the first time, the President received an unfiltered report directly from the heart of the earthquake zone.

Alex turned north on I-55, hoping the overpasses ahead remained in place. He and Tina could see the smoke rising in the distance, above Caruthersville.

Though displacement of several sections of the roadbed made driving difficult, nothing serious enough to stop the SUV appeared until they came to a lake stretching across the roadway. Water covered the highway for at least a quarter of a mile ahead, and Tina shouted a warning. "Alex, be careful. You don't know how deep it is or what's under the water."

"I think it's okay. The highway runs right next to some catfish ponds along here, and my bet is they've slopped out of their banks. Look, there's one of the fish swimming across the pavement." Alex dropped into four-wheel drive and moved with care up the road through the six inches of water. The road remained intact to the dry section beyond.

As they approached the interchange with I-255, they saw a line of cars stopped at the top, just short of a fallen overpass. People stood along the edge of the abyss, looking down at some activity on the road below. Alex turned to the right onto I-255 and drove east toward the next exit off the freeway.

"We'll have to ask how to get to the hospital," he said.

As they neared the edge of town, Tina commented, "This looks like Cooter. Most everything's destroyed." Debris lay everywhere, but people had already collected some of the trash and piled it alongside the road, ready for the next run of the waste disposal trucks.

As Alex neared the major intersection at the edge of town, a deputy sheriff's car parked across the middle of the road blocked his way. The deputy walked up to Alex's side of the car. "Do you folks live here?"

"No, sir. We came up from New Simon. We have a friend we need to get to the hospital."

"If you don't live here, you can't come into town. We're having troubles with flooding downtown, and no one's allowed in. We don't want looters, and the townspeople have short trigger fingers."

"But we need to get Chris to a doctor."

The deputy stepped back and put his hand on his gun. "Sorry, you'll have to leave. It's for your own safety that you just turn around and head back where you come from. You don't want to cause trouble, now do you?"

Alex drew back and called out the window. "No, sir. We won't bother you. But can you tell us where we can find a doctor?"

"Sorry, you'll just have to go look somewhere else. I've heard all the roads are closed north of here. So turn around and leave." The deputy looked perturbed.

Alex did a tight U-turn in front of the patrol car and headed back to the freeway. Tina exploded. "How do you like that? That guy thinks he owns this place."

"Tina, that's the way it is. Everyone's starting to look out for themselves, and they don't have enough to pass around. We're strangers, so we have to get out." Alex fumed as well, but he didn't see any way around the situation in Caruthersville. "Maybe we can find help across the river in Dyersburg."

Chapter 30: Rescues Begin

President LaPorte looked over the young man Homeland Security had sent from FEMA. "Well, did you find anything to help give us a better estimate of the damage?"

"Mr. President, in 1991, FEMA funded a study entitled "*Damages and Losses from Future New Madrid Earthquakes*" at Southwest Missouri State to produce a Central U.S. Earthquake Intensity Scale map. It's still a baseline document for doing scenarios to estimate earthquake damage in the central United States."

The FEMA representative handed the President a dog-eared copy and spread before him the colorful map of the states and counties in the eastern half of the country, color-coded for expected shaking intensity from blue to red. The reddest counties marked the locale of the New Madrid Fault.

"Thank you. What does this tell us?"

"Sir, the study provides a county by county assessment of the expected level of damage for various sized earthquakes along the New Madrid. It also estimates the effects on people, the land, buildings, bridges, and utilities as a function of the level of damage." The young man coughed and pulled his tight collar away from his throat. He had not addressed the President before.

"Based on the last census and using the report's intensity scale maps, a magnitude 7.9 earthquake is expected to result in the total collapse of 1,600 bridges and almost 69,000 commercial buildings. Another 1,500 bridges and 350,000 buildings will be severely damaged."

He coughed again. "Five million people will be displaced from their damaged or destroyed homes. The analysis predicts 20,000 plus fatalities and over 100,000 injuries. However, taking into account the flooding we are experiencing, these figures are expected to climb to 60,000 fatalities and 300,000 injuries with more than six million displaced."

"My God, man, you can't be serious. The reports I have been handed so far only talk about fatalities …" The President searched for the note on his desk. "Here it is, in the 8,000 range. That's the total of the estimates received so far from the Governors. Of course, they did say the numbers might rise. But in the World Trade Center on 9-11 the first estimates were way, way too high. I expected these to go down."

The young man fidgeted and looked embarrassed. "Mr. President, these numbers are consistent with other studies that have been made but not made publici. We didn't want to frighten the populace about what seemed to be such a low probability event. And remember, this is based on a scientific study, not the actual numbers."

"Which do you believe?" The President's piercing eyes bored into those of the FEMA rep.

"Sir, we have so far been able to contact less than a third of the local Emergency Operation Centers in the most stricken region. Given the state of communications at this point, I think the report provides an accurate picture of what to expect."

The President leaned back into his chair. His shoulders slumped. He chewed on his pencil eraser. "I'm afraid you're right. Sixty-thousand dead. I'm afraid those numbers are what we are going to have to deal with." He slammed his fist down on the desk. "Damn."

More bits of light broke the darkness of the trap where he lay. JQ could identify the objects around him. His head rested beneath his desk, and he could see the open lower left drawer. Realization and memory came to JQ. "Wonder if my pistol's still there?" He reached up and over the edge to feel around. At the tip of his fingers he felt the cold metal of the pistol's barrel. He strained and clawed at the gun, trying to pull it within his reach.

"Come on baby, get a little closer. Come on." He twisted his back to move his arm further into the drawer, and then he felt the barrel move away. "God-dammit. If I had you I could fire shots and people would know I'm here. Come on." He strained farther, but to no avail. Now the pistol had shifted out of his reach.

The straining and twisting began to hurt his back, and he relaxed to roll to the other side. In that position he could see where a fallen ceiling beam had broken the cabinet beside the couch. Its skewed door lay open and inside he saw the corner of the briefcase he had stored there yesterday morning. "No shit. Here I am trapped in a building right next to $100,000." JQ laughed in cynical humor.

He reached in and pulled the shiny leather briefcase from the cabinet, patting it lovingly on its side. Then the debris settled closer around him as the earth shook again.

"Pamela, how did you get here? What happened to you?" Marion looked at the young woman in amazement. Covered with dirt, she looked like she must have been in a fight. The tear in her baggy sweatshirt and the back of her scratched and bloody hand confirmed the violence.

"I drove through hell part way in, then had to walk the rest of the way. I came the last ten blocks from over near the University and by the jail. It's getting very mean out there, Marion. A couple of gang-members who used to reside in the jail decided they wanted my body and my clothes, and I had to kick some ass to get through."

Pamela sat down on the nearby stone planter and rubbed the back of her arm. "I forgot a lot of what I learned from the marines, but not everything. Boy, am I out of shape." She stretched her back in obvious pain.

"Should I ask how the opposition fared?" Marion smiled at the thought of thugs tangling with Pamela.

"Oh, they probably won't speak to anybody for the next week or two, at least until their lips grow back together." She asked, "How are we doing here? Who's made it in? Do you have any reports on what happened?"

Marion took a deep breath and tried to give a calm answer. "I'm the first one here. A couple of other city employees showed up in the last few minutes, and I directed them to go to the Emergency Operations Center to set up their functions. Can you believe it, they didn't know where to go.

"As you can see the seismic offices are out of commission. There's no power, so my laptop's running on battery and about to go out. The phones are kaput, and the 800 MHz system trashed after the transmitter towers fell. I'm borrowing a hand-held radio from the police when I need it, but we need to find our own radio link so we can communicate with other city officials."

"Marion, what about Glenda? Yesterday, she said something about coming in this morning to catch up. Have you seen her?"

"No, I haven't seen her around." He looked at the City Building. "If she's in there, there's not much chance."

"Any reports on what happened? Where's the epicenter, and how big was it?"

"Not sure. A guy from the Water District said a fellow on short-wave radio heard reports of destruction as far away as St. Louis, Nashville, and Little Rock. From what I felt and what I see around here, the New Madrid fault obviously experienced a great earthquake. Damage is characteristic of intensity IX and X."

"Have you heard anything from other parts of the Memphis area?"

"We've been listening to scattered reports on hand-helds from the police and fire department. There's massive destruction all over Memphis. We can see the high-rise buildings are down along the bluffs. Nothing's left standing on Beale Street, but that's about what I'd expect. There are a number of fires and more are starting. Water pressure's dropping or gone everywhere." Marion's voice cracked. "This is the big one we've been talking about. The whole city's really in trouble."

A policeman walked up holding out his hand-held radio and interrupted Marion. "Mr. Roberts. I have a call on the radio asking for you, but I can't figure out who it is. It's coming in on one of the internal frequencies, one of those we use for internal security."

Marion took the radio and put it to his ear. Thumbing the transmit button he spoke, "This is Marion Roberts. Who's calling?"

A small voice whispered in response. "Mr. Roberts. This is Glenda. Help me. Please, help me."

Marion's mouth dropped open. "Glenda, where are you?" He turned the radio away from his ear so Pamela could hear the other side of the conversation.

"I'm in the office, and that earthquake crack came through here just like the girls in Finance said it would. It came right across the middle of the room."

"Glenda, listen to me. Exactly where in the office are you? Can you see anything and tell me?"

"Yes. I'm up against the wall in the filing room farthest away from the hall. The emergency lights came on so I can see. The filing cabinets are keeping the ceiling from falling on me."

"What else do you see?"

"The crack is about ten feet away from me. It goes across the floor and right up both walls. The whole other side of the building dropped down when it was shaking. After it stopped I grabbed the radio that belonged to Fred, the guard at the front desk. His floor dropped down so he was even with me for a while. A column fell on him, and he was dead. Then the ground shook some more, and his floor went even further down. Now there's nothing but broken concrete on the other side of the crack."

"Glenda, just stay right where you are. Hang in there. We'll start a search party on its way to reach you. You'll be safe."

"Please, Mr. Roberts, please save me."

"We'll do the best we can, Glenda. Now just sit quietly and rest while we get to work." He put the radio down and took a deep breath.

As Pamela listened to the litany of Glenda's plight, her shoulders slumped. She shook her head. "I know Glenda's going to die." She started crying. Marion grabbed her shoulders.

"Hey, stop that. We'll get Glenda out okay." He shook her a bit more then pulled out his handkerchief and handed it to her.

She wiped her eyes and said, "I'm sorry, Marion. It's just so crazy."

"I know. We just have to work together now. Here, you talk with Glenda and keep her calm while I organize a search team. And after a bit she's going to have to turn off the radio for a while so she doesn't use up the batteries. Come on, let's get to work and get your mind off morbid stuff like dying."

"…and now this news report from Nashville. There has been substantial damage in the older district of Nashville with many broken windows in the financial district. The Ryman Auditorium, original home of the Grand Ole Opry, is burning. Authorities are asking everyone to stay near their homes. Turn off all the main gas shutoff valves and stay away from damaged buildings."

Tom looked behind him. A mixed crowd of people gathered, staring at the small TV screen. He explained, "I have **NWS** on my satellite TV."

"What happened, man?" asked a stout black fellow in a torn tee shirt and shorts.

"I'm just finding out, but I believe we had a gigantic earthquake on the New Madrid Fault just west of here," Tom answered. "I'm hoping to get more information from the TV." He pulled the portable set on the floor nearer the door so more of those gathered around could see and hear.

On screen Harold Owens shuffled a few papers and then looked back into the camera. "We now have confirmation from the USGS that at 9:34:09 this morning, local time, a major earthquake began on the New Madrid Seismic Zone under the Arkansas and Missouri border near the small town of New Simon. It extended southwest toward Marked Tree, Arkansas, and northeast toward Tiptonville, Tennessee, for a distance of over 60 miles. The earthquake lasted more than 20 seconds and is now estimated to be a magnitude 7.9 earthquake. It is the largest earthquake to strike this region since 1812."

A chorus of comments swelled from the gathering, and Tom called out, "Hey, keep it quiet so everyone can hear."

"… felt as far away as New England, Atlanta, Florida, New Orleans, Texas, Denver, and Wyoming. Major damage is reported in New Orleans, St. Louis, Nashville, Little Rock and numerous smaller areas. There are reports of almost total destruction from the region around Memphis and to the west along the trace of the fault in Arkansas and Missouri, but very little information is available because all power and communications have been lost in that region."

"You mean that was an earthquake?" asked one incredulous woman. "We don't have no earthquakes here. Our city councilman told me not to worry. It jest don't happen here." She shook her head in denial and still mumbling to herself, turned to walk away. "We don't have no earthquakes here. We jest don't."

Mel started the engine of his big truck and pulled the trailer away from the broken warehouse. Less than half of the front walls still stood in the cloud of dust. He could see in the rear-view mirrors piles of boxes and containers covering the dock. The roof had caved in on top of the materials stored within the building. Men staggered out of the building from time to time and dropped off the dock to the pavement below.

More dust clouded the air as the walls and roof sections crumbled and settled in the aftershocks that followed from time to time. Thin tendrils of smoke appeared from several heaps of rubbish back of the warehouse near the estuary. The tendrils grew into plumes then to columns, the columns into towering, billowing pillars of smoke.

"Breaker. Breaker. Who's out there? Come back. Come back." The voice from the CB sounded frantic.

Mel picked up his mike and keyed it as he spoke. "This is Big Mel, Breaker. I hear you okay. What's your twenty?"

"Big Mel, this is Nashville Jack. I'm at the Malling Warehouse on President's Island. Everything around me has fallen down and there's some fires starting to burn. Where're you, and what's it like there?"

"Jack, I'm up at Consolidated Freight and Barges at the end of Dock just down from Channel Street. You must be down between Channel and Harbor on Wharf, if I remember right. Most of the warehouses around here came down in the big shake. I've pulled my rig away from the wreckage. There's smoke starting to show up around me, too. My rig's still okay and running. How's yours?"

"Mel, my rig's running okay, but that's a good idea to pull away from the broken buildings. I'm doing the same. What d'ya think? What do we do now?"

The sound of another frantic voice came over the airwaves. "Hey, this is Charlie O. My trailer's caught under the warehouse overhang at Wally's on Harbor."

Mel shook his head. "Charlie, this is Big Mel. You better see if you can jerk it clear. Otherwise, unhitch the trailer right now. You may need to get out of there quick."

"Roger that. Thanks, Big Mel."

"Nashville, I think we should maybe try to get out of here. What're you carrying?"

"I was getting ready to unload canned fruit from California. Why?"

"Well, I'm just thinking that whatever we have in our trailers may soon be the only supplies around these parts. I just got in carrying a load of medical supplies myself. Hey, Nashville, seems to me this smoke's getting thicker."

Ten minutes had passed since the earthquake ended. Suddenly a tremendous explosion ripped through the heart of the chemical complex on Treasure Island in the middle of the estuary. Mel felt the tractor-trailer lurch forward and to the side from the blast. Looking into his rear-view mirrors he could see an immense black cloud filled with flashes of orange and red flame rising into the sky from the estuary.

At the warehouse where Mel had docked his truck, the backside of the building opened to the waters for barge access. The blast blew down the remains of the warehouse, and with the building down, Mel's rig now lay exposed to all the fury and heat that blew across the water.

The cloud of smoke covered the sky. It grew darker and darker. Mel keyed the mike again. "Holy shit. That must've been everything on Treasure Island or something in the channel between here and Riverside Park. Nashville, are you okay after that?"

"Mel, that fire's starting to burn my truck. It's too damned hot." Mel could hear the strain in Nashville's voice.

"Nash, get the hell out of there. Head back to Harbor then north. I'll meet you there. We gotta get off this island before the rest of this complex blows to smithereens."

Already Mel could feel the heat from the flames through the side glass. He could see the paint peeling from the hood of his truck in front of him. Reving the big diesel engine, he threw the tractor into gear and headed across the warehouse lot toward the gate. Behind him through the dust and smoke he could see several other rigs starting to head the same way.

Turning left on Dock Road, Mel headed away from the water. At Channel he saw the railroad crossing bars were down and the red lights flashing. "Now what's happening?" Nothing moved on the tracks. He keyed the mike again. "Nashville, I'm at Channel. The railroad bars are down, but the only thing I can see is an engine on its side about 100 yards north. Damned gates must be running on battery power."

"Mel, I'm turning right on Harbor. Yeah, the train gates were down here too, so I just drove right through them. Didn't seem to be the right time to wait for them to go back up."

Taking Nashville's suggestion, Mel gunned the engine of his tractor and plowed through the gates, pushing them to the side.

A group of people had gathered around an automobile that had crashed off the road at the intersection with Harbor, tending to the injured on the ground. Mel waved but pulled out into the intersection and turned right. Back down the road he could see another rig coming toward him. "Nashville, I just turned onto Harbor. Is that you behind me?"

"Yeah, Mel. Coming up right behind you. I got a couple of others behind me, so we're starting a convoy. Looks like you got the lead. Where're we heading?"

"I'm all for ditching this island. With all the chemical plants around the estuary, I figure there's going to be some horrendous fires here. They just haven't had time to get started."

The convoy grew as Mel continued on the road to the north. A quarter of a mile away from the estuary the heat lessened, and he could see well enough through the smoke to navigate the big rig. Several cars and rigs had been thrown into the chain link fence alongside the road. Some of the electrical wires hung down from those utility poles still standing. Mel drove right through the wires and around the wrecked cars up the main road until he came to a halt behind a line of stopped cars and trucks.

He called on the CB. "Hey up there. This is Big Mel heading north on Harbor. I'm trying to get to the causeway. What's the holdup?"

A gruff voice came over the airways. "Big Mel, your journey's over. Harbor Road's closed. The Jack Carley Causeway has collapsed into the mud. There ain't no other way off this island. Ain't none of us a'going anywhere."

CHAPTER 31: DON'T LET YOUR GUARD DOWN

In the TV studio, Sherry Kent tilted her head to the side, listening to the tiny speaker in her ear, "I understand that we are now ready to show a live video feed from a remote camera crew in Cape Girardeau, Missouri. Tim Pacino is there and provides this live report. Tim?"

A face view of Tim appeared on the screen and he began speaking. "Sherry, this is Tim Pacino reporting for **NWS** from the crumbling banks of the Mississippi River in Cape Girardeau, Missouri. Forty-five minutes ago, this entire television crew experienced one of the most awesome events we could ever imagine. We're just happy to be alive after all that violence. Even now from time to time I can feel more shaking going on.

"We are standing in Missouri Park, atop the bluffs, two blocks from the levee wall that formerly held the river back from this town." The camera panned around to show a small city park, full of people standing around, holding onto one another. Tree limbs littered the ground and one tall cottonwood had fallen, pulling its roots from the black earth below.

"This seems to be the safest place at the present time, even though some of these trees have taken a beating and the courthouse has fallen. Buildings of downtown Cape Girardeau along the riverfront have almost been totally destroyed by this gigantic earthquake, and are now flooded by the encroaching waters."

The camera zoomed out to show scenes of the levee wall, the river, the town. "You can see destruction all around us. The historic courthouse just up the hill lies in a crumbled heap, and we can see that several buildings on Main Street and elsewhere have toppled to the ground, in part or entirely, including the landmark KAPE-TV offices. Most electrical and telephone wires have fallen from the poles, and many of the poles are broken or leaning.

"There is a growing crowd of people gathering in this park and in the parking lots to get away from the buildings. They are afraid of what might fall upon them, and from time to time you can hear the sounds of falling buildings coming from the town. A few brave souls are venturing around the fallen buildings, looking and listening for people who might be trapped."

Tim wiped his forehead and then put the handkerchief to his eyes and his mouth, struggling to control his emotions. "The earthquake lasted more than a minute. The crew and I were standing next to the banks of the river at that time filming the local fishing derby for our St. Louis station.

"During the shaking parts of the floodwall dropped into the water. It looked and felt like the whole front block of the town would slide into the river. That was when we all high-tailed it back to this park as fast as we could. Luckily, our TV truck was parked partway up this hill, so it remained operational, though we initially lost contact with the satellite."

Sherry broke in, "Tim, what can you tell us about the condition of the river and the levees there at Cape Girardeau?"

TIm took a deep breath. "Sherry, the river here is several feet above flood stage. We're above the river where we stand, and we can see the levees on the far side. It's too far away to be sure, but the tree line on the other side appears to have slumped in many places. It is hard to tell if there is significant flooding. On this side of the river the levees and lands next to the river have sagged toward the river, and there's significant flooding along the old riverfront.

"The river itself is still very choppy and unsettled. During the most vigorous shaking we saw water wash part way up the banks from the waves rushing across the water in all directions. I can see boats on the river that are still moving along, but they seem to be moving very slowly, very cautiously. Several boats docked downstream were pitched up on shore or torn loose from their moorings. The riverfront area is a mess.

"Listen, Sherry, we can hear people calling from across the street. I don't know if it's someone trapped or one of the searchers calling for help. I need to take my camera crew into the town to get some close-up shots of the damage and to interview some of the people there. Let me get back to you later."

"Thank you, Tim. We will indeed come back to you soon for an update on the status of Cape Girardeau."

Sherry looked into the camera, "That was Tim Pacino in Cape Girardeau, reporting live on damage along the Mississippi River. Scenes like this must be happening all around the countryside near the New Madrid Fault. No one alive has ever experienced an earthquake of this magnitude in this region. The devastation is immense, and it keeps growing."

NWS had completed their first 50 minutes of earthquake coverage. In that time seismographs around the world had recorded the vibrations from the earthquake, and the entire planet rang like a bell as the waves reverberated back and forth through its core.

"Come on, you guys. We gotta get outa this smoke. It'll kill us if we don't." Mel led the group of seven along the side of the road on President's Island. At least down in the drainage ditch they were protected somewhat from the intense heat of the raging fires on the estuary.

Mel stopped to catch his breath. "Now, up ahead, we're going to move over to the road. We walk along the road through the water. The levee's sunk, but it's no more than three feet deep, so long as you stay on the upriver side. The current's not too strong. Just keep your legs pressed against the railing. It's just under water but you can feel it."

He took several deep breaths. "And for God's sake, keep hold of the belt of the guy in front of you. If you drop off, you're liable to get sucked downstream by the current along with all the people behind you. So don't let go of either the belt or the railing. Got that?"

Mel had lead three groups across the channel on the sunken Harbor Road causeway, a harrowing, but necessary experience for those trying to reach safe ground in Memphis, just 200 feet away.

"Now we won't have the protection of the bank from the heat, so if you get too hot just dip your face down into the water. Don't let go. All right, everybody, line up and grab hold the belt in front of you. Nashville, you ready?" Feeling his CB buddy, the second man in the line, wrap his hand around the belt, Mel moved ahead and around the embankment, searching with his feet for the edge of the road he hoped would still be there under the muddy water.

Touching the concrete with his boot, he reached into the water up to his elbow and located the railing. He called over his shoulder to those that followed, "See where I put my hand. That's the railing. Just reach down and find it as you come to this place. Now let's go. I'll move slow to start."

One by one the men came to the launch point and found the bridge. Left hand on the railing and right hand around the belt in front of them, the troop headed across the sunken roadway into the stronger current.

"Whoa, my feet slipped out from under me," yelled Charlie O, the fifth man in line, the shortest of the group. The man in front crouched and held on to the railing while the man behind pulled the smaller Charlie back toward the railing.

"Charlie, you son-of-a-bitch, grab hold of the railing. Don't let go next time." The group continued.

As they moved out onto the crossing, they left the shadow of the embankment that shielded them from the flames. Though the fires burned 400 yards away, the intense heat blistered their faces.

Looking back at the line of trucks stopped before the sunken causeway, Mel saw several of the trucks had already started to smoke. Fire lapped up the tires on two of the trucks. The smoke from the burning rubber added to the acidity of the choking air.

Mel paused to get his breath. "Here's the hardest part—where the current is strongest. Be extra careful here," Mel called back in warning. He moved ahead, knowing that if he and the group stopped, they could be swept away by the current trying to push them into the flame-covered estuary.

"Hang tight. There's a crack in the pavement about here. You'll feel it with your feet. It's two feet wide, so you can just step over it. Don't worry."

Yard by yard the group moved across the channel. They tired from fighting the current trying to push them away from the railing, shoving across their legs and feet. Mel kept moving ahead.

Without warning, a tremendous explosion blew from behind them. A flash brighter than the sun scorched their backs. Their ears rang from the smash of the blast. Mel turned and looked back. Something in the line of trucks had exploded big time, and he could see debris falling from the cloud above. He yelled, "Quick, both hands on the railing and drop down into the water up to your necks. Get down, quick, but don't let go the railing." He dropped into the water as flaming pieces of the truck started to fall around them, sizzling in the water as they hit.

"What the shit was that?" asked one of the group.

A second offered an explanation. "I was carrying a load of fertilizer, ammonium nitrate. Maybe it got too hot."

The rain of fire ended, but the flaming trucks behind them added to the heat blistering the backs their necks.

"Hey, Mel, the last two guys are gone," came the call from Charlie O. Mel stood and looked back, then to the south. Twenty yards away he saw two frantic men swimming against the current, trying to return to the railing. Though the current flowed less than two miles per hour, they made no headway against it to reach safety. One grabbed the other's shoulder for support, dunking him beneath the water. The five that remained could hear their sounds of panic. Nothing could be done to help.

"Come on now. We've got to get to the other side. Grab the belts and let's go." He reached for the hand behind him to guide it to his belt, and then bent forward to push on through the water toward Memphis and safety on the bank ahead.

Alex turned south onto I-255 toward Tennessee. Even with no traffic, he kept his speed low as he checked the roadway. The highway, built on a raised earthen embankment, had slumped in numerous places.

To the east he could see the waters of the Mississippi River flooding the area between the levees and the highway. "There's part of the flood that's coming in. The levees below Caruthersville must have failed. That'll back water up into the town."

Alex looked ahead at the large bridge structure that would take them over the river. "I'm not happy about having to cross that bridge. It's obviously shaken pretty hard through here and I don't know what condition the bridge might be in."

Tina asked, "But the deputy said the roads north are closed. We already know the roads south are closed. This is our only choice, isn't it, Alex?"

"Afraid so, unless we take the country roads to the west." He looked over his shoulder. "Hey, Chris is waking up."

Tina turned and reached back to touch Chris's shoulder. "Chris, can you hear me? How do you feel?"

Chris reached up with his bloody hand to grasp Tina's arm. "The earthquake happened, didn't it? Where am I?"

"Yes, we've had a major earthquake, and there have been some really bad aftershocks. You were almost crushed in your pickup by the falling overpass. Alex and I are taking you to the hospital in Dyersburg."

Chris stared upwards then closed his eyes. "It was bigger than I expected. Nelson said it would be bigger, but I didn't believe him. Why did it have to be so big? Why?" Tina could see tears filling his eyes.

"You rest easy, Chris, and we'll get you to a doctor as soon as we can."

Two miles down the road Alex stopped behind a line of cars blocking the highway at the start of the bridge. He and Tina got out of the SUV to walk ahead, and then stared in wonder at the southbound causeway. It had pulled away from the dirt anchor of the embankment on which they stood. The fallen roadbed lay 15 feet below amongst the trees and water on the flood plain. Water covered the farther sections of the roadway.

"Alex, what happened to the road?" Tina stared at the spectacle. "It looks like this end of the bridge just got tired and laid down on the ground. Do you think anyone was on the road when it fell?"

A fellow observer commented. "A couple of cars went off over the edge, but you don't see them anywhere now. They went over the side into the water.

And there were at least two down at the far end." He pointed to a perturbation in the road a mile and a half away.

"What are we going to do now, Alex? We can't take this road across the river." Tina looked at Alex, hoping he could think of a good idea.

"Well, I agree, but look, the northbound lane of the bridge is open." Leaving the people watching the action on the bridge Alex led Tina back to their car. Making a U-turn he headed back toward Caruthersville.

As they passed a Wrong Way sign at the side of the roadway, Tina exclaimed, "Alex, we're going the wrong way."

"Yep, I always wanted to do this. So what's the alternative?" He laughed, and when Tina caught the sardonic humor of the situation, she laughed along.

Alex explained, "I'm going back to a turn-around I saw and try the other side."

"Then we'll be going the wrong way on the other side. This is all just too crazy." Tina giggled. She found relief in the ridiculous moment.

Alex did his U-turn at the turnaround and returned to the causeway on the northbound lanes of the freeway, waving to the people standing at the end of the southbound lanes.

He met a delivery truck coming from the south. He waved it down, and the two drivers talked. "Yeah, the bridge is open over to Dyersburg. The Highway Patrol's stopping people from coming this way, but I snuck around. I've got a rush delivery of flowers for Caruthersville. They'll dock my pay if I don't make the delivery by noon."

Alex grinned in relief at Tina. "Well, at least we know the bridge is open to the Tennessee side." But he remained cautious. Driving at 30 miles per hour, he watched for signs of damage to the structure over which they traveled, climbing the causeway to the truss spans over the shipping channel.

As he drove under the trusses, Alex saw where the southbound pavement over the main shipping channel had fallen and disappeared into the waters of the river, leaving the trusses holding up thin air.

"Oh, God," he exclaimed. "It took out the whole other side of the road. Let's take a look at the river below." He pulled to a stop near the side.

"Alex, what are you doing?" Tina yelled. "Don't you think we should be going on?"

"We'll be okay. Come on, let's see what happened." He jumped out of the car and ran to the side so he could look down into the water below. The water churned around a large object just beneath the surface. "That must be the bridge section there, standing on end in the water." He pointed it out to Tina.

"Alex, let's go—I'm worried."

"Tina, don't worry. Everything's fine. Just a minute more." He walked down the roadway to get a better look and saw an old man standing far below on the pier around the columns holding up the bridge. He waved, and the old man waved back.

"Alex," she shrieked.

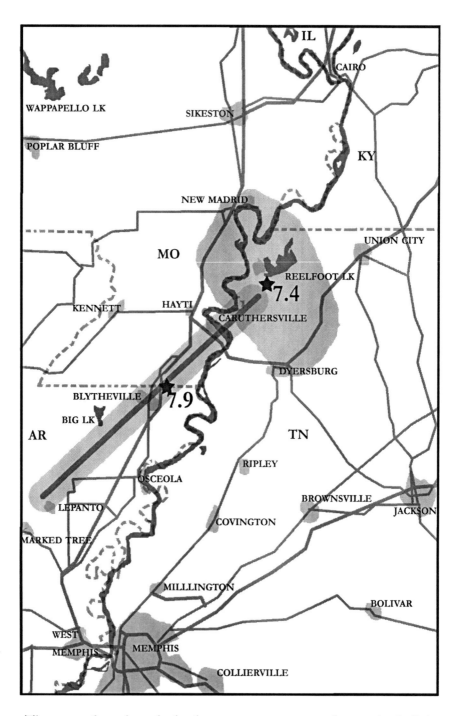

The second earthquake in the sequence measured magnitude 7.4 in the thrust fault under Tiptonville with a strike of 30 degrees.

CHAPTER 32: AFTERSHOCKS HAPPEN

Before heading back to the University Seismic Station in Berkeley, Todd explained to the group standing around the TV in San Ramon, "The New Madrid Seismic Zone has a history of producing a sequence of major events after a giant earthquake. In 1811 there were two aftershocks within hours with magnitudes in the high-7 range after the initial 7.9 magnitude event, and there were two even large events in the next two months, estimated by some to be in the 8.5 range.

"That's what the folks back there have to watch for now. There may be some additional horrendous earthquakes about to happen."

The next major event occurred one hour and forty minutes after the initial temblor. It began 14.3 kilometers beneath the surface with its epicenter just two miles southwest of Tiptonville, Tennessee, near the place where the initial fracture had ended. It spread like a fan from that point, opening up from the northwest to the southeast.

With a magnitude of 7.4, the new earthquake occurred in a thrust portion of the fault zone, fracturing another 500 square miles of the fault surface.

The crust to the northeast dove under that to the southwest along a fracture plane thirty degrees from the horizontal. The fracture extended over an area roughly shaped like a trapezoid with corners at Obion and Dyersburg, Tennessee, and New Madrid and Portageville, Missouri.

The maximum displacement along the fault measured 11 feet, and the maximum vertical lift was four feet near Ridgely. It took 15 seconds for the fracturing to complete along this new break in the crust.

Cities and towns to the north felt the brunt of the seismic waves. Intensity XI shaking tore apart Tiptonville, Bessie, New Madrid, and Marston, assuring that nothing remained standing. Caruthersville and Dyersburg were hit with intensity X seismic waves. Cape Girardeau and Paducah felt another round of intensity VIII shaking. Evansville and St. Louis were subjected to another 60 seconds of intensity VII seismic waves.

The major casualties from this event were the rescuers and the yet to be rescued. Most others who were able to move had taken refuge in whatever open spaces they could find, away from the crumbling ruins.

"Alex, let's go." Tina called, already back in the SUV. As Alex reached for the door handle, he heard the growing rumble of another temblor. He jumped in and slammed the door. Chris struggled to sit up on the platform behind the seat and look around.

Alex turned the key to start the SUV. The rumbling grew louder.

Tina screamed. "Alex, we're having another big earthquake. This is what it sounded like when the first one hit." The bridge jerked from side to side and then forward and backward, up and down. Over the next 21 seconds the bridge tossed and churned about, this time with the epicenter of the fracture in the fault only 18 miles away. The direct waves ended and three seconds later the reflected waves from the mantle pounded the bridge for another 24 seconds.

Alex's SUV tossed about and up into the air. Alex pressed the accelerator through the floor, smoking his rear wheels as he accelerated down the mile-long causeway into Tennessee.

Chris looked backward. "Alex, the causeway from Missouri, it's pan-caking and dropping into the water. There's a line of cars that are following us." He cried. "They're all falling into the water with it."

To the south, Alex could see the causeway rocking and rolling. He pressed harder on the accelerator as he heard the transmission shift to a higher gear. He struggled to keep the vehicle pointed down the roadway. After eleven seconds the heaviest shaking eased. "We're gonna make it. Hold on," Alex yelled. "The bridge is hanging together." He drove like a maniac toward the levee and firm land in the distance.

The SUV had traveled half the distance to the Tennessee embankment when reflected *S-waves* pounded in from the mantle. As the flood plain mud completed its liquefaction, the *Love-* and *Rayleigh-waves* built again, and the causeway sections began to vibrate at their resonant frequencies. All hell broke loose. Thirty-six seconds after the shaking had begun, the causeway began tearing itself apart, almost as if hit by explosives, with different sections twisting and falling in different directions.

Alex's speed had reached 95 miles an hour and the SUV was less than a quarter mile from safety. As the bridge tore apart, the SUV skidded toward a chasm between two adjacent sections. The vehicle leapt over the gap and continued its skid onto the next and last section. Pointing the wheels toward the solid road, Alex pressed harder on the accelerator. The vehicle vaulted off the end of that section onto the embankment, tipping onto it's side, then slid down the road, coming to rest 200 feet beyond the causeway.

The airbags exploded upon impact, bracing Alex and Tina. Chris catapulted into the backs of their heads then fell back. Everyone in the SUV was unconscious as the wheels spun in the air and gasoline leaked into the passenger compartment.

JQ struggled through and against the debris. When the last aftershock shifted material above him, he extricated his leg from under the timber that held it down. With the added room he could now reach into the drawer of his desk. He again heard bricks falling somewhere off to the side from time to time.

Like a worm he squirmed along the sloping floor of the former penthouse, pulling the briefcase along behind him. The pistol he had finally rescued rested in the back of his belt. He decided against firing the gun when he smelled the gas leaking from somewhere within the building. He would use it as a last resort.

"I'll be damned. There's a tunnel." JQ clammered through the makeshift crawl space littered with bricks and ceiling tiles. He caught his back on a protruding nail. It tore a three-inch gap in the seat of his pants and a one-inch gash in the skin on his thigh. He twisted around and bent the nail back up and to the side, sure it would find him again if he left it sticking out like that.

With a little more light he recognized the passage as the hall leading to the stairs and service elevator. The two sides of the hall had kept some of the weight on top from crushing down to the floor below. JQ crawled on through the space, hoping he could find a way to the outside at the end of the hall.

"Oh, my back. Oh, God. Please jest let me die." The soft masculine voice from somewhere ahead surprised JQ. Someone else lay buried in the debris with him. Twisting around JQ realized he lay next to the shaft of the service elevator. Through the slight crack between the doors JQ could see into the broken elevator car. Its dim emergency light lit the interior.

"God, please take my soul and send me to heaven. My body's all broke and don't work no more. I'm ready to join You in heaven if Ya would just take me. Please, God, Please." The old man in the elevator sobbed. JQ could now see him leaning against the side of the elevator, his lower body crushed beneath the metal wheels of the elevator lift mechanism from the roof.

"Joe, is that you?" JQ called, recognizing his janitor, the man he remembered seeing like at the end of a play in the penthouse. "What are you doing here in the elevator?"

"Is that you, Mr. McCrombie? Is that you?" Joe looked toward the door, but he could not see beyond it into the dark tunnel.

"Yes, Joe. This is JQ. I thought you went fishing. What are you doing in the elevator? You had time to get out of the building and leave, old man. You should've been outside, where it was safe."

"But I had to come back for you, Mr. McCrombie. The building started shaking as I went out the door, and I figured ya would need some help, so I come back and took the elevator up to find you. Only, half way up when the shaking really got bad, and the elevator broke loose and fell. I remember bouncing hard when it hit bottom, and I lay there shaking with everything else." He choked and coughed from the dust.

"Then the stuff from above fell through the roof and pinned me here in the elevator. Now my legs are crushed, and I think my back's broke. The legs don't feel at all, but my back's shore painful."

"Joe, God-dammit, Joe." JQ cried. "You dumb old man. Why didn't you stay outside? You shouldn't've tried to find me." Stricken with grief, JQ sobbed. "You dumb old man."

Joe had been the closest thing to a parent JQ had had when he grew up. JQ remembered how the old man raised him alongside the river and took care of him after his parents had discarded him. JQ grew up sharing whatever the two could harvest from the river. Once JQ found work, he always found a place for the old man, someplace where Joe could be a part of JQ's success. JQ had such a debt to pay to the old man, but he could never find a way.

"Jonathon Quincy McCrombie, somebody had to come and find you and save you. This jest seemed the time."

"Joe, that growling sound. There's another quake coming. Hang on." The rumbling of the Tiptonville event coursed through the building, followed by intense shaking. In the dim light JQ watched the one-ton elevator mechanism settle and grind into the old man. Joe screamed as the weight shifted. He screamed again and then fell back, taking one last breath. At last he lay still as God answered his last prayer.

JQ cringed from the shaking and shifting but could not take his eyes from this link to his past. He could not reach the old man to touch him and give him any comfort. He could not offer the solace he had received as a child. He could do nothing. He dropped his head onto the floor and sobbed into the dust and shards around him.

Pamela walked through the stricken city streets. She stepped over the fallen bricks and glass. Crushed cars lined the sidewalk. Very few of the buildings stood more than ten feet high. Those any higher she avoided, afraid that yet another aftershock would topple them as well.

Cracks in the pavement showed in many places, and parts of the sidewalk heaved up, creating barriers and pitfalls for those who did not watch where they tread.

She caught the garlic odor of gas from time to time, escaping somewhere from the tumbled remains, mixed with the stench of raw sewage from the broken lines running beneath the streets.

Pamela heard the sound of a crying child. It came from the remains of a second story apartment above a small boutique. A mannequin lay on the sidewalk trapped in the front of what had been the store window. The roof had fallen and the floor of the apartment was now almost level with the street.

"Hey, there's a baby in this building. I just heard it crying." Pamela subscripted the first able-bodied person who walked by. They listened. The faint cry came again.

"I hear it, too." He turned and yelled. "Charlie, there's a kid trapped in this apartment. Get over here."

Three more men and two women appeared on the scene. They all listened for the faint sounds of life. "Hey, quiet, people. We're trying to find a kid." The crowd around responded in an instant, and the silence became profound.

The crying came again from within the ruins. "He's inside, the other side of this window. We have a kid inside right here." Two of the men approached the street high window and pulled the broken glass out of the casing and onto the littered sidewalk, making a safe port of entry into the wreckage. One put his foot over the sill into the room.

As he stepped down, his weight proved enough to tip the scales, and the building fell another six inches, settling even harder onto the small shop beneath its floor. The body of the mannequin crushed with a loud crack. From inside the apartment now came a loud wail as the child screamed in fright.

"Come on, hurry up and get this kid out." The two men crowded to enter the window, hurrying to the rescue before the roof caved in on the apartment's occupants. Pamela stood to the side, fascinated at the way in which the men took chances to save the child, as if on a crusade.

From inside the room came a call. "I found the kid. He's not even three. He's still in his highchair." Sounds came of materials being moved inside the room. More sounds came of the wreckage settling even more.

A second voice yelled, "Hey, here's another kid, about six. She's got her foot caught under the table. Charlie, help me lift the table." Pamela heard sounds of grunting and shifting. "Got her. Oh shit, her leg's broke." The younger child screamed again.

More sounds of scurrying came from within the building. Then the first man appeared at the window with the six-year-old girl draped unconscious over his arm and her leg dangling at an awful angle. He stepped out of the window with the girl in his arms.

Charlie appeared at the window, the two-year-old in his arms. As he lifted his leg, the Tiptonville event rocked the city, and the upper floor of the building sagged, dropping the top of the window frame across his shoulders.

"Here, Ma'am, take the baby. Quick." Pamela reached out to take the child from Charlie's arms. He pushed against the frame, holding the building up while he put his arms on the side of the window and pushed his leg out over the sill.

Then he could hold it no longer, and the building dropped, crushing Charlie's head down to his thigh on the windowsill. Pamela heard a loud snap and a large grunt as the window frame broke his back and crushed the air from his lungs. Dust billowed out of the window, obscuring the gruesome scene.

Pamela stumbled backwards, the child in her arms. The baby wrapped his arms around her neck and buried his face in her hair. He screamed into her ear, but her eyes remained fixed as the dust settled on Charlie, another rescuer who had given his life to save a child.

People continued to come near, but no one searched through the pile of brick and old timber that had once been the Walker Hotel of Memphis. They all knew no one could be found there.

A gunshot sounded from within the debris. A passerby stopped and called. "What was that?"

"Must be somebody in there, signaling," said another.

A crowd clambered up the pile of rubble and started tossing bricks off to the side. Another gunshot sounded. They searched for an opening, somewhere to look. A *whoomph* sound followed by billowing smoke exploded from the bricks, lifting the debris a foot before it settled back. Smoke poured from between the cracks, then small flames.

The crowd scurried off the pile. "Oh God. That gunshot must have exploded the gas. Whoever's in there don't stand a chance." More flames appeared, and then rose higher from the funeral pyre. The crowd watched in fascination.

"The Lord take his soul," said one of the more pious. Then the entire group turned aside to look elsewhere for someone else whom they could save.

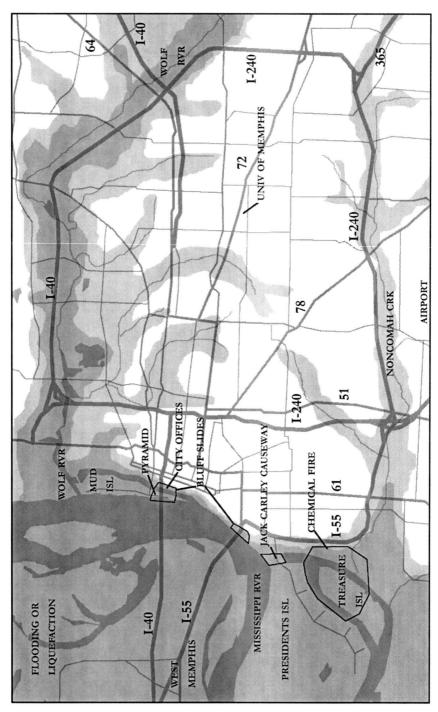

Memphis area: intensity VIII-X throughout; major slides, slumps, and fires outlined in black; liquefaction and flooding in gray.

Chapter 33: Status and Prophecies

"Mr. President." The military liaison officer handed the quarter-inch thick report to the President and saluted. "Here is the status report for the military units that can immediately provide help in the stricken zone."

"Thank you, General Lopez." Taking the proffered document, Frank LaPorte scanned a few pages. "In a nut-shell, where do we stand?"

"Sir, all military units within 150 miles of the New Madrid fault zone are out of commission. Traffic across the Mississippi River is not possible throughout the stricken area, from St. Louis to Vicksburg, so we are using airborne units to service the damaged cities along the river. We will supplement those units with land forces from further away as soon as we can mobilize them."

"How is it going with FEMA?"

"Sir, HomeLand Security and FEMA are working to get things together. They have some communications established with the local Emergency Operations Centers, but they were not prepared for such a widespread event. We will transport their resources whenever they need help, but it appears the Army and Air Force will be providing the bulk of the manpower, at least for now."

The President looked the General in the eye. "What about Memphis? That seems to be one of the most heavily damaged areas and the place without any nearby hope of help."

"Troops from Fort Knox and units stationed near Oak Ridge are already underway. Others will follow. An airborne company and a field hospital unit are scheduled to lift off from Fort Bragg in a couple of hours. They'll drop into the Memphis airport by seven this evening."

"Have you heard anything from the National Guard units in the affected states?"

"Yes, Sir. Most of the communication is that the National Guard is awaiting orders from their respective governors. They promise to coordinate with the U.S. Armed Forces as needed, but they're making no commitments to act on our behalf. They say that since no national security issue is involved, they remain in state control."

"That's what worries me. The governors want to run their own show, and they're not getting their butts in gear very fast." The President's brow creased from the strain.

An aide stepped into the Oval Office and interrupted. "Mr. President, two minutes to time for the broadcast."

"Be right there, Bill. Thanks, General. Keep me abreast of what's going on. I've got to tell the nation about my orders for a National Emergency and Martial Law. It won't go down well, especially with some of the states involved, but so be it."

As the General departed, the President rose from behind his desk to follow his aide to the Press Room, meeting his wife as she came through the door.

He halted. "Mary, have you heard anything more?" He reached out to massage her shoulder the way she liked.

"No, Frank. I keep worrying, no matter what I do." The First Lady leaned into his shoulder.

"It's in the hands of God now, Mary. We just have to wait for news."

Jerry Worthall appeared at the door, a distressed look on his face. "Mr. President, I must speak with you—and Mary."

"Jerry, come on in, but make it quick. I've got the press conference."

Jerry stood with his head bowed. "Sir, we have bad news from St. Louis. Sheila and her people were killed in the collapse of the auditorium at the Union Station, along with over 400 others. There was nothing anyone could do. They just recovered her body. I'm sorry."

Frank turned to put his arm around his wife. Together they sobbed as they held to each other tightly. Finally breaking away for a breath, he said, "Thank you, Jerry. Please tell them to hold the conference and leave Mary and me alone for a few moments. I'll be out shortly to attend to things. You understand."

"Yes, Sir. I'll be outside." Jerry stepped out the door and quietly closed it. Then he too leaned against the wall and cried.

"Mom. Mom." Judy looked up, hearing a familiar cry, not knowing from where it came.

"Tom? Did you hear that? It sounded like Jenny."

"Mom. You're safe." Jenny rode up on her bicycle, skidding to a halt at the side of the street. Dropping the bike into the gutter, she ran forward to throw her arms around her mother.

Judy bawled. "Jenny. It's really you. Jenny, Baby." She hugged her daughter and swung her back and forth.

Jenny pulled back when she saw Tom with his leg propped on the bumper. "Dad. Are you okay?"

Tom grinned and reached up to take his daughter in his arms. "I'm okay, just a little sprain I picked up a bit ago. But everyone's taking care of me. And you look good." He choked and buried his face into Jenny's hair. Judy hugged the two of them together.

Tom looked up at the tall man who had followed Jenny into the camp on his bike. "Is this Chris?"

Jenny blushed. "Oh, no. This is Dr. Kenton. He's Chris's thesis advisor. I'm helping him catalog the damage around the city for the USGS." Turning to Paul she made the introductions. "Paul, these are my parents, Tom and Judy Fox."

With introductions over, Paul's eyes quickly focused on the TV image. "What's that?"

Tom looked over and answered. "**NWS** is showing footage of areas around the epicenter. All the levees have failed with the Mississippi above flood stage. The water from the Kentucky Dam is due to reach that area tonight. They say the eastern quarter of the state of Arkansas will be underwater by tomorrow evening. The only people with a chance of surviving are those that can reach high ground, mostly the freeway overpasses."

Tom's voice broke. "They say there may be no way to rescue those people for at least another week."

Paul dropped to the ground on his knees to better see the screen. Jenny reached over to lean on his shoulder. She asked, "But where could Chris go if he was at New Simon? Oh. No." She hung her head and cried.

Paul stared into the image showing the expanse of water. The announcer narrated as the camera view moved on. "As you can see, the epicenter is being totally inundated. The small towns of Steele and Cooter have disappeared beneath the waters, and in the distance, you can see the remains of a grain elevator marking the location of Caruthersville. The destruction in this area is total."

The joyous gathering ebbed into despair. Tom commented, "There are times when TV tells us more than we really want to know."

At three o'clock all senior staff from the city and county who had come to the City Offices gathered on the lawn outside the Memphis City Building for a status review. A throng of refugees crowded around the periphery.

The Mayor pushed her glasses up the bridge of her nose and addressed the gathering. "Ladies and gentlemen, we'll make this quick, because I know you all have important matters to handle."

She waited a moment for quiet. "We begin by becoming accustomed to our plight. We have no power so there is no air conditioning. There are no printed materials to read. However, you will find a small supply of pens and paper at the table to your right if you want to take notes. We have no sound system, so speak up so everyone can hear and keep quiet if you're not speaking so everyone can hear whoever is speaking.

"I've asked Marion Roberts, our Director of Seismic Safety, to prepare an overview for us all. After he speaks we will have reports from others on the staff, and then we have some time for questions and discussion."

Several of the assemblage retrieved supplies to record the discussion, then returned to sit on the grass, boxes, and an assortment of rescued chairs.

"Marion, your report, please."

Marion stood at the side of the card table and spoke from his hand-held notes.

"As most of you know by now, the New Madrid Fault experienced a monstrous earthquake at 9:34 this morning. Reports from satellite TV, courtesy Mr. Tom Fox camped down in Lee Park, tell us that seismologists in Georgia and California have pegged the event at magnitude 7.9."

He took a sip from a bottle of water then waved it in the air. "By the way, a bottle of water like this is priceless. And save the plastic bottle."

"We hear that there has been substantial damage from Little Rock to Nashville, from Natchez past Saint Louis, and up the Ohio drainage as far as Indianapolis and Cincinnati, making this the most ruinous earthquake to strike the United States in the last 200 years.

"The locks on the Kentucky Dam have been breached, and the lakes are draining into the Ohio River, flooding the countryside. The flood surge will reach New Madrid later this evening and then flood the Mississippi valley to the south. It reaches Memphis tomorrow afternoon. Estimates are that the river will rise about four feet here; it rose 15 feet on the Ohio at Paducah.

"Here in Memphis, we have liquefaction, aftershocks, major landslides, destroyed buildings, fires, and broken utilities. Everything that our Emergency

Management people have been telling us for years has happened. In some cases it is even worse than they warned.

"Over two square miles of the city, between Route 23 and the Wolf River, has suffered severely from liquefaction, where the ground turned to slush. All the buildings in that area sank or cracked into pieces. Liquefaction along I-55 and I-240 to the south along Nonconnah Creek also tumbled a number of buildings and made a mess of the chemical plants in that area."

He coughed from a gust of dust and smoke. "The northern half of the city along the Mississippi, Wolf, and Loosahatchie Rivers experienced especially severe ground motion. Damage in the downtown section of Memphis around us is consistent with a shaking intensity level of X to XII, at the top end of the scale.

"A major casualty of this shaking has been some of the chemical plants around the DuPont facility. There have been gas leaks that are still being evaluated. We know a large number of people have been killed there, but we don't yet know just which chemicals have spilled. Luckily for us here, the wind remains from the southwest and it has not affected the city.

"Aftershocks continue to happen along the fractured fault. Two or three aftershocks strong enough to cause more damage here in Memphis occur every hour. TV reports the last big one was as high as magnitude 7.4."

"Marion, when will these aftershocks quit?" asked the Fire Chief.

"We don't know, only that there will be more. And the New Madrid has a reputation for having very large secondary earthquakes, what they call a sequence. Until you officially hear otherwise, assume that the danger of big aftershocks exists. That means avoid places where more damage can occur, like near unstable walls."

Marion looked down at his handwritten notes. "The damage in the heart of Memphis has been staggering. The hardest hit area is along the riverfront and the northwest side of the city. As most of you know, the huge earth slide from Jackson Street south destroyed the old downtown area. The slide ripped through the Pyramid, tore apart the I-40 Bridge approaches, destroyed our Convention Center, and cut through the bluffs from here at the City Building between Main and Front Streets all the way south to Union Street. Buildings on the slide were totally destroyed. Buildings east of the slide have faired only a little better. Beale Street is now flat."

He took another sip of water.

"Over 90% of all commercial buildings between here and I-240 have been destroyed or are so damaged, they will eventually be torn down. East of

I-240 probably 60% of the buildings have been destroyed or severely damaged out to Germantown. We understand there is considerable damage in Germantown, Bartlett, Collierville, and sections further east.

"Of the 14 major hospitals in the county, two are totally destroyed, and rescue work continues there. The others all have major damage and for the most part they have been evacuated, but their staff continues to operate to some extent, mostly in the parking lots. They are currently at maximum capacity.

"The latest count of injuries exceeds 18,600. We've compiled reports of 1,485 fatalities in Shelby County so far. Expect both of these numbers to climb dramatically. As I remember, the FEMA estimate for Shelby County in an earthquake of magnitude 7.9 equates to 40,000 injuries and 8,000 deaths."

Marion wiped his face with his handkerchief and looked over the assemblage. "I am asking for volunteers to join me after this meeting to discuss the problem of burials. This will become an urgent matter very quickly.

"Residential housing throughout the city has been damaged but much of it came through rather well. The biggest problems are again in the northwest sections where most homes were thrown off their foundations or affected by liquefaction. Older houses, especially those without ties to their foundations, have been the most damaged.

"A major fire continues to rage on President's Island and in the estuary. The ruptured fuel and chemical tanks have mixed their contents out on the water and are feeding a huge conflagration that must simply burn itself out. There is no method for extinguishing that blaze. There is growing concern about the toxicity of the smoke that is blowing from the southwest across the city, but we don't know how dangerous it is.

"There are toxic spills all across the city. They have been marked as well as possible, but more work is needed to determine the extent of the danger.

"We have lost a far too large portion of our fire-fighting capability. Without any warning, too much of the equipment and too many of our brave fire fighters were lost behind closed doors. As a result, there have been —and there continues to be—a substantial number of fires throughout the city. I think Chief Charlesworth will tell you of that situation. Right, Chief?"

The Fire Chief spoke with his head bowed. "Yes, Marion, I have a partial count of the fire damage and personnel losses."

Marion took the opportunity to cough again, then continued. "All bridges over the Mississippi are gone at this point, including the railroad bridges. They are not repairable in the near future. Over 30% of the freeway overpasses and on- and off-ramps in the city have fallen. The streets are passable —with much care.

"Power is gone. It will not be re-established in the foreseeable future. We have reports that the power plant on President Island was totally destroyed. All other power plants within 100 miles of the fault have apparently been wiped out as well. High-voltage lines coming into Memphis are all down. A limited number of emergency generators are in operation, but fuel supplies for these are limited, and most are expected to need more fuel within the next 36 hours.

"Natural gas supplies to the city have been turned off because of the many breaks in the underground lines. The rupture and explosion of the large gas main at Walnut Grove and Poplar near the EMA headquarters has severely affected our ability to respond. I heard an estimate of three weeks before any natural gas supplies can be restored, but that seems optimistic to me. I expect that all major pipelines into our area have been destroyed, so there is no way to replace the fuels we use.

"There is no water pressure. There is no water. There are so many breaks in the water lines that there does not appear to be a chance for it to be restored anytime soon. People must begin saving what water they can from their hot water tanks and swimming ..."

Marion stopped and listened. A low growl rose from the ground. "Hear that sound? It's the *P-wave*. The longer it goes on, the stronger the *S-wave* will shake us." He waited with the rest of the audience as the rumbling peaked then died away. "The shaking will start in 15 to 30 seconds. It will be strong." People sat or stood, waiting, silent, tense, praying.

The Mayor raised her hand. "Please remain here for the temblor to end. I want everyone to hear these reports."

Down Main Street they could hear people calling to the searchers and rescuers, warning them, yelling for them to, "Get out. Get out, now."

Suddenly the ground heaved, then shook from side to side. People cried, screamed, yelled. The sounds of crumbling and falling brick again filled the air with a rising cloud of dust. For 15 seconds the earth shook and groaned. Then the quiet returned.

As the dust settled, Marion coughed several times then resumed his report. "I was saying that people must save whatever water they can find in their hot water tanks, swimming pools, or wherever. Use it sparingly.

"I hope you all realize that without water the sewage system is useless, even if it weren't broken in so many places. Expect this to be one of our more serious problems within a week or so. Epidemics of cholera, dysentery, and typhoid are distinct possibilities.

"Food supplies are running low. We sent crews out to confiscate as much as they could find in the schools, warehouses, and grocery stores in the city, but at the present we have no more than two more days of supplies in our coffers. And most of that is allocated to feed the rescue and response people. We've already seen evidence of a Black Market in food.

"There have been three flights into the airport of Air Force planes carrying emergency supplies, but the runways are severely damaged, and that source is not yet reliable. People will become very hungry before we have enough food for everyone."

The earth trembled again, agitated that someone would ignore its unrest. Marion stood resolute.

"Communication with the outside world is very limited. We are receiving reports via satellite, but we must use short-wave radio or satellite telephone for transmission. The 800 MHz system used by the Fire Department is mostly down; only the EMA and amateur radio networks are truly operational. The phone lines are all down, including the cellular system we had hoped would work in the event of an emergency. Cellular is probably down for hundreds of miles around our area."

Marion turned to the Chief of Police. "Chief Robinson will now tell you about the problems with looting and other forms of disorder in the city, but from my perspective, we have already lost control." His voice cracked. "Ladies and Gentlemen, Memphis has been destroyed." He dropped his face into his hands and squeezed his scalp against his headache.

"How're you feeling now, Chris?" Alex helped Chris move to a more comfortable position as he leaned against the broken tree on the bank of the flooded Mississippi. From their vantage point they looked across an expanse of water that covered most everything from the river to the west as far as they could see.

"Where do you think New Simon is?" Chris avoided Alex's question.

Alex looked into the distance. "As I remember from when I was skydiving, it was about 20 air miles from Dyersburg to the jump field. So maybe 17 miles west of here. Hard to tell, but it looks like it's flooding all the way over there and beyond."

Chris stared at the destruction. His eyes looked dull and his voice sounded listless as he spoke. "I guess my body's okay, but when I look at this scene, I feel like I tried to play God and made a real mess of it."

"Hey. There's no need for you to feel guilty. You didn't cause the earthquake."

"Are you sure? Why should someone like me know what's going to happen like that? It's not right." He shook his head. "No, I must have done something to make it happen. And I had a chance to warn everyone, but I didn't. I was so determined to prove I could predict an earthquake and to get all the glory. I didn't let the world know what was coming."

"Come on, Chris, I heard about it. You told Tina. So you did tell people."

"But I didn't tell the world. Even when I got my model working right, I didn't believe it. Nelson told me a gigantic earthquake was going to happen, but I wasn't sure."

Alex shook his head. "But what good would your telling them have done anyway? Nobody could stop it from happening. They couldn't evacuate the whole Mississippi valley. And besides, everyone with any sense knew something like this was bound to happen some day. They should have prepared."

Tina limped up to the two young men sitting in the shade and said, "I talked to some of the folks up the hill. They said things are a mess all over. There are still people streaming out of Dyersburg. There may be some kind of soup kitchen set up over at the Interstate in a couple of hours. Maybe we can get something to eat there."

Alex stood. "Chris keeps blaming himself for this earthquake. He's got some crazy idea he caused it all with his prediction and with not telling the world about it."

"Chris, you know that's not true. You just happened to be the one person who figured out when it would happen. Just because you were right doesn't make you guilty of anything."

Chris stared at the ground. "Well, whatever, I'm through with seismology." He stood and took his laptop computer from his backpack. He stared at the gray box. "Everything I learned is on this laptop, the model, the data. Alex, you're right. The world doesn't need it."

He reached back and flung the computer like a discus out over the floodwaters. As the ripples from its splash washed the shore he said, "There. It's gone."

Alex and Tina stared in horror. Tina cried out, "Chris, why did you do that?"

Chris shook his head and choked. "Someone told me it hurts to be a prophet. I can't remember who—but he was right. Now it doesn't hurt so much."

Epilogue

Some people estimate that it will take 35 years for Memphis and the Mississippi River Delta—indeed, for our whole country—to recover from a giant earthquake on the New Madrid Fault. The story of *The 7.9 Scenario* is but six hours old—a tragedy that has only just begun.

Twenty-three and a half seconds of fracturing have ravaged the eastern half of the United States and portions of Canada with over 13 minutes of shaking. This earthquake, smaller than some in the 1811 and 1812 sequence, has put at risk over 32,000,000 people, and our country's economic future.

The great transportation and flood control systems on the Ohio and Mississippi Rivers are broken. Levees and dams have ruptured, and water has flooded the surrounding land. Those who ply these waters must save themselves as they fight their way downriver to what they hope is the relative safety of Memphis.

Memphis itself is a lost city. Help can only trickle in—there are simply too many other cities throughout the country that also require aid. Those who would rescue and support Memphis have been injured themselves.

Nearly a million people in the Memphis area are cut off from the rest of the world. Aftershocks pummel the land, and people begin to fight amongst themselves for what few supplies remain. The fate of Memphis rests in the hands of those who are there. They must save themselves.

Many will realize that Memphis and the Mississippi Valley can no longer support those trapped there, especially the very young and old. Their only choice is to leave. A mass exodus begins, some walking east and some south, some floating downstream on the river, looking for safety and solid land.

The story and characters that you have heard here are fiction, but the events will become reality someday when, not if, the next major earthquake strikes on the New Madrid Fault.

Will the United States prepare and plan ahead for how to recover from the worst natural disaster it has ever seen? That decision rests in your hands.

#

Appendix A: Glossary

Asperity – an uneven place along a fault caused by a cross-fault, a bend in the fault, or a change of material.

Calavares Fault – an off-shoot fault from the San Andraes Fault in the San Francisco Bay Area.

Department of HomeLand Security – the cabinet-level department responsible for all aspects of the security of the United States.

EOC – Emergency Operations Center, the central control location responsible for coordination emergency operations in each municipality .

Epicenter – the point on the earth's surface directly above the focus.

FEMA – Federal Emergency Management Agency, the agency in HomeLand Security responsible for preparing for disasters in the US.

Focus – the physical point in the earth's crust where the fracture creating the earthquake started; also called the hypocenter.

g – a symbol for an acceleration equal to that of gravity, producing a force that makes a one pound mass weigh one pound on the surface of the earth.

Hypocenter – another name for focus.

Intensity, Shaking – a measure of the shaking from an earthquake at a particular place; it depends upon the magnitude of the earthquake, distance from the focus, and local geology.

Love-wave – a surface wave that moves the ground horizontally to the right and left perpendicular to the direction of propagation.

Magnitude – a measure related to the total energy released in the fracture of a seismic event. The logarithmic Richter Magnitude was the first well-known measure; now seismologists most often use a method called the Moment Magnitude. See Appendix B.

Model – a computer program that uses input data to predict a result based upon some theory; sometimes called a scenario model.

Modified Mercalli Intensity Scale – In this scale the measures for the intensity of the shaking from an earthquake are expressed as Roman Numerals on a closed scale from **I** to **XII**. See Appendix B.

New Madrid Fault or Seismic Zone – a seventy-mile-wide active seismic region running from east-central Arkansas to near Cairo, Illinois.

P-wave – a pressure wave with dilation and compaction of the media. In air, this is sound.

Rayleigh-wave – a surface wave that moves the ground in a circular motion up, forward, down, and backward like a water wave washing up on the beach.

Reverse Fault – a fault where one face moves away from the opposing face.

Rift – a reverse fault that pulls the faces so far apart that there can be significant sinking of the land and/or an upwelling of magma to form volcanoes.

Sequence – a series of giant earthquakes in a relatively short time. In 1811 and 1812 there were three giant earthquakes within two months plus two giant aftershocks within hours after the first.

S-wave – a shear wave that physically moves an elastic media back and forth. It cannot propagate into air or water.

San Andraes Fault – the major slip-strike fault separating the North American Plate from the Pacific Plate along the coast of California.

Scenario – an imagined result from some possible event. If it is a scientific scenario, it is based upon some underlying physical theory.

Seismology – the study of seismic events in the earth's crust that produce earthquakes.

Slip Fault – a fault where the faces move horizontally with respect to each other.

Strike – the downward angle of a fault; a vertical strike is 90 degrees from the horizontal surface.

Thrust Fault – a fault where one face moves over or under the opposing face. A thrust fault has a strike less than 90 degrees.

USGS – United States Geological Survey, the agency responsible for the data collection and analysis of seismic activity in the United States.

APPENDIX B: EARTHQUAKE SCALES

Magnitude Scale – Earthquake magnitude is an analog for the relative energy release of a seismic event.

In the 1930s Charles F. Richter and Beno Gutenburg introducted a graphical method using seismograph recordings to compare the speed of ground shaking at a particular distance from the epicenter of an earthquake. Each time their magnitude number increased by one unit, it meant the ground moved ten times faster.

Seismologists determined that the magnitude is proportional to the energy release of earthquakes in California on a logarithmic scale, with a 32-times increase in energy released for each unit of magnitude.

More recently seismologists have used computer algorithms to analyze much more of the shaking spectrum and estimate the torsional moment of the fracture to deduce the total energy release. They have converted this into a Richter-like number called Moment Magnitude for communication to the public.

Moment Magnitude depends upon the total area of the fracture and other factors. It is consistent over a wide range of energy releases and distances from the epicenter. It tracks with the Richter magnitude in the lower ranges but diverges in higher magnitude events.

The following shows the description and fracture size associated with various magnitudes.

Magnitude	Description	Fractured Area
< 2.9	micro	< 13 acres
3.0 - 3.9	minor	13-130 acres
4.0 - 4.9	light	130-1300acres
5.0 - 5.9	moderate	2-20 sq mi
6.0 - 6.9	large	20-200 sq mi
7.0 - 7.8	major	200-2000sq mi
> 7.9	great	> 2000 sq mi

Modified Mercalli Intensity Scale – In this scale the measures for the intensity of the shaking from an earthquake are expressed as Roman Numerals on a closed scale from **I** to **XII**.

Extracted from Bruce Bolt's *Earthquakes – Newly Revised and Expanded*, Appendix C, W.H. Freeman and Co. 1993.

MMI I.   Not felt except by a very few under especially favorable circumstances.

MMI II.   Felt only by a few persons at rest, especially on upper floors of buildings. Delicately suspended objects may swing.

MMI III.   Felt quite noticeably indoors, especially on upper floors of buildings, but many people do not recognize it as an earthquake. Standing automobiles may rock slightly. Vibrations are like passing of truck.

MMI IV.   During the day felt indoors by many, outdoors by few. At night some awakened. Dishes, windows, doors disturbed; walls make creaking sound. Sensation like heavy truck striking building. Standing automobiles rocked noticeably.

Acceleration is 0.015g-0.02g, Average Peak Velocity (APV) is 1-2 cm/sec.

MMI V.   Felt by nearly everyone, many awakened. Some dishes, windows, and so on broken; cracked plaster in a few places; unstable objects overturned. Disturbances of trees, poles, and other tall objects sometimes noticed. Pendulum clocks may stop.

Acceleration is 0.03g-0.04g, APV is 2-5cps.

MMI VI.   Felt by all, many frightened and run outdoors. Some heavy furniture moved; a few instances of fallen plaster and damaged chimneys. Damage slight.

Acceleration is 0.06g-0.07g, APV is 5-8cps.

MMI VII.   Everybody runs outdoors. Damage negligible in buildings of good design and construction; slight to moderate in well-built ordinary structures; considerable in poorly built or badly designed structures; some chimneys broken. Noticed by persons driving cars.

Acceleration is 0.10g-0.15g, AVP is 8-12cps.

MMI VIII.   Damage slight in specially designed structures; considerable in ordinary substantial buildings with partial collapse; great in poorly built structures. Panel walls thrown out of frame structures. Fall of chimneys, factory stack, columns, monuments, walls. Heavy furniture overturned. Sand and mud ejected in small amounts. Changes in well water. Persons driving cars disturbed.

Acceleration is 0.25g-0.30g, APV is 20-30cps.

MMI IX.   Damage considerable in specially designed structures; well-designed frame structures thrown out of plumb; great in substantial buildings, with partial collapse. Buildings shifted off foundations. Ground cracked conspicuously. Underground pipes broken.

Acceleration is 0.50g-0.55g, APV is 45-55cps.

MMI X.   Some well-built wooden structures destroyed; most masonry and frame structures destroyed with foundations; ground badly cracked. Rails bent. Landslides considerable from river banks and steep slopes. Shifted sand and mud. Water splashed, slopped over banks.

Accelerations are more than 0.60g, APV is more than 60cps.

MMI XI.   Few, if any, (masonry) structures remain standing. Bridges destroyed. Broad fissures in ground. Underground pipelines completely out of service. Earth slumps and land slips in soft ground. Rails bent greatly.

Accelerations approach that of gravity, Peak velocities are off the scale.

MMI XII.   Damage is total. Waves are seen on ground surface. Lines of sight and level distorted. Objects are thrown into the air.

APPENDIX C: THE 7.9 SCENARIO

A scenario is defined as "an imagined account of possible events resulting from some happening."

The art of building scenarios came out of the Cold War Think Tanks, when the strategists thought through the possible ramifications of nuclear war. They borrowed a term from the movie industry to try to explain to others what they were doing.

By the mid-1980s the development of scenarios for almost everything had become very popular, and much effort was applied to produce scenarios for possible earthquakes, first on the West Coast and then in the central United States. Scenario maps were produced to show where the worst shaking would be to help the planners and designers know where to apply their efforts. But they did not tell me all I wanted to know.

I developed a series of spreadsheets to estimate the overall effects of a giant earthquake in the central United States. I used the most recent US census data and shaking intensity maps at the county level developed in the early 1990s at SouthEast Missouri University for FEMA These spreadsheets were parameterized so I could study the effects of time of day, day of the week, flooding, epicenter location, and magnitude.

I chose to focus on a repeat in today's world of the earthquake that struck the New Madrid Seismic Zone on December 16, 1811. That set of calculations is the foundation for what I call *The 7.9 Scenario.*

Moment Magnitude = 7.9

Epicenter at 36N0 latitude, 89W51 longitude

Focus depth = 17.5 km

Slip-strike fracture 4,000 km^2 in area, 110 km long running N42E

Date and time assumed to be a Saturday morning in May

River condition averages 6 feet above flood stage, St. Louis to Vicksburg.

APPENDIX D: CASUALTIES

Two scenarios are considered, the Mississippi River is high and above flood stage, or it is low and not flooding.

ST	Pop	At Risk	w/floods					w/o floods				
			inj	fatal	displ	bldg	brdg	inj	fatal	displ	bldg	brdg
AL	4,464	2,760	1.3	.3	189	3.1	0.1	1.0	.2	184	.2	
AR	2,692	1,667	32.6	6.5	632	248.3	6.9	12.8	2.6	268	38.0	1.2
GA	8,384	1,706	1.1	.2	114	2.1		1.1	.2	114	2.1	
IL	12,446	2,901	12.9	2.6	514	98.0	1.5	7.3	1.5	417	49.4	.4
IN	6,115	3,242	6.7	1.3	637	36.4	.2	6.7	1.3	637	36.4	.2
IA	2,923	103	.2	-	12	-		.2	-	12	-	
KS	2,695	579	.2	-	8.9	-		.2	-	8.9	-	
KY	4,066	3,364	11.7	2.3	681	90.2	1.5	7.0	1.4	556	29.6	.5
LA	4,465	87	141.0	28.2	2,204	1,101.3	13.9	.1	-	2	-	
MS	2,858	1,948	18.5	3.7	539	147.7	2.9	2.7	.5	290	27.2	.3
MO	5,630	5,309	18.8	3.8	899	134.1	1.7	18.8	3.7	827	91.4	1.0
NC	8,186	25	.1	-	1	-		.1	-	1	-	
OH	11,373	3,011	2.2	.4	440	1.0		2.2	.4	440	1.0	
TN	5,740	4,981	49.7	9.9	1,307	204.7	1.9	49.7	9.9	1,179	145.8	1.5
Totals	31,683		298.7	59.5	8,179	2,062	30.7	110.8	22.1	4,936	416.7	5.3

Legend: ST is the state; Pop is the 2000 population At Risk population are those living where shaking intensity is VI or higher; inj is injured by earthquake or flood; fatal is fatalities; displ is the count of people displaced from their residences; bldg is the number of buildings destroyed, severely damaged, or flooded; brdg is the number of bridges collapsed or severely damaged. All numbers are x1,000.

APPENDIX E: ECONOMIC IMPACTS

The United States economy is severely impacted in The 7.9 Scenario. The Gross Domestic Product will slip by 6% to 10% within days. The following factors contribute that impact:

Immediate property damage from an earthquake this size will range between 1.0 and 1.5 trillion dollars.

Insurance companies will immediately fail because of the large number of expected claims and the investment of insurance reserves in the damaged region.

20% of the nation's cargo tonnage passes by Memphis on barges or through Memphis by air, rail, truck, and pipeline.

6% of the nation's warehousing and transportation centers reside in the areas of damage along the Mississippi River and are expected to be put out of commission.

10% of the nation's chemical plants, those that line the Mississippi, will immediately be put out of commision by damage, lack of power, or lack of raw materials.

All the rail and vehicle bridges between St. Louis and Vicksburg will be severely damaged or collapse, stopping all commercial traffic from crossing the river in that region.

The Mississippi River will be made impassable from Cairo, IL to Helena, AR by collapsed bridges, slides from the bluffs, and the cutoff at Bessie's Neck.

The failure of the locks at Kentucky Dam will not be catastrophic because of the locks at Barkley Dam, just a few miles away. However, there will be little traffic down to the Mississippi.

The failure of the Old River Control Structure between Natchez and Baton Rouge reroutes the Mississippi River into the Atchafalaya basin, wiping out the I-10 and I-20 corridors and inundating the ports in and around Morgan City.

Without adequate water flow down the old river channel, the mouth of the Mississippi will close, leaving the ports of New Orleans, Plaquemine, and Baton Rouge (comprising the second largest seaport in the United States) sitting beside a stagnant slough.

Fuel and power supplied by the western states to the southeast will be cut off along with supplies of food, lumber, and grain.

The lose of power, fuel, and raw materials will have a ripple affect over time, multiplying the impact of the damage by a factor of 1.5 to 2 when businesses must close their doors because they cannot get the raw materials they need.

Up to a third of the people living in the most damaged zones will migrate away, leaving behind those less able to cope and accomplish a recovery.

Estimates are that it will take 35 years before the devastated areas recover from an earthquake this size.

The chance for an asteroid like the one that killed the dinosaurs striking the earth in the next fifty years is smaller than one in a million, maybe as often as once every 500,000 years.

The chance for Yellowstone erupting into a super volcano in the next 50 years may be as high as one in a thousand. A caldera forming eruption happens somewhere on the earth about every 50,000 years.

The official USGS estimate for the chance of a giant earthquake on the New Madrid Fault sometime in the next 50 years is 7% to 10%, depending on the earthquake model used. Call it one in ten. This kind of earthquake happens an average of every 400 years.

Appendix F: Books of The 7.9 Scenario

What does the future hold?

The novels of *The 7.9 Scenario* continue. The second in the series is *Broken River,* a book that tells of what happens to our country's river system in a great earthquake on the New Madrid. Two boat captains are on the river near Caruthersville when the shaking starts, and what would have been a short day's journey to Memphis becomes a four-day ordeal as they fight their way downriver to the city on a river that has been destroyed.

Broken River was published October, 2004 by TwoPenny Publications.

The third novel in the series, to be published in 2006, is entitled *Phoenix of Memphi.* It tells of the efforts of the people of Memphis and of the nation to recover from a disaster that threatens the very existence of the country. The characters of the first two novels continue their struggles as they take part in the Herculean effort of recovery. The backdrop for the action describes how well and how poorly Memphis and the nation have planned and prepared to survive and recover from this kind of disaster.

A fourth book in the series, entitled *The 7.9 Scenario, Analysis and Writing,* is being serialized on the Internet at www.the79scenario.com. It tells of the background for the novels and the research that was done to develop the scenario calculations. Details of those calculations are provided along with explanations for how someone can ask "what if" quesitons for different size earthquakes in different areas. It will be published in hardcopy form when it is finished.

428564

Made in the USA